CHASING JUSTICE

Also by H. Terrell Griffin

Matt Royal Mysteries

Found

Fatal Decree

Collateral Damage

Bitter Legacy

Wyatt's Revenge

Blood Island

Murder Key

Longboat Blues

Ethan Fitzgerald Novels

The Assassin's Game

Thrillers: 100 Must-Reads:
Joseph Conrad, *Heart of Darkness*
(contributing essayist)

CHASING JUSTICE

A Matt Royal Mystery

H. TERRELL GRIFFIN

Oceanview Publishing
Longboat Key, Florida

ISBN: 978-1-60809-141-6

Published in the United States of America by Oceanview Publishing
Longboat Key, Florida

www.oceanviewpub.com

10 9 8 7 6 5 4 3 2 1

PRINTED IN THE UNITED STATES OF AMERICA

Dedicated to

Jessie Elizabeth Jones Royal
"Dandy"
1880-1965

ACKNOWLEDGMENTS

Writing, for me, is a team effort. I have the good fortune to live in both Maitland, an Orlando suburb, and Longboat Key, that paradise off the west coast of Florida. I do most of my writing on my sunporch overlooking Sarasota Bay or at the Maitland Starbucks, where I am surrounded by my coffee-swilling buddies and the gracious baristas who take such good care of us.

Longboat Key has a plethora of bars and restaurants where my island friends gather each evening for a little good cheer and, on occasion, boozy fellowship. We enjoy the beaches, the golf courses, tennis courts, fishing, and some of the best boating in the world. The ideas for my stories spring from these relationships, these friends who people my life and bring me such joy. I value their ideas, their support, and the fact that they often buy me drinks.

My readers are the ones who sustain my passion for writing. I hear from you by email and reviews on Amazon. I learn something from every communication, positive or negative, and they do make me, hopefully, a better writer. I appreciate that you take the time to read my books. I hope that what you read brightens your day a little and takes you into a world that you enjoy, the island world of Longboat Key, an oasis of calm in an ever more complex world, a sun-drenched bit of land surrounded by a turquoise sea where bad guys appear and murders occur only in my imagination.

I have been helped immeasurably in writing this book by my brain trust: Peggy Kendall, David Beals, Lloyd Deming, Chris Griffin, and Jean Griffin. They edit the copy as it comes out of the printer, listen to my endless prattle about the book, and give me ideas on how to better the story. I don't always listen to them, even when I should, so any errors in fact or prose or plot are solely my fault.

I can't say enough about the gang at Oceanview Publishing: Patricia Gussin, Bob Gussin, Frank Troncale, David Ivester, and Emily Baar.

Their support and encouragement through the writing process is invaluable. They have become friends who always have a kind word, a pat on the back, or a kick in the butt as needed. Without them, there would be no Matt Royal.

Finally, there is my wife Jean, who gives me reason to get up every morning. I met her while I was in college, and badgered her, stalked her, and begged her until, I think in desperation, she agreed to marry me. My life has been better than I deserve, but without her, it would all have been meaningless. She gave me three sons whom I cherish, and one of the boys gave us a wonderful daughter-in-law and two grandchildren, Kyle and Sarah, who are probably the best little guys in the whole world.

Thank you all for your patience and for putting up with me. I couldn't do it without you.

CHASING JUSTICE

"To be neutral between right and wrong is to serve wrong."
—Theodore Roosevelt

PART I

THE INVESTIGATION

CHAPTER ONE

Detective Jennifer Diane Duncan looked around the large room in which she was standing. Opulent, she thought, and a bit ostentatious. She looked at the nude body lying at her feet and wondered if the woman had been some rich man's trophy.

The dead woman appeared to be in her late thirties, about the detective's age. She had a lot of blond hair, now matted with blood. Her face was classically beautiful, perhaps too perfect. Her breasts had obviously been surgically enhanced, so maybe her face had, too. She wore makeup that had been applied with care and expertise to accentuate her features. Her skin was the bronze of the Florida sun-worshiper, and she had apparently done her worshiping in the nude. Her dark pubic hair had been trimmed into a heart shape. The detective smiled, wondering whether that had been done for her lover or just on a lark, a bit of whimsy perhaps.

There was no sign of trauma, other than the small pool of blood under her head and in her hair. The deathblow must have been to the back of her skull. But then, she would have fallen forward and would be lying facedown. Somebody had moved the body, turned her over onto her back. Not Steve Carey, the first officer to arrive. He would have known not to disturb the crime scene.

The room's ceilings were at least fifteen feet high. Expensive hardwood floors were covered at intervals by Oriental carpets, each of which probably cost more than her car. The furniture was large, on a scale to fit the room. Tall French doors opened onto a patio that contained an infinity pool, and off to the right, a summer kitchen. On the left, a wall rose along the periphery of the patio, providing an area screened from the beach. An oversized hot tub, more like a small pool, took up a corner, and three lounge chairs sat in the shade on a tiled floor. Later in the day, the area would be flooded with sunshine. An open door led to a dressing room.

Beyond the patio and the white sand beach, the tranquil Gulf of Mexico gleamed under the morning sun, its turquoise placidity at odds with the violence that had been done on its shore. Officer Carey stood near the front door.

"Do you know anything, Steve?" she asked.

"Nothing. The maid found the body when she came to work this morning. Says it's the lady of the house, Jim Favereaux's wife, Linda."

"Where's the maid?"

"I asked her to stay out on the patio. Didn't want her to have to sit looking at the body."

"Did you know the people who live here?"

"Not really. I worked a burglary here about two years ago, before you came to the island. I met them then. He's a lot older than she is. Was."

"Is he here?"

"No."

"They must have a lot of money. Do you know anything about that?"

"Nada."

"What was taken in the burglary you worked?"

"Nothing much. It looked like some kids came up from the beach and broke into the back of the house. The only things the maid could find missing were a couple of bottles of hooch. Bourbon, I think."

The detective left Officer Carey and walked around the living room, into the kitchen and dining room, upstairs to the bedrooms, looking for anything that seemed out of the ordinary. Nothing. She went out to the pool dressing room. A towel hung from a hook. No sign of a struggle.

The crime scene people arrived and began their search for evidence, moving about the rooms with determined patience. The house seemed sterile, as if it were a showplace where nobody lived, where people came to admire the décor and the furnishings and the view of the Gulf. She got no feeling of people living there, eating, sleeping, loving, arguing, the ordinary things that take place in any family home.

The detective shivered in the air conditioning. Somebody had cranked it down to the point that it felt frigid inside the house. It was the first day of April, April Fools' Day, she thought grimly. Not your typical Monday morning on Longboat Key. The weather outside was unseasonably warm, but the temperature inside made her wish she'd worn a jacket. It had certainly skewed the time-of-death calculation for the medical examiner's assistant. He had taken the body's temperature when he arrived shortly after eight o'clock and told her that his best estimate was that she had been dead for six or more hours. "Could've been ten or twelve," he'd said. "Maybe Doc Hawkins can be a little more precise when he does the autopsy. Sorry."

The medical examiner's people were ready to transport the body. "Can you turn her on her side so I can see the back of her head?" the detective asked.

"Sure." The ME's assistant placed one hand on the dead woman's shoulder and another on her flank. He rolled her onto her left side. The back of her head was bloody and blond hair was matted into a depression. Somebody had bashed in her head.

The detective moved back and watched the two young men lift the body onto a gurney. They placed a sheet over it and wheeled the gurney toward the front door. Duncan went to one of the crime scene techs whom she knew. "Kevin," she said, "have you found anything that might be the weapon that killed her?"

"Not yet. I looked at that gash on the back of her head though and got some pictures. We'll keep looking, but there's nothing obvious in this room."

"Thanks," said Duncan. "Let me know if you come up with anything."

* * *

A small woman with brown skin and black hair cropped short sat on a divan on the patio, tears running down her face. She appeared to be in her twenties, early thirties, maybe. She wore a black dress with a white collar and belt, sheer hose, and sensible white shoes. A maid's uniform.

Duncan walked out to the patio and sat next to the maid. "Do you speak English?" she asked.

The maid nodded. "I grew up here. In Bradenton."

"I'm Detective Duncan, Longboat Key Police. People call me J.D. What's your name?"

"Selena Rodriguez."

"Officer Carey tells me that you found the body and called the police."

"Yes."

"What time?"

"About seven-thirty. I'm supposed to be at work by eight, but the bus drops me off up the block at seven-fifteen. The next one wouldn't get me here until eight-fifteen. I don't want to be late."

"Did you move the body, touch it in any way?"

"No."

"Was she face-up when you found her?"

"Yes. I didn't touch anything. I used my cell phone to call 911."

"Have you worked here long?"

"Two years in February."

"What can you tell me about the people you work for?"

"They're real nice," Selena said.

"What's their name?"

"Mr. and Mrs. Favereaux."

"Do you know their first names?"

"James and Linda."

"Do you work every day?"

"Monday through Friday. I'm off Saturday and Sunday."

"This is a pretty big place to keep clean," Duncan said.

"This house has almost twelve thousand square feet, but the Favereauxes only live in a couple of bedrooms and not much of the downstairs."

"They didn't share a bedroom?"

"No."

"Do you know any reason for that?"

"No."

"How old is Mr. Favereaux?"

"I don't know."

"What's your best guess?"

"Probably about sixty. Maybe a little older."

"And Mrs. Favereaux?"

"Thirty-nine. She had a birthday last week."

"Do you know how long they've lived here?"

"I think they hired me as soon as they moved in. So, just a little over two years."

"Selena, I'm embarrassed to ask you this question, but I need to know for my investigation. I'm not with customs or the Border Patrol, and I assure you, your answer will go no further. Are you in the United States legally?"

Selena smiled, ruefully. "I get that question a lot," she said. "I was born here. My parents were illegal but they were given amnesty back in the eighties and now have green cards. I'm as much American as you are, Detective."

"I didn't mean to offend you."

"You didn't. I know you had to ask."

"Do you know where Mr. Favereaux is?"

"No."

"Was he here on Friday?"

"He was here when I left work on Friday afternoon."

"Okay, Selena. That's all I have for now. I'm going to need your contact information, address, phone number, that sort of thing. Where do you live?"

"East Bradenton."

"I'll get an officer to drive you home."

"Thanks, but I'll take the bus. I don't want my neighbors seeing me getting out of a police car."

CHAPTER TWO

"Good morning, Matt."

"Ah, Longboat Key's best detective."

"And the only one."

"And the most beautiful."

"I'd normally love to hear your sweet nothings, but I caught a murder case this morning."

"I told you it would have been better had you stayed at my place last night."

"Yeah, but I needed some sleep. You tend to keep me awake."

"I thought you liked it."

"Your snoring?"

"Oh, that."

The voice coming through my phone was that of Jennifer Diane Duncan, known as J.D., the police detective whom I loved. "Where are you?" I asked.

"I'm standing in front of that huge new house on the beach, the one they built a couple of years back when they tore down that little hotel just south of Pattigeorge's Restaurant. Somebody murdered the lady of the house last night."

"Who's the victim?"

"Linda Favereaux. You know her?"

"I met her once at Pattigeorge's. Sammy introduced me to her and her husband. I never saw them again. Any idea who killed her?"

"Not yet. The husband seems to be away. We'll see."

"I guess that means we're not going to Egmont today."

"Afraid not. I'll see you tonight."

"My place?"

"Yes. I'll bring my earplugs." She hung up.

This was supposed to be a day off for J.D. We'd planned to make a picnic lunch and take my boat to Egmont Key and sit on the beach all day. Egmont is a state park accessible only by boat. It's about a ten-mile run from my house, and with the gorgeous weather we were having, it would have been a salubrious day.

My name is Matt Royal. I'm a lawyer and mostly retired. Other than handling the occasional legal matter for a friend who couldn't afford a lawyer, I stay away from the courts and the practice of law. I was once a soldier, went to war and then to law school. I'd been a trial lawyer in Orlando, and when I grew tired of the rat race, I sold all my possessions and moved to Longboat Key. I'm young for retirement, but if I'm careful, the money I have will last the rest of my life.

My home is a cottage on the bayside of a wonderful little island about ten miles long and half a mile wide at its broadest point. Longboat Key lies off the southwest coast of Florida, south of Tampa Bay, about halfway down the peninsula, bordered on the east by Sarasota Bay and on the west by the Gulf of Mexico. I live in Longbeach Village, the oldest inhabited part of the is- land, if you don't count the Indians who lived there hundreds of years ago. The village sits on the north end of Longboat Key and is populated by the best people on earth. Most of us spend our time in a sort of modified stupor, enjoying our days on the beach or fishing or boating. Our evenings are spent in restaurants and bars with our friends and neighbors. Some of the village people still work for a living, and we have an eclectic group ranging from industry moguls to carpenters and commercial fishermen. Every- body fits in.

J.D. Duncan had come into my life about a year and a half before, when she was hired as Longboat Key's only detective. She'd worked for the Miami-Dade Police Department for fifteen years and risen to assistant homicide commander. Her mother had lived on Longboat Key, and when she died and left her condo to

J.D., the detective decided to give up life in the fast lane that was Miami and move permanently to Longboat Key. My buddy Bill Lester, the chief of police on the island, had jumped at the chance to hire her.

J.D. and I had become friends and, more recently, lovers. She had changed my world and made living on an island paradise even better than I had thought possible. But she was a cop, and sometimes that meant that she had to take on ugly jobs.

I spend most of my days working at being a beach bum. It isn't hard. Our island is full of people who have adapted to life on the key and spend their days lying on the beach, fishing, boating, and drinking in the bars. When I first moved to the key, I thought I might eventually be able to ease out of the fast lane and work my way into that island lifestyle. It took me all of two days to do so, and I became a confirmed beach bum. This life is a lot simpler than that of a trial lawyer. I was happy and satisfied and surrounded by friends. J.D. was the icing on the cake.

I called my buddy Logan Hamilton, and we loaded a cooler with ice and beer, stowed rods and reels aboard my boat, *Recess*, a twenty-eight foot Grady-White, and headed for the fishing grounds. I'd once read a t-shirt that said, "Longboat Key is an island of drinkers who have a fishing problem." I always thought that pretty much captured the essence of our key. As the Bard said, "Truth will out."

CHAPTER THREE

Officer Steve Carey looked agitated as he walked across the living room toward J.D. "Robin Hartill is outside."

"Crap. What does she want?"

"What do you think? She wants to talk to you. She's got her notebook and camera."

"Okay. Tell her I'll be there in a couple of minutes."

Robin and J.D. were friends and often had a beer together at Tiny's, a small bar on the north end of the key. But Robin was a reporter for the local weekly newspaper, the *Longboat Observer*, and J.D. had hoped to keep the press at bay for at least a few hours.

She went to the front door. "Hey, Robin. You sure got here quick. I was hoping to keep this under wraps for a bit. How did you find me out?"

Robin laughed. "The island telegraph. Gwen Mooney was on her way to work at Doc Klauber's when she saw your car and a couple of cruisers parked out front. She called and told me something was up. What's up?"

"Can we talk off the record for right now?"

"Will I get anything out of you that I can use today for our Internet edition?"

"Sure," J.D. said, "just not now. I need a few hours before this gets out. I'll call you this afternoon and cut you loose before the local TV stations go on air for their six o'clock news."

"Sounds fair. What's going on?"

"The woman who lives here, Linda Favereaux, is dead. It looks like murder. Did you know her?"

"No, but Gwen did. Said she was an asshole, excuse my language."

J.D. smiled. If Gwen didn't like someone, then he or she joined the list of assholes that Gwen maintained in her head. The list was fairly long. "Do you know why Gwen thought that?"

"No," Robin said, "but you know it doesn't take a whole lot to get on that list."

"That's for sure. I've got to get back to work. I'll call you this afternoon."

The morning dragged on. The forensic people were going through the large house with great deliberation. The body had been taken to the medical examiner's morgue. The autopsy would get underway quickly, as it always did when the victim came from the high-dollar precincts. There was no sign of the husband. J.D. searched his bedroom for any indication of where he might have gone. She found nothing. A laptop computer sat on a desk in the corner of the room, but it was password protected. J.D. called the police department geek and asked him to come over and pick it up. See if he could get past the security.

It was nearing noon when J.D. left the crime scene. She needed to get back and start the paperwork. Her phone rang just as she was turning into the station at mid-key.

"Detective, this is Dan Murphy at the ME's office. We ran the fingerprints on Mrs. Favereaux. There's a problem."

"Uh, oh. What?"

"The prints don't belong to Mrs. Favereaux. They came back as those of a woman named Darlene Pelletier. She was arrested twenty years ago for shoplifting in New Orleans. That's the reason she's in the system."

"Maybe Pelletier was Linda Favereaux's maiden name," said J.D. "Maybe Darlene is a first name and Linda is her middle name."

"Could be. I thought you'd like to know."

"I do, Dan. Have y'all finished with the autopsy yet?"

"Dr. Hawkins is working on that now."

"Thanks for the call. I'll see what I can find on Darlene Pelletier."

J.D. parked in front of the station and was getting out of her car when her phone rang again. "Good morning, J.D. This is Harry Robson."

"Hello, Harry. How are things on the mainland?" Robson was a detective with the Sarasota Police Department.

"A little hectic right now. Do you know a man by the name of Nate Bannister?"

"Never heard of him. Why?"

"He's one of your citizens, I think. At least that's what his driver's license says. Apparently, he's been living on the mainland, in a condo in one of those new high rises on Main Street. We found him dead this morning. Or at least his housekeeper found him in the living room of his condo and called us."

"Foul play?"

"Gunshot to the head. Left temple."

"Suicide?"

"Not unless he got rid of the gun between the time he shot himself and the time he died."

"Well, as a trained detective, I'd begin to think it was murder. Good luck on the case. I'll ask around and see if anybody knows him."

"He's pretty well known, I think. The Longboat Key address on his driver's license is on Gulf of Mexico Drive, but he'd been living in a condo downtown for at least the last couple of months. He just moved into the condo two weeks ago. I'm told he has an estranged wife somewhere, maybe on the key. Do you have time to check out his house and see if it looks lived in?"

"And notify the wife if she's still there?"

"That would be super." Death notifications were the hardest part of a cop's job and J.D. hated doing them, but Harry had done her some good turns, and she owed him.

J.D. made a U-turn in the police parking lot and drove several blocks north to a large bayside home. She rang the bell, waited, and then knocked on the door. No answer. She scrawled a note on the back of a business card asking that Mrs. Bannister call her as soon as possible. She stuck the card between the door and the jamb and left.

* * *

The police station was busy. Three people in shorts, t-shirts, and flip-flops were sitting in the waiting room, looking anxious. A uniformed officer was sitting quietly in another chair. He nodded to J.D. Iva, the civilian receptionist, was on the phone, and waved a finger as the detective came through the door leading from the parking lot. Deputy Chief Martin Sharkey was coming toward her as she walked down the hall toward her office. "What's that all about in the waiting room?" J.D. asked.

"Their car was broken into yesterday, and they want to file a report for insurance purposes."

"Where was the car?"

"In the airport in Minneapolis."

"You're kidding. Why didn't they talk to the police up there?"

Sharkey laughed. "They said they were running late for their flight and one of them had to go back to the car to retrieve something. The driver's side window was smashed out, but he had to get back to the gate."

J.D. shook her head. "Was anything missing?"

"The guy didn't take time to look."

"Good luck with that one," J.D. said, as she moved on.

As she passed Chief Bill Lester's office, he called to her. "Got time to bring me up to date on that murder?"

J.D. went into his office and took a seat. "Not much to report," she said. "The husband's in the wind. No one's seen him since Friday. The back of her head was bashed in. That's probably the cause of death. She was nude, and there were no other marks on the body. She probably fell face first, but the body was on its back on the floor, so somebody must have turned her over before we got there."

"Sexual assault?"

"No obvious signs, but she's on Doc Hawkins' table now. We'll know more this afternoon."

"Any gut feelings?"

"You mean other than that the husband did it?"

The chief laughed. "The odds are usually pretty good on that."

"We'll see. Do you know a man named Nate Bannister?"

The chief's face clouded a bit. "Yeah. I know him. A real piece of work. Why?"

"I got a call a few minutes ago from Harry Robson at Sarasota PD, asking about him. It seems that somebody found Bannister dead in a condo downtown this morning."

"That's not going to be any great loss," Lester said.

"I didn't know him. What was his problem?"

"He was just a mean son of a bitch. He was a developer here on the key until we got built out, and then he started developing on the mainland. Condos, mostly. He was rough on his subcontractors. Lots of complaints about shoddy work from the people who bought his places.

"We had to pull him off his wife a couple of times when he beat the hell out of her. She refused to press charges both times. She finally kicked him out a couple of months ago, filed for divorce, and got a restraining order against him."

"Where is she now?" asked J.D.

"She's still living in the family home on the bay."

"Any children?"

"No."

"How old was he?"

"Forty-five, maybe. Maggie, the wife, is about ten years younger."

"Harry asked me to check the house and see if anybody's

there and to deliver the death notice. Nobody was home. I'll try later."

"I'll go," Lester said. "I've known Maggie for a long time."

"Thanks, Chief. That's a load off."

CHAPTER FOUR

The call came at three in the morning, a time when a ringing phone can only mean trouble or tragedy, or maybe both. I fumbled in the dark, finally grabbing the receiver and answering.

"Matt," the voice on the other end said, "this is Bill Lester. The FDLE just arrested Abby."

"FDLE?"

"Florida Department of Law Enforcement."

"I know what it is." My head was clearing itself of sleep. "What's going on?"

"I don't know. Two agents showed up, knocked on the door, and told me they had a warrant for her arrest and a search warrant for our house. They took her computer, gave her time to get dressed, and then put her in cuffs. They just left."

"Where are they taking her?" I asked.

"Sarasota County Jail, they said."

"What are the charges?"

"Murder."

"Murder?" No way in hell, I thought. Abby didn't have it in her. "Bullshit," I said. "Who is it she was supposed to have killed?"

"Nate Bannister."

"That prick?"

"Yeah, that prick."

"What's Abby's connection to him?"

"None that I'm aware of. I don't think she knew the man."

"What else do you know, Chief?"

"Nothing about why Abby's involved in this thing. I knew the man had been murdered."

"How did you know that?"

"Harry Robson called J.D. yesterday asking about Bannister. Apparently, he was shot in his condo in downtown Sarasota. I went to see his wife and told her about his death."

"How did she take it?"

"She wasn't broken up, that's for sure. He spent a lot of years beating the hell out of her before she screwed up the courage to throw his worthless ass out."

"Harry's Sarasota PD," I said. "Why is the FDLE involved?"

"I don't know."

"Anything else?"

"That's it. I need you to go play lawyer and find out what you can. I told her not to say anything until you got there."

"Okay, Bill. Let me get a shower, and I'll head downtown. You sit tight until you hear from me. Don't talk to anyone. Got it?"

"Got it. Matt, Abby's not capable of murder. She didn't know Bannister and she sure as hell didn't go to his condo and kill him. Something's terribly wrong about all this."

"I'm sure you're right, Bill. I'll be in touch as soon as I meet with Abby. I may not get a whole lot of information until the clerk of courts' office opens and I can see all the paperwork."

"Let me know something as soon as you can."

"I'll talk to you as soon as I see Abby."

J.D. had stirred when the phone rang, and by the time I hung up, she was sitting on the edge of the bed. "Bill Lester?" she asked.

"Yes."

"What was that all about?"

"His wife was arrested by FDLE a few minutes ago."

"Abby? For what?"

"Murder."

"You're kidding. Who's the victim?"

"Nate Bannister."

"This is nuts. Abby didn't do this. She's not a killer."

"I agree, but they must have some pretty good evidence to arrest the wife of a police chief."

"Harry Robson's working that case," she said. "He called me about it yesterday afternoon."

"I'm going downtown to see what's going on. I'll call you when I know something."

"Want some company?"

"No. Go back to sleep. I think I need to do this by myself. Maybe we can meet for breakfast. I'll call you."

* * *

Gulf of Mexico Drive, known to the locals as GMD, is the only road that runs the ten-mile length of the island between the Longboat Pass Bridge on the northern end and the New Pass Bridge on the southern. The night was moonless, dark, and a bit foreboding. A gentle fog lay on the island, the humidity of the early spring air conflating with the cooler water that surrounded us. Lights on the outside of the few commercial buildings were shrouded in the humid air, giving off a mystical glow that somehow matched my morose mood. There was no other traffic. My headlights danced in the gloom as I drove through the darkness, feeling a bit out of place, like a space traveler flung unexpectedly into a strange galaxy.

I sipped from a cup of coffee I'd made before leaving my cottage. I was concerned about Abby Lester and confused about the FDLE's involvement. Abby and Bill had been married for about fifteen years, but had never had children. She was a high school history teacher in the Sarasota County School system. I had come to know Abby well over the years and I liked her. I'd gone to dinner with her and Bill on a number of occasions, and we ran into each other at the social functions that were part of our island life. Although Bill had never mentioned it, I'd heard through the island grapevine that there had been some rocky patches in the marriage. I'd never heard any details and wasn't inclined to listen to the gossip about two good people.

The Florida Department of Law Enforcement was a police agency that reported to the Florida cabinet. It had statewide jurisdiction and was usually called in when a case involved multiple counties. Sometimes, the agency investigated crimes that were tied to the police agency that would normally have jurisdiction.

Florida's Suncoast was small enough that there was always good cooperation among the police and sheriff's departments that made up the law enforcement community. This was particularly true with the Sarasota and Longboat Key Police Departments. I suspected that the Sarasota police chief had called in the FDLE as soon as he realized that the Longboat Key police chief's wife was a suspect.

I had known the victim, Nate Bannister, and didn't like him. He was one of those guys always looking for a fight. He'd been a successful builder, and as his wealth grew, so did his power in the community. But he wore on everybody he dealt with, from employees to subcontractors to buyers of his condos to the people on the key. I hadn't seen him around for several months and hadn't thought a lot about it. I guess his departure from the island had gone without much notice. He just faded from the islander's consciousness, like a bad dream.

The Sarasota streets were empty, and I parked right in front of the six-story jail that sat on a corner on the edge of downtown. I showed my Florida Bar card and my driver's license to the deputy at the control desk in the lobby and told him I was representing Abigail Lester and would like to see her. He picked up his phone, told somebody that Mrs. Lester's lawyer was in the lobby, listened for a moment, and hung up. "Somebody will be right down," he said. "You can make yourself comfortable over there." He pointed to the plastic chairs grouped around a silent television set.

I had barely sat down when the door opened and Detective Harry Robson appeared. I stood and we shook hands. I'd known

Harry for a while. He was a straight shooter who worked his cases with a methodical determination and no preconceived notions about the guilt or innocence of any suspect. He was a good cop.

"What's going on, Harry?" I asked.

"Let's sit for a minute. Can I get you some coffee?"

"No, thanks. I had a cup on the way here. Why was Abby arrested?"

"This is a touchy one, Matt. I've known Bill Lester for years. But evidence at the scene pointed to Abby, and I didn't have any choice. I took what I had to my chief, and he called in the FDLE. He did the right thing, but the investigation is now out of my hands."

"But you're here," I said.

"I knew they were going to arrest Abby. I tried to get the FDLE agent to wait until a reasonable hour and let me bring her in. I've met her a number of times, and I wanted her to see a familiar face."

"Why the rush? Why go roust her and Bill out of bed at three in the morning?"

"No reason other than that Wes Lucas is an asshole."

"The FDLE agent?"

"Yeah. He's out of their Tampa office. He's got one of the highest conviction rates in the agency, but he's also had an inordinate number of cases thrown out by judges because the evidence was too thin, or there was some impropriety in the investigation. I think he's been on the hot seat with the director several times, but he seems to have some pull with somebody high up in state government."

"Sounds like a fun guy to work with."

"Are you going to represent Abby?"

"Probably not. Bill called me and asked me to come down and see what's going on. I'll talk to him this morning, and we'll see about getting somebody to take the case. Can you tell me what you found that pointed to Abby?"

Harry hesitated for a moment, mulling it over. "I think I'd better let Lucas fill you in."

"Okay. What are they charging her with?"

"Second-degree murder."

"Will the state attorney be going for an indictment for first degree?"

"Probably, but it won't be Jack Dobbyn. The chief called him before he called FDLE. Jack will recuse himself later this morning, and the governor will have to appoint one of the other state attorneys to prosecute."

John Dobbyn, who went by the nickname of Jack, was the elected chief prosecutor for the three-county area that made up the Twelfth Judicial Circuit. There were twenty such circuits in Florida and each elected its own state attorney. If a state attorney in a judicial circuit decided for whatever reason that he could not prosecute a case that arose in his circuit, he would notify the governor's office, and the governor would appoint a state attorney from another circuit to prosecute.

The same procedure would take place if the circuit judge assigned to the case recused himself and all the other judges in the circuit did the same. The governor would appoint a judge from another circuit to try the case.

In Abby's case, the trial would take place in Sarasota County before a Sarasota County jury, but it would be prosecuted by a state attorney from another part of the state, and probably presided over by a judge from another circuit.

"Where is Abby now?" I asked.

"She's in an interview room just down the hall. I'll take you to her."

I followed Harry down a corridor lined with empty holding cells. They would be busy in a couple of hours as the previous day's arrestees were taken before a judge for their first appearance. Some would be released on bail, and others would return to lockup to await their trials.

We stopped before a door with a glass partition. I looked inside and saw Abby sitting at a table, her wrists cuffed in front of her. She was a small, pretty woman who seemed younger than her forty years. Her blond hair was in disarray and she wore no makeup. She looked wan and disoriented. She was shaking her head at the man standing over her, his fists balled, his face angry.

Harry opened the door, and I walked in.

"Who the fuck are you?" the man asked.

Abby looked up. "Oh, Matt. I'm so glad to see you."

I offered my hand to Wes Lucas and said, "I'm Matt Royal, Mrs. Lester's lawyer. You must be Agent Lucas."

He just looked at my hand until I withdrew it. "You can leave now," I said.

"Just who the hell do you think you are?"

"I just told you. Now leave."

"I'm not going anywhere, Counselor."

I grinned at him and pulled out my cell phone and dialed a number. "Harry," I said, "would you have the jail supervisor come down here with a couple of his men and remove Lucas? My client wants to exercise her right to counsel, and I can't very well talk to her with this asshole hanging around."

As I returned the phone to my pocket, Lucas moved toward the door. "Don't think this is over, Counselor. You don't get away with calling me an asshole."

I smiled at him. "We'll see. Close the door on your way out."

He left, slamming the door behind him.

"He's a bully," Abby said. "I'm awfully glad you're here."

"Did you tell him anything?"

"No. Bill told me to keep my mouth shut until you got here."

"Do you know why they arrested you?"

"For the murder of Nate Bannister."

"Did you know him?"

"Are you going to be my lawyer, Matt?"

"I'll talk to Bill later today and see about getting you somebody good to represent you."

"I want you, Matt."

"Abby, I'm retired from all this."

"You tried a murder case a few years ago and got an acquittal."

She was right. About three years before, I had come out of retirement to represent my friend Logan Hamilton when he was accused of murdering his girlfriend. "That was different," I said.

"How?"

"That was for a friend who'd been wrongly accused."

"I'm a friend too, Matt. And I'm innocent. Did you know I have a trust fund? It's not huge, but I can pay you."

"Abby, you know this isn't about money."

"I didn't think so."

"It's bad practice to represent friends. Sometimes, the lawyer's objectivity is colored by that friendship. It makes it easier to miss some piece of evidence that might be crucial. A lawyer can believe in his client's innocence, but he can't lose the objectivity that keeps everything in perspective."

"You did it your last time out. I watched most of that trial in Bradenton. You can do it again. I trust you, Matt. I trust your instincts and your abilities, and I trust you to bow out if you ever start to doubt my innocence."

"Let me talk to Bill," I said. "He'd have to be on board with this."

"If you're my lawyer, anything I tell you remains confidential, right?"

"Right. Unless you tell me you're planning to commit a crime. Anything you tell me about this case is absolutely confidential."

"Does that mean that if I tell you something I don't want Bill to know, that you won't tell him?"

Ouch. I think that's what they call a sticky wicket. "That's what it means," I said. "But to be fair, I'm going to have to make sure Bill understands that and agrees to it."

"Okay. Come see me when you decide."

"I'll either be back later today, or I'll send you a lawyer I trust."

"Please do this, Matt. I need you."

I kissed her on the cheek and left.

CHAPTER FIVE

Harry Robson was standing in the waiting room as I came out. "I don't know what you did to Lucas, but you sure pissed him off."

"I called you and asked you to bring the jail supervisor and a couple of deputies and kick his ass out of the interview room."

"You called me?"

"Well, I might have dialed the wrong number. I actually got the answering machine at Tiny's Bar out on Longboat."

Harry laughed. "Are you sure you want to get on the wrong side of Lucas?"

"Ah," I said, "the better question is, does he want to get on the wrong side of me."

"There's going to be a lot of testosterone flowing around this case. Are you going to represent Abby?"

"Not sure yet. I need to talk to Bill Lester. See what he thinks. I'm not going to get anything out of Lucas about the probable cause for the arrest. What can you tell me?"

"Abby's fingerprints were found in the condo. She was a school teacher, so her prints were in the system. Bannister's computer had lots of emails from and to Abby. Most were suggestive of an affair. But the worst one came from Abby. It was a threat to kill Bannister. It was dated two days ago."

I took a deep breath. What they had was a long way from enough evidence to convict, but it certainly wasn't good for Abby.

Harry continued. "There was a wine glass on the bedside table in Bannister's bedroom that had Abby's fingerprints on it. The sheets on Bannister's bed were rather ripe with semen and vaginal fluid. Those are at the crime lab. We should have some DNA evidence back soon."

"That's not good," I said.

"No. Are you going to tell Bill?"

"Not yet. I'll want to talk to Abby some more before I let Bill know about this."

"He's got friends in our department. Including our chief. He might have his own sources. He'll probably find out."

"I can't do anything about that, but right now I've got a confidential relationship with Abby. I'll have to see how this plays out. Has the ME determined the time of death?"

"Doc Hawkins said he was probably killed about ten o'clock on Sunday evening."

"Doc's usually on the money."

"Is there anything I can do?" Robson asked.

"See if you can get Abby into some sort of isolation. I don't think it'd be a good idea to put the chief's wife in general lockup."

"I'm sure I can get that done. I'll talk to the corrections lieutenant, James Forrest. He's a good guy."

"I appreciate that."

"Good luck, Matt."

"Thanks, Harry. And thanks for being a friend. Watch your back with Lucas."

"Don't worry. I can handle him."

* * *

It was only a little after five when I got back into my Explorer. Too early to call J.D. so I called Bill Lester instead. "You got coffee on?"

"Where are you?"

"Just leaving the jail."

"It'll be ready by the time you get here."

Bill and Abby lived in a small house on a canal near the south end of Longboat Key. He was waiting at the door with a cup of black coffee in his hand. "Well?"

"Let's sit, Bill."

"Of course. Sorry."

I took a seat on a sofa and he sat in a recliner facing me. "What did you find out?"

"Not much. She's accused of killing Nate Bannister and she's charged with second-degree murder. But you already knew that. Harry Robson says that Doc Hawkins puts the time of death at about ten on Sunday evening. Was Abby here with you?"

"I wasn't here. I'd gone to visit my mom in a nursing home. I didn't get home until almost midnight. Bad timing, huh?"

"That's not too big of a problem. If you testified that you were here with Abby at the time of Bannister's murder, the jury might not put much credence in it anyway. You being the husband and all."

"Who's handling the case?"

"The FDLE assigned an agent named Wes Lucas. Ever heard of him?"

"Yeah. Just rumors. But never anything good."

"He's a hardass," I said. "And a bully. He likes to throw his weight around." I told him about our encounter in the interview room.

"You never did take well to threats."

I shook my head. "Jack Dobbyn has already recused himself, and I wouldn't be surprised if all the judges in the Twelfth Circuit did the same thing."

"How soon do you think the governor will appoint somebody else?"

"I'm guessing he'll do it quickly. He'll be worried about the publicity, so he'll want to get everything in place as soon as possible."

"What about bail?" Bill asked.

"I don't know. Second-degree murder carries a twenty-five year to life sentence, and I wouldn't be surprised if the new prosecutor takes the case to a grand jury and ups the charge to first-degree murder. The rules make exception to bail in these kinds of cases, but the prosecution has to show that the charge is based on a substantial amount of evidence and a likelihood of prevailing in order for the judge to deny bail."

"What was the evidence that led somebody to think Abby killed that bastard?"

"I can't discuss that with you right now. I'm sorry, but at least for now, I'm Abby's lawyer and I'm bound by all kinds of confidentiality rules."

Bill nodded and was silent for a moment. "Will you represent her?"

"Do you think that's a good idea, Bill? I've been out of it for a long time."

"You couldn't tell that when you were representing Logan."

"Let me talk it over with J.D."

"We've got quite a bit of money saved," he said. "Abby has a small trust fund, and we've been living on our salaries and putting that money away. We can pay you."

I shook my head. "That would ruin my amateur status. But if I take the case, I'll have to hire an investigator and maybe an assistant to take care of some of the paperwork. I'd probably be able to get a second-year law student at Stetson to help. They'll need to be paid."

"Whatever you need."

"There's another issue, Bill. If I'm Abby's lawyer, anything she tells me will be confidential. I won't be able to share it with you. She can tell you, but if she's in jail, I don't want you two talking about anything dealing with the case. You don't have any right to privacy, and they record those conversations. I'll only be able to tell you what she allows me to say. Can you live with that?"

"I guess I'll have to."

"Bill, your friendship means a lot to me, and I don't want to get into a situation where you're mad at me for not telling you everything I know."

"That won't happen."

"Okay. I'll be having breakfast with J.D. and then I'll get

back to you. If I decide to take the case, I'll go downtown and meet with Abby. I'll talk to you by ten this morning."

* * *

It was nearing six o'clock as I drove north on GMD. The fog had cleared, but it was still dark. Harry's Corner Store was just opening. I pulled in, bought the morning paper, and drove on home.

I heard J.D. stirring about in the bedroom and then the shower running. I prepared some eggs for scrambling, put bacon in a frying pan, and started a pot of grits. I filled the coffeemaker with water and coffee and turned it on. Breakfast would be ready by the time she was dressed.

She came into the kitchen just as I was putting the food on the table. J.D. was beautiful any time of day or night, but the mornings always brought a smile from me. She was dressed in what she called her cop uniform; black slacks, a white polo shirt with the logo of the Longboat Key Police Department embroidered above the breast pocket, and comfortable shoes. Her dark hair just touched her shoulders and she was showing that smile that could bring a grown man to his knees. "I smelled the bacon," she said. "We sure are domestic this morning."

"Nothing's too good for my sweetie."

We sat and ate. "Do you want to talk about this morning?" she asked.

I went through the whole thing. I told her about the charges, about Harry Robson and Wes Lucas and our confrontation in the interview room. And I told her about the evidence that I knew about. "You know you can't tell anyone any of this."

"I know. How's Abby holding up?"

"Actually," I said, "she's holding up pretty well. She and Bill want me to represent her."

"What did you tell them?"

"That I wanted to discuss it with you."

"It's your decision, Matt."

"But it could affect you. And us."

"How?"

"If I lose this case, your job could be in jeopardy. Bill Lester wouldn't be happy with me, and by extension, maybe you. And he probably wouldn't hold on to his job either. The husband of a convicted murderer isn't going to be working as a cop. His career will be over. Maybe yours, too."

"I'll take that chance."

"Are you sure?"

"Matt, you want to take this on. I can see it, all that energy radiating from you like some physical force. Do you know why you feel like you have to do it?"

"I'm not sure."

"Do you think you still have something to prove? That you're still a great lawyer, maybe?"

"No. I'm satisfied with the reputation I built before I got sick of it all. Anyway, that's not really important anymore."

"How is your lack of regard for the legal profession going to play into this case?"

"I don't know. I think I can put it aside for this one case."

"Think about this, Matt. Why do you want to take this on?"

I sat quietly, thinking through the whole situation. I had nothing to gain and perhaps a lot to lose by getting back in harness. But nobody should play with the system. Justice creaks along in our society, but it usually does the right thing. And it does it right, because, for the most part, the men and women who work in the system, the judges, lawyers, and cops, are honest people doing honest jobs.

It's an adversarial process, but that doesn't mean it has to be an all-out war. There are rules that have been hammered out through a trial-and-error process that evolved over eight hundred years of Anglo-American jurisprudence. But every now and then, somebody like Agent Wes Lucas comes along, and just out of sheer meanness, or stupidity, or both, skews the system.

"Matt," J.D. said again. "Why do you want to take on this case?"

"Because Wes Lucas really pissed me off."

"That's a good enough reason. You go kick some butt."

CHAPTER SIX

J.D. was perusing the reports that had come in overnight from the crime scene technicians. They had discovered a lot of fingerprints in the Favereaux mansion, and were checking them against people who had reason to be in the house. It was a process of elimination, an effort to discover the identity of anyone who had no reason to be there.

Two experts had examined the computer found in James Favereaux's bedroom, and neither was able to crack the sophisticated encryption code that protected it. J.D. was surprised that a retired businessman would have any need of such security. It didn't make sense.

One of the reports was a biographical sketch of James Favereaux. He was sixty-four years old, and a graduate of a high school in New Orleans. He'd served in the army in Vietnam and earned a Bronze Star for valor when he was nineteen. He'd saved the life of his platoon leader, a young lieutenant, whom he dragged wounded out of a firefight.

When Favereaux got out of the army, he used the GI Bill to study at Louisiana State University, graduating with a degree in business. He'd spent his life as an investor, putting money into one project after another, and making substantial profits on every venture. When he was in his mid-forties, he got married in New Orleans to a woman named Linda Fournier, who was twenty-five years his junior.

J.D. picked up her phone and called Dr. Bert Hawkins, the medical examiner for the Twelfth Judicial Circuit. "Bert, it's J.D."

"Ah, the loveliest detective on Longboat Key."

She laughed. "That's easy to do when you're the only detective."

"Well, you're a lot prettier than Martin Sharkey."

"So is everybody else."

"I guess it's a good thing he got promoted to deputy chief," Hawkins said. "You're calling about Mrs. Favereaux?"

"Yes."

"Cause of death was blunt force trauma to the back of her head. There were no other injuries to the body. She died real quick."

"One of your techs called me yesterday and said the fingerprints you ran came back as those of a woman named Darlene Pelletier."

"Yeah. Probably a maiden name."

"I don't think so, Bert. I just got some information on Mr. Favereaux, and he married a woman named Linda Fournier. Can you double check those prints for me?"

"Sure. I'll take them again and have somebody run them through the system."

"Thanks, Bert. Let me know what you find."

"As soon as I know."

J.D. hung up and thought about what she had learned. If Linda Favereaux was really Darlene Pelletier, then who the heck was Linda Fournier Favereaux? And where was her husband?

The chief had not arrived for work at his usual hour of seven o'clock. J.D. checked her watch. It was almost ten. She went to Lester's office. He still wasn't in. She stuck her head into the deputy chief's office. "Martin, have you seen the chief?"

"I don't think he'll be in today. He called. Said he'd talked to the town manager who told him to take the day off."

"I'm getting some strange information on that murder yesterday. You got a minute to talk?"

"Sure. Take a load off."

J.D. took a chair across the desk from Sharkey. "I don't think our victim is who we think she is."

"What's going on?"

"Her fingerprints came back as belonging to a woman named

Darlene Pelletier who was arrested in New Orleans twenty years ago for shoplifting. She was nineteen at the time."

"Maybe that was her maiden name."

"My report on the husband says he married somebody named Linda Fournier in New Orleans twenty years ago."

"What do you make of all this?" Sharkey asked.

"I don't know. By the time he got married, Favereaux was a successful businessman. Why would he be marrying a nineteen-year-old shoplifter?"

"Maybe he didn't know about that. Maybe she was some kind of debutante who was shoplifting for the fun of it. Do you have any more information on the Pelletier woman?"

"Not yet. I've asked Doc Hawkins to run the fingerprints again. If he confirms that they belong to the Pelletier woman, I'll dig into her background."

"Sounds like you're doing everything you can at this point."

"Can you think of any reason a retired businessman would have a laptop with world-class encryption software?"

"Nope."

"How's the chief?" J.D. asked.

Martin gave her a quizzical look.

"Did Bill tell you why he wasn't coming in today?" J.D. asked.

"He did."

"Abby?"

"What do you know?"

"Not a lot. I know about Abby's arrest and the charges," J.D. said. "Matt is going to be representing her."

"Bill didn't mention Matt's involvement."

"He saw Abby at the jail early this morning. I think he was going to see Bill today and let him know he'll take the case."

"I'm glad. There're not many lawyers as good as Matt."

"Have you heard anything more through the grapevine?"

"No," he said. "I called a friend of mine at Sarasota PD, and all he could tell me was that FDLE had taken over. He did tell me that Jack Dobbyn had recused himself and the governor got busy first thing this morning and appointed the state attorney from Jacksonville to prosecute the case."

"That was quick," J.D. said.

"They probably want to move on this one. There's going to be a lot of press."

"I guess. I hope Bill can survive it."

"He will, if Matt gets an acquittal."

"Matt's worried about that," J.D. said. "About both Abby and Bill. It's a lot of pressure."

"Surely he knows that. If it's a problem, why take the case?"

"He's a bit of a cynic about the way law is practiced these days, but he's a believer in the system. He's worried that an out-of-control FDLE agent out to get a prominent defendant, coupled with an irresponsible press, is going to make it difficult to get a fair trial. He won't admit it, but he thinks he's good enough to overcome all that."

"Is he?"

"You've known him a lot longer than I have, Martin. What do you think?"

Sharkey grinned. "Ain't nobody better, sweet cheeks."

J.D. made a face. "Sweet cheeks?"

"Well, you know what I mean. Detective."

* * *

J.D.'s cell phone was ringing as she walked back to her office. Robin Hartill. J.D. answered. "Hey, Robin."

"Morning, J.D. I heard that Abigail Lester was arrested for murder. Anything you can tell me?"

"If you'll make me a confidential source, I'll tell you who to contact for all the information."

"You got it."

"And everybody calls her Abby. Not Abigail."

"Okay. The booking report had her full name. Whom do I talk to?"

"Matt."

"Matt? Your Matt?"

"Yep. He's going to be her lawyer."

"Where can I reach him? If I get this written in the next couple of hours, I can get it in Thursday's edition."

The weekly newspaper came out on Wednesdays, even though the masthead dated it for each Thursday. Since the paper was printed on Tuesday night, Robin's deadline would be fast approaching.

"Call his cell. You have the number?"

"I've got it. Thanks, J.D."

CHAPTER SEVEN

I was at Bill Lester's house at eight o'clock. He invited me in and poured me a cup of coffee. "Well?" he asked.

"I'll take the case, Bill. But we have to understand each other."

"Okay."

"I'll be Abby's lawyer. Not yours. There may be things I can't discuss with you, or I might take a position you don't like."

"I can live with that."

"You have to understand that I won't do anything to hurt Abby's case and I'll run everything by her before I do it."

"I'm okay with that."

"I won't be running that stuff by you."

He sat quietly, sipping his coffee, mulling over my comments. "Matt, I'm not some rookie. I've been a cop for more than twenty years. I know things you might not know about how cops work."

"You surely do, Bill, and I'm going to be asking you for advice and relying on it. But I have only one client, and it's not you."

"Matt, Abby's my wife."

"Yes, and my client. I can only answer to one person. Abby. Not you. If you can't live with that, we'll find another lawyer."

"Why are you willing to take this case, Matt? Because I asked you to?"

"Partly, and because Abby seems to want me. There are other lawyers around here who would be excellent choices for you. But, I know Abby, and I know she isn't a killer. That gives me a slight edge. I won't let her be railroaded into some bullshit plea deal, because I know she's innocent."

Bill chuckled. "There goes your objectivity."

He was right, of course. I couldn't know she wasn't guilty. My affection for her was already coloring my thinking, but I thought that would work in my favor. I was pretty sure I could turn off the subjectivity if the evidence started to pile up against her.

"You're right," I said. "But that may not be a bad thing."

"We need to talk about money. Do you want to bill us by the hour or on a lump sum basis?"

"I won't practice law for money. Not anymore. You can reimburse me for any out-of-pocket expenses, like paying for an investigator and a maybe a law clerk."

"You sure?"

"I'm sure."

"Thanks, Matt."

We shook hands and I left to see my client.

* * *

My phone rang as I was nearing the county courthouse. I answered.

"Matt, this is Robin Hartill."

"Good morning, Robin. How're you doing?"

"Great. I hear you're going to be representing Abigail Lester."

"Where would you hear such a thing?"

"Confidential source."

"That confidential source wouldn't be some cop I'm sleeping with, would it?"

"You're sleeping with a cop? I'm shocked."

"A gentleman never kisses and tells."

"Are you?"

"What, sleeping with a cop?"

She laughed. "Representing Mrs. Lester."

"I am."

"What can you tell me about the case?"

"She's innocent."

"You defense lawyers always say that."

"Yeah, but this time, it's true."

"Then why did they arrest her?"

"I don't know, Robin. I haven't actually been retained by Mrs. Lester, yet, but I think I will be in the next few minutes."

"Don't the police have to have probable cause to arrest somebody?"

"They do, but I haven't talked to the prosecutor yet, so I don't know why they arrested her. Have you talked to the arresting officer yet?"

"I've got a call in to Agent Lucas, but I haven't heard back from him."

"Why don't you call his boss at the FDLE office in Tampa? See what you get."

"I can do that."

"Good. Let me know what he says."

"Quid pro quo?" asked Robin.

"I'm on my way to talk to my client right now. Get what you can from FDLE, and I'll give you whatever I can."

"Fair enough. Talk to you later." She hung up.

* * *

I found a parking place near the jail, went through security, and was led to the same interview room I'd been in early that morning. Abby was sitting at the small table, dressed in an orange prison jumpsuit. She looked tired and drawn.

"Did you get any sleep?" I asked.

"No. They put me in a cell by myself, but there's so much noise in here the dead couldn't sleep."

"Did they feed you?"

"In a manner of speaking. I guess you could call what they gave me food. I wouldn't serve it to a pet rat. Are you going to represent me?"

"There are some ground rules we need to establish first."

"Like what?"

"You have to tell me the absolute truth. No omissions, no sidestepping, no shading."

"Not a problem."

"Abby, if I ever find out that you've lied to me or not told me the entire truth, I'll drop you like the proverbial hot potato."

"I won't do that, Matt. What else?"

"I haven't seen any of the evidence yet, but I've been told about a couple of things that are going to prove embarrassing. They'll come out, and we need to get ahead of them."

"Like what?"

"Like an affair you had with Bannister."

"I—"

I held up my hand. "Not yet. If I become your lawyer, I'll expect you to tell me if it becomes relevant, but we're not there yet."

"Okay. What other rules?"

"You talk to no one but me, or perhaps my investigator, about this case. No discussing it with other inmates or even Bill. Any conversation you have in the jail is probably monitored, and the prosecution can use anything you say against you."

"Agreed." She looked at me expectantly.

"The next rule has to do with me. I will never discuss anything you tell me with anyone other than my legal team, unless you give me specific permission. That includes your husband. I've already explained this to him, and he's on board with it." I crossed my fingers on this one. I'd surely talk to J.D., but I knew that whatever I said to her would stay between us. I sat silently, thinking.

"Is that it?"

I nodded. "Something else may come to mind. If so, I'll let you know."

"What about your fees?"

"Bill and I have worked that out."

"Then you're my lawyer?"

"I am. For better or worse."

"Where do we go from here?"

"The first thing we'll face is a lot of press. Word of the affair, if that's what it was, is going to get out. So is the fact that they found your fingerprints in Bannister's condo. Bill's going to learn about it, so, after you explain it all to me, I'd like your permission to tell him. I don't want him reading it in the newspaper."

"Okay. What about bail? I'd really like to get out of here."

"I'm going to push that through during your first appearance. That'll probably be this afternoon. It has to be done within twenty-four hours of your arrest. I don't know which judge we'll get, but I imagine it will be somebody from another circuit."

"Will I get out?"

"It's dicey, Abby. Right now you're charged with second-degree murder, which carries a twenty-five year to life sentence. The charge is one of the two exceptions to your right to bail, the other being a first-degree murder charge. However, the prosecution must show that the proof of guilt is evident, or that the presumption of guilt is great. I don't think they can show that at this point. I'd like to get this behind us now, rather than try for a bail hearing later. The downside is that the prosecution's belief that you had an affair with Bannister is going to be front-page news tomorrow."

"Let's go for it."

"I hoped you'd say that."

CHAPTER EIGHT

The first appearance hearing was going to be held via video conferencing at three o'clock in the afternoon. I had gone to the clerk of courts' office and gotten the paperwork moving, including filing a motion for bail and my notice of appearance on behalf of the defendant, Abigail Jane Cooper Lester. Both would be transmitted to the prosecutor and the judge before the hearing.

I was told that the governor had appointed the state attorney from Jacksonville to prosecute and because all the Twelfth Circuit judges had recused themselves, the governor had appointed a Tampa judge to preside over the case. That judge would handle the first appearance.

Robin Hartill called to tell me she had talked to the First Circuit state attorney's office in Jacksonville and was told that an assistant state attorney named George Swann would be the lead prosecutor.

"He's tried twenty-two murder cases and won them all," Robin said.

"Big deal," I said.

"That's a lot of wins, Matt. You might be in for some trouble."

"The prosecutor always gets to pick the cases he tries. If the case is too difficult, they often grab a plea deal. We'll see what this guy's made of when we get into the courtroom."

"Can I quote you on that?"

"That sounded kind of arrogant, didn't it? I'd rather you not quote me on that. No sense in pissing Swann off this early."

"Maybe later, on the quote?"

"We'll see. Did you find out anything else?"

"Did you know they found your client's fingerprints in Bannister's condo?"

"Yes."

"Did you hear about the emails between Abby and Bannister?"

"I heard about them, but I haven't seen them yet. Did you get a look at them?"

"No, but I'm told one of them was pretty threatening."

"Did you talk to FDLE?" I asked.

"Tried. Got a strange response."

"What?"

"I talked to the agent in charge of the Tampa office, a man named Stan Strickland. He said he couldn't discuss this case, but asked if I worked for Matt Walsh. I told him I did, and he said he'd call Walsh."

"Strange."

"Very. Your turn. I need more for my story."

"Okay. I don't know much, but we're going to turn the first appearance this afternoon into a bail hearing. I doubt Mr. Swann is going to be expecting that. Make sure you're in the jail video conference room at three this afternoon."

"That's it?"

"You can get the story on your Internet edition before the other papers get it out. I won't talk to anybody else until I get with you. You'll have an exclusive interview with me, for what it's worth, for your Internet edition. And you'll have your print story for tomorrow."

"Okay. See you at three."

* * *

I drove out to Bill Lester's house to tell him what was about to hit the papers. It was not an easy conversation, but I wanted him to know what was coming. "Under the circumstances, Bill, I think you should be at the hearing this afternoon. I want the press to see you as a man standing by his wife, no matter the circumstances.

Don't say anything to the press. Refer all questions to me. Just look resolute and supportive."

"Do you think the judge will grant bail?"

"Hard to say. Probably not. I filed the motion as soon as I met with Abby, but I don't hold out much hope for success. Whoever the judge is, he'll know he's going to be under a lot of press scrutiny. He won't want to appear to be giving Abby a break because her husband's a cop."

"Do you know which judge the governor appointed?"

"Not yet. Typically, the governor would decide on which circuit the judge would come from and let the chief judge of that circuit pick one of his judges for the governor to appoint. The name hasn't been disclosed yet."

We left it at that, and I drove home to shower and put on a clean suit. I wanted to look spiffy for the hearing. I suspected that the local TV stations might be broadcasting a live feed from the jail conference room. If I was going to be on TV, I needed to look the part of a lawyer. I'd been in high-profile cases before, back in my other life in Orlando, and I knew it was important to play to the press. I was certain that George Swann would be doing exactly that.

CHAPTER NINE

Bert Hawkins called J.D. at eleven. "This is very strange, J.D. Mrs. Favereaux's prints are not in any database."

"Wait a minute. Did your office somehow screw up with the first set of prints you ran?"

"No. I took a good look at the first set of prints we took. When I sent them the second time and got the negative response, I printed her again and compared that set to the first set we'd taken. They're identical."

"What does that mean?"

"I don't know. Maybe she's in the witness protection program. Maybe there's supposed to be a stop of some kind on her prints so that it would appear that there are no prints in the system."

"Then how did we get them the first time?" J.D. asked.

"Who knows? Maybe some kind of slip-up in the system."

"Thanks, Bert. You've confused the situation even more."

"Sorry. I'm just a seeker of truth."

J.D. laughed, hung up and sat back to think. Maybe the lack of a response to the second request for the fingerprints was the slip-up. Maybe the system just burped on the second request. She thought about sending the request again, but decided to wait.

She turned to the facts she knew, or surmised, about Linda Favereaux. By the time Favereaux married Darlene—if that was her real name—he would have been a very successful man. Maybe he wanted a trophy wife, or maybe he was in love with her despite the difference in ages. Maybe Darlene wanted to leave a bad life behind, and she completely changed her identity. It might all be innocent, but J.D. didn't think so.

She looked up the New Orleans Police Department on her computer and called the records department. "This is Detective J.D. Duncan in Longboat Key, Florida. I'm hoping you can help me with some old arrest records."

"What do you need?"

"Twenty years ago your department arrested a woman named Darlene Pelletier on a shoplifting charge. She was murdered here on Longboat Key yesterday. She had been living here under a fictitious name. I'm trying to do some background as part of my investigation."

"That'd be a misdemeanor charge. I doubt we'd have anything on it. Even if we kept the file, we lost a lot of records during Hurricane Katrina."

"Would you check on it for me?"

"Sure. How do I get in touch with you?"

J.D. thanked him and left the police station's phone number and her extension.

Her phone rang a few minutes later. A gruff voice on the other end of the line, said, "This is Special Agent Devlin Michel of the Drug Enforcement Administration."

"What can I do for you, Agent Michel?"

"You can tell me why you're looking for Darlene Pelletier."

J.D. was taken aback, and she didn't like Michel's tone of voice. "What interest would that be to you?"

"That's really none of your business. Why are you looking for Darlene Pelletier?"

"That's really none of your business, Agent Michel." She hung up, shaking her head at the lack of manners some people displayed.

The phone rang again. "This is Devlin Michel. I think we got off on the wrong foot."

"You certainly did."

"I apologize, Detective. Your inquiry on the prints rang some very large bells in Washington."

"My inquiry?"

"The one from the Sarasota County medical examiner. Your name was on it as an interested party."

"Why are the bells in Washington ringing?"

"I can't disclose that, but I will tell you we've been looking for her. For a long time."

"You can stop looking for her. She's dead."

"Dead? You sure?"

"A woman named Linda Favereaux was murdered on Longboat Key early yesterday. We ran her prints, and they came back as belonging to Darlene Pelletier."

"I wonder why we didn't see your first inquiry," he said.

"We didn't use her name on the request. Maybe your people are still looking at the prints and haven't yet connected them to Ms. Pelletier."

"Could be. You'll probably have a local DEA agent coming by to verify that Pelletier's dead."

"I've got a couple of questions for you."

"I'll help if I can. Shoot."

"Once you satisfy yourself that she's really dead, will you be able to tell me why you had her on a watch list?"

"I don't know. That's above my pay grade."

"Can you tell me if she's connected to anyone else? That might help lead me to her killer."

"Again, I don't know if we can give you that information."

"Does the name James Favereaux mean anything to you?"

"Not to me."

"How about to your agency?"

"I just don't know, Detective. I'll run all this up the chain of command and see if anyone will talk to you."

"I guess that's all I can ask for, Agent Michel. Thank you."

J.D. sat for a few minutes and picked up the phone again. She called Sammy Lastinger, the repository of most of the island gossip. He had been the bartender at Pattigeorge's, a popular restaurant on the island for many years. He had recently moved to the Haye Loft, an upscale bar on the second floor of a world-class restaurant called Euphemia Haye. He and Eric Bell, the bartender there, formed a team that the islanders were already calling the dynamic duo. Nothing that happened on the island would get by those two.

"Sammy," J.D. asked, "do you know James Favereaux and his wife Linda?"

"Do they drink and live on the island?"

"Presumably so."

"Then assume I know them. I heard Linda was murdered."

"She was. And her husband is missing in action. What can you tell me about them?"

"Not much. They'd come in sometimes, usually have a drink or two and leave. They weren't very talkative."

"Did they ever come in with anybody?"

"Not usually, but I did see them with Mike and Lyn Haycock one evening a couple of weeks ago. The four of them came into the bar for a drink. I think they'd had dinner downstairs."

"Thanks, Sammy. See you soon."

She was getting nowhere. The Haycocks were her friends, and she'd stop by and see them when Mike got home from work. Maybe they could shed some light on the Favereauxes.

She pulled the murder file out of her drawer and went through it again. She concentrated on the crime scene photos, pulling each of the eight-by-ten color prints out one at a time and staring at it, hoping to see something she'd missed. She was about halfway through the stack, and was looking closely at a photo of the body, when she noticed what appeared to be a small tattoo high on the underside of the victim's right arm. It was hard to tell for sure.

The body was facedown and the arm was lying on the floor at an odd angle, palm turned up. J.D. could just see the top of the tattoo. The arm had probably flopped over when J.D. asked the techs to turn the body so that she could see the back of her head.

J.D. pulled the autopsy report out of the file. She found a description of the tattoo buried deep in a long paragraph describing the body. It was about two inches square and was described as an abstract design with squares and circles. There were no pictures attached to the report, but J.D. knew the ME would have taken some. She called Bert Hawkins' office and asked his assistant to email her any pictures of the tattoo they had. They arrived ten minutes later.

The tattoo was simple. It was a square within a square with small circles within the squares. What was that all about? J.D. emailed it to the department geek and asked him to search all the tattoo databases to see if he could find one that matched.

CHAPTER TEN

The video conference room was small, so the deputies had ar-ranged for the press to use a bigger room down the hall. The video hearing would be transmitted to a large flat screen TV for the reporters and to the TV trucks parked on the street out front. We'd be live on TV screens all over the country. Nothing like a juicy murder story to send the media into a feeding frenzy. This one had all the elements: a resort town, a wealthy developer murdered, a sordid affair, and the wife of a local chief of police charged. Who could resist?

The video conference room had two tables positioned on ei-ther side of the room; one for the prosecution and the other for the defense. A flat screen hung from brackets in the ceiling at the front of the room. Two cameras were positioned so that one was trained on each table. A technician sat at a small console in a corner of the room. He would manipulate the feed from the cameras so that the person talking would be the one the judge saw on his screen. In this instance, he would also be getting a feed from the prosecutor's of-fice in Jacksonville and the judge's chambers in Tampa. He told me he would use a split-screen effect so that I could see both the judge and Mr. Swann at the same time. A court reporter sat next to the technician, her steno machine in front of her.

I had settled into one of the counsel tables and was waiting for the deputies to bring in Abby. I was surprised to see Agent Lu-cas walk into the room along with a man in his late thirties. Both were wearing suits and the man with Lucas was carrying a brief-case. Lucas saw me and whispered to the other man who came to my table, offering his hand.

"Mr. Royal, I'm George Swann. I'll be prosecuting this case."

I stood and introduced myself and shook his hand. "I wasn't expecting you here in person. I thought you'd be on TV."

"I thought so too, until I got your motion for bail. I chartered a plane and here I am."

"Welcome to paradise," I said. "I hope we'll be able to get through this mess on a professional basis."

Swann smiled. "I'm sure of it. I'll be going to a grand jury as soon as we can get one empaneled. You'll have to get a death case-certified lawyer to take over."

Uh, oh, I thought. Looks like we're going to be comparing genitalia size here. "I'm certified, Mr. Swann. I think I'll be able to muddle through."

He looked surprised, but the smile, or maybe the smirk, was still on his face. "I heard you were retired, living on an island, working as a beach bum."

"You heard right."

"And you're going to try a murder case?"

"Yep. I heard you've tried a few and got some verdicts."

"I'm twenty-two zip on murder cases. Never lost one."

Just what I needed. An arrogant prick. I smiled now, a genuine, you're-my-best-buddy kind of smile. "Maybe you ought to dismiss this case," I said. "You'll be able to preserve your sterling record."

He laughed. "I've never tried a case against a beach bum. We'll see." He walked back to his desk.

The door in the back of the room opened and a corrections deputy escorted Abby into the room. She was still wearing the jumpsuit and her wrists were cuffed in front of her. She sat at the table and gave me a tired smile. I leaned over and whispered, "Hang tough, Abby."

"I've got the judge up," the technician said, and the big screen came to life with the image of the Honorable Wayne Lee Thomas. I'd known Judge Thomas for a number of years, tried a few cases before him back in that other life I'd traded for the beach. He was a good man, a judge who was a stickler for the rules and courtroom decorum, who loved the law, understood it, and brooked no nonsense from those lawyers who would abuse it. He was fearless in his rulings and always fair. In short, he was the perfect judge for this case.

"Good afternoon, gentlemen," the judge said. "Please identify yourselves for the record."

Swann stood and identified himself. I followed suit, and the judge said, "I take it, Mr. Royal, that this retirement isn't working out too well for you."

"I just help out a friend now and then, Your Honor."

The judge chuckled. "Are we ready to proceed?"

"Yes, sir," Swann and I said in unison.

"If the defendant will stand, I'll read the charges," the judge said.

I stood. "Your Honor, we'll waive the reading of the charges. My client pleads not guilty. I filed a motion for bail that I'd like heard this afternoon."

"Okay, Mr. Royal. Mr. Prosecutor, did you get a copy of defendant's motion for bail?"

"I did, Your Honor. Of course, we object."

"What's the basis of your objection?"

"The defendant is charged with second-degree murder, and I think that will be increased to first degree as soon as we get to a grand jury. Because a gun was used in the murder, the defendant would be subject to a sentence of life in prison even if she were only convicted of second degree. The rules provide that there's no bail under those circumstances."

"I'm familiar with the rules, Counselor. And there's an exception. There's always an exception. What is your evidence of a high probability of conviction?"

"The Florida Department of Law Enforcement agent who is leading the investigation is here to testify, Your Honor. Agent Lucas."

"Okay. Agent Lucas, we don't have a witness stand in this room, so you can stay where you are. Please stand so that I can swear you in."

When Lucas was duly sworn, the judge said, "Your witness, Mr. Swann."

Swann stood and looked at Lucas. "State your name for the record."

"Wesley Lucas."

"Your occupation?"

"I'm an agent with the Florida Department of Law Enforcement."

"What is your job in relation to the case we're here on?"

"I'm the lead investigator."

"Have you reviewed the evidence that led to the arrest of the defendant, Abigail Lester?"

"Yes, sir."

"Did you order her arrest?"

"Yes, sir."

"Based on what?"

"The evidence at the scene points to her guilt."

"What evidence did you find?"

"Her fingerprints were in the victim's condo."

"Where did you find the fingerprints?"

"On a wine glass on a bedside table in Mr. Bannister's bedroom."

"Anything else?"

"There were emails from the defendant to the victim on the victim's computer."

"How many?"

"About ten."

"Over what period of time?"

"The week leading up to the murder."

"Have you read those emails?"

"Yes, sir."

"Was there anything in them that led you to believe the defendant was more than just an acquaintance of the victim?"

"Yes, sir."

"Please tell the court what that was."

"The emails were a bit salacious."

"What do you mean?"

"You know, sexy. Like sex talk between lovers."

"Anything else?"

"In the last email, the defendant threatened to kill the victim."

"What was the date of that email?"

"March thirty-first."

"The day Mr. Bannister was killed," Swann said.

"Yes."

"Anything else?"

"There was semen and vaginal secretions on the bed sheets in the victim's room."

"Have you checked for DNA?"

"Yes, sir. The semen was the victim's. We weren't able to compare the DNA in the vaginal secretions to the defendant."

"Why not?"

"We have no exemplars of her DNA. We'll be getting a court order for that."

"Anything else?"

"The bullet that killed Mr. Bannister was from a thirty-eight caliber revolver. We found the casing in the bedroom and the bullet in his brain."

"What significance is that?" asked Swann.

"The defendant is the registered owner of a thirty-eight caliber revolver."

Swann looked at the camera, giving Judge Thomas a big smirky grin. "That's all I have for now, Your Honor."

"You may cross-examine, Mr. Royal." the judge said.

I stood. "Thank you, Your Honor. Good afternoon, Agent Lucas."

"Good afternoon."

"When did you decide that Abby Lester was your target?"

"I wouldn't say she was a target. She was the person the evidence pointed to."

"Okay. When did you come to the conclusion that Abby was probably the murderer?" I wanted to humanize my client a bit. I would use the same tactic with the jury. Using her first name made her more of a real person than simply calling her the defendant or the accused.

"After we finished processing the evidence."

"And what time of day was that, Agent Lucas?"

"Probably mid-afternoon."

"Mid-afternoon of yesterday?"

"Yes."

"Do you know what time the crime scene technicians discovered Abby's fingerprints?"

"Not exactly."

"You weren't part of the investigation until after the fingerprints had been processed, were you?"

"That's right. The Sarasota police chief called my boss in Tampa and told him that Mrs. Lester might be a suspect and he wanted to get our agency involved."

"Did the chief use that term? 'Suspect?'"

"I wasn't privy to that conversation."

"So, you don't know exactly what was said in relation to Abby Lester?"

"Not exactly."

"So, the word 'suspect' is your word. Right?"

"Yes, sir."

"May I remind you, Agent Lucas, that you're in a court of law and sworn to tell the truth?"

"No. I'm well aware of where I am, Counselor."

"So, would it be unfair of me to ask that you stick to what you know and not give us rank speculation?"

"Objection, Your Honor." Swann was on his feet, outrage evident. It was a pretty good act.

"What are your grounds, Mr. Swann?" asked Judge Thomas.

"Mr. Royal is arguing with the witness."

"Didn't sound like argument to me. The witness stepped

over the line, and Mr. Royal, quite adroitly, I thought, brought him back. Overruled."

"But, Your Honor—" said Swann, before being cut off by the judge.

"Was there something you didn't understand about my ruling, Mr. Swann?"

"I understood it, Your Honor, but—"

The judge cut him off again. "Then sit down, Mr. Swann. I've ruled."

I smiled to myself. Old Wayne Lee hadn't changed. He ran a tight courtroom. Most good trial lawyers appreciated that. Nonsense wasn't allowed, and woe be unto the lawyer who engaged in it. Thomas would cut him off at the knees and not worry a whole lot about the mess a couple of bloody stumps would leave in the jury's mind.

"You may proceed, Mr. Royal," the judge said.

"Thank you, Your Honor. How did you come to be assigned to the case, Agent Lucas?"

"I was already in Sarasota on another matter, and my supervisor called me and asked me to get involved."

"What time of day did you decide to arrest Abby Lester?"

"After we reviewed all the evidence and had agreed to rule out the other people whose fingerprints were in the condo. About mid-afternoon, I'd say."

"About three o'clock yesterday afternoon?"

"Yes."

"So, by then, the fingerprints had been identified as belonging to Abby," I said.

"Yes, sir."

"Had you found the emails by then?"

"Sarasota PD had those. Yes, sir."

"Who made the decision to arrest Abby?"

"I did."

"And that was based on the fingerprints and the emails?"

"Yes, sir."

"Did the technicians find any other fingerprints in the victim's condo?"

"Yes, sir."

"Of how many people, Agent?"

"About ten."

"Have you identified any of those?"

"Yes. Most of them, I think."

"Did you arrest those people?"

"No, sir."

"Why not?"

"Why would we?"

"Well, you ordered Abby's arrest based on the fingerprints, didn't you?"

"And the emails."

"Did you find Abby's finger prints anywhere in Mr. Bannister's condo other than on the wine glass in the bedroom?"

"No, sir."

"Didn't you find that odd? Wouldn't you have expected to find her prints in other parts of the condo?"

"Not necessarily. With the exception of the glasses Mr. Bannister and Mrs. Lester were drinking out of, all the glasses and dishes had been washed. There were no prints of anyone on them."

I switched gears. "How did you know the emails came from Abby?"

Lucas couldn't help himself. He chuckled and shrugged his shoulders. "I don't know. Maybe because she signed them?"

"You mean she had an electronic signature attached to them?"

"No. She just typed her name at the bottom of the emails."

"Including the email that contained the threat to kill Mr. Bannister?"

"Yes."

"Couldn't someone else have done the same thing? Typed her name in?"

"Why would anybody do that?" Lucas asked.

"Why would anybody as smart as a high-school history teacher like Abby put her name at the bottom of an email threatening to kill the man she was supposedly having an affair with?"

"You'd have to ask her," Lucas said.

I let the silence hang for a moment. "I have," I said.

I shuffled some papers, letting the silence run on for another few seconds. "Agent Lucas, why did you wait twelve hours, until three in the morning to arrest Abby?"

"It's safer to arrest somebody in the middle of the night."

"Safer than going to her house at a reasonable hour in the afternoon, or the next morning?"

"Yes."

"Were you afraid she was going to shoot you? Maybe beat you up?"

"You never know, Counselor."

"No, I guess not. Not when you're after a hardened criminal. Or a history teacher. Did you confiscate Abby's computer?"

"There was only one computer in the house, and we got it."

"Were you able to determine if Abby used that computer?"

"She did."

"Did you look at her emails? The ones she'd sent from her computer?"

"Yes."

"Did you find copies of the emails she'd supposedly sent to Mr. Bannister?"

"No."

"Didn't you find that odd?"

"Not particularly. She could have erased them."

"Do you know who her Internet service provider is, Agent Lucas?"

"Verizon."

"And any emails she sent from her computer would have gone through Verizon, right?"

"That's my understanding."

"And wouldn't Verizon have had all that information stored somewhere?" I asked.

"Supposedly."

"Did you reach out to Verizon to see if they could track the emails?"

"One of the technicians did."

"And did Verizon have that information?"

Lucas looked over at Swann, as if waiting for some direction. He got nothing. He looked back at me. "I'm told that Verizon had no record of any emails between the defendant and the victim."

When one is ahead, one sits down and shuts up. "Nothing further, Your Honor," I said.

"Redirect, Mr. Swann?" Judge Thomas asked.

"No, sir."

"Do you have any witnesses, Mr. Royal?"

"Perhaps, Your Honor. I'd like to put my client on the stand to testify about her ties to the community, which goes to the risk of her fleeing the jurisdiction of this court and which is germane to your decision on my motion for bail. However, I'd like a stipulation, or better yet, an order from you, that the only testimony elicited from my client would have to do with her residency and such and that this would not prejudice in any way her right not to testify at trial, if she decides not to take the stand."

"Will you so stipulate, Mr. Swann?" the judge asked.

"No, sir."

"Then I rule that the defendant can testify and no prejudice will attach. Mr. Swann, you may not examine on the merits of this case."

The judge swore in my client. I stood and directed my questions to Abby. "State your name for the record, please."

"Abigail Lester."

"Where do you reside?"

She gave her address on Longboat Key.

"That's in Sarasota County?" I asked.

"Yes, sir."

I went through a litany of questions and elicited that she had lived her entire life in Sarasota County, graduated from Sarasota High School and gone to college at the University of South Florida's Sarasota campus. She had taught in the Sarasota County school system for seventeen years and had been married to Bill Lester, the Longboat Key chief of police, for fifteen years. Her father was dead and her mom lived in Sarasota in the house where Abby had been raised.

When I finished, Swann said that he had no questions.

Judge Thomas looked at his notes for a moment and then said, "I'm going to grant bail of one hundred thousand dollars with conditions. Mrs. Lester, you will have to wear an ankle monitor that will alert the sheriff's office if you go more than one hundred feet from the base unit that will be in your home. If you need to leave your home for any reason, such as meeting with your attorney or going to the doctor, you will need to get permission from the probation officer who will be assigned to you. Do I make myself clear?"

"Yes, Your Honor," Abby said.

"Anything else, gentlemen?" the judge asked.

"Your Honor," I said. "Can you order the sheriff's department to set up the monitoring system today so that we can get my client released?"

"I'll transmit the order within a half hour or so. You should be able to take her home today."

"Thank you, Your Honor."

"Anything further?"

Swann and I both said no.

"Court is dismissed," the judge said, and the TV screen went blank.

CHAPTER ELEVEN

It was almost five o'clock when J.D. called the Haycock home. Lyn answered. "It's good to hear from you, J.D.," she said. "How have you and Matt been?"

"We're fine, Lyn, but I need to come by and talk to you and Mike."

"What's up?"

"It's part of an investigation I'm involved in."

"Well, sure, J.D.," Lyn said, a bit hesitantly. "You're always welcome. You know that. Mike just called to tell me he's on his way. He should be home in a few minutes. Come on over now, if you'd like. Is this about Linda Favereaux?"

"It's not a big deal, but I'm just trying to get a little background on her and her husband. Sammy told me you'd had dinner together recently, and I thought maybe you could shed some light on them."

"I'm not sure how much we can help, but I bought a bottle of Villa Maria Sauvignon Blanc from Publix this morning."

"I'll be there in half an hour."

* * *

Mike and Lyn lived in a bayfront townhouse not far from the police station. They were gracious hosts who threw Super Bowl parties that had become legendary. Mike, who was nearing retirement, was an executive with a multinational company with offices in Bradenton. He and Lyn had lived on the island for a number of years and had no plans to leave.

"Sit down, J.D.," Lyn said. "I'll get you a glass of wine."

"I shouldn't. I'm still on duty."

"We won't tell," Mike said.

"Well, then," J.D. said, "you talked me right into it."

"Lyn said you've been talking to Sammy."

J.D. nodded. "Everybody on the island knows if you need to know something about anyone, Sammy's the source."

Mike laughed. "You can say that again. I'm afraid we can't be much help. We didn't really know the Favereauxes that well."

"How long have you known them?" J.D. asked.

Mike looked at Lyn. "A year, maybe?"

"That's about right," Lyn said. "We met them at the bar at Pattigeorge's one night, but they weren't regulars. We saw them a few times after that, and a couple of weeks ago, Jim invited us to dinner. That's how we ended up at Euphemia Haye."

"Did they tell you anything about their backgrounds?"

"No," Mike said. "I did ask what he did, and he told me he was retired. When I asked what he'd done before, he just said he had been an investor. He sounded sort of guarded, but that might have been my imagination. I didn't push it."

"How did they seem together? Any animosity, that sort of thing?" J.D. asked.

"There was quite an age difference," Lyn said, "but I didn't see that there was a problem. Linda said they'd been married about twenty years, so I guess it was working. But, well, I probably shouldn't say anything."

"You never know what might help," J.D. said.

"I just felt like there was some kind of barrier between them. I can't put my finger on it, but there seemed to be, maybe not a barrier, but some distance or something. You know how married couples are. There's an easiness between them, something unspoken. I can't explain it, and I probably ought to keep my mouth shut, but it left me feeling like I was out with two people who were friends, not mates. Does this make any sense?"

"Actually, it does," J.D. said. "I've met people like that. You just know intuitively that something's not right. Like maybe it was more of a business proposition. He needed or wanted a trophy wife, and she liked his money."

"That could be," Lyn said, "but it seemed a little more than that."

"Have you heard anything about Linda having an affair?" J.D. asked.

Mike laughed. "That didn't exactly come up at dinner."

J.D. smiled, "I guess not."

"But, that might explain my feelings about them," Lyn said. "Like maybe their relationship was a bit strained."

The Haycocks had nothing else to add. The conversation moved on to mutual friends, Sammy's new job, and his most recent girlfriend, the latest in a long line of beautiful women.

CHAPTER TWELVE

J.D. and I were having a quiet dinner on the sunporch of her condo overlooking Sarasota Bay. It was nearing eight o'clock and we were both tired. The sun was setting over the Gulf, its dying rays reflecting off the low-lying clouds to the east, painting the still waters with a patina of liquid gold.

We had gone over my day, and she was telling me about hers. I was fascinated by this wondrous creature who loved me. She was tall, about five-seven, and her daily workouts kept her slender and shapely. Her dark shoulder-length hair framed a face that in another time would have graced a Grecian urn. Her green eyes twinkled with good humor, and when occasion demanded, flashed with anger. Her smile was a high-wattage killer, her laugh big and contagious.

My cell phone rang. I answered. "This is Matt Royal."

"This is Matt Walsh."

"Hello, Matt."

"Hello, Matt."

It was our shtick, a silly greeting between old friends. He often reminded me that he was older than I, and thus had seniority in the use of the name. Matt Walsh was an old-school journalist and the publisher of one of our local weekly newspapers, the *Longboat Observer*. "I've just had a troubling telephone conversation with Stan Strickland, the agent in charge of the Tampa FDLE office," he said.

"Troubling how?"

"One of my reporters called him earlier today about the Abby Lester case. He wouldn't talk to her because he would be breaking all kinds of rules if it got out that he was giving a reporter any information. So he called me."

"Why call you?" I asked.

"He's an old acquaintance. We met several years ago through Kiwanis, and we run into each other occasionally. He said there was some funny stuff going on with this case, and he's tired of the pressure he gets from people in high places. That, and the fact that he trusts me to keep my mouth shut on what he called deep background."

"And you're calling me?"

"I told him that you and the Lesters were friends of mine, and if what he had to tell me would have an impact on Abby's case, I would want to be able to discuss it with the three of you. He wouldn't agree to let me talk to the Lesters, but he said I could pass it on to you. He said he'd be protected by the attorney-client privilege, and you couldn't talk about what he had to say."

"Actually, the work-product privilege would protect the information, but it serves the same purpose. I can keep it all confidential. What did he have to say?"

"He's not happy with the agent investigating Abby's case."

"Wes Lucas," I said.

"That's the one. Apparently, there's some bad blood between Strickland and Lucas."

"Then why assign Lucas the case?"

"Lucas told Strickland he wanted it, and Strickland felt he had to give it to him. It seems that Lucas has some highly placed friends, and what Lucas wants, Lucas gets. Strickland is sick of dealing with it, and thinks that maybe a little publicity about how Lucas barged into the Lester case might have some effect on the higher-ups who are pulling the strings."

"Highly placed in FDLE?" I asked.

"Higher than that."

"Did he tell you who?"

"He doesn't know, but he's had pressure before when he tried to discipline Lucas for stepping over the line in cases he was working."

"Lucas said he was in Sarasota working on another matter when FDLE was called in. That's the reason he was assigned to Bannister's murder."

"Strickland says that wasn't the way it happened. Lucas called him on the morning the body was discovered and said he wanted to be the lead investigator. The thing is, Lucas called before Strickland even knew there was a murder."

"That's strange. I wonder if Lucas was in Sarasota and heard about the case and Abby's possible involvement."

"Don't know, but Strickland said Lucas was very insistent that he get the assignment."

"Are you going to follow up on this?" I asked.

"Maybe. But, Matt, I won't be able to keep you informed on what we find. If I can print it, you'll see it, but I can't let my people become part of your investigation."

"I understand, and I appreciate your calling me on this. Do you think it'd be okay for me to talk to Strickland?"

"I don't see why not. He specifically gave me permission to talk to you."

"Thanks, Matt."

"You're welcome, Matt." The line went dead.

I told J.D. what Walsh had said. "Lucas must have a direct line into Sarasota PD. Somebody's leaking him information."

"Maybe not," she said.

"I don't know of any other way he could have known about the murder so soon."

"Unless he was part of the murder and the framing of Abby in the first place."

I hadn't thought about that possibility. "You have a devious mind. I wonder, though. You might be onto something. I'll look into it."

"I'd like to know who is protecting a scumbag like Lucas," she said.

"So would I. What were we talking about when Walsh called?"

"My murder case. I haven't heard back from New Orleans on my record request. I don't know if the files on Darlene Pelletier even exist, or whether everybody out there is just too lazy to look for them."

"What are you hoping to find?"

"I don't know. I'm just stirring the pot, hoping some bit of information will float to the top. I have nothing at this point, except that the husband has disappeared. We've tagged his credit cards, but there have been no hits anywhere. Late this afternoon, Tampa PD found his car in a long-term parking lot at Tampa International, but nobody named James Favereaux has taken a flight out of there since last Friday. And we know he was home on Friday afternoon when the maid left for the day."

"Nothing else from the DEA?"

"Nothing. I thought I might get a call back from Agent Michel, but not so far. Maybe he'll call tomorrow."

"I wouldn't bet on it. If you don't have information to trade him, he's got no reason to give you anything. He was looking for Darlene Pelletier, and you told him she's dead. He'll follow up on that to make sure your identification was good, and that'll be the end of DEA's involvement."

She frowned. "I'm afraid you're right. I'll just have to keep digging. Where are you going with Abby's case?"

"I'm not sure yet. I don't think she killed Bannister, and I don't think the state can prove she did. At least not with the evidence they have so far."

"What about the DNA on the sheets?"

"If it's hers, that would be a big hurdle to get over. I guess we'll know in a few days. I need to find somebody who can tell me about those emails. I'd like to know where they came from since they weren't sent from Abby's computer."

"Our department geek could probably explain that to you."

"I don't want to have any appearance of help from your people. That could end up biting me in the butt at trial."

"You're right," she said. "I hadn't thought of that."

"I'll have to hire an expert who can testify, if need be."

"Who do you think did kill Bannister?"

"I don't have any idea, but I need to come up with some suspects to give the jury a plausible alternative to Abby as the murderer. That produces reasonable doubt, which means acquittal."

"I thought you were pretty sure the state didn't have enough evidence to convict."

"I don't think they do, now, but we've got several months to go before trial. And there's the DNA question hanging out there."

"Did Abby have an affair with Bannister?"

"I don't know. I haven't asked her."

"Isn't that important?"

"It may be, but not right now."

"Why not?"

"Abby's fingerprints in Bannister's condo mean nothing in and of themselves. Except that she's been in the house. But so have a lot of other people. If the DNA isn't Abby's, that shoots a hole in the prosecution's theory that it was an affair gone bad. The emails certainly made it look like there had been an affair, but they didn't come from Abby's computer. So unless Swann and Lucas can tie the emails to Abby in some way, or find a witness who will testify that he or she has some knowledge of an affair, I think we'll be in the clear. If that theory is dead, I don't need to know about an affair. And frankly, I just don't want to think that Abby would do something like that."

"You need to be very careful of your objectivity, Counselor."

"I know," I said. "I'm counting on you to help me with that."

"Even if someone wanted to kill Bannister, and from what I hear, there may have been a lot of them, why would they pick Abby to pin it on?"

"If I can find the answer to that, I'll know who the killer is."

"Are you going to stay here tonight?" J.D. asked.

"No, I want to get on the computer and do a little research. I wouldn't be good company."

"You're always good company."

"Well, your expectations are minimal."

"Hmm. You're probably right. I do the best I can with what little I've got to work with."

"Are you saying that what you have to work with isn't a lot?"

"No, sweetie," she said, "it's not. But we women put up with a lot, or a little, in the name of love."

"Wasn't that a song?"

"Roberta Flack. 'When you feel it, you can't let go.'"

"Geez," I said. "I'll see you tomorrow."

CHAPTER THIRTEEN

It was nearing ten in the evening when I walked into my cottage. It had been a long day and I was tired. I felt my bed calling me, but I had a few things to do if I didn't want to lie awake all night worrying about them.

I rummaged around in my desk drawer and found the external hard drive on which I kept all kinds of legal things left over from my years of law practice. I had forms for most of the pleadings I would be filing during the course of *State of Florida vs. Abigail Lester*, lots of statutes and case law, which I needed to update, and other miscellany. I might be able to muddle through without hiring a law clerk.

I would need an investigator. There were too many questions that needed to be answered, and although the state attorney was supposed to provide me with much of the information I'd need, I was afraid that George Swann would be a master at the game of hide the ball. It was unethical, of course, but, too often prosecutors forgot their charge to see that justice was done rather than the need to win at all costs.

J.D. had introduced me to a Sarasota police detective named Gus Grantham, with whom she'd worked in Miami before he moved to Sarasota PD a few years before. J.D. and I had gone to dinner with him on several occasions. He had recently retired, gotten his private investigator's license, and opened an office in a building across from the Ringling School of Art and Design on North Tamiami Trail. I decided to give him a call the next morning.

I needed to find out more about my opponent. I Googled Swann and found several articles about him and his trials that had run over the years in the *Florida Times-Union*, the Jacksonville newspaper. He'd been a climber, starting out in the misdemeanor division when he graduated from law school at Florida State University. He'd moved up quickly to the felony division and within a few years was trying murder cases. He'd been with the state attorney's office for thirteen years, was thirty-nine years old, and a native of Orange Park, a suburb of Jacksonville. A few of the articles about his murder cases mentioned the names of his opposing counsel, usually a member of the public defender's staff. I made a mental note to call a couple of them.

I did a quick survey of the case law, updating my digital library, downloading a few recent cases, and cataloging them by subject matter. They'd be close at hand if and when I needed them.

I was restless, my mind churning, gnawing at the case I'd taken on. There was so much to learn, so much to do, so much riding on the decisions I made, the strategies I relied on. I was probably closer to Abby than a lawyer should be to his client. There were so many reasons I should not handle this case, but while our system of justice was the best in the world, it wasn't foolproof, and I had come to the conclusion, perhaps unsupported by facts, that Swann and Lucas were glory hounds who would not be above manipulating the process to score a win, no matter the guilt or innocence of the defendant.

My problem with the practice of law was that I was an idealist. I thought the law should be somehow immaculate, above the machinations of mere mortals. Yeah, I know, that's kind of stupid, and I had not been a lawyer very long before I began to see how outrageous my expectations had been. It was a rat race and the rats were the lawyers who plied their trade in the courtrooms all over the country. Winning, not justice, was the name of the game, and I became one of the rats. Alcohol consumption made it easier to go to work every day, and I began to exist in a haze of good bourbon. I had once been a proud soldier, an officer leading a group of men who were the best fighters in the world and the most honorable people I'd ever known. Honorable men in the honorable profession of soldiering. Then I went to law school.

The terrible contradiction of the law was that it was peopled for the most part with idealists who had to lower their sights to survive in the real world of daily practice. Most of the lawyers I knew were honest, forthright, and hard working. But there were enough of the other kind that the practice lost its allure for me.

My wife Laura, the only woman I'd loved before I met J.D., worked hard at our marriage, but finally gave up in the face of my intransigence. She left me, got a divorce, and remarried. I woke up one morning a couple of years later, looked around my empty house, said the hell with it, sold everything I had, and moved to Longboat Key to start over. It was the best decision I'd made in a long time.

Maybe it was that innate idealism, the little flicker of what was left of it that still endured deep in my soul that was dragging me back into the courtroom. Maybe that wasn't a bad thing. But was I doing this for Abby Lester, or myself? I'd have to chew on that some. And my house, on this night, was very empty. I picked up my phone and called J.D.

"I need a place to sleep," I said. "I'm not real choosy about where or with whom."

"You did say sleep."

"Yes."

"Just sleep?"

"I think so. I'm tired."

"Then come on over. I'll make room for you."

CHAPTER FOURTEEN

I slept in on Wednesday morning. At some point I heard the shower running and a bit later, I felt J.D. kiss me on the forehead as she was leaving for work. I went back to sleep until a little after nine and woke up feeling like I could take on the world.

I showered in J.D.'s oversized shower, dressed, and drove the mile and a half to the Blue Dolphin Café for breakfast. Most of the locals had already left and the place was full of tourists. I sat at the counter and read the *Tampa Bay Times* while I ate. I was aware that someone had taken the stool next to me, but I was engrossed in the latest news out of Washington, which really wasn't news, just a rehash of the same old political battles that were so meaningless to most people.

"Back to the courtroom, huh, buddy? You must be bored."

I looked up to find my friend Logan Hamilton sitting next to me. I laughed. "Hey, Logan. You look a little peaked. Long night?"

"Tiny's was jumping. I thought you and J.D. might stop in."

"We had a quiet night. I got a pizza and salad from Ciao's and we ate at her place. Anything special going on at Tiny's?"

"Nah. A lot of snowbirds winding up their stays on the key. Most of them are headed north. I guess they wanted to make sure there wasn't any liquor left on the island. Are you sure you're doing the right thing by taking on Abby's case?"

"I think so. What do you think?

"Matt, there's no better lawyer in the state than you are. If anybody can get her off, it's you." He sat quietly.

"I appreciate the compliment, but you still haven't said whether you think I ought to be on this case."

"You think she's being railroaded, don't you?"

"Yes, but I don't know why."

"You want to get up on that white charger of yours and go do justice, don't you?"

I laughed. "Yeah, you're probably right."

"Then go do it. If somebody else takes this case, and she's found guilty, you'll never get over it."

"Suppose I take the case and she's still found guilty?"

"You'll do everything you can to see that doesn't happen, won't you?"

"Of course."

"Then you won't have any regrets."

"If I lose, I will. I remember every case I ever lost. I regret them all."

"In the cases you lost, were any of the clients innocent?"

"Probably not. But I still lost."

"You were supposed to lose, buddy. Can't have those guilty bastards on the streets."

As usual, Logan had a point. "Well, I'm in it now." I said. "For good or bad."

"You'll do fine. When are we going fishing?"

"October, probably."

"October? Are you crazy?"

"Trial will be over by then."

"You're full of crap, Royal. You won't be able to wait that long."

"You're probably right. How about Saturday?"

* * *

I went back to my cottage and called Gus Grantham. "I might have some work for you, Gus. Can you have lunch today?"

"Abby Lester?"

I was surprised. "How did you know about that?"

"You were on the front page of the *Herald-Tribune* this morning. Big piece about a beach-bum lawyer coming out of retirement to take the case. Don't you read the paper?"

"I haven't seen today's Sarasota paper. I'll pick up a copy. But, yes, this is about Abby's case. Is that a problem?"

"Not at all. Where do you want to have lunch?"

"How about Cha Cha Coconut's on the Circle. At noon."

"See you then."

I cranked up my computer and called a lawyer I knew in Jacksonville who had tried a case against George Swann. I identified myself and told him about my upcoming trial.

"I heard you had retired and were living the good life down in the keys."

"You heard right, except that I'm on Longboat Key, near Sarasota. What can you tell me about Swann?"

"He's a snake," the lawyer said.

"Don't mince words," I said. "Tell me straight up."

He laughed. "I wouldn't usually talk about a lawyer like that, but Swann is just a bad guy."

"Tell me about him."

"First of all, he's very particular about the cases he tries."

"How do you mean?"

"If there's a solid defense, or even a chance of a defense, he'll either plead it out or dismiss the case. He only goes to trial on slam dunks."

"Give me an example."

"One of his wins had to do with a murder where a man with a record as long as my arm killed a cop. Three other cops witnessed the shoot-out. Swann opted to go for the death penalty and wouldn't agree to anything less. The public defender put up as good a defense as he could, but the trial took one day. Swann put the three cops on the stand, the defense put on no case, and the jury was out for twenty minutes."

"Are there others like that?"

"You mean big wins?" he said, sarcastically.

"Yes."

"Most of them."

"What about the case you tried against him?"

"Pretty much the same kind of case. I was appointed because the public defender had a conflict. My guy was guilty and the evidence was pretty much stacked against me. I tried for an insanity defense because there was no other chance. I think Swann was afraid his precious win record might be compromised, so he did everything he could to screw with me. I had a hell of a time getting the discovery done. Everything I filed was contested, put off with motions, anything he could do to keep me from getting the stuff I was entitled to."

"Your judge didn't do anything about it?"

"He ruled with me every time, but refused to order sanctions."

"Why?"

"The state attorney is a big political power up here, and the judge has to run for reelection. He wasn't about to piss off the man."

"How did your case come out?"

"The judge ruled against us on the insanity plea and we lost. I won in the penalty phase, though. No death penalty. But Swann still puts that one in his win column. In fact, a lot of those wins are where he had slam dunks, and he got the conviction, but lost the death penalty. The defendants still went away for life without parole."

A little small talk and I thanked him and hung up. I made two more calls to lawyers in Jacksonville, and got pretty much the same opinions. Swann was not an ethical man, and it didn't sound like his boss was either. My suspicions were confirmed. I'd have to keep my eyes open and expect the worst kind of lawyering. But then, two could play that game.

CHAPTER FIFTEEN

The department geek had left a report on J.D.'s desk concerning the tattoo on Linda Favereaux's arm. He had found its twin in a database that was restricted to law enforcement agencies. Over the years, the federal agencies had collected thousands of pictures of tattoos found on drug dealers, terrorists, white supremacy groups, criminal gangs, and others who would do harm to the rest of us. Curiously, Linda's tattoo matched the secret logo of a neo-Nazi group that, according to the geek's report, was still marginally active in Louisiana. A web address was included.

J.D. typed it into her computer and up popped a picture of a man in a brown shirt wearing a red armband bearing the swastika of the Nazi party. His right arm was straight out in the Nazi salute. A banner above him screamed, "TAKE AMERICA BACK FROM THE MONGRELS." The group's name was emblazoned across the bottom: "THE WHITE AMERICA PARTY."

The text made J.D. wince. It was an exhortation to kill black people, brown people, Jews, and Muslims; anybody who wasn't of the Aryan race, whatever that was. The party seemed to be small, but was proud that it had existed for more than forty years, doing its best to transform America into what the Founders had envisioned, a democratic utopia where the white race could achieve its God-given rights to life, liberty, and the pursuit of happiness, without the nettlesome problems presented by the inferior races.

J.D. clicked off the site and sat for a few minutes, wondering at the insanity of these people. What could have happened to them to cause such hatred, such paranoia? She shook herself out of her reverie and called Lyn Haycock to ask her if either of the Favereauxes had ever said anything racist in their meetings.

"No," Lyn said. "To the contrary, I know they had some black friends. I've seen them on the island at least twice with a black couple who live on the mainland. They introduced them to Mike and me as old friends."

"Do you remember their names?"

"I can't come up with a last name, but their first names were Mark and Julie. They're both professors at the Sarasota campus of the University of South Florida."

"Thanks, Lyn. That'll narrow the search substantially."

The USF branch at Sarasota only enrolled a couple thousand students, so the faculty would be fairly small. It shouldn't be too hard to find the professors. She called the Human Resources Department and asked to speak to the director.

"This is Detective J.D. Duncan, Longboat Key police. I'm trying to identify a couple of your professors who might have some information about a case I'm working on."

"I don't know what I can tell you, Detective," the woman on the other end of the line said. "We have a lot of privacy concerns here."

"Actually, I just need a last name. The professors are married, they're black and their first names are Mark and Julie."

"Oh, I know just who you're talking about, but I wouldn't feel comfortable giving out any information on them. Suppose I take your number and ask one of them to call you?"

"I'd appreciate that," J.D. said, and gave the woman the phone number of the station.

An hour later J.D. picked up her ringing phone. "Detective Duncan?" the voice said.

"Yes."

"This is Julie Erickson. The human resources director at USF said you were looking for me and my husband."

"Thank you for calling, Professor. I'm investigating the murder of Linda Favereaux."

"Oh, my. I heard about that. It's just terrible."

"I have a very sensitive question to ask you, but I assure you it has a place in my investigation."

"Okay."

"Are you and your husband African-American?"

There was a bit of surprise in her voice. "Yes."

"I apologize for having to ask that. I understand that you and your husband were old friends of the Favereauxes. I have also developed some information that the Favereauxes may have at one time been involved with a white supremacy or neo-Nazi group?"

"Aren't they the same thing?"

"Usually," J.D. said. "Did the Favereauxes ever indicate any racist feelings to you?"

"My Lord, no. They were the most color-blind people I've ever known. We first met them a couple of years ago when they endowed a chair that my husband and I now jointly hold."

"An endowed chair is a fund set aside to support and pay a professor for teaching in a particular subject area, right?"

"Right."

"Do you mind my asking in what academic discipline the chair is funded?"

"African American studies."

"Oh."

"Yes. That doesn't sound like something a couple of racists would do, now does it?"

"No, Professor. It certainly doesn't. Let me ask you something else. Have you heard from Mr. Favereaux in the past few days?"

"No, we haven't. We read in the paper that he'd disappeared. We're concerned about his safety."

"Did you see any indication that there was trouble in their marriage, or that they were concerned about anything?"

"Nothing."

"When was the last time you saw them?"

"We had dinner last Thursday at Michaels on East."

"Anything out of the ordinary come up?"

"No. It was just a pleasant evening. Like so many others we've had."

"Would you mind giving me your contact information in case I need to get in touch with you again?"

Julie Erickson gave J.D. an address and a phone number.

"Thank you for your cooperation, Professor. I apologize again about the question about your race."

"Don't worry about it, Detective. I know you're just doing your job. Don't hesitate to call if you need anything else."

CHAPTER SIXTEEN

I drove south on the key, headed for St. Armands Circle, one of the premier shopping and dining venues in Florida. It was a gorgeous spring day, the temperature in the mid-seventies, and the air drifting off the Gulf was sweet with the smell of the sea. The sidewalks were full of walkers, joggers, and bicyclists, all jockeying good-naturedly for space. I had the sunroof of the Explorer open and was listening to soft classical music on the radio. A guy just can't beat living in paradise.

Gus Grantham was waiting for me when I walked into Cha Cha's, a restaurant and bar on St. Armands Circle. I was wearing a pair of cargo shorts, a t-shirt with a beach scene airbrushed on the back, and boat shoes.

"You look more beach bum than lawyer," Gus said.

"That's what I am, truly," I said. "The lawyer thing is just temporary."

"How's J.D.?"

"Covered up on a murder case."

"I read about that one, too. She's good. She'll crack it soon enough."

"I hope you're right."

"It's good to see you, Matt. Are you going to be able to spring Abby?"

"That may depend on what a good investigator can turn up. Are you interested in taking on the case?"

"Sure."

"Abby has money to pay you. So this won't be pro bono."

"That's always good to hear. What do you need me to do?"

"Maybe some things that aren't quite aboveboard."

"Uh, oh."

I grinned. "Nothing illegal. It's just that I'm told my opponent is a slimy bastard who isn't going to be very compliant with
the discovery rules."

"I'm not sure how much I can get from the FDLE. I know
the guy who's running the investigation, Lucas. Talk about slimy."

"Doesn't the FDLE have to keep the locals in the loop on
their investigation?"

"They're supposed to. I'm not sure they always do. What do
you need first?"

"The Sarasota crime scene techs collected a bunch of fingerprints from the victim's condo. I'd like to know who those belonged to. Abby's were there, but I need to know who else had
been in that condo in the days leading up to the murder."

"You know," Gus said, "that some of those fingerprints could
have been there for years."

"Yeah. But Bannister had only been living there for a couple
of weeks. I'm hoping maybe he had everything cleaned before he
moved in and that most of the prints would be recent."

"I'll check it out."

"I need anything on the ballistics. I don't think they found
the revolver, but I'd sure like to know everything else, such as
whether the gun had been used in any other crimes. Whatever the
techs turned up."

Gus was making notes as we talked. He looked up. "I should
be able to get this to you pretty quickly. I have a good relationship
with the guy who heads up the forensics unit."

"I'm told there were some bed sheets that had recently been
the scene of sexual activity. The techs got DNA samples. I'd like
to know who the DNA belonged to."

"Are you going to let the state get a sample from Abby?"

"I probably won't be able to stop it if the lab can't match the
DNA to anybody in the system."

"Was Abby screwing Bannister?"

"I don't know. Unless the state can come up with some evidence that they were sleeping together, it won't be relevant to the case."

"The DNA," Gus said.

"The DNA might tell the tale. But even if there's not a match, evidence could pop up that Abby and Bannister were having an affair. I'll cross that bridge when we get to it. If we get to it."

"Anything else?"

"If Abby didn't kill Bannister, and I don't think she did, that means there's somebody else out there. My job is to make the state prove that Abby is the murderer, and I don't think Swann and Lucas have the evidence to do that. But you never know. Things turn up, theories change. I have to be ready to make a plausible case that somebody else had reason to kill the victim. Somebody other than Abby. And I think the emails are the key to that."

"The *Herald-Tribune* didn't say much about emails."

"Several were sent to Bannister that appeared to come from Abby. I haven't seen them yet, but they seem to indicate an affair. The final email was sent the day of the murder. This was the email in which Abby threatened to kill Bannister. The problem is that the emails didn't come from Abby's computer. The only reason they point to her is that her name was typed at the bottom of the messages. I think it was a crude attempt to frame Abby. Do you know a computer guy who can help us out?"

"I've got the perfect one. He's a computer science professor at USF."

"Good. Let's get him on board. Can you get the emails from the police?"

Gus grinned. "Can a fish swim?"

"Okay. I think that about does it for now."

Andy Brock, the waiter who had worked at Cha Cha's since the place opened, brought our food while we talked. We finished our meal discussing old friends and the major league baseball spring training that was going on in the area. By one-thirty, I was in the Explorer driving north onto Longboat Key, headed to the Lester house.

Abby invited me in. She was wearing shorts and a blouse and was barefoot. "You like my new anklet?" she asked, pointing to the device that surrounded her leg just above her ankle.

"Chic," I said.

"Beats a cell, I guess. I really appreciate your getting me out of there."

"That's my job, Abby. Where's Bill?"

"He went back to work this morning."

"I'm glad you're home. Even with the restrictions."

"Me too. Anything new?"

"Not really. I've hired Gus Grantham to do the investigation for us. He'll be getting us the names of the people to whom all the fingerprints belonged. I was surprised that there were only ten sets."

"Harry Robson told me Bannister had the place painted before he moved in about two weeks before his death. The place wasn't furnished, so he bought all new stuff."

"Well, that explains that."

"I guess you want to know about the affair that wasn't."

"Wasn't?"

"Wasn't. I did not have an affair with Nate Bannister."

"Abby, let's not talk about this right now."

"Isn't that the crux of the state's case? That I was doing the dirty with that creep Bannister?"

"We don't know that yet, and I don't want to intrude on your private life any more than I have to."

"Matt, when we talked yesterday about you representing me, one of the things you were concerned about was your objectivity. If you had never met me before, wouldn't the first question you would have asked be, 'Did you have an affair with the victim?'"

"Maybe," I said. "But, if I thought my client might lie to me, I wouldn't ask the question."

"You think I'd lie to you?"

"Maybe. Under the right circumstances, everybody is capable of lying."

"I thought we were better friends than that."

"We are, Abby, and there lies the rub. It's only natural that we want those we care about to think highly of us. Sometimes, we shade the truth to make ourselves appear better to our friends than we really are. I'm bound to confidentiality about what you tell me, and you know I won't break that bond. But, you also know that I might think less of you if you tell me that you've done things that aren't proper or right, even though I may need that information to defend you. If you lie to me, I could step into a trap set by the state and blow your case. But, if I'm ignorant of your actions, and those actions have no bearing on your guilt or innocence, I can defend you without knowing about them."

"I'm not sure I get all that, but I'll do as you say. What do you want to know?"

We sat for the better part of an hour, with Abby telling me how she came to be involved in Bannister's affairs and a plausible reason as to why her fingerprints were in his condo. We talked about her relationship with her husband Bill, the good and the bad. I made notes that I would type into my computer when I got home. In the end, I was confident of my client's innocence and even more concerned that I could screw up her defense and send her to jail.

CHAPTER SEVENTEEN

J.D. was restless. She was making no progress. Linda Favereaux had a tattoo that indicated she was part of a virulent racist group, yet she and her husband had black friends and supported African American studies at USF. James Favereaux seemed to have dropped off the earth. There had been no activity on any of his credit cards; his car was at the Tampa airport, yet he had not taken a flight from there.

Her lunch had consisted of a sandwich eaten at her desk. Its remains rested heavily on her stomach and she tasted acid in the back of her throat. She reached into her desk drawer and extracted two antacid pills, chewed them, and felt no better.

She walked down the hall to Chief Bill Lester's office, knocked on the door, and stuck her head in. "How're you doing, Bill?"

"Hey, J.D. I'm fine. Come on in. You making any progress on your murder case?"

"Not really. I'd like to bounce it off you. See if you've got any ideas."

They spent the next thirty minutes going over everything she knew, what she surmised, and all the questions that were still rattling around in her mind. "Anything on Favereaux's car?" Lester asked.

"Not yet. The Sarasota sheriffs picked it up yesterday, but so far they haven't gotten to it over at the crime lab."

Bill looked at his watch. "Twenty-four hours, and they haven't touched it?"

"No. I've talked to the lab twice today, and they keep saying they have other priorities."

"This just went to the top of their list. I'll make a call. I think you can get the results first thing in the morning. Are you expecting anything specific?"

"I doubt they'll find anything at all. I suspect Favereaux dropped the car at the airport and grabbed a cab. Maybe he has other IDs and he flew somewhere using an alias. There've been no hits on his credit cards, so I'm thinking he's using a different ID."

"But," asked Lester, "why would a legitimate businessman have false IDs stashed away?"

"And own a computer with sophisticated encryption software. Maybe he's not legitimate."

"Any evidence of that so far?"

"No. Not so far. I haven't pursued that angle yet, but I will."

"Keep me posted, J.D."

"How's Abby?"

"Not bad. Glad to be out of jail, but she's pretty much restricted to the house and yard. She's not happy about that."

"If there's anything I can do..."

"I know, J.D. Thanks."

Back in her office, J.D. went to the Drug Enforcement Agency's website, found the number for the Tampa office, and dialed it. She identified herself to the receptionist and asked to speak to Agent Devlin Michel. "I'm sorry, Detective, we don't have an agent by that name in this office."

"Do you have a list of your agents in other offices around the country?"

"Nothing that I can give out. I'm sorry."

J.D. thanked her and called the Washington headquarters of DEA. No Agent Michel on their staff. She talked to several people, climbing higher up the bureaucratic ladder until she had an assistant deputy director on the line. She explained her dilemma. Michel had called her, but now he didn't seem to exist.

"I'll call you back in half an hour, Detective."

"Thanks. Let me give you my number."

"Not necessary." The line went dead.

J.D. shrugged, went back to her computer and pulled up the FBI's website. She found the phone number for a division that tracked terrorist organizations, called it, identified herself to the receptionist, and asked if she could speak to the agent in charge. She was on hold for a few seconds before the line was picked up. "This is Agent Charles Willits."

"Good afternoon, Agent Willits. This is Detective J.D. Duncan in Longboat Key, Florida. I'm working a murder case down here, and we found a tattoo on our victim that appears to be associated with a New Orleans organization that calls itself The White America Party. I was wondering if you had any information about them."

"A nasty little bunch. They run a website and make as much noise as possible, but they've been pretty dormant for the past few years."

"I'm surprised you know much about them off the top of your head."

He laughed. "Until about two years ago, I was the Special Agent-in-Charge of the New Orleans office. That group was just one of several we kept our eye on."

"You said they've been dormant. What do you mean?"

"They used to have rallies, parade around in their Nazi uniforms, make a lot of noise. They owned some property out in the sticks where they went to shoot guns and raise hell. We were pretty sure they had tried to intimidate some black folks from time to time, but we were never able to pin anything on them."

"What happened to slow them down?"

"Oh, I think most of the members just got old. They weren't getting many new recruits, and the organization was drying up. They sold off their property and sort of disappeared into the woodwork. They're still out there making noise. They put out a monthly newsletter that nobody reads and they keep up their website. Our New Orleans office checks on them periodically, but they're pretty quiet."

"Were they ever into drugs?"

"You mean selling, distribution, that sort of thing?

"Yes."

"They might have been. There was a lot of drug activity around. I always thought The White America Party was on the periphery, buying and selling small quantities to keep money flowing their way, but we could never prove it."

"Do you have any idea why the DEA would still have an interest in one of their members?"

"No."

"One last question, Agent Willits. Do you know a federal agent named Devlin Michel?"

"Never heard of him. I'm pretty sure he's not one of ours."

"I appreciate your help. One more thing. Do you have a list of The White American Party members?"

"I'm sure we do. Probably going all the way back to when they started. Do you need it?"

"Any idea how many names are on it?"

"Not many. Probably less than fifty."

"Well, it's a shot in the dark, but I'd appreciate it if you'd email it to me." She gave him her address and hung up the phone. It rang again almost immediately.

"Detective Duncan, this is Devlin Michel. I understand you've been looking for me."

"You're a ghost."

"Sometimes. What can I do for you?"

"Tell me who you are."

"Devlin Michel, DEA."

"I don't think you're DEA, and I have grave doubts that your name is Devlin Michel."

"I think you're confused, Detective."

"Wouldn't be the first time. Just what is your interest in Darlene Pelletier?"

"Sorry. I can't tell you."

"Listen, Devlin, or whoever you are. I'm investigating a murder, and you're not helping at all. Maybe I ought to be talking to your supervisor."

"That won't do you any good, I'm afraid. Look, Detective, I'm not trying to jerk your chain, but there are things I can't get into with you. If you want to stay in touch, I'll give you a phone number where you can reach me. Who knows? I may be able to help you somewhere down the line."

"If I need you," J.D. said, "I'll call you at your office at Home-land Security."

There was silence on the other end of the line. Then, "I'll give you my cell number. Save you having to go through the switchboard." He laughed and gave her the number.

CHAPTER EIGHTEEN

It was nearing four when I left Abby's. I called J.D. "You've been there since seven this morning," I said. "Ready for a break?

"Yes."

"Tiny's?"

"When?"

"Now."

"Be there in fifteen minutes."

"Wear something sexy."

"Right."

Tiny's was a little bar tucked away in a small shopping center on the north end of Longboat Key. It was a gathering place for the locals, a place that was not attractive to the tourists seeking sun and surf and upscale restaurants. Gwen Mooney had once described the place as the north end clubhouse. That was pretty much what it was.

My friends Logan Hamilton and Cracker Dix were at the bar, arguing good-naturedly over which provided a better high, scotch or marijuana. Tiny's owner, Susie Vaught, was behind the bar. "Hey, Matt," she said, as she came around the bar to give me a hug. "I hear you've been busy the last couple of days."

"Sort of. How are you, Susie?"

"Living the dream, listening to the highly intellectual chatter that appears to be a fixture in my bar."

"They the only ones here?"

"Yeah. Mel Swartz will be here any minute. He gets here at four on the dot. Every day. You can set your watch. Where's J.D.?"

"She's on her way."

"Miller Lite?"

"Yeah. And a white wine."

Cracker said, "Hey, Matt. I hear you're lawyering again."

"Somebody's got to do it."

"Take care of Abby. She's good people."

"She is that, Cracker. Who's winning the argument today?"

"Arguing with Logan is like talking to a puppy. He yaps at you a lot, but he makes no sense whatsoever."

"The English are poor losers, Matt," Logan said. "That's Cracker's problem."

Cracker, the expatriate Englishman who'd lived on the key for thirty years, laughed and gave Logan the finger.

J.D. came in. She'd stopped at her condo to change into shorts, t-shirt, and flip-flops. "You look like a tourist," I said.

"Hush." She went to the bar and kissed both Logan and Cracker on the cheek. "Good to see you guys."

Mel Swartz came through the door. Everybody in the place looked at his watch. Four o'clock on the button. "How're you doing, Mel?" I asked.

"Better now that it's four."

I picked up our drinks and led J.D. to a high-top table in the corner. "You look tired," I said.

"I am. I seem to be hitting nothing but dead ends on this case. How's yours going?"

"Not much to tell. I met with Gus Grantham at lunch and talked for a long time to Abby. Tell me about your day."

"Very strange. I think that DEA Agent Michel who called me yesterday is actually Homeland Security."

"What makes you think that?"

"He's not in the Tampa DEA office. I called Washington and finally talked to an assistant deputy director who shut me down and said he'd call back in half an hour. Guess who called back?"

"Agent Michel."

"Bingo."

"Wouldn't that indicate that he was DEA?"

"I talked to an FBI supervisor in the division that oversees terrorism. He was well aware of The White America Party. He thought they might have been selling a few drugs, but he was never able to prove it. If they don't deal in drugs in a big way, then why would DEA be interested in them?"

"Good point," I said.

"The supervisor also told me he didn't think Michel was FBI. He probably would have flat denied the existence of Michel if he was trying to hide his identity."

"So, if not DEA or FBI, what other agency could possibly have any interest in a nineteen-year-old woman who disappeared twenty years ago?"

"Exactly. And when Michel called me back, I accused him of being with Homeland Security. He didn't deny it."

"So the question is, why would Homeland Security have an interest? They weren't even in existence twenty years ago."

"There's more," J.D. said. "The FBI guy sent me a list of the names and most recent addresses of people who had been members of The White America Party over the years. It wasn't ever very big. There were only fifty-two names, but guess who showed up?"

"Darlene Pelletier?"

J.D. shook her head. "Close. The party was formed about forty years ago. One of the founders was named Bobby Pelletier."

"Too much of a coincidence. Is he still running the show?"

"No. I checked back with the FBI. Bobby was shot dead about ten years ago. The case is still open. New Orleans PD has jurisdiction since it was a local murder, but the FBI has been monitoring the investigation all this time because of Pelletier's connection to a group on the terrorist watch list."

"I take it the list didn't include Darlene Pelletier."

"No, but it did have a woman named Connie Pelletier. She was apparently Bobby's wife."

"Is she dead, too?"

"Nope. She lives in New Orleans."

"I wonder if Favereaux knew of his wife's connection to that bunch of maniacs," I said.

"He must have seen the tattoo."

"Yeah, but that wouldn't mean anything in and of itself. She could have told him it was just something she picked out at the tattoo parlor."

"Maybe the husband found out about her past and killed her," J.D. said.

"What would be his motive?"

"I don't know. I'm just grabbing at straws."

"Did you ever hear back from New Orleans PD about Darlene's arrest?"

"No. I'm thinking about going out there to see what I can turn up. I'll ask Bill if he has any travel money in our budget."

"Want some company?" I asked.

She smiled. "Maybe, but don't you have a case to work on?"

"Gus Grantham is trying to get me some evidence. I don't think we'll have anything on the DNA for a few days, so there's not much I can do for now."

"I'll call Bill at home this evening. See if he'll let me go. Tell me about your day."

"It wasn't as exciting as yours." I told her what I'd found out and discussed the direction I thought the case might take. "Of course, at this point, that's mostly speculation. This thing will unfold slowly over the next few weeks."

"You want another round?" Susie called from the bar.

I looked at J.D. She nodded, and said, "Let's go sit at the bar. Catch up on the gossip."

CHAPTER NINETEEN

One would think that you could take a flight straight across the Gulf of Mexico from Tampa to New Orleans. Not so. The gods of flight have decreed that you must stop first in Atlanta. Thus, a flight that should take an hour or so, turns into a five-hour ordeal, including a less-than-exciting tour of the world's busiest airport: Atlanta.

We had driven the hour trip from Longboat Key to Tampa International Airport, lugged our bags through Atlanta's never-ending concourses, and were on final approach to New Orleans. We'd gained an hour when we crossed into the central time zone, and it was now a little after noon.

J.D. had called Bill Lester when we got home the evening before, brought him up to date on what she'd learned, and got him to agree for her to go to New Orleans. She asked if he had a problem with me going along. He told her he would call the New Orleans police chief to give him a heads-up on J.D.'s visit, and would tell him that he was also sending along his department's legal adviser.

I'd made reservations at an elegant little hotel on the edge of the French Quarter, a place I'd stayed in frequently when I was practicing law. We took a taxi from the airport to the hotel and dropped our bags with the concierge. We walked across the street to a little joint that was locally famous for its po-boy sandwiches.

After lunch, another taxi took us to the New Orleans Police Department headquarters on South Broad Street. I was wearing a suit and tie, wanting to look like what I thought a police legal adviser ought to look like. That is, if anybody cared. We were escorted to the chief's office and introductions were made. "How can I help you, Detective Duncan?"

"I don't know how much Chief Lester told you." J.D. said, "A woman was murdered on Longboat Key early Monday morning, a very wealthy woman who lived in a Gulf-front mansion. When we ran her prints, it turned out that she wasn't who she was supposed to be. Twenty years ago, she was arrested here on a misdemeanor shoplifting charge. She would have been about nineteen years old at the time. We're trying to backtrack to see if there's anything in her past that might lead us to the killer. I'm hoping you still have the records of that arrest."

"I'll check. What's the woman's name?"

"Darlene Pelletier."

The chief buzzed his secretary and asked her to dig up any records on Darlene Pelletier. He gave her the approximate date of the arrest. "Do you have any suspects?" he asked J.D.

"Not yet. The husband is a possibility. He seems to have disappeared."

The chief grunted. "The husband's always a possibility."

We sat for a few minutes making small talk until the secretary came back into the office. "Chief, that file was checked out on Tuesday."

"To whom?"

"That's the funny thing. There's no card on it."

"Then how do you know it was checked out on Tuesday?" the chief asked.

"The paper log shows that a detective asked for it and was sent back to the stacks. But, the detective's name is redacted. Blacked out."

"That's odd as hell." The chief looked at J.D. "When somebody checks out a file, they have to leave a card with their name and badge number written on it. The card is put into the space where the file would be, and a notation is made on a paper log kept by the custodian. That information is later put in the computer."

CHASING JUSTICE 99

"I called here about that file on Tuesday," J.D. said.

"Who did you talk to?" the chief asked.

"I didn't get a name. A man answered the phone in the records department."

"What time did you call?"

"Late morning," J.D. said. "Just before lunch. Our time."

The chief turned back to the secretary. "Check on who was working there on Tuesday. Probably some kind of paperwork error."

"Wouldn't the Pelletier case file be in your computers?" I asked.

"Afraid not. We haven't bothered to digitize the misdemeanor cases that far back. If it'd been a felony, we'd have it for you."

The secretary came back in a couple of minutes. "Officer Jim Tatum was the custodian on Tuesday. He was off yesterday, and he hasn't shown up yet today."

"What time was he due for duty today?" the chief asked.

"Seven this morning."

"Did you talk to his sergeant?"

"I checked with him. He said he'd tried to call Tatum this morning and got no answer. He sent a car by his house, but nobody was home. The sergeant put him on report. He told me that he thinks Tatum got his days off mixed up, and didn't realize he was supposed to be at work this morning. He said Tatum was a good cop and always showed up for work on time. Never missed a day."

"Thank you, Mildred," the chief said. The secretary left, closing the office door on her way out.

The chief looked at J.D. "Tatum will show up tomorrow morning, and I'll get to the bottom of this. I'll call you first thing tomorrow and you can swing by and pick up the file."

J.D. gave him her cell phone number and we left. "What now?" I asked. "Time for one of those funny Bourbon Street drinks with the little parasol in it?"

"Ugh. Let's go see if we can find Connie Pelletier."

We waved down another taxi, gave the driver Connie Pelletier's address from the list, and were driven into a spooky area of town. The houses lining the narrow asphalt street were old and decrepit, their front yards more garbage dump than lawn. Young men stood on street corners, smoking cigarettes or dope or something, their steely gazes locking onto the taxi. A police patrol car drove slowly toward us from the opposite direction, the two officers surveilling either side of the street as they passed.

The place looked like a city in a war zone, one of several I'd seen when I was a soldier. The young men were just there, waiting for something, anything, their fate maybe, staring into a future that demanded death at a young age or incarceration that would take them into middle age.

The cabbie stopped before a small shotgun house. I asked him if he would wait for us. I told him it would be worth an extra fifty bucks. He shook his head and gave me a card with his cell number on it. "I ain't staying in this blighted place," he said. "But there's a police substation about four blocks from here. I'll wait there. Call me when you're ready to leave, and I'll come pick you up. Don't leave the house until you see me pull up out front."

"That bad?" J.D. asked.

"Worse, lady. Lots worse. I'll sit here until you get in the house."

We got out of the car. "You got your gun?" I asked.

"You bet. You?"

"Yep." We'd checked them with our luggage and retrieved them before we left the hotel.

"I'm legal," J.D. said. "Cop's perk."

"If anybody gets upset about me having a gun, I'll tell them you gave it to me."

"You're a wuss, Royal. Let's go."

I knocked on the door, and in a minute or two a woman opened it. If this was Connie Pelletier, she would have probably been in her mid-sixties, given the time frame for the inception of

The White American Party. She looked ninety. She was stooped, her back twisted by the prominent widow's hump, her gray hair sparse and in disarray. She was absently scratching at a sore on her left wrist, her eyes staring blankly at us, her cheeks pasty and flaccid. She wore an ancient housedress with a faded floral design. She was barefoot, her toenails discolored and fractured and so long they curled under the ends of her toes. The odor of old smoke and sour whiskey billowed from the house as she opened the door.

"Yes?" she said, her voice raspy from cigarettes.

"Are you Connie Pelletier?" J.D. asked.

"Who wants to know?"

"I'm Detective J.D. Duncan." I noticed she didn't identify which police department she was with.

"What do you want?"

"Do you know Darlene Pelletier?"

"No." Something passed across her rheumy eyes like a fleeting shadow. It was so quick that if I hadn't been watching for it, I would have missed it. She was lying.

"Mrs. Pelletier," said J.D. "I'm not here to cause you trouble or sadness." J.D. had seen the same thing I had. "But Darlene has a tattoo identifying her as a member of The White America Party. It's just not possible that in such a small organization, you didn't know somebody with the same last name as yours."

"She's dead."

"May we come in?"

"I guess so. I don't want no uniforms breaking down my door in the middle of the night. Not with all them darkies they got on the force these days."

We stepped into the living room. A mess. The furniture was old and stuffing was falling out of most of it. A filthy green shag carpet from the 1960s covered the floor and the place smelled of unwashed dog. I saw a small terrier cowering under the sofa, shivering, its skin showing through where patches of fur had been destroyed by disease. Despair seeped from the walls, enveloping all who entered with a miasma of hopelessness and regret. It was per-haps the most depressing place I'd ever seen.

J.D.'s reference to the tattoo had gotten us in the door. We didn't know for sure that Darlene's tattoo had existed at the time of her arrest, and that was one of the things we wanted to find out from the arrest file. Still, it was a good bet that the tattoo was once worn with pride, and I was betting that Connie was Dar-lene's mother, or at least a relative.

When we were seated, and I was trying to think of the name of a spray product I could buy to take care of any cooties I might pick up in this dump, J.D. said, "Who was Darlene?"

"She was just one of the girls who hung around. She was screwing my husband Bobby and took to using his name. They didn't make any secret of it, they just went at it like rabbits and didn't care what I thought about the whole thing."

"Where did she come from to join your group?" J.D. asked.

"I think she was some kind of orphan. Maybe from one of the homes around here. She just showed up one day. She was a pretty little thing, and old Bobby was on her like the hound dog he was."

"Didn't that bother you?" J.D. asked.

"Ah, I guess. He was like an old alley cat, though. Always looking for the next score. And he had a way about him. Women just loved him. I did too."

"How did Darlene die?"

"She got sick and went into Charity Hospital and never came out."

"Sick with what?"

"Hell if I know. I always thought it might be AIDS. The way she screwed around and all."

"Did you see her in the hospital?"

"No."

"Do you know anything about her getting arrested for shop-lifting?"

"Which time?"

"There was more than once?"

"Yeah. I think she got passes on all but the last one. Taking care of the cops, you know." She made an up-and-down motion with her closed hand. "That last one was just before she got sick, so nothing ever come of it."

"How did Bobby die?" J.D. asked.

"Somebody shot him down like a dog in the street. Just outside that front door. He was coming home from work and a car drove by and somebody took him out with a shotgun. It's been ten years, and the cops don't have any idea who killed him. I don't think they tried very hard."

"Do you have any idea who killed him?" J.D. asked.

"Nah. I guess about half of Orleans Parish would be reasonable suspects."

J.D. had been making notes in the little book she carried with her at all times. "What was your maiden name, if you don't mind my asking?" J.D. asked.

Connie laughed, a bitter cackle, carrying no trace of merriment. "Going to check into my background?"

"It's just routine, ma'am."

"Nobody's called me ma'am in a long time. It was Rohan."

"Is there anything I can do for you, Mrs. Pelletier?"

"Nah. I got my social security, and Bobby paid off the house before he got killed. I do fine. I'm just hanging around waiting to die. Can't come too soon."

"I'm sorry, ma'am. I truly am. I'm going to leave my card. If you think of anything that you think might help, will you let me know?"

Connie Pelletier nodded. "You never did tell me why you're looking for Darlene."

"I'm not looking for her, Mrs. Pelletier. A woman was murdered on Longboat Key, Florida. We have reason to believe the victim might be Darlene. I'm hoping to find something in her background that will help me find her killer."

"It's not our Darlene. She's been dead twenty years. I saw the body at the funeral home, just before they cremated her."

I was pretty sure she was lying again, but we weren't going to get any more out of her. I used my cell phone to call the cabbie, and he showed up in less than five minutes. We got in and drove out of the hell that was once a decent subdivision.

CHAPTER TWENTY

We were sitting at a table in The Court of Two Sisters restaurant in the French Quarter, Creole dinners spread before us, their aromas tickling my senses with anticipation. My phone buzzed to alert me to an incoming text. "I've got the fps. DNA tomorrow. Gus"

I texted back. "Email me fps."

"What's that all about?" J.D. asked.

"Gus has the fingerprint information from Bannister's condo. He's emailing it to me. I should get the DNA results tomorrow."

"Good. Maybe something will turn up."

J.D. was beautiful in the faux candlelight emanating from the table. She was wearing a form-fitting dress of deep green to match her eyes. Her dark hair fell to her shoulders, and her smile was playing its usual tricks with my heart. "What were we talking about?" she asked.

"Sex."

"No, we weren't."

"Want to talk about it?"

"No."

"Are you being difficult?"

"No."

"Then why not talk about sex?"

"Why talk when we can do," she said, throwing that thousand-watt grin at me.

"You ready to go back to the hotel?"

"We haven't eaten yet."

"Oh. I guess that means you're hungry."

"Quite. And when I finish this, I want one of those flaming desserts and then a drink or two at a bar, listening to Dixieland."

"And then?"

"Sex. Maybe."

I was a happy man. Her maybes always turned into yeses.

* * *

The ringing of J.D.'s cell phone woke me a little before seven. She was in the bathroom and came padding out to answer it. I heard her say, "Oh, Chief. That's terrible. I'm so sorry." Silence, and then "Okay, I'll be in touch."

"Bill Lester?" I asked, alarmed by J.D.'s end of the conversation.

"No. The New Orleans chief. They found Officer Tatum dead this morning. Shot in the back of the head."

"Tatum? You mean the records guy?"

"Yes."

"Crap. Where did they find him?"

"A deputy sheriff in the St. Barnard parish south of here found him just before dark yesterday on the side of a rural road that leads into a swampy area. He had his police ID on him. The medical examiner thinks he'd been dead for at least twenty-four to thirty-six hours."

"So he was probably killed on Tuesday evening. We know he was working during the day on Tuesday. What do you make of it?"

J.D. took a deep breath. "I think I got him killed."

"That's not rational thinking," I said. "If Tatum got killed over your document request, it's probably because he was dirty."

"How so?"

"That file didn't disappear on its own. Somebody had to let the person who took the file redact his name, and there is no paper log of the file going out. Maybe Tatum was part of that and planned to put the information into the computer later, maybe using a fake name for the detective. Maybe Tatum was going to set it up so that it looked like another clerk had let the file go out the door."

"You're probably right. I can't imagine that file would be important to anybody until I called about it. How did someone know I was looking for it? It had to be the person I talked to on the phone, and that was most likely Tatum."

"Maybe Tatum was a little cog in a bigger machine," I said, "and somebody was just shutting down the lines of communication."

"Probably. There's nothing we can do about it now. Why don't you check your email and see about those fingerprint IDs Gus sent you?"

* * *

The list had seven names on it, including Abigail Lester's, and three prints that could not be identified, but there had been enough of those prints that the crime scene techs thought them significant. Gus had made a notation after each name, giving his or her reason for being in the condo. He'd also sent me a note telling me that Bannister had his condo, including all the cabinets, painted just before he moved in about two weeks before his death, so the prints found on various surfaces would all be current. The only prints found on unwashed glassware and plates were duplicates of other prints found in other places in the condo, with the exception of the prints on the wine glass on Bannister's bedside table. There were no prints on the clean ones. The hot water and detergent in the dishwasher would have obliterated those. There were a number of unidentified prints on the furniture, but it was all new and most of the prints probably belonged to the men who'd moved it into the condo. Nobody had bothered to run those prints down.

Of the six other names on the list, three had been identified as workers who painted the place. Three of the prints could not be identified from available databases. Three others belonged to Maggie Bannister, the dead man's estranged wife, someone named

Victoria Madison, and another person named Robert Shorter, who, according to Gus' notes, had been arrested twice in Sarasota for assault and battery. He'd been sentenced on the first one to probation and anger management classes. Apparently the classes didn't take, and on the second offense, this time against Nate Bannister, Shorter was sentenced to thirty days in the county jail. He had been released two years before.

I told J.D. what Gus had found. "At least the three unknowns might be of some use if I can match those prints to a suspect."

"Good luck," she said, sarcastically.

"Right. I'll get Gus to run down the two we do know, Madison and Shorter. The guy sounds like a prospect. Apparently, he has anger issues. He might be one of Bannister's less-than-satisfied customers."

"From what I've heard, there are a lot of those."

I sent Gus a text asking him to see what he could find out about Madison and Shorter. "Let's see what Gus turns up," I said.

"Aren't you going to get out of bed today?"

"I'm just enjoying a little postcoital torpor."

She laughed. "Right. I guess you deserve it. Now get up and take a shower. We've got a plane to catch."

"Yes, ma'am."

CHAPTER TWENTY-ONE

Our flight was scheduled for late afternoon. We talked the hotel desk clerk into a late checkout and took a taxi back to the police station. I was wearing a pair of khaki slacks, golf shirt, and loafers. J.D. was in dark slacks, white blouse, and low-heeled pumps. Her gun was in an ankle holster, as was mine. Our IDs got us through security once again, weapons and all, and we were escorted to the chief's office. I noticed that the officers manning the security station were wearing black bands across their badges.

The chief was wearing full uniform this morning, black band and all, and was in a somber mood. "Detective," he said after ordering coffee for us, "I think Tatum's death must have something to do with your investigation. Otherwise, there's just too much coincidence."

"I agree," said J.D. "But I can't put the pieces together. Not yet."

"My guess is that coming from a small island like Longboat Key, you probably haven't had much experience with murder cases."

J.D. smiled coldly. I knew that look. The chief had insulted the lady, and she didn't handle insults well. "Chief," she said, her voice flat, "I've been with the Longboat Key Police Department for less than two years. Before that, I was the assistant homicide commander of the Miami-Dade County Police Department. *My* guess is that I've handled more murder cases than anybody in your department, including yourself."

I couldn't help but smile. My woman would go toe to toe with anybody, anytime. And she sure had made her point.

"I'm sorry, Detective," the chief said, "I didn't mean to insult you. I just assumed..."

"No problem, Chief." She favored him with a smile. "It was a reasonable assumption. I didn't mean to sound so sharp. But I'm not a rookie."

"I can see that. Why don't we put our heads together on this? One of my detectives, Brad Corbin, is monitoring the investigation of Officer Tatum's death, but the St. Barnard Parish Sheriff's Department is handling it, since that's where the body was found. Corbin will be looking into things on this end." He picked up his phone and asked that Detective Corbin come to his office.

"Corbin's been doing this for a long time," the chief said. "He's a good cop and knows this town inside and out."

"Has he ever worked with the gangs or hate groups?" J.D. asked.

"A lot. He worked with the gang unit before he moved to homicide. Why?"

"The woman we're looking into, Darlene Pelletier, was part of a group called The White America Party. They're some sort of Nazi group and they don't seem to like anybody but other white people. And that doesn't include Jews."

"Sounds like a bunch of crazies. I don't think I've ever heard of them."

"They've always been a small group, but they've been around for about forty years," J.D. said.

"Maybe Corbin will know something. Here he comes now."

Detective Corbin was a man of about forty, dressed in a beige suit set off by a red-and-blue tie and a powder-blue shirt. The chief introduced us and Corbin took a seat. "Brad, don't let the small-island cop thing fool you about Detective Duncan. She used to be the assistant homicide commander at Miami-Dade PD. I think she probably knows her way around a murder case."

Corbin smiled. "I hope we can help each other out, Detective, but I'm not sure I understand why you need a legal adviser with you."

"I really don't, Detective," J.D. said. "Matt's just my boy toy of the week."

"Ouch," I said.

Corbin and the chief both laughed at my obvious discomfort.

"Well," I said, "at least say something about how well I do my job?"

"He's a great lawyer," J.D. said.

Another round of laughter.

"Actually," said J.D., "Matt does give legal advice to our department, and he's been a great help in other investigations. He's ex-Army Special Forces, so he's pretty good in a firefight, too."

"You have firefights on Longboat Key?" the chief asked.

"More than you'd think," J.D. said.

"I think I'll be changing my vacation plans," the chief said. "Why don't the three of you get your heads together and see if you can come up with something."

I took that as our invitation to leave. Corbin suggested we go to his office, and we followed him through a maze of hallways to a small cramped space with a desk and couple of side chairs. He took a seat behind the desk. "Tell me what you're doing here," he said, looking at J.D.

She told him about the murder of Linda Favereaux who, according to the fingerprints, was Darlene Pelletier, and about the tattoo, the association with The White America Party, and our visit to Connie Pelletier. "I'm trying to find some kind of connection that will lead me to her murderer. I thought it might be in her past."

"I'm familiar with The White America Party," Corbin said. "They're an unpleasant little group that never caused much trouble. They sometimes hang out on street corners holding racist signs and hollering at passing cars."

"Do you know anything about Bobby Pelletier's murder?" J.D. asked.

"I followed that pretty closely. I was working gangs at the time, so I had an interest in what happened. We never did find any evidence of who shot him. I thought it might be one of the black gangs who did it, but we had pretty good intel on them and we never heard a whisper."

"Do you have any theories?" I asked.

"Yeah, lots. Bobby was a real bastard and he'd pissed off a lot of people. We had so many suspects we couldn't even begin to narrow them down. He ran with a lowlife bunch, and a lot of them hated his guts. His murder was just about inevitable."

"Were they ever involved in illegal activities?" J.D. asked. "Drugs, guns, that sort of thing?"

"If they were, we never found any evidence of it."

"Do you have any ideas on why Officer Tatum would be killed right after a misdemeanor file disappeared?" I asked.

"No, other than they're probably connected."

"How so?" I asked.

"I think it would take a lot of coincidences to have that file disappear just after Detective Duncan called about it, and then to have Tatum killed the same day."

"I agree," J.D. said. "But what could be in that file that would cause somebody to murder a cop?"

Corbin shrugged. "Got me."

"We went to see Bobby Pelletier's widow yesterday," J.D. said. "She's in bad shape."

"Connie," Corbin said. "She was quite a character in the day."

"How so?"

"Bobby was the leader, but Connie ran the show."

"How was that?" J.D. asked.

"Most of their followers were ignorant shit-kickers who couldn't earn a living if their lives depended on it. Come to think of it, I guess their lives did depend on making a living. Anyway, Connie was able to get most of them jobs, menial things like wash-ing dishes in third-class restaurants or cleaning toilets in what they used to euphemistically call gentlemen's clubs—bars where they water the drinks and feature topless dancers. She gave her members a place to sleep in an old warehouse down by the river. It wasn't much, but it was better than the streets."

"Where did they get the money to support their activities?" I asked.

Corbin emitted a short bark of a laugh. "What activities? Other than the street corner sign thing, they didn't have any activities."

"Can we get a look at the murder file on Bobby Pelletier?" J.D. asked.

"Sure," Corbin said. "I don't know what good it'll do you, but I'll run you a copy." He turned to his computer and booted it up. He entered some commands, stopped, frowned, and entered some more. He picked up his phone and punched in a four-digit number. "Bubba," he said, "I can't find a file in the system. Can you pull it up for me? The Bobby Pelletier murder. Happened about ten years ago."

Corbin hung up and said, "Some kind of glitch in the system. Bubba's the information technology guy. A real wizard. He'll have it for us in a minute."

The phone rang. Corbin answered. "What do you mean, gone?"

Silence on our end, then, "Goddamnit, Bubba, how does a file disappear with all the security you've rigged into the system? This is the goddamned police department, for Christ's sake." He slammed the phone into its cradle, looked up and said, "Bobby's file's disappeared from the system. Let me check the records room and see if they have the original."

Within a few minutes, we knew that the original file was gone, too. It had apparently been checked out by the same detective who took Darlene's file.

CHAPTER TWENTY-TWO

By mid-afternoon, J.D. and I were in a taxi on the way to the airport when Brad Corbin called with the news that Connie Pelletier's body had been found in her living room. She'd been shot in the back of the head. At first glance, the forensics people thought the bullet was the same caliber as the one that killed Officer Tatum. They'd know more when ballistics finished with it.

"I think we'd better stick around another day or so," J.D. said.

I nodded. "Driver, can you take us back to our hotel?"

"It's kind of sad," J.D. said. "She was a pitiful excuse for a human being, but she'd seen so much grief and hatred in her life, and look where it ended. In that hovel she lived in with a bullet in the back of her head. Do you think she saw it coming?"

"She probably did, and she probably welcomed it. She was just tired of living."

"I wonder what happened in her early life to set her on that path."

"We'll never know," I said. "Sometimes the gods just drop a bag of crap on some children and they never get out from under it. They just can't figure it out. Life is difficult and they give up at an early age and just go with the flow. And the flow is like sewage running downhill. For some of those people, hate becomes a shield that tempers the stark reality of their lives. And it's a vicious cycle. Each generation breeds another generation of broken people, as mired in hopelessness as those who went before."

"How did you get out of it, Matt? You were born into a family of alcoholics. They were poor, lived a hardscrabble life, didn't have much education, and yet, you became a successful lawyer."

"I don't understand it, J.D. Some make it out, and others don't. Maybe it's pride. Or raw ambition and a willingness to work hard and sacrifice everything that makes life sweet, just to feed the ambition monster. I don't know the answer, but I know what despair feels like. It can be a killer. And I felt it in that little house yesterday."

J.D. kissed me on the cheek and called Detective Corbin to tell him we were coming back to town. He suggested we meet him at Connie's house. I called the hotel and booked us another room.

The taxi took us to the hotel, and we again dropped our bags with the concierge. He'd put them in our newly assigned room. Then we went back to that little bit of hell where Connie Pelletier had lived and died.

Two police cruisers were parked in front of the house next to an unmarked Crown Victoria that was so obviously a cop car I wondered why they even bothered to keep it unmarked. A crime scene van was parked behind the cruisers.

A uniformed cop was standing on the little front porch. J.D. told him Detective Corbin was expecting us. We walked into the living room to see that nothing had changed, except for the twisted body of Connie Pelletier lying on the shag carpet. Technicians were working the scene, so we hung back at the edge of the room, waiting for Corbin to finish talking to another cop.

"Do you have a time of death?" J.D. asked, when Corbin joined us.

"The medical examiner's man thinks she was probably killed last evening. Between six and midnight."

"Who found her?" I asked.

"One of the neighborhood kids heard the dog barking and came up on the porch and looked in the window and saw the body. His mom called us. The kid said the dog hardly ever barked, so it got his attention."

"Where's the dog?" I asked.

"Animal Control just left with him. They aren't sure they'll be able to save him. He's pretty bad off, and really old."

"Any idea who shot Connie?" J.D. asked.

"No. So far the techs haven't turned up anything. The scene's clean as a whistle."

"Professional?"

"Probably. If it turns out that the same gun killed Tatum, I'll put money on both murders being professional hits."

"I wonder if it has anything to do with my investigation," J.D. said.

"Maybe. I'd like to get a complete statement from you guys about your visit with Connie. I should be finished here in a few minutes. Maybe we could go somewhere for a drink."

"Do you mind if we look around a bit?" J.D. asked.

"No, but would you mind if I have one of the crime scene people go with you? If you see anything you think might be pertinent, I'll want a record of it."

J.D. nodded and Corbin waved over one of the techs and introduced us.

* * *

The rest of the house was as untidy as the living room. A hall led toward the back of the house, with a kitchen and bath on one side and two small bedrooms on the other. Connie had slept in one of the bedrooms and used the other as an office of sorts. It contained an ancient roll-top desk, a chest of drawers, a dresser, and a bookcase. The few books stacked on the shelves seemed to be self-published racist screeds, of little interest to anyone other than idiots.

"Have you checked the drawers?" J.D. asked.

"We haven't gotten to them, yet," the tech said.

"Do you mind if I take a look?"

"Go ahead, but put these on." He handed her a pair of latex gloves.

J.D. found it in the third drawer she searched. An old snapshot of a woman holding a baby. She showed it to me. We couldn't be sure, but the woman could have been Connie, when she was young. J.D. laid the photo on the dresser and took a picture of it with her cell phone. She put it back in the drawer where she'd found it and finished searching the others.

"Nothing but old handouts and bills for printing, that sort of thing," J.D. said when she'd finished the search. She thanked the tech and we left him to his investigation. Corbin asked us to meet him at a bar in the French Quarter in one hour. He said it would be quiet and he'd bring his tape recorder.

* * *

The bar was empty at five o'clock. It was a small place, cozy, even elegant. There was a bandstand set up for a three-piece combo, about a dozen tables scattered around the floor, and a bar in the back that stretched across the width of the room. Other than the three of us, the bartender was the only person in the place.

"It'll get a little rowdy later," Corbin said. "They play some wonderful jazz here, and there are quite a few regulars."

"Are you one of them?" I asked.

"Yep. I love good jazz." He put his digital recorder on the table and switched it on. "Tell me about Connie."

We told him about our visit, what was said, our impressions of Connie, our suspicions that she was lying to us about Darlene and maybe some other things. J.D. told him about the picture she'd found in the desk drawer in Connie's house. The interview took about thirty minutes, during which I sipped a Miller Lite, J.D. had a white wine, and Corbin drank sour mash whiskey, straight.

"Are you headed back to Florida tomorrow?" Corbin asked.

"Unless you need us for something else," J.D. said.

"Nah. If something comes up, I'll give you a call."

"Will you make sure to get a DNA sample from Connie?" J.D. asked.

"We will. I'll send you the results as soon as I get them."

We had one more drink while J.D. and Corbin told old cop

stories and laughed about their jobs and the peccadillos in which they sometimes found themselves.

I called the airline and made a reservation for a six a.m. flight to Tampa. Via Atlanta, of course. That meant we had to leave the hotel by four to get to the airport by four-thirty. It would be a long day. J.D. and I had a quick meal in the hotel restaurant and went to bed.

CHAPTER TWENTY-THREE

It was nearing one o'clock on Saturday afternoon when we crossed the Manatee Avenue Bridge onto Anna Maria Island. We stopped at Duffy's for a burger and drove onto Longboat Key. I had called Maggie Bannister, the widow of the man Abby Lester was accused of killing. She agreed to see me mid-afternoon. I took J.D. with me.

I'd never met Maggie Bannister, but that wasn't all that unusual, even on a small island. While our off-season population was probably no larger than three or four thousand residents, the winter crowded the island with twenty-five thousand people. We had an ever-shifting population, so I regularly met someone I probably should have known, but didn't.

The Bannister home sprawled along a choice piece of bay-front property just south of Longbeach Village, where I lived. The lot was large and stretched from Gulf of Mexico Drive to the bay. We drove down a winding lane lined with Royal Palm trees until we came to a house that appeared to be one of the few remaining homes built in the 1960s. Most of the others had met the wrecking ball, and their lots were now filled with mansions. I knocked on the door and was greeted by a woman in her mid-thirties. She was attractive, blond, and smiling.

"Mr. Royal," she said. "Do come in."

I introduced J.D., and we followed her into the living room where we had a view of the bay and the Sister Keys. She offered us something to drink. We both declined. We sat, J.D. and I on a sofa and Maggie Bannister in a chair across from us. She was sipping from a tall glass of something clear. Water, I hoped. "I appreciate your seeing us, Mrs. Bannister," I said. "I know this is a difficult time."

"Please call me Maggie," she said. "I'm surprised our paths haven't crossed before, Matt. It's a small island, after all. I heard you're representing Abby Lester."

"Yes. I'm sorry for your loss."

Maggie laughed. "Matt, let's get off on the right foot here. That bastard's death is not a loss to me. In fact, it's a great relief. He was mean clear through, just plain evil. He thought nothing of beating the hell out of me when he felt like it, and he was always dipping his wick in some little slut he found in bars or whorehouses, or God knows where. I'm just glad he's gone."

I realized then that she had been drinking. She hid it well, but the cadence of her speech was just a little off, and there were squint lines at the edges of her eyes, like she was trying to focus. "Did you kill him, Maggie?" I asked.

She sat, her face still, no expression whatsoever. Then, "A reasonable question, Matt, under the circumstances. But no, I didn't kill him. I might have, given the chance, but I have a perfect alibi for the time he was murdered."

"May I ask what that alibi is?"

"I was with a person of impeccable credentials who'll testify to my whereabouts."

"Who was that?" I asked.

Maggie smiled. "I can't divulge that, Matt. I'm sorry, but it might put a good man in an impossible situation."

"I can find out, you know. Depositions and all that."

"I'm sorry, but I won't talk even if the court orders me to. If I'm charged with the crime, and I don't think I will be, my friend will testify on my behalf, but that's the only way it'll happen."

"Why didn't you leave your husband?" J.D. asked.

"Good question. I wish I had an answer. The shrinks have lots of answers, but I could never figure out which ones applied to me. I just stayed. A couple of months ago, a friend convinced me to take action. I did. I kicked the bastard out and got a restraining order. My friend gave me a gun, and I learned how to use it. I told Nate that if he ever came near me again, I'd shoot his sorry ass."

"He believed you?" J.D. asked.

"Not at first. But the day after I served him with the restraining order, he showed up here and threatened to kill me. I stuck the pistol in his gut and told him I was going to pull the trigger if he didn't leave." She laughed. "I think he wet himself. I never heard from him again."

"When was that?"

"Three weeks ago? I could check the restraining order, if you like."

"That's not necessary. Did you ever visit him in his new condo?" I asked.

"No. I had no reason to see the bastard."

"Was Nate having an affair with Abby Lester?" I asked.

"I have no idea. I've never met Abby, but from what I hear, she's not the kind of lowlife Nate was usually drawn to."

"How long were you two married?" J.D. asked.

"Ten years."

"How did you meet, if you don't mind my asking?" J.D. said.

"Oh, I don't mind. I was working as a bartender over at the Hyatt Regency on the mainland. He was a semi-regular and seemed a little shy. One night he asked me out. I was young and dumb and pretty impressed that this rich guy wanted to take me out. He brought me out here. He was a perfect gentleman. He was ten years older than me and divorced, but I had stars in my eyes, I guess, and they blinded me to the reality of that bastard. We danced for three months, and then had one of his judge friends marry us down at the courthouse."

"When did the trouble start?" J.D. asked.

"About three months after the wedding. He came home drunk one night and stunk of cheap perfume. I accused him of screwing around and he hit me. Only once, but it gave me a black eye. He apologized and begged me to forgive him. What a crock. I didn't realize that was the start of a ten-year ordeal."

"Did it ever get better?" J.D. asked.

"There were some good times. Nate was very generous and we lived pretty well. He took me on some real nice vacations, and we got along most of the time. I learned to overlook his affairs and tried not to cross him on anything. I didn't want to make him mad. I guess I was afraid of him, but I never really thought of it in those terms. Over the past couple of years, it got to the point where he'd beat me for no reason. At least, none that I could see. Just the meanness percolating out of his gut, I guess. Something went wrong at work, I'd get hit. Somebody dinged his car door in a parking lot, he'd take it out on me. He was careful not to hurt me enough that I had to seek medical attention, but it was pretty bad. I'm glad somebody killed the bastard."

"Do you know a woman named Victoria?" I asked.

"Yes. She goes by Tori. She worked for him at a project he was doing over in Lakeland. She was his assistant on some other things he was doing, but she was pretty much running the Lakeland site."

"You seem a bit skeptical about her job," I said.

"She was his latest squeeze. She's young and pretty and, I think, very smart. She has a degree in business. But there were problems. I'm not sure what they were, but I think Nate had given Tori too much responsibility and she was screwing up. He told me before I kicked him out that he was planning to fire her, but I think he was also trying to figure a way out of the affair he was having with her."

"What can you tell me about Tori?" I asked.

"Not much. I only met her once, and that was at a cocktail party in Lakeland when Nate was setting up the sales office for the project. I think she'd just shown up and applied for a job Nate had advertised. My guess would be that it was her body more than her credentials that got her the job."

"Where did she get her degree?"

"I have no idea. She might not actually have one. That could just have been part of Nate's smoke screen. Give him a reason for hiring a hottie. Who knows?"

"Do you have any idea about who might have wanted him dead?" I asked.

"Sure," Maggie said with a smile. "Anybody who ever bought one of his condos, or worked for him, or with him, or screwed him, or even met him. He was one mean and ruthless son of a bitch."

There was nothing else. She was running out of bile, her anger dissipating as she talked, as if just telling the story unburdened her. J.D. and I left and drove the short distance to my cottage.

"She's pretty bitter," I said.

"I wonder why," J.D. said, her voice dripping with sarcasm.

"Yeah. She has a lot of reasons. Most of those are also reasons to kill him."

"Do you think she did it?" J.D. asked.

"I don't know. She had every reason to do so."

"She lied when she denied ever being in his condo."

"Yeah, I caught that. Her fingerprints were on the list Gus sent me."

"Why would she lie about that?" J.D. asked.

"Maybe she either killed him or was there when someone else did."

"There's that. I wonder why FDLE didn't charge her. She had a lot more reason to kill her husband than Abby did. Even if Abby was having an affair with him."

"I've been thinking about that since Gus sent me the prints," I said. "Charging Abby might have made sense if Maggie's prints weren't in the condo. But since they were, you'd think she would be the prime suspect."

"Maybe FDLE didn't know about the violence in their marriage."

"I'll have to look at the court file, but I'm pretty sure a judge wouldn't have issued a restraining order without some evidence that Nate was at least threatening Maggie. That should have been enough, even without evidence of the beatings, to point FDLE or Sarasota PD to Maggie instead of Abby."

"Maybe Gus can come up with a reason Sarasota PD didn't follow up on that."

"Yeah. I'll give him a call."

CHAPTER TWENTY-FOUR

Sunday brought one of those bright mornings we Floridians live for. The island lay still in the gentle sun, and the aroma of frangipani blossoms filled the soft air as J.D. and I jogged toward the beach. We crossed the dunes on the wooden bridge at the end of North Shore Drive and turned south. The Gulf was an infinity of turquoise, flat and inviting. The hard-packed sand squished under our sneakers, gulls cackled, joggers and walkers smiled and waved, the contrails of a high-flying jet slashed across the otherwise flawless blue of a crystalline sky. "Paradise," J.D. said. "It just doesn't get any better than this."

"And you're the angel that makes it complete."

She punched me on my arm. "You're a sickie, Royal."

"You didn't think that poetic?"

"I didn't even think it was cute."

"I guess we have a day with nothing to do," I said. "You got any ideas?" I wiggled my eyebrows. Or at least I tried to wiggle them. It's harder to do than you might think. It didn't seem to make the impression I was trying for.

"We could go to the Longbeach Café for breakfast."

"Okay. Then what?"

"Moore's for lunch?"

"Okay."

"Finish up with dinner at Mar Vista?"

"Is eating all you ever think about?" I asked.

"It's all I'm thinking about right now."

"So we'll make a day of it in the village. Doing nothing."

"Maybe Gus will call," she said. "Or Detective Corbin."

"Gus said it'd probably be Monday before he could talk to one of his buddies at Sarasota PD. And I doubt that the New Orleans medical examiner is going to spend his weekend doing an autopsy on as undistinguished a victim as Connie Pelletier."

"You're probably right."

We came to the mid-rise condo building that marked the two-mile turnaround point for our four-mile run. I looked at my watch. Almost seven o'clock. We started back north, our breath getting a little shorter now. The conversation stopped, and we plodded on, making good time.

We cooled down on our walk from the beach to my cottage, took a quick shower, put on clean clothes, and walked back to the Longbeach Café, a tidy little diner in the same small shopping center that housed Tiny's Bar. Bob and Shannon Gault were sitting in a booth. They waved us over and asked us to join them.

"You guys look pretty chipper for this early in the morning," Bob said.

"She dragged me out for a run," I said. "Kind of gets the blood flowing. How have y'all been?"

"Fine," Bob said. "We just got back from San Diego and heard you're coming out of retirement."

"Sort of. I think I've got one more case in me."

"We knew Nate Bannister," Shannon said. "Terrible little man."

Colleen, the owner and cook, came and took our order and left.

"How did you know Bannister?" I asked.

"We talked to him a couple of years ago about building our house," Shannon said. "He didn't get along with the architect, he didn't like the plans, and he called me sugarplum and told me I had no business making suggestions to him about what kind of house I wanted."

"Sugarplum?" J.D. asked, laughing.

"Yeah. I thought Bob was going to hit him."

"I guess you decided to go with another builder," I said.

"Yes. I think Bannister got the message when Bob kicked him off the property."

Colleen brought our breakfast, and we ate as we talked.

"Did you ever meet his wife Maggie?" I asked.

"Once," said Bob. "Bannister took us to dinner when we first contacted him about the house. We got rid of him about three weeks later."

"What was your impression of the wife?" I asked.

"She seemed nice," Shannon said. "Kind of quiet; reserved, I guess."

"How did they seem as a couple?" J.D. asked.

"Fine," Shannon said.

"Did you ever meet anybody else who worked with Bannister?" I asked.

"Just his assistant," Bob said.

"Tori?"

"Yes. I think that was her name."

"What was she like?"

"She seemed pretty much in charge," Bob said. "At least when we were talking money. But one time he almost bit her head off."

"Tell me about that."

"I think she was talking about allowances for different rooms," Bob said. "You know. Things like how much we could spend on crown moldings, flooring, that sort of thing. Suddenly, out of the blue, Bannister called her a stupid bitch and said he'd explain it all to us."

"What did Tori do?"

"Nothing," said Shannon. "She just sat there and didn't say another word. I'd have slapped some of that arrogance out of him if he'd talked to me that way."

Bob grinned. "I thought Shannon was going to take him out when he called her sugarplum."

"There was something else," Shannon said. "I think Bannister and Tori were having an affair."

"What made you think that?" I asked.

"I'm not sure. There was just something between them. She was quite a bit younger than he, and he was certainly in charge of whatever relationship they had. I can't quite put my finger on it, but I'd bet good money they were an item. She looked genuinely hurt when he called her stupid."

"She also looked mad as hell," Bob said.

"That too," Shannon said.

"Did you ever see them again?" I asked.

"I saw him a couple of times on the island, once at the post office and another time in Publix," Bob said. "I just nodded at him. Never had another conversation."

"What about you, sugarplum?" I asked.

Shannon burst out laughing. "That's not funny, Matt. But no, I never saw him again. I did see Tori once."

"Here on the island?"

"No. I was downtown with some friends having lunch and I saw Tori in a restaurant. She was sitting in a corner with a man about her age. Not much to him. He was wearing one of those tight t-shirts that showed off his biceps, only he didn't have any. I couldn't see them as a couple, but they were holding hands and talking quietly. Kind of looking into each other's eyes. That kind of stuff. I don't think she even noticed me."

"When was this?" I asked.

"Two weeks ago? Maybe three. I can look at my calendar and pinpoint it exactly if you need the date."

"Don't worry about it now. Can you describe the guy?"

"He was skinny as a rail, but tall. It was hard to tell with him sitting down, but I'd guess maybe six-two. He had blond hair that he wore long. I don't think he washed it regularly. That's about all I can tell you."

"How about eye color, facial hair? Any distinguishing marks?"

"I didn't get a good enough look at his face to tell you about his eye color, but I don't think he had a beard or mustache. No scars that I saw."

"Are you thinking they might have had something to do with Bannister's murder?" Bob asked.

"Not really, but you never know what's going to turn up. I *am* sure that Abby Lester didn't kill him. But somebody did."

Bob looked at his watch. "We've got to go. We're going to take the boat on a run down to Venice with Woody and Sue Wolverton and grab some lunch at the Crow's Nest."

We said our good-byes, and Bob insisted on picking up the check.

Our day was just as J.D. planned it. She sat on the patio reading a book, and I read up on case law to make sure I wasn't missing something I'd need for Abby's case. We walked to Moore's for lunch, back to my cottage, more reading, more sunning on the patio, more conversation about things of no importance, then to Mar Vista for a light dinner and home to bed. Not a bad way to spend a beautiful Sunday in paradise.

CHAPTER TWENTY-FIVE

Monday mornings are busy times at the Longboat Key police station. The cops who were off for the weekend are catching up on what had happened since their last shift ended, paperwork is flowing to the deputy chief's office and on to the chief's. The Sunday night shift is getting ready to check out for the day and the calls of snakes in pools and dogs loose on the beach start coming in. There is little crime on Longboat Key, but the island never sleeps. Dogs bark, neighbors quarrel, snowbirds drive slow on Gulf of Mexico Drive, raccoons raid trash cans, car keys get lost, lovers walk the beach after midnight, landscapers start working before eight; a never-ending litany of calls presenting problems that the officers respond to and sort out.

J.D. had closed her office door, muting the cacophonous din echoing down the corridor. She was contemplating the email she'd received early that morning from Detective Brad Corbin in New Orleans. It contained a DNA analysis on Connie Pelletier and a note explaining that the ballistics people at the Orleans Parish crime lab had determined that the gun used to kill Connie was the same one that had killed Officer Tatum. The connection to the murder of a police officer spurred the lab to a frenzy of overtime, resulting in a quick turnaround on the DNA.

J.D. emailed a copy of the report to Bert Hawkins with a note asking him to compare Connie's DNA to Linda Favereaux's, and imploring him to let her know something as soon as possible.

Corbin's email also told her that he had found regular cash deposits into Tatum's bank account beginning two years before— at about the same time that he became one of the records clerks.

Corbin had also checked the bank account of Tatum's predecessor, a civilian who had held the job for twenty years. He'd received monthly cash deposits for most of that time.

J.D. looked at her watch. Almost nine. Corbin would be at work. She dialed his cell phone, identified herself, and told him she appreciated his email and the rush on the DNA. "What more can you tell me about the money going into the records clerks' accounts?"

"Not much," Corbin said. "They were cash deposits, probably made by the account holder. But they were regular as clockwork. During the first week of every month, Tatum's predecessor made a five-hundred-dollar deposit. Apparently, Tatum got a raise. He was depositing a thousand bucks a month."

"The other guy was a civilian. Why did they replace him with a cop?"

"I asked the chief about that. It seems that internal affairs had some indication that when Tatum was a patrol officer, he was on the take from some pretty bad people down in the Quarter. Apparently, just penny-ante stuff for the most part. Look the other way on small crimes like prostitution being run out of some of the bars, that sort of thing. They never could get the goods on him. The chief didn't have the grounds to fire him, so he brought him in-house to take care of the records. He figured Tatum couldn't get into trouble in the records room."

"Looks like the chief was wrong," J.D. said. "Did you follow up with the civilian to find out where the money was coming from?"

"Unfortunately, no. He died about six months ago. Heart attack."

"Did the money going to him ever stop?"

"There were no more cash deposits after he retired."

"Were you able to check to see if any of your other records are missing?"

"I've got our information technology people on that, but they may never find anything. We've got thousands upon thousands of files, and a few could have been taken out and not returned, and we'd never know, unless we were looking for a specific file."

"What about the computer files? Wouldn't the IT people be able to find out if any of those were erased?"

"They're trying to reconstruct that now. We'll know more in a couple of days."

"Thanks, Brad. I've sent your DNA results on Connie to our ME for comparison with my victim's. I'll let you know what turns up."

J.D. hung up and went to her computer. There were still no reports of any activity on James Favereaux's credit cards. She dug through her inbox. Junk mail, memos about nothing important, and a report from the Sarasota County crime lab on Favereaux's car that had been found at the Tampa airport.

J.D. groaned out loud. The report was dated the Wednesday before. It'd probably shown up in her inbox on Thursday morning while she and Matt were en route to New Orleans. She had forgotten about it.

The report was detailed, giving a description of the meticulous search of every part of the vehicle. Nothing out of the ordinary was found. Just the typical detritus found in most cars after they'd been driven awhile. There was a McDonald's bag on the floorboard of the back seat. It contained, among other things, the remains of a meal and a receipt for a Big Mac, fries, and a Diet Coke, bought at an all-night McDonald's on Cortez Road at twenty-five minutes past midnight on Monday morning, the night of his wife's murder. Was this before or after she died?

J.D. remembered that the ME's assistant could only give an approximation of the time of death. She pulled the autopsy report from the file and found the estimated time of death. Midnight, Sunday, give or take an hour. She thought about it. If Linda had been killed early in that two-hour window, James would have had time to kill her and get to the McDonald's shortly after midnight. If she had died late in the window, James would have had time to get his burger and drive home and kill his wife. Was he that devoid of humanity, that big a monster? It didn't fit with the fact of his philanthropy to USF, the endowed chair in African-American studies.

She went back to the forensics report and found the mileage that showed on the car's odometer at the Tampa airport parking garage. She toyed with that, but since she had no way of knowing what the mileage was when he pulled into McDonald's, there was no way to determine if James had driven straight from the restaurant to the airport or had made a detour to the key to kill his wife.

It hit her like a lightning bolt. Cameras. The town had recently installed cameras near the bridges at either end of the island, part of a system known as Automatic License Recognition System. The cameras took pictures of the license plates of any vehicle that entered the island or left it. The plate numbers were instantaneously fed to a computer that checked the plates against those listed for stolen cars or ones owned by people who had suspended or revoked licenses, or a myriad of other things. A number of islanders had complained about Big Brother, but the cameras had been installed and were being tested. Maybe they caught James Favereaux's plates.

She called Sharkey and asked how to find out the information she needed. He said he'd run it for her if she could give him a plate number. She gave it to him and in a few seconds, he said, "Here it is. He left the island on the Longboat Pass Bridge at eleven-fifty on Sunday night and returned at twelve-forty-five in the morning. He left again via the Longboat Pass Bridge at twenty minutes after one."

"Okay. So he has a Big Mac attack and goes to McDonald's. He crosses the bridge at eleven-fifty, takes about thirty-five minutes to get to the restaurant, order his meal, and start home. He comes back across the bridge twenty minutes after he pays for the meal. Not much traffic that time of night, and it would be about a fifteen to twenty-minute drive either way."

"Sounds about right," Sharkey said.

"So what about the fifteen-minute gap? There was thirty-five minutes between the time he left the island and the time he paid for the meal, but it took him only twenty minutes to get home."

"Maybe he stopped for gas. Maybe the Cortez Bridge was up on his way to McDonald's and he had to wait for a boat to pass. Any number of things could have delayed him."

"You're right. Thanks, Martin." She hung up and thought some more. It didn't make sense that James killed Linda, went to McDonald's, and then returned to the island. When he came back from McDonald's, he crossed the bridge at twelve forty-five, and would have driven the ten minutes farther to his house. That would have put him at home within the kill window. She knew those windows were not very precise. They could be off by an hour or more depending on a lot of variables.

Still, Favereaux could have murdered Linda, left his house at ten minutes after one, and crossed the bridge at one-twenty. The time frame fit. Did something happen, a violent argument perhaps, within the fifteen minutes or so between the time he arrived at the house and the time he left?

What happened in that fifteen minutes? What was the murder weapon and where was it now? Probably in the Gulf of Mexico. Something didn't fit. A man leaves his house, drives a half-hour to McDonald's at midnight, eats his sandwich in the car on the way home, kills his wife, and leaves again. She shook her head. Could she assume that he ate the sandwich? Did it make any difference? The remains of the sandwich wrapping were in the car. The sandwich was gone. Maybe he threw it out the window, but why would he do that? Suppose he wanted to establish a time line by leaving the time stamped receipt in the car. Did he know about the cameras on the bridge? A lot of islanders weren't paying attention to them yet, so maybe it wasn't something he thought about. If he'd thought about it, he would have known that the cameras would have established his time line.

If he knew about the cameras and planned to kill his wife, why take the chance that somebody could figure out the time line that put him in the house during the period when the murder took place? And if he were just trying to establish a time line with the McDonald's receipt, why not stop for gas at the 7-Eleven store at Cortez Road and Palma Sola Boulevard? It would have been closer, and the gas receipt would have served the same purpose.

She had no answers, but her growling stomach was telling her that it was lunchtime. Her phone rang. Bert Hawkins. "I don't know what you're working on, J.D.," he said, "but the DNA report from New Orleans makes things interesting."

"How so?"

"The dead woman in New Orleans was, without a doubt, the mother of Linda Favereaux."

CHAPTER TWENTY-SIX

It was time for me to have a conversation with Robert Shorter, the man with anger issues who had left his fingerprints in Bannister's condo. I drove twenty miles south to a Siesta Key condo that sat on the bayshore near the southern end of the island. I knew from my search of the Sarasota County property appraiser's website that the building in which Shorter lived was only about five years old, but it was not wearing well. Stucco was peeling from the underlying concrete block, leaving bare patches in the walls. The wooden trim appeared to be rotting away, the landscaping was minimal, and neighboring condo buildings nearing completion were encroaching too closely on Shorter's building and severely limiting the view of the bay. It made me wonder if someone had greased the palms of a building official to get the necessary permits to build.

The man who answered the door was squat, about five feet six and two hundred pounds. He appeared to be in his mid-thirties. His belly, not quite covered by a thin t-shirt, overflowed the waistband of his shorts. He was wearing flip-flops and a scowl. "Whadda you want?" he asked.

I stuck out my hand. "I'm Matt Royal, Mr. Shorter. I'm a lawyer—" I got no further.

"Get the fuck outta here." He started to close the door.

I put my hand out to stop the door. He pulled it quickly, opening it all the way. "I'll kick your slimy ass," he said.

I smiled. "I guess the anger management classes didn't take."

He threw a punch. I saw it coming. There was a split second there when his eyes squinted and his right shoulder twitched and the fist started upward. I reacted instantly, old army training kicking in. I stepped back and his fist whizzed past my chin, missing completely. His body followed his hand, the momentum twisting his torso to his left, opening up his right rib cage. I reacted reflexively, no thought, no debate about the wisdom of my response, or the consequences. Just action. I jabbed him with a left, hard, just below his right ribs. I'd learned long ago that when you punch somebody, you don't aim for the place you're planning to hit. You aim several inches beyond, so that when you connect, it's with all the power you can generate. That stopped his forward movement and turned him toward me. I followed up with a right to his solar plexus. He went down, gasping for breath, falling into his apartment.

I followed and closed the door behind me. I stood over him, waiting for him to catch his breath, hoping for a return to lucidity, and feeling a bit sorry for the man. I had reacted to his assault without thinking, but it was never a contest, and I probably didn't have to hit him the second time. He looked kind of pitiful lying there on the floor, and I felt like a bully.

His breathing became shallower, his eyes focusing on me. "Who are you?"

"I was telling you when you went all Rambo on me. I'm Matt Royal. I'm a lawyer, and I'm representing the woman accused of killing Nate Bannister. I think we might have gotten off on the wrong foot. Can we start over?"

"You bastard," he said. "I ought to call the cops." He still had some fight left in him, or maybe just anger. He was lying on the floor, seething.

"Who do you think the cops will believe? A scumbag arrested twice for assault and battery, or an icon of the Bar, a lawyer of impeccable standing, the epitome of all that's right and good in our society."

"You have a pretty high opinion of yourself," he said.

"Alas, I may be the only person in the whole world with that opinion, but I'm certainly not a scumbag."

"Are you calling me a scumbag?" The feistiness was back.

"No, sir. I'm just pointing out how you might appear to an officer of the law."

"Okay. Tell me why I ought to talk to you. You sucker punched me."

"You swung first."

"Yeah, but I missed."

"Let's look at the situation we're in, Mr. Shorter," I said. "I can just kick the shit out of you and call an ambulance, or we can sit down and have a rational discussion, just like regular human beings."

"You think you can take me?"

"I already did."

"You've got a point," he said. "What do you want to know?"

"Get up off the floor and we'll talk."

"You're not going to hit me again, are you?"

"Do I have to?" I asked.

"No. We're okay."

He pulled himself up and sat in a chair, massaging his side. "You pack a hell of a punch," he said. "For a lawyer."

"Why did you swing at me?"

"I don't like lawyers."

"Most people don't," I said, "but generally they're at least civil to me."

"I didn't kill that bastard, if that's what you're thinking."

"Why would I think that?"

"You're here, and I was arrested a couple of years ago for taking a swing at Bannister."

"Why did you go after him?"

"Did you take a look at this place?"

"Yes. A quick look."

"It's falling apart. The construction was shoddy and somehow Bannister managed to build on a lot that was too small. When the buildings on either side went up, they were built so close they ruined our view."

"What do you do for a living?"

"Nothing."

"Nothing?"

"I'm what you call a trust-fund baby."

"Big trust?" I asked.

"You think I'd live in this dump if it was big?"

"You could get a job."

"I've tried that. Never worked out too well."

"Why not?"

"Some people say I've got anger issues."

"Was that the last time you saw Bannister? The day you hit him?"

"No. I saw him again about two weeks ago."

"Where?"

"His condo. Downtown."

That would explain his fingerprints in Bannister's home. At least Shorter wasn't lying. "How did that come about?"

"I called him. Made an appointment to see him. He told me to come to his condo."

"Was anybody else there?"

"His assistant."

"The assistant's name?"

"I don't remember. She was a young woman, a real fox."

"Tori?"

"What?"

"Was her name Tori?"

He was quiet for a moment. "Wait a minute," he said. "She gave me a business card." He pulled out his wallet and riffled through it, pulling out folded pieces of paper, a couple of twenty-dollar bills, and several business cards. "Here it is," he said, finally. He handed it to me. The name on the card was Victoria Madison.

"Why did you go to see Bannister?"

"Some of the owners here are threatening to sue him over the building problems. I thought I might be able to work something out."

"What do you mean?"

"You know. A settlement."

"Were you there on behalf of the other owners?"

"Not exactly."

"What does that mean?"

"I guess you could say I was there on my own behalf."

"I'm surprised."

"Why? Oh, you're kidding."

"So," I said, "why were you there?"

"I wanted to make a deal."

"What kind of deal?"

"I offered to help him out if he'd buy this place back from me."

"Did you give him a price?"

"Yes.

"Big price?"

"Reasonable price."

"How reasonable?"

"I just wanted a little profit out of the deal."

"How much profit?"

He took a deep breath. "I told him I'd sell it back to him for three times what I paid for it."

"Little profit, huh?"

"Well, I think I ought to be paid for the aggravation he put me through."

"Aggravation?"

"Yeah. I spent thirty days in lockup because of that bastard."

"You hit him. Remember?"

"Yes, but I wouldn't have hit him, if he weren't such a bastard."

"That probably didn't stand up too well as a defense in court."

"No. You damn lawyers are too picky."

"What was your part of the deal?"

"What do you mean?"

"What were you going to do in return for the money?"

"Oh. I told him I would join the lawsuit with my neighbors and keep him informed about what was going on."

"A spy," I said.

"Well, more like a consultant."

"What did Bannister think of the deal you proposed?"

"He said he wanted to think about it. Said he'd get back to me."

"Did the assistant have anything to say?"

"She was all for it. Tried to talk Bannister into making the deal right there."

"Did you ever hear from him?"

"Not from him, but his assistant called me and said Bannister wanted to meet with me again."

"When did you get that call?"

"A week ago Friday."

"Two days before he was killed."

"Right."

"Did you set up the meeting?"

"Yeah. I was supposed to meet him at his condo on Sunday evening."

"The same night he was killed."

"Right."

"Did you go?"

"No."

"Why not?"

"The neighbors set up the meeting with their lawyer for the same evening. I found out about it Sunday afternoon and called Bannister's assistant. She told me it was very important that I meet with them as planned. I told her I needed to go to the meeting with my neighbors if I was going to learn anything that would help Bannister out. She was really pissed, but said Bannister would call me on Monday and reset our meeting. I never heard from him. Bastard."

"You didn't hear from him on Monday," I said, "because he was dead."

"Well, hell. I didn't know that on Monday. I figured he was stiffing me."

"Make you mad?"

"Damn straight."

"What'd you do about it?"

"I tried to call him a bunch of times, but never got an answer."

"Where was the meeting with your neighbors on Sunday evening?"

"Here. In the activity room. We had to bring our own chairs 'cause that bastard Bannister never furnished the place."

"Who was the lawyer you all met with?"

"I don't remember the guy's name. I can get it for you."

"How long did the meeting last?"

"Four hours or so. Damn neighbors are boring as hell. They just wouldn't shut up."

"Were you there the whole time?"

"Yeah. I wanted to be able to give Bannister a full report."

"What time did the meeting break up?"

"Around eleven."

"Can you give me the names of some of the neighbors?"

"Sure." He grinned. "Checking my alibi, huh?"

"Something like that."

CHAPTER TWENTY-SEVEN

My phone rang as I was crossing the bridge from Siesta Key to the mainland. J.D. "Hey, sweetie," I said.

"You ever call me that in public, I'll shoot you."

"Not to worry. I don't have a death wish, Detective."

"That's better. Got time for lunch?"

"Sure. Where do you want to eat?"

"Where are you?"

"Just leaving Siesta Key. I've had an interesting morning with Robert Shorter."

"Who's that?"

"The guy whose fingerprints were found in Bannister's condo. The one who assaulted him a couple years back."

"Sounds like fun. I've had a really big morning."

"Yeah?"

"Yeah, but you've got to buy me lunch to hear about it. Marina Jack?"

"Sounds good. It'll take me thirty minutes in this traffic."

"See you then."

* * *

Marina Jack was a sprawling marina and restaurant that took up a lot of space on the bayfront in downtown Sarasota. The docks were full of boats and expensive yachts, some semi-permanent residents, some day-trippers who pulled their small boats into the slips provided for the restaurant, and others who stopped in for a few days while cruising Florida's west coast. The restaurant was crowded with a mixture of boaters, business people, and professionals from the downtown office buildings.

J.D. and I were at a table overlooking the Intracoastal Waterway. The sun was high and bright and warm, the air still, the bay flat, a perfect day for boating. It made me miss my other love, *Recess,* which was tied to her dock behind my cottage. I had neglected her of late, and I think she resented it. I'd make it up to her. Spring was upon us, the weather was magnificent, and I lived in a boating paradise.

"Tell me about your morning," I said.

"Linda Favereaux was Connie Pelletier's daughter."

"Wow. That *is* big news. Kind of changes things in your case."

"It does, but I haven't figured out how. Yet."

J.D. told me what she'd found out about the midnight trip of James Favereaux, the evidence from the bridge cameras, her speculation about the timing, and the DNA evidence from New Orleans.

"Maybe," I said, "James came home and found Linda with somebody else. Both nude. It could piss a guy off."

"I thought about that, but James was only gone an hour. Surely, Linda wasn't dumb enough to invite a boyfriend over while her husband ran out to get a hamburger."

"Maybe she didn't know her husband was coming back. What if he was leaving on a trip and forgot something and returned to the house? Or changed his mind about leaving and was coming home? She might have thought he was gone for the night and called her boyfriend."

"Possible. But then what happened to the boyfriend, if there was one? Nobody's come forward."

"Might be a married man who's not interested in having his name associated with the murder of his girlfriend."

"You're not helping, Royal. You've got more questions than answers."

"Yes, but questions lead to answers and answers lead to truth."

"There are times when you're insufferable."

"Like now?"

"Nah. You're kinda cute when you go all philosophical."

"The value of a liberal arts education."

"I guess. But you're right, you know. Something like that could have happened. There was indication in the autopsy report that Linda had recently had sex."

"Any indication as to whom she had sex with?"

"No. She had been in the hot tub on the patio and the chlorine would have compromised any trace evidence. The autopsy showed no trace of semen."

"If the boyfriend arrived right after the husband left," I said, "they would have had an hour or so before he got back. Maybe they let the time slip up on them, or took up too much time fooling around."

"Yeah. Maybe the boyfriend puts more value in foreplay than you do."

"Ouch."

"Just kidding. I'm a satisfied detective." She laughed. Not the big one that shivers my timbers, but the little one, the one that tinkles like little silver bells, and melts my heart.

"What do you think about the connection between Linda and Connie?" I asked.

"I don't know what to make of that. Connie lied, obviously. But why? What happened to cause her to deny that Linda was her daughter?"

"If Linda really was screwing around with Bobby, that would certainly drive a wedge between them."

"Incest?" J.D. asked.

"We don't know that Bobby was Linda's father."

"That's a good point. I wonder if we can get the marriage and birth records from Louisiana. Linda had Bobby's last name, so maybe he adopted her."

"Time to call our buddy, Corbin," I said. "See if he can turn up the records."

"I've already called him about the DNA match. I'll get back to him this afternoon about the family records. I think adoption records are usually sealed. We probably won't be able to get them, but it's worth a try."

"Do you think the murders of Connie and Linda are connected?" I asked.

"I don't know, but it seems to be a reasonable assumption. Connie was killed after we went to see her about Linda. And she was Linda's mother. Why would that be a secret? Or important enough to kill Connie?"

"Another point to consider," I said. "Connie was killed by what appears to be a professional hit man. Linda's murder looked more like a crime of opportunity or passion, something that wasn't planned. If a pro did it, wouldn't he just have shot her? Like the one who did Connie?"

"I've been thinking about that. There's really nothing that ties the murders together other than the family relationship and the fact that Connie was killed right after she talked to us."

"The timing might have been nothing more than a coincidence."

"Maybe so," she said. "How did your morning go?"

"Pretty good, after I beat the crap out of the witness."

"Right."

"Actually, I did."

"You're kidding."

I told her about the altercation. "It was just reflex. He swung, and I hit back."

"I hate to tell you this, but that's not a very good way to win friends and influence witnesses."

"This time, it worked," I said, and told her about Shorter's meeting with Bannister and Tori and his alibi for the night of the murder.

"You didn't accomplish a lot, then."

"Well, maybe not a lot, but I did eliminate a suspect, and we found out that Tori wasn't above a little illegal activity."

"Have you heard from Gus?"

"I talked to him after you called. He's on his way over here. Says he's got some news."

"Good or bad?"

"Didn't say. Here he comes now."

Gus Grantham was a slender six feet of distinguished-looking manliness. He moved through the restaurant with an assurance that comes from the years of self-confidence that a badge and gun give a man. He was smiling as he approached. J.D. stood and hugged him. I settled for a handshake. He joined us at the table.

"Good to see you," J.D. said. "It's been a while."

"Too long, J.D. I miss seeing a lot of the old people we worked with for so many years."

"Do you miss being a cop?" she asked.

"Sometimes, but I like being my own boss."

"You like the work?" I asked.

"About half the time. When I get a case like yours, it gets the juices flowing. I depend on lawyers for most of my work, and that means I have to take their crap along with the good stuff."

"Crap?" J.D. asked.

"Divorces."

"I see what you mean," I said.

"Did you ever do any divorce work, Matt?" Gus asked.

"No. A lot of the guys who did criminal defense work did divorce as well. But it's like my old buddy Bill Barnett once said, 'In criminal defense you find the worst people on their best behavior, and in divorce work you find the best people on their worst behavior.' When I wasn't handling criminal cases, I did a lot of complex civil litigation. What do you know about why somebody decided to charge Abby with murder?"

"Okay. This came from a very reliable source, an old friend of mine at Sarasota PD. When the fingerprints first came in, Harry Robson caught Abby's name on the list and took it immediately to the chief. Both of them realized that they had to dump the case on FDLE, or they'd face legitimate criticism for pursuing a case where the wife of the police chief in a neighboring jurisdiction was at least a potential witness. The file was turned over to FDLE with no recommendations about what or whom to pursue."

"So," I said, "somebody at FDLE made the decision to pursue Abby. I can't believe those emails would have been the deciding factor. Especially since they didn't come from her computer. Do you have any idea who made the decision, or why?"

"I'm pretty sure the decision was made by Wes Lucas, but I don't know why. There were other fingerprints in the condo, including those of the victim's estranged wife. She would have seemed to me to be a better possibility than Abby Lester. FDLE must have something that Sarasota PD isn't aware of."

"They would have had to dig it up pretty quick," I said. "There were only a few hours between the time the case was given to FDLE and the Jacksonville state attorney charged Abby."

"I'm not sure Lucas waited for the state attorney before making his decision. It looks to me like he decided to arrest Abby, and then told the state attorney to charge her. They haven't been real quick to take the case to a grand jury."

"I noticed that," I said. "I wonder if they're going to stick with the second-degree murder charge. It'd make more sense to go with manslaughter. Better chance for a conviction."

"That's for you lawyers to figure out," Gus said. "They also got results from the DNA found on the sheets. Some of it was Bannister's, but the female DNA isn't in the system."

"I'm not surprised by that," I said. "Unless somebody's been arrested before, it won't be there."

"They're probably going to request a swab from Abby," J.D. said.

"I know. I may fight them on that."

"Why?" asked J.D.

"If Abby was having an affair with Bannister, it wouldn't do us any good to have that go into evidence. If she wasn't, and that's not her DNA, maybe our fighting them on the production will send the prosecution off on a wild-goose chase."

"Aren't they likely to get the sample from Abby?" asked Gus.

"I don't think so. Not with the evidence they have. Judge Thomas isn't going to let them go off on a fishing expedition. They're going to have to show him reasonable cause for taking the sample. If they have something we don't know about that would rise to reasonable cause, they're going to have to show their evidence. I've got nothing to lose by fighting their request for Abby's DNA, but potentially, a lot to gain."

"My computer guy's been out of town," Gus said, "but he's back. If you can get me Bannister's computer, I can have him take a look at it. See if he can figure out where those emails came from."

"I won't be able to get possession of the computer, but I should be able to get your guy access to it. I'll file a motion tomorrow. I'd also like you to check out this assistant, Tori. See what turns up. It sounds like she's not too hung up on ethics."

"Even if the deal had gone down between Shorter and Bannister," said Gus, "I don't think they would have been breaking any laws."

"I agree," I said, "but from what Shorter said, Tori sure seemed to be quick to buy into something dirty."

"She may just be an opportunist," J.D. said.

"Maybe," I said. "Anything on the ballistics on the murder weapon?"

"Nothing," Gus said. "They haven't found the gun, and the slugs were pretty beaten up, so it was hard to get enough information off of them to find a match to any other weapons used in crimes. Nothing showed up in the databases."

"Any luck in getting copies of those emails?" I asked.

He pulled seven sheets of folded paper from the inside pocket of his suit coat and handed them to me. "This is all of them," he said, "and you didn't get them from me."

"Good work, Gus," I said.

CHAPTER TWENTY-EIGHT

J.D. called me late in the afternoon. I was at home drafting a motion to allow our expert to examine Abby's computer. I had just finished researching the case law concerning the threshold of evidence that was needed for a court to order a defendant to provide a DNA sample.

"Brad was able to get hold of what appears to be Linda Favereaux's birth certificate," she said. "He tracked it through Connie's maiden name, Rohan. She had a baby girl thirty-nine years ago. She named her Darlene Rohan."

"Father?"

"Unknown. Connie married Bobby Pelletier two years later. It could have been Bobby's baby, but who knows. I'd think if Bobby was the father, Connie would have listed him on the birth certificate."

"What about adoption records?" I asked.

"Sealed. We can't get them."

"How important are they?"

"Probably not much. I don't see what Darlene's adoption would have to do with her murder."

"Maybe the adoption records would have the natural father's name," I said.

"That's a possibility, if Connie really knew who he was. But what bearing would that have on the murder?"

"I can't think of any. I just don't like loose ends."

"Neither do I," J.D. said. "But sometimes they're just not important enough to pursue."

"If we had Bobby Pelletier's murder file, we might have a shot at his DNA."

"Maybe that's why it's missing," J.D. said.

"Probably. I wonder how Darlene Pelletier became Linda Fournier and then married James Favereaux. Did she legally change her name?"

"If she did," J.D. said, "there's no record of it in Louisiana. Brad checked that out."

"But there's a record of the marriage?"

"License issued in Orleans Parish and the wedding was performed by a notary public."

"Do we have any information on the notary?" I asked.

"Dead for fifteen years."

"Not much of a lead."

"Not much," she said.

"Are you coming over after work?"

"I'll see you in about an hour."

My phone rang as soon as I hung up. Gus Grantham. "I've got some information on Tori."

"That was quick."

"Just computer stuff. But it should give you something to discuss with her."

"Shoot."

"She's twenty-five years old, grew up on the wrong side of Tampa, dropped out of high school in the tenth grade, did a stint in juvie, arrested twice as an adult for drug possession, once for drunk driving and has a tattoo on her lower back. I think they call that a tramp stamp. She worked as a bartender in one of those topless joints on Dale Mabry in Tampa, but it doesn't look like she was a dancer. Kept most of her clothes on, I think."

"Ever do time?"

"I can't get hold of the juvenile records. They're sealed. She got probation on the first drug charge and did thirty days in the Hillsborough County lockup on the second one. She pled the drunk-driving charge down to reckless driving and paid a fine and did some community service."

"Any sign that she ever went to college?"

"None."

"Do you have an address for her?"

"She lives in an apartment in Sarasota. Commutes to the project in Lakeland." He gave me the address and also the address of the office where she worked. "Are you going to see her?"

"Tomorrow."

"Want me to come along?"

"I don't think so, Gus. It might not rattle her as much if I just come alone. I'd like you to go to Tampa and see what you can find out about her background. Family ties, friends, ownership of the club she worked in, how she got the job with Bannister when she seems absolutely unqualified for it, that sort of thing."

"I'll get on it first thing tomorrow. Is there anything specific you're looking for?"

I told him about the young man Maggie Bannister had recently seen Tori with at the downtown restaurant. "It's probably nothing, but I'd like to know who he is without asking her directly."

"You think he might have had something to do with Bannister's murder?"

"I don't know. It's a possibility. Then again, I might be chasing ghosts."

CHAPTER TWENTY-NINE

I grilled steaks on the patio while J.D. tossed a salad and toasted garlic bread in the oven. We ate outside, sitting at the picnic table overlooking the bay. It was a quiet evening, the sky still lit with the rays of the sun sinking into the Gulf on the other side of the island. We watched the boats going by on the Intracoastal, mostly small craft, each with a couple of retired guys heading home after a day of flats fishing.

"What did you think of the emails?" J.D. asked.

"Not much. I can't see Abby using some of the gutter language that was in them."

"I agree. It sounds a lot more like something a man might come up with."

"The one in which Abby supposedly threatens to kill Bannister is just a bit much. If we give any credence to the earlier emails, it would appear that Abby was in love and had become a sex maniac to boot. Why would she have gone from that to threatening to kill her lover within the space of twenty-four hours?"

"Crazy people might do that," J.D. said, "but there's no indication that Abby went nuts."

"The emails are frauds. I think we can make some points with them. Women on the jury wouldn't think Abby would write that sort of garbage."

"Unless they think she's nuts."

"Well, there's that."

"And what if you get an all male jury?"

"You're not helping me here, sweetie."

She grinned and changed the subject. "Why do you think Tori was so adamant about Shorter going to Bannister's condo on Sunday night?"

"I've been thinking about that. Could Tori have been setting Shorter up to take a murder rap?"

"It's a possibility, but why would Tori want to kill her meal ticket?"

"Good question," I said. "Maybe we'll have a better idea when we know more about Tori's background."

We finished our meal and cleaned up as darkness dropped in, the sun finally giving up and sinking into the Gulf. We walked down to Tiny's for a nightcap and a little conversation with friends. It was a pleasant and ordinary way to end our day, a way to relieve the stress of two murder investigations.

Cracker Dix and Logan Hamilton were at the bar, and based on their slurred conversation, they had been there awhile. The Tiny's regulars didn't worry much about driving drunk, because someone would always take them home. If everyone was too drunk to drive, Susie, the owner, would leave the least drunk person in the bar in charge and drive the soused ones home. It was just part of the small island community's ways.

"Cracker," I said, as J.D. and I took seats at the bar, "you know everybody on this end of the key. Do you know Maggie Bannister?"

"Sure."

"What can you tell me about her?"

"Not much. She was married to a real bastard, and now she's a widow. I think she's a lot happier."

"Have you seen her lately?"

"Yesterday."

"Where?"

"At her house."

"What were you doing there?"

"I stop by now and again."

"You're friends?"

"I guess you can say that."

"Cracker," J.D. said, "you're not telling us she's one of your married women friends with benefits."

"Nah. Maggie was never into messing around. She put up with that bastard of a husband because she didn't know what else to do. But she didn't screw around. Well, not until recently, anyway."

"You mean she started up with somebody?" I asked.

"Pretty sure."

"Do you know who?"

"Think so."

"You want to tell me?" I asked.

"Not really." He screwed up his face and looked squarely at me. "A gentleman doesn't carry gossip." The slurring was getting more pronounced.

"Ah, what the hell," Logan said. "Tell him, Cracker. It's Bill Lester."

"No. You're mistaken," I said.

Cracker nodded. "No, Logan's right."

"Are you sure?"

"Pretty sure," Cracker said.

I was truly shocked. "How did you know about this, Cracker?"

"I went to visit Maggie one night after leaving here and I saw the chief pull into that long driveway of hers. I was near the house and watched her come out and greet Bill. She was wearing some sort of flimsy negligee and had a glass of wine in her hand. She gave ole Lester one of those big wet kisses. I could almost hear it from where I was standing. Then they disappeared inside."

"When was this?" I asked.

"A couple of months back."

"Do you think it was a one-time thing?" J.D. asked.

"No," Cracker said. "Maggie told me she had a boyfriend. She was all excited and said she thought she was in love."

"Did she tell you it was Lester?"

"No. She wouldn't give me a name. But I saw him pull into her place again a couple of weeks later."

"Damn."

"Don't let him know where you got this," Cracker said. "The last thing I need is the chief of police breathing down my neck."

"Mum's the word," I said.

J.D. made a zipping motion across her lips.

* * *

Cracker and Logan left an hour later. Logan said he was sober enough to drive, and he did seem pretty steady. Cracker, as usual, was walking. J.D. and I moved to a high-top table in the back corner, by the silent jukebox. I wanted to get her thoughts on what we'd learned about Bill Lester and Maggie Bannister.

"That's a shocker," J.D. said. "If it's true."

"It could be true. Maybe that's why Maggie was so sure of her alibi. She sounded as if it was rock solid, and she did say the man she was with had impeccable credentials. Maybe it was Bill."

"Why would Bill get involved like that? He's married."

"Married men do stray sometimes," I said. "And Bill and Abby have had some rough spots."

"Do you think Abby found out about Bill's affair and was screwing Bannister for revenge?"

"I don't think so. Abby's got too much class for that."

"Yeah, but I thought Bill did too," J.D. said.

"If Bill was the one Maggie was with when Bannister was killed, they're each other's alibi. That might just be a little too neat."

"I was thinking the same thing. Are you going to confront Bill about this?"

"I'm going to have to think about that. He told me he was visiting his mother in a nursing home when Bannister died."

"Bill could have killed him," J.D. said. "He and Maggie could have concocted a story about Bill being with her, when Bill was really downtown putting a bullet in Bannister's brain."

"Motive?"

"Two, maybe. He found out that Abby was having an affair with Bannister and decided to take him out, or maybe he was taking care of business for Maggie."

"Taking care of business?" I asked.

"Bannister had come out to the key to threaten Maggie not too long before the murder. Remember? She said she stuck a pistol in his gut and threatened to kill him if he ever bothered her again. Maybe he came back, and Bill decided to kill him to protect Maggie."

"If that were the case, why would he try to frame Abby?"

"Frame Abby?"

"Somebody's trying to," I said. "Those fake emails are pretty strong evidence of that."

"Suppose the emails aren't fake," J.D. said. "Maybe she got carried away with the sex talk. Maybe she sent them from somewhere else. A library, for example."

"I guess that's possible. Gus' computer guy should be able to tell us about that. But I can't see Bill doing that to Abby. He might have been having an affair with Maggie, but I think he loves Abby. I just can't see him trying to set her up for murder."

"Suppose Maggie set it up."

"How do you mean?" I asked.

"She knew Bill was going to kill Bannister. She was part of the plan. She could have seen her chance to take out Abby and Bannister at the same time. Give herself a better chance of reeling Bill in. No Abby, no conflict."

"You have a devious mind, Detective."

"That's why I'm a detective."

"Then how did Abby's fingerprints get in Bannister's condo?"

"Maggie could have used some pretext to get Abby into that condo. Maybe she and Maggie went together. Part of the plan.

Maybe Maggie didn't plan on leaving her prints, but wanted to get Abby's there."

"Plausible," I said. "This is giving me a headache."

"It's probably those two Miller Lites you had. Let's go home. Maybe things will be clearer in the morning."

CHAPTER THIRTY

Lakeland was only about an hour's drive from Longboat Key, and I didn't plan to get there too early. I wanted to catch Tori Madison off guard. I had already decided not to call her for an appointment. I was just going to show up in her office. So, I took my time on that Tuesday morning, eating a leisurely breakfast of cereal and coffee with J.D., and taking a jog on the beach after she left for work.

The morning was clear and a bit cool. I ran hard on the packed sand, thinking about my case and J.D.'s. I was slowly coming to the conclusion that James Favereaux was dead. Nothing else made sense. How could a retired businessman just disappear? Why would he take off right after his wife's murder? Unless he killed her, and the time line J.D. had worked out didn't lend much credence to that theory. Maybe he'd returned home to find his wife dead and the murderer still in the house. The killer had a gun and made Favereaux get in his own car and drive off the key. The cameras at the bridges only recorded license plates. They did not take pictures of the car or its occupants.

The lab folks had not found any blood or other evidence that anybody had been killed in Favereaux's car, or that a body had been there, or that there had been a passenger. But there was no evidence at the house either. If the killer was a pro, he could have taken Favereaux without much effort and without leaving any evidence. On the other hand, why would a professional killer beat Linda to death rather than taking a quick shot with a silenced pistol?

The big question was whether there was a connection between

the two murders in New Orleans and Linda's murder in Longboat Key. And if a professional killer had murdered Linda, and not an enraged husband, why was she a target?

Lots of questions, but so far not many answers. I was just starting to turn Abby's case over in my mind, when my phone rang. I slowed to a walk and answered. Gus Grantham.

"I think you need to come up to Tampa."

"What's up?"

"Quite a bit, actually."

"You must have gotten an early start."

"I arranged to meet an old buddy of mine who's a detective with Tampa PD. Had to meet him at seven this morning and buy him breakfast."

"I'm running on the beach. Do you really need me up there?"

"I think it'd be worth your while. I want you to talk to my buddy before you go see Tori."

"Okay. I've got to go home and clean up. It'll be close to noon by the time I get there. Where do you want me to meet you?"

"Let's have lunch on Dale Mabry. There's a diner that the cops up here like. I'll bring my buddy with me. His name's Clay Adams." Gus gave me the address.

* * *

I met Gus and Clay Adams at the restaurant, and after a quick lunch, we drove a few miles to a place that appeared to be part of a slum from a third-world country. I was staggered by the devastation before me. A building fronting the narrow street that ran off North Dale Mabry Boulevard was mostly cinders. Pieces of it littered a large area surrounding the foundation, about the only part of the building still standing.

A trailer park, or what had once been one, stood behind the ruin. There were perhaps twenty trailers, all in disrepair, sides crumbling into dust, roofs dented by falling tree limbs, broken windows, some covered by plywood, rickety wooden steps leading to a single door. The trailers were small, only big enough for one bedroom and maybe a small living area. They all sat on concrete blocks, their tires rotted and wheels removed some time in the distant past. There was no grass, no trees or shrubs, just bare ground. The trailers set haphazardly about the property, no order, no roads, and no cars. Trash littered the grounds and rotting garbage was stacked by the doors of some of the trailers. Electrical transmission lines ran from nearby poles to the trailers.

A lone woman, wearing a faded housedress, walked barefoot from one trailer to another. She was not young, but probably not as old as she looked. She was let into the second trailer by another woman of indeterminate age.

There was no other sign of human activity. Early afternoon and everybody asleep? Were they in hiding because they sensed a cop in the neighborhood? Had they all died of some alien infection that had fallen from the sky that morning? They were living one rung above animals. A place of despair and broken dreams resting under the Florida sun. A slum. A ghetto of the damned. How in the world did human beings sink to this?

"What happened here?" I asked.

"The building was a nude dance joint called Buns that doubled as a drug supermarket," Detective Adams said. "We'd been trying to close it down for a long time, but there's somebody in the body politic with enough juice to override mere cops."

"Who?" I asked.

"We don't know. We know the man who was listed as the owner, but nobody's sure he actually owned the place."

"So what happened to the building?" I asked.

"We finally got code enforcement to take a look at it. They scheduled a surprise inspection for a couple of weeks ago, but somebody must have gotten word of it. The night before the inspection was scheduled, somebody blew the place up. Dynamite. A professional job."

"Looks like it pretty much destroyed the trailer park, too," Gus said.

"Didn't touch it. That place has looked like that for years."

"How many people live there?" I asked.

"It's full of residents," Adams said.

"People are living in that mess?" I asked.

"Yes."

"What's it called?"

"Palm Paradise. What a joke."

"Why doesn't some government agency do something about it?"

"Our code enforcement people don't seem to be able to get anything done. The people who live here are the forgotten ones. Drug addicts, alcoholics, prostitutes. Nobody cares. Social Services won't touch the place. Too many of their people have been run off. These folks don't trust the government."

"Why blow up the bar?" I asked.

"We haven't figured that one out yet. Maybe there was too much evidence in there about the owners and God knows what else. Probably just easier to blow the place to smithereens than try to clean up all the evidence, or burn it down and miss destroying something if the fire department got here too soon."

"I take it this is where Tori Madison worked," I said.

"This is it," Adams said. "She lived here, too."

"In one of the trailers?" I asked.

"Yep. She lived with her mom, Nina. Tori was raised in those trailers."

"Is her mom still around?"

"No. She died a couple of years back. AIDS."

"AIDS?" I asked.

"Yeah. She was a prostitute. Must have caught it from one of her johns."

"There's treatment for that now," I said.

"She didn't get any. Didn't want to."

"Did you know her?"

"Yeah," Adams said. "She was one of my snitches. I knew her for a long time. Knew Tori, too, when she was a kid."

"When's the last time you saw Tori?"

"Long time. I moved to Homicide about five years ago and lost contact with Tori and her mom."

"Do you know who Tori's dad was?"

"I didn't know him, but he was a pretty big drug importer. Lived in a big house over on the Gulf with Tori and her mom. This was all before I met them."

"How did they end up in this place?" I asked.

"The dad got busted. I wasn't involved in the case. It was before my time, but the guy had been pretty much bulletproof until the Hillsborough Sheriff's detectives were able to somehow get an undercover guy inserted into the drug organization. They got the goods on the dad and the government confiscated everything he owned. A judge sentenced him to twenty years. He didn't last a week in prison before somebody stabbed him to death in the shower."

"And Tori and her mom ended up here."

"Yep. A really big comedown."

"How old was Tori when all this happened?"

"Nine or ten, I guess."

"Kid never had a chance," I said.

Adams nodded. "I know she dropped out of school and went to work in the club when her mom got sick. She stayed with her mom. Took care of her. When Nina died, Tori disappeared."

"Was Tori a dancer?"

"No. Bartender."

"Gus tells me she had a record."

"Nothing serious. A couple possession busts and a DUI."

"But, there may be things the police never found out about."

"Probably so," Adams said. "Probably so."

"You have nothing on the owners?" I asked.

"No. I checked with Vice after Gus called me, and they have nothing either. They don't think the drug sales have stopped, but they can't find where the new operation has set up. They've been monitoring all the titty bars along the strip, but so far, nothing's turned up."

"I appreciate your help on this, Clay," I said. "Would you let me know if something does turn up?"

"I will, Matt. I've asked Vice to keep me in the loop."

* * *

"That was pretty dismal, Gus." We were sitting in my Explorer at the restaurant parking lot where we'd met earlier. Clay Adams had gone back to work.

"I thought you ought to see it firsthand. I didn't think I could adequately describe it."

"I don't think John Steinbeck could have adequately described it."

"I wonder how Tori went from that place to being Bannister's squeeze?"

"I was thinking about that, too," I said. "Could Bannister have been mixed up in the drug business that was being run out of that sleazy bar?"

"Good question. I'll see what I can find out."

"I ought to go see Tori, but I don't think today is the time."

"Sit on it for a day or two," Gus said. "Let me see if I can dig up anything on Bannister that would tie him to the drug sellers."

"Okay, Gus. Let me know if anything pops up."

CHAPTER THIRTY-ONE

At mid-afternoon J.D. was sitting at her desk plowing through paperwork when her intercom buzzed. "There's a man out here to see you," said the receptionist. "Says he's an old friend named Devlin Michel."

"Send him back," J.D. said. She left her desk and walked down the hallway to meet him.

A six-foot tall man and a pretty blond woman were coming down the hall. "You must be Agent Michel of Homeland Security," J.D. said, emphasizing the agency's name.

"I am," he said, "and this is my colleague, Agent Katrina Stevanovich. And you must be the very perceptive Detective Jennifer Diane Duncan."

She smiled. "My friends call me J.D. You can call me Detective Duncan."

"A little touchy, huh?"

"Mostly curious. Come on back to my office. Want some coffee?"

They sat in J.D.'s office, steaming cups of coffee in front of them. "May I ask why Agent Stevanovich is here?"

"She's just returned from a tour at our embassy in Croatia, and the bosses assigned her to help me while they're deciding on her next assignment. She also happens to be my fiancée."

Katrina smiled. "I think I'm here mostly to look after him. I'm actually the senior agent."

"So, what can I do for Homeland Security?" J.D. asked.

"You can show me your file on the Favereaux murder."

"That's not going to happen."

"Suppose I have my director call your boss and okay it?"

"My boss won't care what your director says," J.D. said. "It's my case, and sharing the file is left to my discretion."

"You're sure about that?" he asked.

"Yep. But you should know that I'm not above a little quid pro quo."

"How so?"

"You show me yours and I'll show you mine."

"You told me that on the phone," Michel said.

"Offer still stands."

"Okay. Let's play twenty questions. I ask a question, you give me an answer, and then you ask a question, and I'll give you an answer."

"Fair enough," J.D. said. "You go first."

"What do you know about James Favereaux?"

"Nothing much. He was a hero in Vietnam, went to college, became an entrepreneur, got rich, married a trophy wife, retired, and moved to Longboat Key."

"What if I told you that you were wrong on all counts?"

"Then I'd ask you to correct my many misimpressions."

"I'm not sure I can do that," he said.

"Why not?"

"A lot of this is highly classified. You have to have all kinds of security clearances for most of this stuff. You don't have the clearance."

"Gee," J.D. said, "we're about two questions in and we're at a stalemate. Let me ask you this. Do you think James Favereaux killed his wife?"

"I can't answer that."

"Another one then. Do you think somebody else killed her?"

Michel grinned. "I bet that sort of questioning works with the perps you deal with. Let me put it this way: I think somebody killed the lady."

"You're just a font of information, Agent Michel."

"I understand you went to New Orleans."

"I did. Ate at the Court of Two Sisters. Great food."

"And you talked to Brad Corbin."

"Yes. Real nice man."

"And Connie Pelletier was murdered right after you visited her."

"My, Agent Michel, you do get around. If you know so much, why are you here?"

"In part, because Detective Corbin said he wouldn't talk to us about this case without your permission."

"Brad's an honorable man. So, how do we solve this impasse?"

"What do you know about Nate Bannister?"

The question caught J.D. off guard, and she hesitated for a moment. "He's dead."

"You didn't see that one coming, did you?"

"Your question or the murder?"

"My question."

"No, I didn't," J.D. said. "Is the Bannister case related to the Favereauxes in some way?"

"It might be."

"Do you know who is charged with Bannister's murder?"

"Abigail Lester, your chief's wife."

"We're getting onto shaky ground, here," J.D. said. "Bill Lester's not only my boss, he's my friend. And the lawyer representing Abby Lester is also a friend of mine."

"Matt Royal."

"You've done your homework."

"Yes, and I gather Mr. Royal is more than just a friend."

J.D. grinned and said nothing.

"You find this Bannister thing intriguing, don't you?" Michel asked.

"Let me ask you a serious question. What if your director ordered you to tell Matt Royal and me everything you know about both of these cases, would you be completely honest with us?"

"My director isn't going to order me to do any such thing, but hypothetically speaking, if he did, I'd tell you everything. But I'd want your word that you'd open your file to me."

"You know Matt wouldn't be in a position to do the same."

"I'm well aware of the attorney-client privilege, Detective Duncan, and I wouldn't do anything to breach that."

"Where are you staying?"

"At the Hilton."

"Why don't Matt and I meet you at the outside bar there this evening? Say five o'clock?"

"We'll be there, but I'm not confident we're going to get any-where with all this. I'll talk to my boss. See what he thinks."

"The director?"

"No. There are a lot of pay grades between my boss and the director."

CHAPTER THIRTY-TWO

I was pulling into my driveway when J.D. called. "How would you like to have a drink with Homeland Security this evening?"

"Wow," I said. "I'd be pretty impressed, I think. What's going on?"

"Agent Devlin Michel showed up in my office a little while ago. He says he can't tell me anything about the Favereauxes, but he wants everything I know."

"I don't imagine he got very far with that."

"No, but he said if he got permission from his boss, he'd spill the beans."

"Is that going to happen?"

"He says it won't."

"Then, why are we meeting with him?"

"I was thinking that maybe we knew somebody who could shake up Michel's director and get us the information."

"Jock?" I asked.

"Jock."

"I thought you didn't like to go outside channels like that?"

"I don't, but necessity breeds necessity."

"I don't think that's the adage."

"Close enough," she said. "What do you think?"

"I'll give him a call."

"We're meeting at the Hilton at five."

"That gives me about an hour."

"I've got faith in Jock," she said.

"What about me?"

"I've got a lot of faith in Jock." The line went dead.

* * *

Jock Algren had been my best friend since junior high school. He was an agent for an intelligence agency that was so secretive it didn't even have a name. Jock did the deepest of undercover work, killed the worst of our enemies, and faced death regularly on those shadowy battlefields where so much of the world's dirty business is transacted, the places where terrorists thrive and men like Jock hunt them down and exterminate them like the roaches they are.

Jock was well known in certain government circles, because he was one of the few intelligence operatives who talked directly to the President of the United States, and because he had become legendary for his exploits around the world.

Jock was a regular visitor to the island. He had his own room in my cottage where he stashed clothes and toiletries and several weapons. J.D. and I considered him family, and we were the only family he had. He hadn't visited in almost a month, and that meant he was busy in some godforsaken part of the world. We communicated regularly by email or phone, but I missed having him around. I called him. "Hey, podna," was the way he answered.

"Jocko, I need a little help." I explained what I wanted, and he said it'd be done by the time I got to the Hilton. He also told me he was finishing up a project and would be coming to the island soon.

* * *

The outside bar at the Hilton overlooks the Gulf of Mexico and is adjacent to a patio where meals are served by the restaurant. It's my favorite spot for watching the sunset, which on clear days transforms the sea into a palette of colors. My buddy Billy Brugger was tending the bar where he had been for more than thirty years. He was nearing retirement, and I would miss my regular sunset watches with him.

We were early and took seats at the bar and chatted with Billy. When Michel and his blond colleague arrived, J.D. introduced me and we moved to a table, taking our drinks with us. "You've got some powerful mojo, Detective Duncan," he said. "I don't know who you talked to, but he or she must be pretty powerful. My director called me personally, and he doesn't talk to people at my level. He told me to give you anything and everything I had and he let me know that if I held anything back, or didn't cooperate fully, my head would be on the chopping block. He said his orders came from the very top of the government food chain."

J.D. smiled, "Please call me J.D. I think we're going to be good friends."

Michel laughed. "I hope so," he said. "I've only been with the agency for a year. I'm mostly an errand boy at this point."

"What were you doing before?" I asked.

"I was in the navy, and before that, college."

"What'd you do in the navy?"

"I was a SEAL."

"I'm impressed," I said.

"I checked you out, too, Mr. Royal. You were Army Special Forces. I always liked those green berets you guys got to wear. They're cute as hell."

I laughed. "Spoken like a true swabbie. So, what can you tell us?"

"The director said that his orders included you, Mr. Royal, but that I had to extract a promise from you that none of this would go further."

"We'll be discreet," I said. "And call me Matt."

"Katrina is fully briefed on these cases," Michel said, "and she's been with the agency longer than I have. She can fill in any blanks."

Katrina nodded. "Some of this is black ops."

J.D. and I nodded.

Devlin Michel took a deep breath. "You're actively looking for Jim Favereaux, right?"

"Yes," J.D. said. "Do you have any ideas about his whereabouts?"

"We have him."

"Homeland Security?"

"Yes. He's one of ours."

"That's going to take some explaining," J.D. said.

"He's one of our deepest cover agents. He's been with one or another intelligence agency since he got out of college, starting with the Defense Intelligence Agency."

"I thought he was an entrepreneur," J.D. said. "That's what's in our files anyway."

"Part of his legend. He's been living rich for quite a while now."

"Tell us about him."

"I guess you saw that he pulled a lieutenant out of the line of fire and saved his life in Vietnam."

"Yes," said J.D. "He got a medal for it. Was that true?"

"It was true. Did you get the lieutenant's name?"

"That wasn't in the file, or if it was, it didn't mean anything to me."

"Does the name Zebulon Etheridge ring any bells?"

We both shook our heads.

"He was the Army Chief of Staff at the time Favereaux saved that lieutenant's butt. The lieutenant was Zebulon Etheridge, Jr. He wasn't quite a year out of West Point, and his dad was very happy that Jim Favereaux saved his son's life."

"So that's how Favereaux ended up working for the government."

"In a roundabout way. Jim had grown up in New Orleans, in one of those horrible neighborhoods that kids don't usually escape from unless they hook up with criminals. Jim got out of the army and went to LSU on the GI Bill. Got a degree in business administration."

"That was in the file."

"He picked up the legend about the time he graduated. In other words, that's when we started manufacturing his life."

"Homeland Security wasn't even in existence then," I said.

"No. By the time Jim graduated, General Etheridge had retired from the army and become the civilian head of the DIA, the Defense Intelligence Agency."

"Could the government function without acronyms?" J.D. asked.

"Probably not. There was a lot of stuff going on in New Orleans that had some bearing on defense issues. Some very bad people were using the port of New Orleans to ship arms and ammunition to Central and South America. Jim managed to infiltrate one of the biggest of the gangs. He had contacts in his old neighborhood and he called on his friends and let them know he was looking for a job. Turns out a lot of the bad guys were excited to have a college grad and bona fide war hero in their crew.

"He rose quickly in the organization, and pretty soon, he'd accumulated a small fortune. When the DIA took down the bad guys, they made sure to leave Jim alone. There was some subterfuge that allowed him to escape. The DIA let him keep the money and stay in place in New Orleans. He built up quite a reputation among the darker elements over there, and he was willing to use his funds as seed money for some of the criminal enterprises. The DIA took down some very dangerous people because of Jim Favereaux."

"I'm surprised that DIA would let him keep the money," J.D. said.

"It was all aboveboard. Jim reported all the funds, and his accounts were audited closely by DIA. He needed to have the appearance of a man getting rich on criminal enterprises, and he needed money to invest in new ones."

"Nobody ever got on to him?" I asked.

"No. Well, not until a couple of weeks ago, anyway. But DIA was very cautious and loaned him out to the FBI and the

Drug Enforcement Agency, so he worked deals that wouldn't have excited the DIA, or in any way connect Jim to the DIA. The agencies kept moving him around the country. He became a criminal entrepreneur and was crucial in shutting down a lot of operations. Finally, he moved to Homeland Security because a lot of his contacts in the underworld were involved in things that touched on our responsibilities, such as drugs, guns, money laundering, and moving terrorists about the world."

"You'd be surprised at how many things we keep our eyes on because of the threats to our security from terrorism," Katrina said.

"You think somebody recently figured out who he really was?" I asked.

"We're not sure," Devlin said. "Jim had set up here to burrow into a large drug-importing business. We think the drug sales were being used to support a terrorist group working out of South America. Getting Jim involved was a slow process, but he had made a lot of progress. We were getting close."

"What happened?" J.D. asked.

"He sent a coded message about three weeks ago saying he thought he was being followed. We sent in another agent to follow the follower, but we were never able to find anybody that seemed too interested in Jim. Then early Monday morning, Jim called our duty officer and told him that Linda had been killed and he needed to come in. He'd be leaving Tampa International with a false ID and would fly to Atlanta. It was a prearranged escape route. One of our people met him in Atlanta and took him to a safe house in the North Georgia mountains."

"I'm surprised he'd run off and just leave his wife dead on the floor of his mansion," J.D. said, the sound of contempt creeping into her voice.

"She wasn't his wife," said Michel.

"What was she?" J.D. asked. "Just part of the cover? A trophy wife to enhance the image? Kind of a throwaway doll that if necessary would be sacrificed on the altar of national security?"

Michel's face suddenly looked hard, as if anger was creeping up on him and he was fighting it off. He stared at J.D. for a moment, and then, his voice tight, said, "Linda wasn't Jim's wife. She was his daughter."

CHAPTER THIRTY-THREE

"Oh my God, Devlin," J.D. said. "I'm so sorry. Sometimes my mouth overloads my brain."

"It's okay, J.D.," Michel said. "You couldn't have known, but Jim is devastated. He really loved Linda. And I mean he loved her in a fatherly way."

"Linda was his daughter?" I asked. "She was also the daughter of a woman in New Orleans named Connie Pelletier."

Now, Michel looked surprised. "How the hell did you know that?"

"Didn't you know we went to see Connie?" I asked.

"I did. But how did you make that connection?"

"After Connie was killed," J.D. said, "I asked Brad Corbin to send me the results of her DNA. We compared it with Linda's and got a hit. Connie was definitely Linda's mom. You didn't know that?"

"We've known it for years. Linda was one of our agents, too. I thought we'd covered her tracks so that her old identity was pretty much buried."

"Darlene Pelletier?" J.D. said.

"Yes. How did you get onto her?"

"We got the fingerprint hit. When we ran Linda's prints the first time, up popped a New Orleans arrest twenty years ago of a young woman named Darlene Pelletier. Then the DNA connected Darlene and Connie."

"You ran them twice?"

"Yes," J.D. said. "You caught it the second time and blocked the identification. Instead, you called me."

"Geez. I thought we'd cleaned up all of Darlene's history. Her prints are supposed to be flagged and if somebody comes looking for them, they won't show up in any database. I know the Sarasota PD and FDLE ran her prints, but we caught that, just like we caught your request. I didn't know you'd had another request. Somebody's going to catch hell about those prints."

"I can't imagine that had anything to do with Linda's death," I said. "Somebody with access to the law enforcement databases would have to have a reason to check Linda's prints against Darlene's. That's a big stretch."

"It should have been caught," Devlin said. "It's a very important part of how we protect our agents."

"Why was Linda posing as Favereaux's wife?" J.D. asked.

"Twenty years ago, when Linda was still Darlene, Jim came across some information that a contract had been put out on her from Los Angeles. When he saw the name, Darlene Pelletier, he got to thinking about a girl from his old neighborhood, Connie Rohan. He'd had a short affair with her when he first returned to New Orleans after college. He was aware that Connie had married a lowlife named Bobby Pelletier and wondered if Darlene could be Connie's daughter."

"Why would somebody in Los Angeles put a hit on Darlene?" I asked.

"Darlene was a mess. She'd been raised by her grandmother, Connie's mother, in a shack down in the delta. When Connie married Bobby, he wouldn't let the little girl stick around, so Connie's mom took her in and moved south to the area where she had grown up. The grandmother died when Darlene was fifteen, and she came back to live with Connie and Bobby. She took the name Pelletier, although she was never adopted or legally changed her name."

"No wonder we couldn't get hold of the adoption records," J.D. said. "There weren't any."

"No," Michel said. "Darlene just moved in, and Bobby started having sex with her. He was keeping her doped up and even pimped her out a few times. It got to be too much for Darlene, and she left with a creep she'd met in a bar. The creep was a drug runner from Los Angeles, and off they went to California. Six months later, the creep was murdered by his own people, and Darlene witnessed it. She knew the killers. Somehow she survived the murder and got back to New Orleans. The people who killed her boyfriend put the hit on her."

"So what was Favereaux's part in this?" J.D. asked.

"He looked up Connie and offered to provide protection for Darlene. Connie told Jim about the sexual abuse from Bobby and said that Darlene needed to get as far away as she could. Jim thought he was just doing her a favor. He asked Connie if she wanted him to take care of Bobby. Told her the incest alone would be enough to send Bobby away. That's when Connie told him that he was the father, not Bobby."

"Jim accepted that?"

"No, but he took Darlene in and had DNA tests run. The tests weren't as precise back then, but they were good enough to convince Jim that he was Darlene's father. Jim was either going to leave the agency or get some help from DIA. The agency accepted Jim's assurance that the test results were positive and decided to give Darlene a new identity and move Jim out of New Orleans. He was ready to move on, anyway. The DIA set him up in Atlanta."

"Do you think that old contract got executed?" J.D. asked. "That somebody found her and killed her this many years later?"

"No. Jim took care of the contract. He knew where it came from, and let's just say that the ones who put out the contract don't exist anymore."

"You said Linda was an agent," I said.

"Yes. Jim thought the best way to cover her trail was to marry her. He wanted her to have a rock-solid legend. DIA got her a new name, new documents, and even carried out a sham wedding. It always seemed like overkill to me, but I was in grade school when all that was going on."

"What if Jim ever decided to get married? For real. How would that have worked?" J.D. asked.

Michel looked at Katrina. "I guess the agency would have cooked up a divorce and moved Linda into other operations," she said.

"Anyway," Michel said, "it turned out that Darlene was a very smart young lady. With Jim's help, she kicked the drugs and got her life straightened out. Jim thought she had the potential to be an agent and convinced the bosses that she could be a big help to him. So they sent her through the whole training course, and she and Jim have worked together all these years."

"You said they were getting close on the drug group here. How close?"

"Jim hadn't gotten to the top yet. He had worked his way into middle management, mostly by throwing money around, paying for drugs, that sort of thing. He set up a shell company that could launder some of the drug money, and the bad guys were warming up to him. We figured he'd be another year getting to the top."

"What was Linda doing?" J.D. asked.

"She was mostly playing the trophy wife. She'd hang out with some of the wives of the people Jim was sucking up to, picking up what gossip she could."

"When we did a time line on Jim's movements the night of the murder," J.D. said, "it seemed pretty convenient that he was gone for just the time that it took for the murder to take place."

"Jim told us that he'd gone to sleep on the sofa in the living room and woke up about eleven. Said he was starving and craving a Big Mac. Linda was soaking in the hot tub when he left. Nobody else was in the house. He came back and found her dead. He grabbed a pistol and searched the house. Nobody was there."

"What if the killer was just after Linda?" I asked. "He was watching the house and waited for Jim to leave."

"We thought about that. It's entirely plausible. We just don't know who would have had any reason to kill Linda, other than somebody involved in the investigation they were working on."

"If that was the case," I said, "I'd think the killer would have waited around for Jim."

"I agree," Michel said. "So do my bosses. That's why we need to know what you know."

"Who were the drug people Jim was investigating here?" J.D. asked.

"I can give you a list, but I doubt it'll mean much to you. Unless there's somebody in your file who shows up on that list."

"What about Bannister?" I asked.

"What about him?"

"You brought it up when you asked J.D. if she knew anything about the case."

"I guess I did. Katrina probably knows more about that than I do," Michel said.

I looked at Katrina. "Well?"

"When I got back from Croatia, our boss asked me to take a look at the case Jim Favereaux was working on. He thought a new pair of eyes might find something everybody had overlooked."

"Did you find anything?"

"There was nothing in the information Jim and Linda had been sending us, but there were other agents working on other drug-smuggling cases in the Southeast. I went over those and started putting together a matrix, trying to plug all the facts into all the little squares and see if something we'd missed took shape. I wanted to know if anything the other agents were finding had any bearing of Jim's case. If so, I'd alert Jim and he could go from there."

"Did anything pop up?"

"Nothing earth shattering, but I did see one thing that only began to make sense after Bannister was killed."

"What?" I asked.

"We have an operation being run out of Miami, trying to get to the top of a ring of drug importers. We think they have ties to other groups throughout the Southeast. One of the names that came up was Nate Bannister. That, in and of itself, didn't mean anything, because I'd never heard of the man. As I kept looking, the same name popped up in an investigation going on in Atlanta. I thought he might be some kind of conduit between the Miami people and the ones in Atlanta. We ran the name through our databases and came up with three or four people with the same name, but only one was in the Southeast. The one in Sarasota."

"Did you send that information to Favereaux?" I asked.

Katrina shook her head. "I found it on Monday, the same day Jim called the agency duty officer from the Tampa airport. Then, I find out that Bannister was killed the same night that Linda was murdered. I began to wonder if the murders could be connected."

"Was Bannister mentioned in any of Favereaux's reports?" I asked.

"No."

"Did you think that strange?"

"Maybe. Jim had made some headway with the drug people in this area, but he hadn't gotten too far up the ladder. He was salting the trail with lots of money, and was beginning to make real progress. If Bannister was involved with the local drug dealers, I would think Jim might have found that out. Then again, maybe Bannister was so far up the chain of command that Jim hadn't run across him yet."

"Or," I said, "maybe our dead Bannister wasn't the same one who was involved with the drugs."

"There's that," Katrina said, "but if he's involved, I think it's on the money-laundering side. I'd think Jim's money would have drawn Bannister out."

"If he was involved in the drug business," I said, "there'd be a lot of reasons for him to be killed that didn't involve my client or a lover's spat."

"You're right, Matt," Katrina said. "Maybe we can work together and find out what Bannister was up to."

"Why would you care?" I asked. "Now that he's dead."

"Two reasons. We want to shut down this operation, and if we find his killers, maybe we can get them to trade information for a lighter prison sentence."

"And the second reason?" I asked.

"I think whoever killed Bannister may have also killed Linda Favereaux. And there's no walking away when you kill one of our agents."

We talked for another hour. J.D. gave him a copy of her file and answered all his questions. They compared the names on Michel's list with the names J.D. had turned up. There was no connection that we could see.

I went over the details of the Bannister murder, as I understood them this early in the case. I told Katrina and Devlin about what seemed to be a professional hit on Bannister, and the unprofessional manner in which Linda Favereaux was killed. I also told her about my suspicions that Abby Lester was the target of a frame-up, and unless Abby was involved in the drug business, I could see no reason why anybody would want to involve her.

Finally, we called it quits. It had been an informative evening, and a pleasant one as we sat with good company under a great Banyan tree, the rays of a full moon shining through its branches, and the whisper of the anemic surf gently assaulting the nearby beach.

We were walking toward the parking area that adjoined the patio. "One more thing," J.D. said. "I need to talk to Mr. Favereaux."

There was a moment of silence, and then Devlin said, "I'm afraid that's not possible."

"We're supposed to have full cooperation here," J.D. said.

"We've given you everything we have."

"Except Favereaux," J.D. said.

"And we'd give him to you if we could."

"What do you mean?"

"He's in the wind."

"Gone?"

"Yes."

"And you don't know where he is?"

"No. He met our agent at the Atlanta airport and was taken

to the safe house up near Blue Ridge, Georgia. When the Atlanta agent showed up the next day, Favereaux was gone."

J.D.'s voice was tinged with sarcasm. "Didn't that seem a little strange?"

"Of course. We're looking for him. A big manhunt, actually, but the security is real tight on the whole thing."

"Any sign of struggle at the safe house?"

"No. It looks like he just walked away."

"I know Blue Ridge," I said. "It's kind of isolated. How would he have gotten out?"

"We don't know."

"Any cell phone activity?" J.D. asked.

"He left his phone in the safe house."

J.D. was angry. "Don't you think it would have been important for me to know about this? You said your agency had him."

Katrina said, "I'm sorry, J.D., but the word came down from on high in our agency that we were not to volunteer that information unless you brought it up. You brought it up and we told you. We did have him, but we lost him."

"Do you think he killed Linda?" J.D. asked.

"No."

"Then why would he run?"

"We don't know. The safe house may have been compromised, and he decided he had to leave," Katrina said.

"Then why no contact with your agency?" J.D. asked.

"He might be concerned that there's a mole in our agency, and if he contacts us, the bad guys will find him."

"Or," I said, "he might be a rogue who killed his own daughter rather than be found out."

Katrina shook her head. "That's the one that keeps me awake at night."

CHAPTER THIRTY-FOUR

"Is Favereaux the killer?" J.D. asked. We were sitting on my patio overlooking the bay. It was nearing ten, and the moon was high and full, its soft light adding a mellow glow to the mangrove islands that poked out of the water.

"Maybe, but I can't see a man who has gone to such lengths to protect his daughter all these years killing her. It doesn't fit."

"Maybe somebody else killed Linda and Jim knows who it was. He may be after the killer."

"He wouldn't have to do that alone," I said. "His agency would have given him all the help he needed, and would have sanctioned his killing Linda's murderer. Those agencies take care of their own."

"I think he's the key to solving my case. Either he killed Linda or he knows who did. If I can't find him, this case is going to end up in the cold case files."

"Based on what Katrina told us, Favereaux may have some bearing on Abby's case as well. If Bannister was part of the drug business, that might explain his murder."

"For whatever reason, Favereaux is running from his agency. If they can't find him, we don't stand a chance."

"We've got another big problem. What do we do about Bill Lester?"

"I noticed that you left out the stuff about the chief while we were talking to Devlin and Katrina."

"Yeah. I don't know how Bill fits into all this, or if he does, and I don't want a bunch of government snoops looking into it. Not yet, anyway. I guess we could run Bill's tag number through the bridge camera system, but I don't really think that's a good idea."

"I thought about that," J.D. said, "and decided it's a very bad idea. Bill goes through the reports from that system every morning. He'll know somebody was looking for his car. And even if he missed it somehow, I can only get that stuff through Sharkey. He and the chief are tight as ticks, and I don't think Sharkey would do it."

"Would you, if you were in Sharkey's shoes?"

"Not in a million years."

"There you have it then," I said. "Scratch that idea."

"We may be making a mountain out of an ant pile," J.D. said. "All we know, or even have some reason to believe, is that Bill was having an affair with Maggie Bannister. I don't even want to think that's true, but even if it is, that's a long way from putting a bullet in Bannister's brain."

"It would give him motive," I said, "and he would certainly have the means, a pistol. And if Maggie and Bill were each other's alibi, it would give either one of them opportunity."

"Maggie had the means because Bill gave her a pistol and she sure had motive. So why don't we think of her as the killer, rather than Bill?"

"Good point," I said, "but even if Bill—if he was the boy-friend—wasn't the shooter, if he gives Maggie an alibi, and she was the murderer, then he's at least guilty of aiding and abetting."

J.D. slapped at a mosquito that had landed on her arm. "This isn't getting us anywhere, and I'm getting eaten alive. Let's go in."

* * *

The phone rang just as I drifted into sleep. It was almost midnight. Bad news coming, I thought. I picked up the phone.

"Matt, it's Gus. Sorry about the late hour."

"What's up?"

"Somebody tried to kill Robert Shorter a couple of hours ago."

"The witness?"

"Yeah. You awake yet?"

"Just about. What happened?"

"My contact at Sarasota PD just called. Said somebody took a shot at Shorter as he came out of a bar on Siesta Key."

"Was he hit?"

"Yes," Gus said. "Not bad. He took a round through his left upper arm. Didn't hit anything important. The paramedics took him to the emergency room at Sarasota Memorial."

"Has anybody taken a statement from him?"

"A detective talked to him, but he said he didn't know why anyone would try to kill him."

"Was there a fight in the bar, anything like that?"

"Not according to my source. The bar is pretty upscale, so they don't get a lot of that sort of thing."

"Was Shorter drunk?"

"No. He came in late, had a couple of beers, and told the bartender he was going home. Nothing out of the ordinary. Shorter often stops by late in the evening."

"Do you know if they're going to keep him in the hospital?" I asked.

"Overnight. They'll probably cut him loose tomorrow."

"Okay. I'll try to see him first thing. You want to come with me?"

"Yeah. I'll call Harry Robson early, see if he can get us in."

"Thanks, Gus. Call me if Harry says no. Otherwise, I'll meet you at the hospital at ten." I hung up.

J.D. was awake. "Gus?"

"Yeah. Somebody took a potshot at Robert Shorter tonight."

"You think it's connected to Abby's case?"

"Probably not. Given Shorter's personality, I wouldn't be surprised if a lot of people wanted to shoot him. Maybe I'll know more after I talk to him in the morning."

CHAPTER THIRTY-FIVE

I was up before six on Wednesday morning, sitting on my patio with a cup of coffee and a granola bar. Some breakfast. A slight wind blew from the south, rippling the surface of the bay with small whitecaps. In the distance, the dark mass of the mainland was crowned with the glow of the rising sun, still hidden below the horizon, giving the illusion that the world was on fire.

I had awoken with thoughts of Robert Shorter. People like him stumble through life in a fog of anxiety, their anger lurking just below the surface, ready to rise up at the least perceived slight. They make enemies at every turn, but most of those contacts are fleeting; the guy in line at the grocery store, or the lady he cut off at a traffic light. Not the kind of people who would try to kill him.

Could the shooting of the night before be connected to Abby's case? Possibly. I had begun to think more about why Bannister's assistant would be so insistent on Shorter meeting with Bannister on the very evening that he was murdered. Could that have been an attempt at a set-up? A way to tie Shorter to the murder?

But if Shorter was supposed to be framed for the murder, where did Abby come in? Once Shorter called on Sunday to cancel the meeting set for that evening, the killer would only have had a few hours to set up Abby. And the emails supposedly sent by Abby had come days earlier. Maybe she was the fall back position, plan B, in case something didn't work out to make Shorter appear to be the killer.

And, as J.D. had pointed out, Maggie Bannister had more reason than anybody to want her husband dead. Then, like an errant lightning strike, the thought hit me. What about inheritance? How much money would Maggie inherit upon her husband's death? They were headed for a divorce and the court would set the division of property. Maggie would certainly not get as much from a divorce decree as she would if Bannister died. Even if Bannister had tried to leave his estate to someone other than his wife, the law would require that Maggie be given a substantial portion of his assets, regardless of the language of the will. I should have thought of that before now. I'd have to check it out.

* * *

I met Gus at Sarasota Memorial Hospital shortly after ten that morning. The investigation of the shooting the night before had come up empty, and the detectives had decided it was just a random event, a shooting with no motive, or a case of mistaken identity. A man wearing a ski mask shot Shorter at close range in the parking lot. The bullet went straight through his arm and couldn't be found.

There was no security guard at Shorter's hospital room, an indication that the investigating officers did not expect anybody to take another shot at him. "You looking for a client?" Shorter asked as I walked into the room. "Damn ambulance chasers."

"I'm worried about you, Mr. Shorter."

"Right. Call me Rob."

I introduced him to Gus and said, "Who shot you?"

"Not a clue."

"Do you think it was just a random shot?"

"Don't know."

"Can you think of anyone who would want to kill you?"

"Sure, but not one of them would have the guts to try it. What's it to you, anyway?"

"I'm wondering if it's connected to my case," I said.

"I don't see how it would be."

"Did it ever occur to you that somebody may have been trying to set you up for the murder of Nate Bannister?"

"Nah. I don't see that."

"Think about it," I said. "Bannister's assistant, Tori, seemed hell-bent on getting you to Bannister's condo so that you'd be there at the exact time that he ended up dead."

Shorter seemed a bit shocked by that thought. "You think so?"

"It fits. You were on record with a couple of assault charges, and one of them was against Bannister. If you'd been at the condo on Sunday evening, it wouldn't have been too hard to set up a scenario where you shot Bannister and then ended up dead yourself. They'd have found two bodies instead of one. Murder-suicide. Case closed."

"Even if that were the case, what would it have to do with somebody taking a shot at me last night?"

"Maybe they were tying up loose ends. Getting rid of the possibility that you might figure out that you were supposed to be the patsy."

"That means they might come back after me."

"Yes. Do you have someplace to go when you get out of here? Someplace other than your condo?"

"I've got an aunt who lives in Nokomis," Shorter said. "I could stay down there for a while, I guess."

"Might not be a bad idea."

* * *

Gus and I drove east on Highway 60. We were on our way to see Tori Madison. The development that Bannister had been working on was a large condo complex situated on rolling ground sloping down to a lake a few miles south of downtown Lakeland. There were six buildings in various stages of completion, clustered around an open space in which sat two mobile homes that served as the construction offices. We went into the largest trailer and entered a reception area. An attractive middle-aged woman sat behind a desk that bore a nameplate identifying her as Shirlene Girardin. "May I help you?" she asked.

"I hope so. I'm Matt Royal and this is Gus Grantham. I'm a lawyer, and I've been engaged to look into matters surrounding the death of Nate Bannister. We'd like to speak with Ms. Madison, if she's available."

Ms. Girardin picked up her phone and spoke quietly into it. She stood, smiled, and showed us into the inner office.

Tori Madison was in her mid-twenties, but her eyes said she'd lived for a hundred years. They were dark and wary, suspicious, unfriendly, and hard as diamonds. She had blond hair tied in a French twist, her face set off by startling thick black eyebrows. She was medium height and had a lush figure. She was wearing clothes that emphasized her body, and her voice, when she greeted us, was throaty and cultivated. She did not look like the little girl who'd grown up in that dismal trailer park in Tampa.

"I'm in a bit of a time crunch," Tori said brusquely. "I wish you'd made an appointment. How can I help you?"

"I'm representing the woman accused of killing Mr. Bannister. This is my investigator, Gus Grantham."

Those eyes hardened into a stare that reminded me of an army sniper I'd once watched as he lined up his human target, a very bad man who'd been responsible for the death of many innocents. Hers were as focused and deadly as that soldier's, and I had no doubt that Tori was contemplating some horrible end to our meeting. "You said you were looking into Nate's death. You lied."

"I didn't lie," I said. "I am looking into the facts surrounding his death because I want to find out why someone is framing my client for his murder."

"Your client?"

"Yes. Abby Lester."

"I don't have any idea who would do such a thing," Tori said. "Besides, I'm pretty sure your client killed my boss. No need for anybody to try to frame her."

"I'm thinking you probably know some bad people who might have had a reason to kill your boss."

A look of consternation crossed her face. She held it just a bit too long. "I am a respectable businesswoman. Where in the world do you think I'd meet such creatures?"

"The Palm Paradise trailer park, maybe," I said, "or a bar called Buns."

Tori's face closed down. It was immediate, from a look of shock straight to blankness. She stared straight ahead. There was no movement in her features, not even a twitch. It was as if she'd turned to stone. Then she took a deep breath and her lips parted, closed again, and parted. She reminded me of a stroke victim who was trying to talk, but couldn't. Then, suddenly, her body relaxed and she smiled. She'd made the decision not to tough it out. "You got me. What do you want?"

"I want to know who killed Bannister," I said.

"Your client."

"Do you know Abby Lester?"

"I've met her, but I can't say I really know her."

"Do you have any reason to believe she was having an affair with Bannister?"

"Yes."

"What makes you believe that?"

"I know she spent a lot of time in Nate's condo, and he told me they were lovers."

"When did he tell you that?"

"A couple of weeks before he died."

"How do you know she spent a lot of time at his condo?"

"I saw her there several times."

"What time of day?"

"Usually mid-morning."

"Did you ever see her there in the evening?"

"No."

"Did you ever see Abby at Mr. Bannister's on the weekend?"

"I don't think so. She was probably home with her husband."

"Other than what Nate told you, do you have any reason to believe they were lovers?"

"One time when I came over, I heard the shower running, and Nate told me that Abby was in the bathroom. Another time I got a glimpse of her through the bedroom door."

"Are you sure the woman you saw was Abby Lester?"

"Positive."

"Are you aware of some emails that were supposedly sent by Abby to Bannister in the days before he died?"

"Yes."

"What do you know about them?"

"Nate showed them to me."

"Did he tell you they came from Abby?"

"He didn't have to. They were signed by her."

"What was Mr. Bannister's reaction to the emails?"

"The last one threatened to kill him. That rattled him. He said her husband was a cop and he figured she had access to guns. He thought she was crazy."

"Did you have plans to meet with Bannister on the night he died?"

"No. He told me that the Lester woman was coming over that evening. He wanted to cut her loose. Dump her."

This wasn't going well. "Do you know Rob Shorter?" I asked.

"No."

"Does the name mean anything to you?"

"No. Sorry. Never heard of him."

"He is the guy who tried to beat up Bannister a couple of years back. He went to jail for the attack."

"I never heard Nate speak of anybody named Shorter and I don't know anything about somebody trying to beat him up."

"Do you have any financial interest in this project?"

"That's none of your business." Her voice was cold, flat, angry sounding.

"I can find out."

"Then go for it."

"Do you know who owns the project now that Bannister's dead?"

"BLP, Inc. The same company that owned it from the start."

"I take it BLP is Bannister's company."

"Yes. BLP stands for 'Bannister's Lakeland Project.'"

"Was he the only shareholder?" I asked.

"I don't know."

"Do you have the corporate books here?"

"Do you have a subpoena?"

"No, but I can get one."

"Let me know when you do."

"Anything, Gus?" I asked.

He nodded. "Do you have a boyfriend?"

A flash of anger, now. "That's none of your goddamned business," Tori said, her voice rising.

"What's his name?" Gus asked.

"Go to hell. Leave now."

"It's a simple question, Tori," Gus said.

"Get the fuck out of here, or I'll call security to drag your ass all the way back to where you came from." The veneer was gone, and the girl from the Palm Paradise trailer park emerged, angry, profane, and, I thought, a little frightened.

"So," I said. "The Buns bartender still lives in there somewhere. Have a nice day, Tori. I'll see you soon. If the cops don't show up first."

* * *

Gus and I were in my Explorer heading west toward home. My phone rang and the caller ID was blocked. I answered. "Matt Royal."

"Mr. Royal, this is George Swann."

"Call me Matt."

"Mr. Royal," he said, his voice sounding like a sneer might. "I have called to inform you that a Sarasota County grand jury has handed down a first-degree murder indictment on Abigail Lester. We'll be going for the death penalty."

I can't say that I was surprised, but I had hoped Swann might have had better sense. He would have a hard time convicting Abby of second-degree murder, much less first, and the jury would not be excited about the state reaching for the death penalty. "George, I suspect the reason you've gone for the indictment and are putting the death sentence on the table, is that you think it will give you some negotiating leverage on a plea."

"The grand jury indicted her, not me."

I laughed. "I might have fallen off a turnip truck, but it wasn't last night. Give me a grand jury and I can indict you for having sex with a coconut before noon. All that indictment means is that you decided to roll the dice."

"We'll see."

"Okay, George, but write this down. Block letters, so you can read it and remember it. 'There ain't going to be a deal.' We're going to trial."

"As you wish. FDLE will be arresting your client on the new charge within the hour."

"Look, George, why don't you just let me bring her in tomorrow, and we can have an immediate arraignment and get the bail continued."

"No can do. She's going to jail. No bail on this one. You want to rethink a plea?"

"Are you in Sarasota, George?

"Yes."

"Don't leave. I'll see you in a couple of hours."

"I'm not—"

I didn't let him finish. I hung up.

The call had come through the hands-free system in the car, so Gus had heard the conversation. "Prick," he said.

"Yep."

"Is the indictment going to make a difference in the case?"

"Some. Mostly procedurally. Unless the state has some infor-

mation I don't know about. That's the thing that keeps trial lawyers up at night. What do they know that I don't?"

I called Abby and told her to get ready to be arrested again.
I told her I would be at the jail by the time they brought her in.
Then I made a couple more calls and turned onto I-75 toward
Sarasota.

CHAPTER THIRTY-SIX

The previous night's revelations about James and Linda Favereaux were rolling around in J.D.'s head as she sat at her desk sipping her first cup of coffee of the morning. There was a missing piece in the narrative she'd gotten from the Homeland Security agents. An operative as experienced as Jim Favereaux would have at least some suspicion of who killed his partner. These things just didn't happen in a vacuum. Yet, according to Devlin and Katrina, neither Jim nor the agency had any leads or even suspicions as to why she was killed.

She was sworn to secrecy about the things she'd heard the night before. But that didn't mean she couldn't use some of the information as part of her investigation, as long as she was careful not to divulge anything she'd been told. She called Detective Brad Corbin in New Orleans.

"Brad, does the name James Favereaux mean anything to you?"

"The guy whose wife was killed on Longboat Key?"

"Yes, but I was thinking more in line with a man in New Orleans twenty years or so ago."

"That was before my time, but I can ask around. You think he was in New Orleans back then?"

"I've heard he was. I'd just like to know if he ever came to the attention of law enforcement."

"I'll get back to you," Corbin said, and hung up.

She sat and sipped her coffee and thought some more. If Bannister was somehow involved in something that connected him to the Favereauxes, the case took on a different complexion.

If Bill Lester was implicated in Bannister's murder, would that mean that he was somehow involved in the killing of Linda Favereaux? She couldn't see a way to make that connection. Yes, Lester might have had a reason to kill Bannister, either because his wife Abby was having an affair with him or because he himself was having an affair with Bannister's wife and he wanted to make sure that Bannister didn't give Maggie any more trouble. But what possibly could be the connection between Lester and the Favereauxs? Where was the motive? She didn't see one.

She walked down the hall to the deputy chief's office. He was wearing his uniform today, a single gold star tacked to his shirt collars. "Going somewhere important?" J.D. asked.

Sharkey grinned. "A little road patrol. Get the juices flowing. If I didn't get out from behind the desk occasionally, I'd go nuts. Anything new on your murder case?"

"Possibly. I met with the Homeland Security agents last night, and they told me a lot of interesting stuff, but I had to take an oath of secrecy to get them to open up."

"I'm surprised they'd do that."

"I had a little help."

"What?"

"Jock Algren."

Sharkey laughed. "Ole Jock. He talked to the president?"

J.D. grinned. "Who knows? Whoever he talked to built a fire under the Homeland Security director. I wonder if the agents I'm dealing with could get some information from our camera surveillance system without anybody here or anywhere else knowing they were in the system."

"What's going on?"

"I don't know, Martin. They just asked me about getting that done." J.D. didn't like lying to a good friend, but she wanted to protect another friend, the chief.

"I would think they or the National Security Agency or somebody in the government would be able to hack into that system without us knowing a thing about it."

"For some reason, they don't want to do that."

"I don't know what to tell you, J.D. Nobody here can use the system without a password, and we will know immediately when somebody with a password accesses the data."

"Who all gets that information on a regular basis?"

"If there's a hit, that is if a license plate pops up that we need to act on, or if anyone attempts to run a specific plate, the chief and I are both notified in the reports that hit our desks first thing in the morning."

"No way around it?"

"Not that I know of," Sharkey said.

* * *

An hour later, Detective Corbin called back. "I talked to the detective who partnered with me when I was new to this job. He was working the gang units twenty years ago. He knew a guy named Favereaux who was quite the player, but he could never pin anything on him. He seemed to be some sort of money man for some bad guys who ran the rackets on the docks."

"Did your friend know what happened to him?"

"He just disappeared, dropped totally out of sight. There were rumors that he pulled up stakes and moved on to St. Louis or Atlanta or someplace. He was out of our hair, so there wasn't any follow-up."

"Was there anything about him getting married before he left New Orleans?"

"Nothing."

"How about him having a daughter?"

"Nope."

"Was there any connection to The White American Party or Connie Pelletier?"

"No. What are you looking at, J.D.?"

"Just scratching around. Running down rumors. The usual crap."

"Tell me about it. Sorry I couldn't be of more help."

"Not a problem, Brad. Thanks for checking it out."

J.D. sat, drinking a cup of fresh coffee. The remains of her lunch, take-out from Harry's Deli, lay spread out on her desk. She sipped her brew and thought some more. She wasn't going to be able to use the bridge cameras to check out Lester's coming and going from the island on the evening that Bannister was killed without both Lester and Sharkey becoming aware of it. Her queries in New Orleans had turned up nothing. Her case was getting colder by the hour and her frustration level was rising to new heights.

She closed her office door to shut out the quiet din that permeated any office at work. She rested her head on the back of her chair, trying to close out the world. She was tired, and her eyelids drooped, her respiration slowed, her heart beat rhythmically, and vignettes of happy times flashed through her consciousness. Suddenly she was wide awake, completely aware of her surroundings, an idea percolating through her prefrontal lobes, dragging shards of facts from her memory banks.

Sometimes, when you let your brain range free over a problem, allowing it to swoop in and out, examining little bytes of data that you have consciously or unconsciously stored away, when you relax and sip coffee and contemplate the margins of the conundrum, insight strikes like lightning out of a clear sky, unexpected and shocking. A solution begins to take shape. Maybe not the perfect solution, or even the correct solution, but a possible solution at least. And so it was with J.D. that day in her Longboat Key police station office.

She called Bert Hawkins, the Twelfth Circuit medical examiner.

CHAPTER THIRTY-SEVEN

The video conference room at the jail was crowded. Reporters from all the local outlets had settled in, waiting for something juicy to happen. None of them had been kind to Abby. The stories were always a bit salacious, slanted awkwardly against a fine woman. Who knew why journalists sometimes decided to take sides in a case before all the facts became known? When a prominent man was murdered and a policeman's wife charged with the crime, it was too much to pass up. The story was headline material, and the titillating hint of sex got everybody's attention. The scandal would quickly lose its allure if it turned out that Abby was neither the murderer nor the lover of the dead man, or that Bannister's murder was nothing more than a random event.

I'd called the judge's assistant when I hung up with Swann. I told her what had happened, and asked if the judge would hear a bond motion this afternoon. He agreed and called Swann to tell him to be at the courthouse ready to argue the motion.

I'd also called Robin Hartill at the *Longboat Observer*. I could count on her to write the story straight, and I would give her an exclusive interview as soon as the hearing was over. I also owed her boss.

I'd dropped Gus at the hospital where his car was parked and then drove the short distance to the county jail. As I was setting up at counsel table, Swann swaggered into the room. "I was catching a plane to Jacksonville," he said. "Now I've got to stay overnight."

"Sorry, George, my guest room is booked for tonight."

"You want to play games like this?"

"The game began when you indicted my client for first-degree murder and sent your hounds out to arrest her. We could have had a conversation with the judge and skipped a hearing. Just let her keep the bond she's on."

"I'm following the law."

"You're gaming it, George. Or trying to. Are you familiar with the Manatee High School football team?"

"No."

"Well, they're a damn good team, year in and year out. They win state championships. They play in the top class in the state. They're coached by one of the best high school coaches in the country."

"What's your point?"

"In this game, the one you and I are playing, you're the Manatee High School football team. You're good as long as you're playing in your class. But, I'm the Tampa Bay Bucs, and you're playing way above your level of competence. You don't stand a chance."

"Hah," he said. "We'll see."

Sometimes a poke in the eye is good for arrogance. It makes you stop and think, and it makes you mad. The anger is what survives, and anger brings about mistakes. The game that Swann was playing was a head game. I wonder if he understood that.

The TVs cranked up and Judge Thomas was on the big screen in the middle. "Good afternoon, gentlemen."

"Good afternoon, Your Honor," Swann and I said in unison.

"I understand that a grand jury has indicted Mrs. Lester for first-degree murder. I have a copy of the indictment. You want to continue the bond as set, am I correct, Mr. Royal?"

"Yes, sir."

"Any objections, Mr. Swann?"

"Yes, sir. This is now a first-degree murder case. We'll be going for the death penalty. That gives her good reason to flee the jurisdiction."

"Have Mrs. Lester's circumstances changed since the last hearing?"

"No, sir," I said.

"Other than the indictment, I'm not aware of any change, Your Honor," Swann said, "but this is now a first-degree murder case."

The judge rustled some papers on his desk, looked down at them, and said, "I see no reason to change the requirements of the bond. Mr. Royal, will the bonding agent agree to continue the bond in light of the indictment?"

"He will, Your Honor, and I have him in the hallway if you want to question him."

"Your representation is good enough for me, Mr. Royal. The bond will hold over. Anything else?"

"Your Honor," Swann said, "the complexion of this case has changed. It's now a first-degree case."

"Mr. Swann," Judge Thomas said, "I've ruled."

"Yes, sir, but I think you might want to rethink the ruling."

"Mr. Swann," the judge said, his voice tight and low, "when I rule, the argument is over. Don't continue arguing. You've had your say."

"But, Judge, I'm not sure you understand—"

The judge cut him off. "Mr. Swann, do you want to spend the night as a guest of the county jailer?"

"No, sir."

"Then sit down and be quiet."

Swann sat.

"If there's nothing else, court is adjourned," the judge said. His TV screen went dark.

I left the courtroom immediately, not stopping to speak to Swann. I saw Agent Lucas sitting in the back of the room, frowning. I nodded at him. He took no notice. There was a howling pack of reporters in the hallway, all shouting questions at me, the cameramen from the local TV stations jockeying for position to get a shot of me walking. "No comment," was my only answer. I did swagger a bit for the benefit of the cameramen.

Robin was waiting for me by my car. We got in and cranked

up the air conditioning. "Robin," I said, "I don't really have anything for you. I was a little surprised at the judge's quick decision,
but I don't know any more now than the last time we talked."

"Will you ask Abby to give me an interview?"

"Sorry, Robin. I can't allow that. I have to control all the testimony, and if she told you something that might hurt her case, it
might be admissible in court. I can't take that chance. But I promise you'll have first crack at her as soon as this case is over."

"Okay, but keep me in mind if anything comes up."

"You got it. I need to go check on Abby. She should be ready
to go home. Bill's waiting for her at the jail."

CHAPTER THIRTY-EIGHT

The town of Longboat Key encompasses the entire island, but it is divided at mid-key by the Sarasota-Manatee county line. Sarasota County is the southern end and Manatee County takes up the northern end. The Bannisters lived on the northern end of the key, in Manatee County, so probate would be filed in Manatee County.

I took the long way home, through downtown Bradenton. I stopped by the Manatee County Courthouse and went to the clerk of courts' office. Maggie Bannister had lost no time in filing for probate. The will was in the file. It was a simple document that left all Nate's personal and real property to Maggie. There was no list of assets attached to the will, but Maggie's lawyer probably had such a list and would go through the motions of entering into probate everything required by the code, filing the estate tax returns, paying off creditors, and taking care of all the minutia that attends the death of a wealthy man.

I stopped by the property appraiser's office and checked the index to see if Bannister owned real property in Manatee County. He and Maggie owned the house in which Maggie lived and both of them were on the deed to a Gulf-front lot that would be worth a lot of money. There was a right-of-survivorship clause in both deeds, so Maggie would inherit the properties. Neither was mortgaged.

Nate probably owned other properties in other counties. Gus said he could use a computer service to turn those up. I'd have to talk to Maggie to find out anything else. If she was willing to talk to me.

I called Maggie as I drove out to the island, arriving at her house in the late afternoon. She offered me a drink. I declined. She was sipping something clear from a large tumbler. A wedge of lime was stuck on the rim. Gin, I thought. "I appreciate your seeing me," I said.

"I'm glad to help, Matt. You mentioned you wanted some information on Nate's estate."

"I'm just pulling at loose strings, Maggie, but I'm wondering if somebody might have had a reason to kill Nate for money."

"Like me?" she asked.

"No. I stopped by the courthouse and looked at the will. You get everything, but I can't see you killing him over that. You'd have gotten enough out of the divorce to take care of you forever."

"If I'd killed him, it wouldn't have been for the money. I'd have killed the bastard for being the bastard he was."

I smiled. "What about the project in Lakeland? Do you get that?"

"No. Everything was set up in a corporation called BLP, Inc. I assumed he owned all the stock. When he died, I assumed I would get control."

"You didn't?"

"No. When my lawyer started digging into the assets, he found that Nate didn't even own one share of the stock. He was just an employee of the company."

"Were you able to find out who does own the stock?"

"My lawyer's trying to unravel that now, but he says he may never be able to figure it all out. Apparently the stock is owned by some guy I never heard of, but none of that makes sense. Nate set up the corporation, and I'm pretty sure he owned the property individually. It wasn't part of BLP."

"If BLP is operating in Florida, there must be a resident agent for service of process. That would be a matter of public record at the secretary of state's office."

"Yeah. It's some lawyer in Tampa. He won't tell my lawyer anything. Client confidentiality and all that crap."

"Did Nate leave any papers here? Anything that might give us some background on the Lakeland project?"

"No. But Nate did have a safe deposit box at the SunTrust Bank downtown. My lawyer has the key and the court order allowing him to open the box."

"Would you mind if I looked through the documents in that box?"

"Not at all. I'll call my lawyer and tell him to go ahead and get the stuff out of the box and let you see it all."

"Who's your lawyer?"

"Bob Crites. You know him?"

"I do. He's good. Do you think we could get this done so that I can go over the documents tomorrow?"

"I don't see why not. I'll call Bob this afternoon."

* * *

I was tired. My day had started early and I wanted to get out of my suit and tie and into my island clothes; shorts, t-shirt and boat shoes. I called J.D., and she suggested we have a drink at the Haye Loft. I decided I'd have to wait to change.

I left my jacket and tie in the Explorer and climbed the steps to one of the nicest bars on the Suncoast. The downstairs part of the building houses a world-class restaurant named Euphemia Haye, and the Haye Loft Bar on the second floor was a favorite of both locals and snowbirds. It was virtually empty at five-thirty in the afternoon. As my eyes adjusted to the low light of the bar, I recognized Jon and Donna Boscia sitting at a table in the corner of the room. Jon waved me over.

"I just left a message on your home answering machine," he said. "I wanted to talk to you. Join us."

I kissed Donna on the cheek, shook Jon's hand, and sat down. Eric Bell came from behind the bar with a cold Miller Lite and a frosted glass. "Where's J.D.?" he asked.

"On her way."

"Good. She's the part of you I like best."

"Yeah. Everybody says that."

Eric laughed and went back to the bar. I turned to Jon. "I haven't seen you guys around for a while. Have you been away?"

"We were in Europe for a couple of weeks. Just got back this afternoon. I was going over the back issues of the *Observer* and read about the chief's wife being arrested for Nate Bannister's murder. The article said you were representing her."

"That's right. Do you know Abby?"

"Not really. I've met her once or twice, but I can't say I know her. I knew Bannister, though. He was a bad guy."

"How well did you know him?"

"Not well, but he came to me about investing in a project he was trying to put together. I looked at the deal and turned him down. He came back later, with another investor, but said he was still short and wanted me to take another look at it."

"Was the deal any better?"

"I never got that far. You know that before I retired I was in the financial services industry. I called an old friend of mine who has a company that does background checks on people involved in the financial world. I asked him to check out the other investor, a man named Mark Erickson. Turns out, Erickson made his money running a nudie bar up in Tampa called Buns. My investigator friend said that a lot of drugs came through Buns, but nobody ever pinned anything on Erickson. That was enough for me to decline to get involved."

"Are you sure the bar was called Buns?" I asked.

"Oh, yeah. I drove up there to check it out. Ugly-looking place with an abandoned trailer park behind it."

"I know the place," I said. "The trailer park isn't abandoned. People actually live there. Do you think Bannister was involved in drugs?"

"I don't know, but he was close enough to the action that I didn't want anything to do with him."

"Does this Erickson have any other job? Anything that would produce enough income for him to invest in one of Bannister's projects?"

"Not that I could find."

"How much was he planning to invest?"

"Twenty-five million dollars."

"Wow," I said. "That's a lot of dough."

"You said it."

J.D. came in the door, waved at Eric, and joined us. Eric brought over a glass of some kind of white wine, and said, "You and Donna sure do add a lot of class to this table." He kissed her on the cheek and went back to the bar.

"I heard you guys have been in Europe," J.D. said. "Have fun?"

"It was a nice trip," Donna said, "but a bit tiring. We're glad to be home."

"Jon was just telling me about some dealings with Bannister," I said. I gave her a brief recital of what Jon had told me. When I mentioned Erickson's name, I noticed a quick look of recognition cross her face, but she said nothing.

"Jon," J.D. said when I'd finished. "Was this Erickson a big blond guy?"

"No. In fact, he was African American."

We chatted some more, had one more drink each, and J.D. and I took our leave. I thanked Jon for the information, and we made plans to have dinner together in a week or two.

* * *

J.D. followed me to my cottage. As soon as she walked in, she said, "Mark Erickson is our link."

"What do you mean?"

"He's the link between the Favereauxes and Bannister."

"How so?"

"There's a black professor at USF named Mark Erickson. He and his wife share a chair that Jim Favereaux endowed to the tune of a million dollars. I'd be very surprised if there were two black men in this area named Mark Erickson."

"If Favereaux gave the money to the university, it wouldn't necessarily mean that he even knew the Ericksons."

"No, but Lyn and Mike Haycock saw the Favereauxes and the Ericksons having dinner together. Erickson's the link. We need to follow it up."

"Why did you ask Jon if Erickson was a big blond guy?"

"Erickson sounds Scandinavian, and they're all big blond guys. If I'd asked him if Erickson was black, Jon would have known I knew him. I thought I'd keep that our little secret for now."

"You're a devious person."

"I am."

"And I like it."

"What are we going to do about dinner?"

"Les Fulcher brought me some red snapper he caught yesterday. They're in the refrigerator. We could grill them."

"Sounds like a plan."

CHAPTER THIRTY-NINE

Bob Crites was a refugee from Delaware winters. A few years before, he'd moved his estate planning and probate practice to Sarasota. He was a middle-aged man of medium height and sported a head full of silver hair. He was also one of my drinking buddies from the various Longboat Key establishments.

Maggie Bannister had made arrangements for me to meet Bob in his office in a downtown high-rise. The safe deposit box was in a bank on the ground floor of his building, and he'd emptied it as soon as the bank opened that morning.

We were drinking coffee in Bob's conference room, the documents from the safe deposit box spread across the table. "Tell me what you found out about the BLP stock," I said.

"Nothing, really. Bannister owned all the stock in the corporation until last year. He entered into an agreement with a local man and turned the stock over to him. The really strange thing is that the property on which the project is being built was owned outright by Bannister. Last year, as part of the agreement that transferred the stock, Bannister transferred the property to BLP, Inc. The agent for service of process is a lawyer in Tampa, but he won't tell me anything. I'm guessing he set up the corporation since he's listed as the sole incorporator in the corporate papers on file with the secretary of state. But I can't be sure. A lot of times, the incorporator doesn't have any real ties to the company."

"Do you know if he drew the agreement that transferred the property and the land?"

"I asked. He refused to answer."

"Have the names James or Linda Favereaux popped up anywhere?"

"No."

"How about Mark Erickson?"

"I'm pretty sure that's the man to whom Bannister transferred the stock in BLP."

I sat quietly while Bob looked through the documents.

"Here it is," he said. "It's an agreement between Erickson and Bannister, dated last year." He handed me the document.

The agreement was pretty straightforward. Erickson had put ten million dollars into the BLP project that Bannister had approached Jon Boscia about, and would supply another fifteen million when Bannister secured the financing. If Bannister could not arrange for the one hundred million dollars the project would cost within six months of the signing of the agreement, the agreement would expire and Bannister would have to return the ten million to Erickson. It appeared that Bannister had bought the land for the project some years before. According to a report attached to the agreement detailing the property records search by a reputable company in Lakeland, the land was mortgage-free. An attached report by a widely respected real estate appraiser in Tampa, appraised the land at fifty million dollars.

The document required that the project's land be transferred to BLP, Inc. Bob told me that the Polk County property appraiser's office confirmed that the transfer had been made by warranty deed on the same day that the agreement was signed.

I looked at the date of the agreement. "Bannister was killed five days before the expiration date," I said.

Bob continued shuffling through papers as I read. "Here's another one that might be of some interest," he said.

He handed me photocopies of the original incorporation papers and the stock certificates for BLP, Inc. The corporation's charter authorized the issuance of one hundred shares of stock. All the stock certificates were initially issued to Bannister, but on the same day the agreement had been entered into, Bannister transferred all of them to Erickson.

"That was probably security for the ten mil loan," I said.

"Maybe," Crites said, "but why would you use a fifty-million-dollar piece of property to secure a ten-million-dollar loan?"

"Good question. Maybe it's the only thing Bannister had that could secure the loan and there was no way to divide the property up and maintain all the approvals he had from the county to start the project."

"Possibly. But since the property was transferred into the corporation, why not just issue some of the stock in the corporation as security? He could have done that on a pro rata basis, so that the shares given to Erickson would only secure the ten million."

"I don't know," I said. "Maybe Erickson was only willing to put the twenty-five million in if he had all the real estate locked up."

"If Bannister had seventy-five percent of the hundred million he needed, why didn't he just go to a bank for the rest? For that matter, why not just go to a bank for the fifty million, cutting Erickson out all together? Any bank would lend money that's secured in its entirety by real estate."

"I think there may be some drug money in this deal." I told him what Jon Boscia had said about Erickson.

"Are you suggesting that Bannister might have been involved in the drug business?" Bob asked.

"The evidence is starting to stack up. I think he might have been."

"That's too bad. I wonder if Maggie knew."

"Bob," I said, "now that Bannister is dead, what happens to the real estate in Lakeland?"

"Nothing. The real estate is owned by BLP, Inc., and it looks as if BLP, Inc. is owned by Erickson."

"So, Erickson has benefited by Bannister's death."

"Yes. To the tune of fifty million dollars. If that's really what the land is worth."

"What about the ten million Erickson advanced?"

"I'll be willing to bet that money never changed hands," Crites said. "Or if it did, it went right into the corporation."

"Then why the subterfuge with the agreement?"

"It sure makes a nice paper trail, if anybody ever came looking. All aboveboard."

"And," I said, "I guess if some law enforcement type did come looking and found what we did, he couldn't prove anything more than we can. Nothing of a criminal nature."

Crites smiled. "Bingo, Counselor."

PART II

THE TRIAL

CHAPTER FORTY

Florida's new courtrooms have no personality, no history, no ghosts of the past hanging around lamenting like banshees the tragedy that would play out over the next few days. They're just cookie-cutter spaces carved out of the new courthouses that have sprouted throughout most of the counties in the state. Florida's phenomenal population growth over the past thirty years has required county commissioners to build new monuments to themselves, and cost constraints have relegated courtrooms to sterile environments designed by unimaginative architects who eschewed any input from lawyers and judges. The stateliness of ornately carved wood, classical murals, high ceilings, mahogany furnishings, and polished wood floors has given way to plastic, vinyl, and commercial carpeting.

There are never enough elevators and the security measures are too cumbersome and mostly useless, resulting in long lines of people trying to get into the courthouse to do their public business. The result is a cheapening of the jurisprudential experience for all involved; judges, lawyers, litigants, the accused, and the victims.

I was sitting in one of those courtrooms in downtown Sarasota on Monday morning, four days before summer officially began. It was early yet, and the room was deserted and cold. The air conditioning had been cranked up against the mid-June heat that seeped into even the sturdiest buildings. When all the actors arrived, the jurors, court deputies, clerks, court reporter, judge, prosecutors, my client, and the curious who had come to watch the trial, the room would heat up and the air conditioning would blow harder and, hopefully, keep us comfortable.

I had, over the years, made a practice of arriving in court early. It gave me time to think about my case, my client, the law, and the consequences of what I did or did not do during the course of the trial. Somehow, these new courtrooms didn't bring me the solace I sought. They were like Starbucks without the coffee, all eerily similar, yet different in small ways.

The door of the courtroom opened and George Swann, the prosecutor, swaggered in. I wondered if he'd had to learn that swagger or if he'd just never been taught to walk normally. He had an entourage with him, two women who were probably in their late twenties, and a thin young man with red hair and freckles.

I stood and shook hands with Swann. He introduced me to what he called his team. The young man was a law clerk who would be a third-year student at Stetson Law School in the fall. One of the young women was a paralegal and the other an attorney. "Do you particularly want this table?" Swann asked. "I usually take the one closest to the jury."

I had absently sat down at the table nearest the jury box. The other counsel table was across the room, but the room was small enough that it made no difference to me which table I used. But Swann's attitude did make a difference. "I'm comfortable here," I said.

"In the Fourth Circuit, where I come from, the prosecutor sits at the table nearest the jury."

"We're in the Twelfth Circuit. Different rules."

"Are you trying to be difficult, Mr. Royal?" Swann asked.

The battle had already started. Some lawyers, usually those who don't have a great deal of confidence in their abilities, are contentious just for the hell of it. They seem to think they can intimidate their opponents by the force of their personalities, or their reputation, or maybe just their win-loss records. I had learned a long time ago that you took these guys head on, gave no quarter, beat them over the head with your brain and your mouth. And you never raised your voice. "George," I said, "I think you'll know when I decide to be difficult. Now, move away."

He stood over me for a moment, the school yard bully who'd been called to task in front of his posse, and wasn't sure how to proceed. He chuckled. "We'll see, Mr. Royal." He turned to leave.

I couldn't help myself. "George," I called. He stopped, turned and glared at me. I said in a quiet, even voice, "You fuck with me, and I'll bury you."

"Is that a threat, Mr. Royal?"

"No." I smiled coldly. "I want to be your friend."

"Call me Mr. Swann," he said, and turned his back on me.

"Okay, Georgie." Who said I couldn't act like a twelve-year-old?

He stopped for a split second, and then moved on to his table and instructed his staff to unpack the large briefcases that lawyers called trial bags. One of the young women, the lawyer, looked at me and smiled, quickly and furtively, winked, and said loud enough for Swann to hear, "He's never lost a murder trial, Mr. Royal." I thought she probably didn't hold her boss in very high esteem.

Bill and Abby Lester came in and pushed through the rail that separated the lawyers from the spectators. Abby sat down next to me, leaned over and gave me a kiss on the cheek.

Bill said, "I'll be a phone call away if you need me." He would not be allowed in the courtroom because of the rule of sequestration that required all witnesses who would testify to remain outside the courtroom during the trial.

"Did Swann serve you with a subpoena?" I asked.

"No. I was surprised," Bill said.

"He can't make you testify against Abby because of the husband-wife privilege, so I guess he decided not to even try."

"You're going to call me, aren't you?"

"Probably, but if I put you on the stand, we'll lose the privilege, and you'll be subject to cross-examination. I want to see how the evidence goes before I make that decision."

"Call me if you need me. And keep me posted." He left.

Abby leaned over to whisper. "The probation people came

by early this morning and took off that confounded anklet. This is the first time I've been downtown since I was arrested. Two and a half months is a long time."

"We're nearing the end," I said.

"How's it look?"

"Hard to tell." I never wanted to get a client's hopes up too high. I thought we had a good case, perhaps even one that the judge would dismiss for lack of evidence after the prosecution finished putting on its case. But I wanted Abby to remain sharp and focused. I didn't want her to relax, thinking we were going to win her an acquittal.

She smiled ruefully. "I've got faith in you, Matt. You'll get me out of this, and by next week, it'll just be a bad memory."

"I hope so," I said, but my mind flashed to that old saying that no matter what verdict the jury returns, the lawyer goes home. I hoped Abby would be going with me.

There was more activity in the back of the courtroom. I turned to watch the venire, that group of people who had been chosen randomly from the Sarasota County driver's license roll to serve on our jury. There were about forty people in the group, most of them not happy about being there. I had found over the years that the jurors tried hard to see that justice was done, even though jury duty was an imposition. It was, as the judges invariably told them, part of their civic responsibilities. And they took that responsibility seriously.

We would proceed to trial with twelve jurors and two alternates. The alternates' sole duty was to step in if for some reason one of the jurors could not proceed. I thought we'd whittle this crowd down pretty quickly.

The court reporter and two deputy clerks entered and took their seats. The reporter would take down every word said in the courtroom, making and preserving the record. The deputy clerks would handle all the documentary evidence and keep the court minutes, recording all documents offered into evidence, whether admitted or not, and noting the judge's rulings during the course of the trial.

A door behind the bench opened and a court deputy stepped out, stood for a moment and motioned behind him. The judge walked out and climbed the steps to the bench. The deputy intoned, "All stand. Hear ye, hear ye, the Circuit Court of the Twelfth Judicial Circuit in and for Sarasota County, Florida is now in session, the Honorable Wayne Lee Thomas presiding."

A chill ran up my spine. The trial was about to begin; the culmination of all that had gone before, the investigation, the evidence gathering, the depositions, the heartache, and the emotional highs and lows that lawyers and litigants always suffer. I thought I knew how that receiver standing at the goal line felt when the referee's whistle blew, and the kicker on the other team approached the teed-up football. The game was on, and Abby's future rested in the palms of my hands.

CHAPTER FORTY-ONE

The day was grueling. Picking a jury is an art based on gut feelings and the little evidence given by the prospective juror on the form he or she fills out before arriving at the courthouse, and the answers given to the questions posed by the lawyers. Attorneys walk a fine line in their questioning, seeking information but not wanting to irritate the people who will decide the fate of the accused, and in this case, the perfect record of the prosecutor. We lawyers always tell the prospective jurors that we're looking for people who can be fair to sit on our jury. That's a crock. We want the person whom we think will be the most likely to find in our client's favor. At best, it's a crapshoot.

For the most part, the venire was a cross-section of the Sarasota County community. One woman stood out briefly, at least in my mind, because I couldn't figure out why Swann had not dismissed her. According to her information sheet, Judith Whitacre was thirty-four years old, held a master's of business administration degree from the elite Wharton School at the University of Pennsylvania, and worked for a large multinational cosmetic company. She was blond, beautiful, and dressed in a dark-blue suit set off by a white blouse and a pearl necklace.

Swann was at his most charming, his smarmy smile showing dazzling white teeth as he stood. "Miss Whitacre," he said, looking at the blond woman, "what do you do for a living?"

"I work for a large cosmetic company."

"Any particular division of that company?"

"Fragrances."

Swann's smile got bigger. "Are you one of those pretty girls who stand at the door of department stores in the mall and offer people a spray sample of your perfume?"

"No."

"Well, what exactly do you do for your company, Ms—?"

"I'm the manager of operations for the Southeastern division, covering thirteen states."

"Oh." Swann said.

"Yes." Ms. Whitacre said, with a smile.

Swann must not have looked too closely at Ms. Whitacre's form questionnaire. I was pretty sure he would dismiss her, but he didn't. I think he didn't realize how bad a mistake he'd just made. He'd insulted a woman who was obviously proud of her accomplishments and her place in the corporate world. I asked her no questions, and for the rest of the day, she smiled at me and frowned at Swann.

The prevailing wisdom among criminal defense lawyers is that you do not want a juror with ties to law enforcement, either by marriage, blood, or just close friendship. People always talk, and it doesn't matter how many times the judge instructs jurors not to discuss the case, they will talk, and cops usually come down on the side of the prosecution. I thought this one might be different because Abby was the wife of a well-respected officer who had been part of the Sarasota County law enforcement community for more than twenty years. I accepted a woman whose brother was a Sarasota County deputy sheriff. Swann seemed a little smug about what he surely considered a mistake on my part, but I ignored him and hoped for the best.

We worked all day and finally, by late in the afternoon, we had chosen the fourteen people who held the fate of Abigail Lester in their hands. It was an awesome responsibility to thrust on a small body of citizens chosen at random by a computer, and then whittled down to a jury by obsequious lawyers seeking their favor.

Judge Thomas swore in the jury, charged them not to read anything about the case or watch any news of it on television, and dismissed us until nine the next morning.

As Swann's team was packing up, he sidled over to me and said, "Nice work with that cop's sister. I guess retirement dulled your senses." He walked off before I could respond.

Abby and I walked out of the courtroom to find her husband sitting on a bench in the hallway. We waited for the jurors to leave the area and then boarded an empty elevator.

The June air was muggy, the sun still bright and the temperature hovering in the low nineties. "How's it going?" Bill asked.

"Let's find someplace with air conditioning," I said. "I could use a drink and we can talk."

We crossed the street and walked a block to an upscale bar and restaurant favored by the courthouse lawyers in need of a little decompression time at the end of a day of hearings or trials. We found a booth in the back and ordered beer for Bill and me and red wine for Abby.

"I think we've got a pretty good jury," I said. "You never know how they'll play, but I feel positive about this bunch." I told Bill about each of the jurors, why I thought each would be good for our case, which ones I wasn't too sure about and why. "It's always a crapshoot," I said. "You get some you like and some you don't, but they usually surprise me. The ones you think are good turn out to be patsies for the prosecution, and some of the ones you would have liked to have dismissed are your biggest supporters."

"I'm surprised this system works at all," said Abby. "You get a bunch of people who don't want to be there, you ask them personal questions, put them through a wringer, make them sit there for days listening to witnesses and lawyers argue, and still expect them to do justice."

"It does seem rather ludicrous, doesn't it?" I said. "But it works. The system's cumbersome and not very pretty, but it almost always spins out results that look and feel like justice."

"What about when it doesn't?" Abby asked.

"That's what appellate courts are for. Look, the system isn't perfect, but then no system is. Ours is just better than any other in the world."

"What's up for tomorrow?" Bill asked.

"Swann will start putting on his case. My guess is that he'll start with Harry Robson, set the crime scene, and bring in the forensics people, set up the fingerprint identifications, that sort of thing. I wouldn't be surprised if he drags that out so that he can put the FDLE guy Lucas on the stand late in the afternoon, maybe finish with direct but not leave time for cross-examination. That'll mean the jury will go home thinking about the case the way Swann wants them to."

"Is that a problem?"

"No. I'd rather them go home after listening to some of our evidence, but I can't control that. The pendulum swings both ways during a trial. We'll have our time at bat."

"What are you planning to say on opening statement?" Bill asked.

"I'm not. At least not yet. I'm going to wait until we start our case to give my opening. By then, I'll have seen all the state's evidence. My opening becomes a bit of a closing argument, although it's not supposed to. I can pick at Swann's case by laying out our evidence that rebuts his. Then on closing, I just hammer it in further."

* * *

I drove home, tired and looking forward to a quiet evening of doing nothing. Unfortunately, the trial lawyer's day does not end when court does. He has to prepare for the next day, go over deposition transcripts looking for little tidbits that might amount to a weakness in the state's case, reviewing one more time the questions he wants to ask on cross-examination of the witnesses that he expects to be called the next day, and then prepare for those he doesn't expect to be called just in case the other side surprises him and puts the witness on the stand.

It's a never-ending process. You never get enough done, because there's just too much information, too many facts, too many personalities. The fear that the other side knows something you don't is pervasive, always knocking on the edge of your psyche, whispering to you that you're not good enough, that your client is going to jail because of something you forgot to do. No sane trial lawyer ever gets over the fear of failure, that gnawing dread that he's left something undone.

The mental stress of hanging on every word said in the courtroom translates to physical stress, ulcers, insomnia, the need for alcohol, and ever more insecurity. Your mind wants to wander during a trial, but you know you can't let it. You have to focus on every word said for fear of not being ready to object or react or jot down the note that will remind you of something that needs to be asked on cross-examination.

So, as I drove home in the gathering dusk, all I wanted was a couple of drinks, or maybe three or four, and then eight hours of sleep. I knew I would have neither. I'd drunk two beers with Abby and Bill, and that was my limit. I wouldn't sleep, because I never slept well during a trial. The mind won't shut down, the fear won't recede, the dread keeps gnawing at the perimeter of your consciousness. And I had work to do.

I parked in the driveway of my cottage, next to J.D.'s Camry. I opened the front door to the aroma of frying chicken. J.D. was standing at the stove, oblivious to my presence. I put my arms around her and kissed the back of her neck.

"Who's there?" she asked.

"Your friendly neighborhood stud."

"Oh, goody. I was afraid it was the guy who lives here."

She turned to hug me. Over her shoulder I could see pots of rice, gravy, green peas, black-eyed peas, and fried okra. Bread was baking in the oven and a chocolate cream pie sat on the counter next to a pitcher of tea. A Southern meal.

"You've been busy," I said.

"I took part of the afternoon off. I kind of thought my sweetie could use a good meal."

"I didn't know you knew how to do this."

"I'm my mama's daughter and she grew up in Georgia.

Taught me how to cook before I got old enough to be interested in boys."

"Ah, a hidden talent."

"Don't let it out. And don't get used to it. I only cook for special occasions. Like now."

"Now?"

"Like when my honey needs to relax and get his mind off the trial."

The meal and the company worked magic. My mind slowed down, the stress evaporated, and I began to feel human again. When we finished, we cleaned up, put the dishes in the dishwasher, and sat on the sofa, nuzzling.

"Thank you," I said. "You want to hear about my day?"

"Yes, but not now. I want you to go to bed soon, get a good night's sleep, and get ready for tomorrow."

"I've still got a lot of work to do."

"Sleep, and get up early in the morning and start over. You'll feel better."

"Did you make any progress on your murder case?"

"Nothing worth talking about." She patted me on the chest. "I'm going home now. You go to bed. I'll talk to you tomorrow." She kissed me on the mouth, a chaste touching of lips, and was gone.

I slept like a hibernating bear, with a stomach full of good food and a brain empty of any thought.

CHAPTER FORTY-TWO

George Swann was at his most pompous, strutting before the jury box, his voice rising and falling in dramatic fashion as he went through the evidence he planned to present. He talked for almost an hour, and while I thought he was a bit long-winded and his emphasis was sometimes misplaced, overall he presented his case in an orderly fashion. I did notice that Judith Whitacre, the fragrance company manager he'd insulted in voir dire, never looked at him. She kept her head down, and I thought I saw slight frowns cross her face two or three times.

When Swann finished, I stood. I was already tired. I'd been up early to do all the work I hadn't done the night before and the day was already long. I said, "Your Honor, I'll defer my opening statement until Mr. Swann completes his case." I would refer to it as "Swann's case" throughout the trial. No sense in reminding the jury that the state of Florida was the entity prosecuting my client.

The first witness called was the housekeeper who found the body. Swann walked her through her name address and occupation, elicited the fact that she'd arrived for work at eight o'clock on the morning of April first and found Mr. Bannister dead on his living room floor. She immediately called the police. I had no questions for her.

Harry Robson was the next witness. After Swann got his name, occupation, and background into evidence, he asked, "Were you called to the residence of Mr. Nate Bannister on Monday, April first of this year?"

"I was."

"Why were you called there?"

"I was informed that a body had been found in his condo unit."

"What time did you arrive at the scene?"

"My log shows I got there at twenty minutes after eight in the morning."

"Did you identify the body?"

"I did. His driver's license was in his pocket. It was Mr. Bannister."

"How did he die?"

"Gunshot to the head."

That wasn't technically within the purview of the responding officer, but it wasn't enough to argue about. The medical examiner would be called and he would confirm the cause of death. I stayed in my chair.

"Did you find a weapon?" Swann asked.

"No, sir."

"I take it that you ruled out suicide."

"Yes, sir."

"Did you call in the forensics investigators?"

"Yes, sir. Immediately."

"These are the people who're often called the crime scene investigators, right?"

"Yes, sir."

"What did they find?"

"Quite a bit of evidence, but I'd defer to the crime scene supervisor on that."

"Okay, fair enough," said Swann. "Did they find any fingerprints?"

"Yes, sir."

"Did you recognize the names of any of the people who left those prints?"

"Yes, sir. Two people."

"Who were they, Detective?"

"Abigail Lester and Maggie Bannister."

"Who is Maggie Bannister?"

"The wife of the victim."

"And Abigail Lester?"

"The woman sitting at the defense table."

"Did you know her personally at the time of the murder?"

"Yes."

"Were you friends?"

"Acquaintances."

"How were you acquainted?"

Swann was starting to show a little frustration. Normally, the police officer is quite happy to respond positively and volubly to a prosecutor's questions. The problem is usually that the defense lawyer has a hard time keeping the officer from going off on a tangent with his answer.

"Mrs. Lester is the wife of the Longboat Key chief of police, Bill Lester," Robson said.

"And you're a friend of Mr. Lester?"

"Do you mean Chief Lester, Mr. Swann?"

The answer visibly piqued Swann. His voice was hard. "Do you know of any other Lester we're talking about here, Detective?"

"No, sir," said Harry. "But it's common courtesy to call a police chief by his title, and since you didn't, I wasn't sure you were actually talking about Mrs. Lester's husband."

It was a smart-ass answer, delivered in a calm, friendly voice. I noticed a smile cross the pretty face of Judith Whitacre.

Swann was getting angry now, his calm demeanor starting to show cracks. That was good news for me. If that little stab by Harry Robson would get his dander up, I was quite sure I could turn him into a raving lunatic before this trial was over. Juries never like lunatics. I think that is an axiom written down somewhere. Maybe not.

"Didn't you think that your friendship with the defendant and her husband might prejudice you in the performance of your duties?" Swann asked.

"Not at all. However, in an abundance of caution, I took the issue to my chief. He decided, and quite properly I think, to bring in the Florida Department of Law Enforcement to handle the case. He didn't want any hint of scandal to infringe on the investigation."

"When was this decision made?"

"Early. I think we got the initial fingerprint findings about ten in the morning, and I went immediately to my chief."

"Did you ever meet with an FDLE agent?"

"Yes. Agent Wes Lucas."

"What time did you first meet with Agent Lucas?"

"I'm not sure of the exact time, but it was before noon on the same day."

"And you formally turned the case over to him at that time?"

"Yes, sir."

"I have nothing further, Your Honor," Swann said.

I stood at counsel table. "Just a couple of questions, Detective Robson. Did you find a computer in Mr. Bannister's condo?"

"I did."

"What did you do with it?"

"The forensics people took it with them."

"Before they left the crime scene, did they examine the computer in any way?"

"Yes. They pulled up a few days' worth of emails."

"Did you see any of those?"

"I did."

"What were they?"

"Emails to Mr. Bannister that appeared to have come from Mrs. Lester."

"You used the word 'appear.' Were they from Abby Lester?"

"I don't think so. They didn't come from her computer."

That brought Swann to his feet. "Objection, Your Honor. Outside the scope of direct examination."

"Your Honor, he opened the door when he asked about evidence," I said.

"The detective testified on direct about what was in a computer found in the victim's residence," Swann said. "Now, he's being asked about the defendant's computer that was found in her home."

"Sustained," the judge said.

Swann looked at me and smiled. I'd just won a small battle and Swann wasn't even aware of it. I'd planted the thought that Abby couldn't have sent the emails, and the jury wouldn't forget that. When we got to the part of the case where Swann would try to put the emails into evidence, I'd be able to get his technicians to testify that they'd found no evidence that the emails had come from Abby's computer. The jury would have to wonder why Swann had tried to keep that fact out of evidence when Detective Robson was on the stand. Those small wins add up over time.

"Was there anything in those emails of interest to you as the investigating officer?" I asked.

"Yes. There were several that indicated that Mr. Bannister and Mrs. Lester were having an affair. And one of the emails contained a threat to kill Mr. Bannister."

"Objection," said Swann, rising to his feet. "This is outside the scope of direct examination."

It was a poor objection, more designed to knock me off my rhythm than to stop my questioning. But it was an indication that Swann was getting nervous. He hadn't anticipated that I would bring up the emails. He probably assumed I would try to keep them out. And I was stealing some of his thunder. I was pretty sure his plan had been to use Agent Lucas to put the emails into evidence. Score one for the home team.

"This was part of Detective Robson's investigation which Mr. Swann covered extensively in direct," I said.

"Objection overruled," the judge said.

"Was there any indication that those emails had come from Mrs. Lester?" I asked.

"Her name was typed at the bottom."

"No signature?"

"No, sir. Just a typed name."

"Did you give those emails to Agent Lucas when you first met with him Monday morning?"

"Yes, sir."

"Nothing further, Your Honor." I sat down.

"Redirect?" asked the judge.

"No, sir," said Swann. He'd had enough of Harry Robson.

Swann called the county medical examiner, Dr. Bert Hawkins. He established that Dr. Hawkins in the course of his duties had performed an autopsy on Nate Bannister and that the cause of death was a gunshot wound to the head. A thirty-eight-caliber revolver had been used to dispatch Bannister. The victim's blood alcohol at the time of his death was 0.09, just a bit above Florida's legal presumption that one was too impaired to drive. The stomach contents contained a residue of red wine and pepperoni pizza.

Dr. Hawkin's opinion was that Bannister had died at about ten o'clock on the evening of March 31, about ten hours before the maid found his body. I had no questions, but told the court that I reserved the right to recall Dr. Hawkins in my case.

Judge Thomas called for a lunch break, and we stood as the jury filed out of the courtroom. Abby and I sat for a few minutes to let the jury get clear of the area. I didn't want to get caught on an elevator with one of them.

Bill Lester was waiting in the corridor to take his wife to a restaurant. I begged off going with them. I needed a little time by myself to let some of the tension of the courtroom bleed off. I would have enjoyed a walk, but the heat was too much. Florida's famous humidity had enveloped the Suncoast, and the people who lived here spent their outdoor time scurrying from one air-conditioned building to another.

I retrieved my car from the parking garage and drove to the end of Main Street where the Marina Jack restaurant overlooked the bay. I asked for a window seat where I could watch the boats plying the Intracoastal Waterway, eat a leisurely lunch of grilled grouper, and relax.

CHAPTER FORTY-THREE

The afternoon was consumed by the mundane requirements of the law. The prosecutor's job is to build his case, one block at a time. He has to put each little piece of evidence in, paint a picture that the jury can understand, and lay out all the legal elements of the crime. A lot of the presentation was tedious. I didn't object to any of it.

Late in the afternoon, Swann put one of the forensic techs on the stand. He got his name and occupation and his qualifications as a computer expert who had worked for the City of Sarasota crime lab for a decade. "Did you find a computer at the residence of the victim, Mr. Bannister?" Swann asked.

"Yes, sir."

"Did you examine the computer?"

"Yes, sir."

"And you found some emails from the defendant, Mrs. Lester?"

The question was leading and objectionable, but I let it go. No sense in wasting a bullet on something that Swann could get answered easily enough by just rearranging the question.

"Yes, sir," the witness said.

"What were they about?"

"They were for the most part about sex between Mrs. Lester and the victim."

"How do you know they came from the defendant?"

"She signed her name to them."

"How do you mean she signed her name?"

"Her name was printed at the bottom of each email."

"Anybody could have typed in her name, couldn't they?"

"Yes, sir. I suppose so."

I sat up a little straighter on this one. Swann was making a preemptive strike. By bringing this out in the state's case, it would appear to the jury that he was trying to be straightforward. I could make no points on cross-examination by belaboring the issue.

"Did you have occasion to examine the computer that belonged to the defendant, Mrs. Lester?" Swann asked.

"I did."

"Was there any indication that the emails in question were sent from her computer?"

"No. In my opinion, they were not sent from her computer."

"Did that fact cause you to reexamine the computer found in the victim's home?"

"Yes, sir."

"What were you looking for?"

"I wanted to see if I could figure out where the emails originated."

"Were you able to do that?"

"No, sir. I lost the trail in a server somewhere in Europe."

"What does that mean?" Swann asked.

"I couldn't tell where the emails originated, but they'd bounced about the ether from one server to another. Some of the servers are encrypted, and if I couldn't beat the encryption, the trail stopped. I found one I couldn't beat, so I couldn't get past it."

"The emails could have come from anywhere?"

"Yes, sir."

"From a computer in a library or a computer café?"

"Yes, sir."

"So the fact that the emails did not originate in the computer found in the defendant's house would be of little significance?"

"That's correct."

"The defendant could have sent the emails from anywhere."

"Yes, sir."

Swann had the witness testify that the printed copies of the emails were identical to the ones found on Bannister's computer. The judge accepted them into evidence and Swann turned to me. "Your witness."

I walked to the podium and stood there for a minute pretending to study my notes. I looked up at the witness and said, "Sir, you testified that these emails could have come from anywhere, such as a library or a computer café, correct?"

"Yes, sir."

"Then doesn't it follow that they could have been sent by anyone?"

"Yes, sir. They could have."

"Then you wouldn't be surprised to learn that they came from somebody other than Mrs. Lester."

"Objection," Swann said. "Lack of predicate. There's no evidence that anybody else sent those emails."

"There's no evidence that my client sent them either, Your Honor."

"Her name's on them," Swann said.

"Meaningless drivel," I said. "Anybody could have typed the name in and sent the email from a public computer."

"Overruled," the judge said. "The witness may answer the question."

"No, sir, I wouldn't be surprised if someone else had sent them."

"Wouldn't someone have to be a pretty sophisticated computer user to send an email through the complex web of servers that whoever sent these emails used?"

"I would think so."

"Well," I said, "you're a computer expert. In your opinion, would someone who had enough basic knowledge of computers to send routine emails and that sort of thing, be able to hide the source of those emails?"

"Objection," Swann said. "Calling for a conclusion."

"Mr. Swann qualified him as an expert," I said.

"Overruled," the judge said. "You may answer the question, sir."

The witness squirmed a bit in his chair and then said, "I think it would take a lot more knowledge than the average computer user possesses to send emails the way these were sent."

"Thank you. No further questions." I sat down.

The computer expert that Gus Grantham provided me had arrived at the same conclusion as this witness. I'd planned to call Gus's expert in my case to show that the emails had not been sent from Abby's computer. Swann beat me to it, and had made some points with that witness. He'd given the jury an explanation as to how the emails may have been sent by Abby, even though they hadn't come from her computer. I had pointed out the obvious, that anybody could have sent the emails, but I would have made a bigger impact by putting up the same evidence in my case. Maybe old Swann was smarter than I was giving him credit for.

* * *

The last witness of the day was another crime scene technician. Swann qualified him as a fingerprint expert and asked, "Did you find fingerprints belonging to the defendant, Abigail Lester, in the victim's condo?"

"I did."

"Where were the fingerprints located?"

"They were on a wine glass."

"And where did you find the wine glass?"

"On one of the bedside tables in the master bedroom."

"Did you positively identify those prints as belonging to the defendant?"

"Yes, sir."

"Did you find other fingerprints in the condo that belonged to the defendant Abby Lester?"

"No, sir."

"Did you find that a little odd?"

"No, sir. It's very difficult to recover fingerprints from fabric, so she may have used the sofa or one of the chairs, touched the bed sheets, something like that, and the prints wouldn't show up."

"Did you find prints belonging to anyone else?"

"Yes, sir."

"Did you identify them?"

"All but three."

"And did you give all those identities to the FDLE investigator in charge of the case?"

"Yes, sir."

"Were any of the other prints found in the bedroom?"

"Yes. There was one other set of prints, other than Mr. Bannister's and Mrs. Lester's, in the bedroom. We couldn't identify them. They were not in any database."

"No further questions," Swann said.

I had anticipated this testimony. I had taken the witness's deposition in early May. Swann and I had been in the room asking questions, and everything had been taken down by a court reporter. I stood. "Can you describe the wine glass?"

The witness looked puzzled. "It had a long stem and a round bowl, I guess you'd call it."

"Was there any engraving on the glass? Initials, maybe."

"No, sir."

"Did you check Mr. Bannister's cabinets to see if the glass with my client's fingerprints had come from there?"

"Yes, sir."

"The glass with the fingerprints didn't match any of the others in the cabinets, did it?"

"No, sir."

"In fact, Mr. Bannister had a set of wine glasses engraved with his initials."

"Yes, sir."

"Was there wine in the glass with Abby Lester's prints when you found it?"

"Just a residue of red wine. A drop or two maybe."

"Did you find any wine bottles in the condo?"

"Just one."

"Any prints on the bottle?"

"Just Mr. Bannister's."

"Any of Mr. Bannister's wine glasses in the dishwasher?"

"Two. But they had been washed and there were no prints on them."

"Were there any glasses similar to the one found on the bedside table in the dishwasher?"

"No."

"Did you see any other wine glasses in the condo? Other than those in the cabinet and the dishwasher and the one on the bedside table?"

"No, sir."

"Were there any other fingerprints on the wine glass found on the bedside table? Other than my client's."

"No, sir."

"But you did find a smudge on the stem of the glass?"

"I did."

"Did that appear to be a fingerprint?"

"Perhaps a partial. There was not enough of a print to identify."

"Could that smudge on the stem have been a partial print left by somebody other than my client?"

"Anything's possible."

"That's probably not true, but could the smudge on the stem have been a fingerprint of someone other than my client?"

"That's possible, I guess."

"I think you testified that you didn't find any other prints belonging to Abby Lester, other than those on the wine glass in the bedroom."

"Yes."

"This probably sounds like a stupid question, but please bear with me. You said that Mrs. Lester could have left her prints on fabrics in the condo and you wouldn't have been able to find them. Correct?"

"Yes, sir."

"The lack of prints could also mean that Mrs. Lester was never in that condo, couldn't it?"

"Yes, sir. Except that the wine glass was there."

"But somebody else could have put that wine glass in the bedroom, couldn't they?"

"I guess so. Yes."

"Did you find any fingerprints in Mr. Bannister's condo that were identified as belonging to Robert Shorter?"

He consulted his notes. "Yes, sir. Mr. Shorter's fingerprints were found in the living room."

"Thank you. I have no further questions."

I couldn't figure out how that wine glass with Abby's fingerprints got into the master bedroom, unless somebody else carried it there. The location of the wine glass on the bedside table gave more credence to the prosecutor's theory about Abby and Lester being lovers than if the prints had been found randomly in the condo. My cross-examination had been meant only to throw a little mud on the wall. Who knows what might stick in the mind of a juror?

CHAPTER FORTY-FOUR

Judge Thomas recessed for the evening after the last witness. I spent a few minutes with the Lesters, talking about the day and trying to prepare them for the day to come. I warned Abby not to react to whatever she heard from the witness stand, no facial expressions, no comments, no body language. I told her she'd hear some lies, and she had to rely on me to correct them. I excused myself, telling them I had work to do, and that I'd see them in the morning.

* * *

Some years before, Longboat Key had become my refuge from a world of which I had despaired. My life had been a series of ever tightening circles, a pitiless gyre whisking me inexorably toward that final drain. My wife, the only woman I'd ever loved before I met J.D., had divorced me, tired of my inattention, my drinking, the eternal meetings that consumed my evenings, and so much else that a self-centered lawyer chasing the holy grail of success got himself involved in. Over the years, the practice of law had changed almost imperceptibly from a respected profession into a business. Lawyers spent more time chasing the dollar than they did justice. Legislatures whittled away at judicial discretion and froze judges' salaries so that inflation meant that they earned less each year they stayed on the bench. The result was that many qualified lawyers refused to apply for judgeships, leaving the field open to those with little experience, and too often, even less intellect.

The sun was hanging low in the sky as I drove onto the key at the end of the day, another day in a courtroom, the kind of day I thought I'd never see again after I had ensconced myself in this lovely slice of paradise. But here I was, back in the pit with a friend's life hanging in the balance. I had an abiding fear that I may have lost a step in the years away from the daily grind of the trial practice, but during the months since I had agreed to represent Abby, I had boned up on the procedures and substantive law, and the precedents contained in the cases that had been decided by the appellate courts since I'd given up the practice.

I needed a little downtime, an evening away from the travails of the trial and the worry that floated over me like an ominous cloud. The key wasn't a place of refuge on this evening. It was ground zero, awash with talk of Abby and her trial, and by extension, of me and how I was faring. I could go home or to J.D.'s condo and we could hide out, keep to ourselves, but I wanted to sit quietly with her and order a meal and a couple of beers and talk of nothing of consequence.

I called her. "I'm just crossing the New Pass Bridge. I thought I might pick you up and go up to The Bridge Tender Inn for dinner. Just the two of us."

"You think that'll be far enough away to dodge all the interested bystanders?"

"Better than on the key."

"I'll be ready when you get here. Call me when you turn onto Dream Island Road, and I'll come downstairs and meet you."

The Bridge Tender sits on the edge of Sarasota Bay in the small town of Bradenton Beach, which takes up the southern end of Anna Maria Island, just across the Longboat Pass Bridge from Longboat Key. It was an old place and it always brought to mind the Florida of my youth. "Old Florida" we called it, a place that lived mostly in memory now, a place that had been torn down and paved over by the developers in pursuit of progress. I'm not sure that the new was a fair trade for the old, but it was done and there was no going back, except rarely, as on Bridge Street in Bradenton Beach, where the new abutted the old, and the old held on with a tenacity lost to most of our magical state.

We settled into the paneled dining room and ordered seafood so fresh that we knew it had been swimming in the Gulf just that morning. The snowbirds had left us for the summer, and the tourists had not yet made a dent in the idleness of the islands. J.D. and I were seated next to the windows overlooking the bay. Only one other couple was sharing the dining room with us, and they were on the far side of the room. I sipped a cold Miller Lite and let my mind succumb to the quiet, the company, the food, and the beer.

"How're you doing, Matt?" J.D. asked in that quiet husky voice that conveyed her concern.

"I'm fine. Just trying to keep my feet under me."

"Are you on top of this?"

"I think so. We had a pretty good day, but Swann will really come out with his heavy guns tomorrow. Those witnesses are going to hurt us."

"Do you remember Deanna Bichler?"

"Sure. Your lawyer buddy from Miami. The hot, brilliant one who doesn't look her age."

J.D. stuck her tongue out at me. "She says you're the best cross-examiner she's ever seen. And she's no slouch in a courtroom."

"I appreciate her confidence, but I've been out of it for awhile. I might be a little rusty."

"Were you rusty today? Did you not do something you should've done?"

"I was thinking about that on the drive out. I did okay, but there wasn't much contest. Swann was just crossing off the mostly uncontested facts he has to put into evidence. Tomorrow will be different. I've got to be on top of every word, and I'm going to have to destroy a couple of witnesses."

"Which witnesses?"

"The FDLE agent Lucas, and Bannister's business manager, Tori Madison."

"Are you ready for them?"

"Yes, but I'm thinking about holding off on cross-examination. I can call them in my case and do the cross then. It might have more impact with the jury. It'll be closer to the time they go out for deliberation and it'll also be part of the narrative I'm trying to convince them is the truth."

"What's the downside?"

"If I'm really able to destroy their testimony, the judge might be more inclined to grant a directed verdict of acquittal when Swann finishes his case. On the other hand, unless one or both totally recant their testimony, the judge will probably let it go to the jury. I certainly don't think we'll see any recantations, so I might as well follow the game plan I've been thinking about for weeks."

"Go with your gut. Isn't that what you're always telling me?"

I laughed. "You're right. My gut is usually on the money."

"Have you talked to Bill much?"

"No. I try to stay away from that conversation. There are issues I don't want to get into unless I have to. I left him and Abby at the courthouse this afternoon. I told them I had to get home to do a little legal research for tomorrow. How does he seem at the office?"

"He's doing well," she said. "At least by all outward appearances."

Our conversation drifted on to local gossip, the doings at the police station, and other matters of little consequence. Because I would call J.D. in my case, she was bound by the rule that kept witnesses from discussing the case beyond the parameters of her own testimony. We'd been over that a number of times, and she was well prepared.

We finished our meal and dawdled over another drink, then walked out into the night and across the street to my car. "My place or yours?" I asked.

"Is that a proposition?"

"Yes, ma'am."

"Are you sure you're up to it? You have to be in court tomorrow."

"Celibacy is not part of the trial lawyer's creed."

"Abstinence can't hurt."

"You know not of what you speak. Abstinence is counter-productive. It dumbs me down."

"Well, my goodness, we can't have that. Your place is closer."

CHAPTER FORTY-FIVE

It starts to tear at you by the third day of trial. The constant tension, the gnawing fear of failure, the weight of your client's life riding your shoulders. It all wears you down. I knew Swann would start out with an important witness, one that would begin the real process of making his case that Abby Lester did, with malice aforethought, plan and execute the murder of a citizen of Sarasota County, one Nate Bannister. There would likely be surprises, so I had to be alert, ready to diminish the impact of the worst of the testimony. But I had some surprises of my own, and they would play out when I started my case.

The morning was quiet as I drove the length of the key. It was not yet seven and the sun had barely slipped above the eastern horizon. The Gulf was green and flat and inviting. A few walkers and cyclists were out, getting their exercise before the heat and humidity locked them in their air-conditioned homes and condos. I wished I were with them, enjoying the morning and the beauty of our island. Only an idiot trades a week as a beach bum for a week in a courtroom.

I parked and went to sit in the courtroom and plan my day. I was counting on Swann to put either Tori Madison or Wes Lucas on the stand. These would be his best witnesses, I thought, the ones who would tie Abby to Bannister. I had, of course, taken Lucas' deposition, but he had played it coy. That wasn't unexpected. It's what a good cop does when a defense lawyer is questioning him. But, Lucas was dirty, and I thought I could prove it. If I could, whatever he had to say about Abby would be ignored by the jury. People don't like dirty cops. Even arrogant cops rub us the wrong way. The guy in the patrol car who passes you on the highway when you're doing the speed limit and he has no emergency lights on, or the one who parks his marked car in a handicap parking spot while attending his son's Little League game. So when we find a dirty one, we want him off the force, off the taxpayer's payroll, and we don't believe a word he says under oath.

Victoria Madison presented another problem. Her background wasn't pretty, but she had pulled herself up and was doing well with Bannister's development business. I had the feeling that she was involved in some decidedly criminal activities, but so far I hadn't been able to turn up anything.

I'd decided I had to cross-examine both of them. I was afraid that if I let their testimony go without challenging it, the jury would start making up their minds before I had a chance to begin tearing them down.

Trials are always conundrums. The truth is in there somewhere, but in the end juries don't really find truth. They arrive at a consensus based on their collective beliefs about the veracity of each witness and the probative value of evidence, that is the weight they place on a piece of evidence or testimony, and how that adds to the effort to determine the truth. But consensus is, after all, only opinion. In the end, the jury may do its best, but truth is elusive, and opinion is colored by the individual juror's life experiences and prejudices. The trial lawyer's job is to sway that opinion, to get the jury to arrive at a conclusion that exonerates his client and hope that in its wisdom, the jury has arrived at the truth. Because the trial lawyer doesn't know the truth either, and it's not his job to find it. His job is to gain an acquittal.

I thought the truth in this case was that Abby was innocent. If I hadn't thought so, I'd be fishing today, rather than sitting in an empty courtroom waiting for the action to begin. I didn't know whether she'd had an affair with Bannister, because I'd never asked her. Nor had I ever asked if she'd killed him. I didn't need to know either one of those things. She had gratuitously denied the allegations, but could I trust the denials?

I didn't need to know the truth to gain an acquittal. I now had a pretty clear idea of who had pulled the trigger, but I didn't have the direct evidence I'd need to pin the murder on him. I thought I did have enough evidence to point the jury away from Abby as the murderer and make them question the prosecution's contention that Abby was guilty. Reasonable doubt was what I needed to plant in the juror's minds in order to gain an acquittal.

My thoughts turned to Bill Lester and Maggie Bannister. If they were having an affair, they would possibly have reason to kill Bannister, if for no other reason than to get him out of their hair. But what then? Would Bill have divorced Abby? I couldn't imagine Bill setting Abby up as the murderer in order to get her out of the picture. Was he capable of that? I didn't think so, but I had long ago learned that marriages are opaque from the outside. As the old Charlie Rich song goes, "No one knows what goes on behind closed doors."

On the other hand, Maggie had plenty of reason to kill Bannister, or at least she may have thought so, and if she could frame Abby for the murder, she would have a clear shot at having Bill Lester to herself. She'd also be rich, or so it would have seemed. She probably had no inkling that her husband was so close to being broke.

I had not pursued Bill or Maggie as the murderer. I wondered if it had been anybody else, would I have tried to make a case that one or the other of them had killed Bannister, and thus take the spotlight off Abby. Was I letting my friendship for Bill color my thinking? I was, but it was more than the friendship. I'd known Bill Lester for a long time and I thought I knew the man. I simply did not think he could be involved in a murder. I didn't even think he could be involved in an affair. But that was my lack of objectivity coming into play.

I thought Maggie Bannister would have been a good suspect. She had much to gain financially, or at least she thought she did, and Bannister's death would have meant she didn't have to deal with him any further. But I couldn't suggest Maggie as the murderer without bringing Bill into it.

This wasn't the first time I'd had this argument with myself. I understood that I might be jeopardizing Abby's case by not pursuing Bill and Maggie. I had decided to let the trial play itself out. If I got down toward the end and it looked like Abby was at risk, I'd play the Maggie and Bill card. It would ruin Bill's career, but if it would mean my client going home, I'd have no real choice. I'd have to do it. Legal ethics required it, but more than that, it would be the right thing to do. Sometimes, one has to make hard choices when chasing justice.

My reverie was interrupted by Swann and his entourage's entrance into the courtroom. He shot me a quick frown and, behind his back, the young woman lawyer smiled quickly and gave me a finger wave. The gangly law clerk nodded. I'd sure like to know the dynamics of that bunch. My guess was that they didn't like Swann any more than I did.

* * *

The players were onstage. The jury in the box, my client next to me, the judge, clerks, and stenographer in their places, the prosecutors huddled over their table. The first witness was Victoria Madison. She was dressed professionally and walked to the stand with an air of confidence. I had to admire her in a way. She'd survived the swamp that her childhood and young adult years had been, and she had risen to a position of some significance. It was too bad that she hadn't been able to do so legitimately. All she had needed was a small opportunity and she could have been a success. Maybe she found the criminal element more desirable, a way to quicker riches without all the drudgery of college and job seeking. Well, I thought, we'll see what she's made of.

"State your name," Swann said.

"Victoria Madison."

"Your occupation?"

"I'm vice president of BLP, Incorporated."

"What kind of company is BLP?"

"We're a condo developer."

"Do you presently have any projects underway?"

"Yes, sir. In Lakeland."

"Did you know the victim in this case, Nate Bannister?"

"Yes. He was the president of my company."

"Were you social friends as well?"

"Not particularly. We spent a fair amount of time together, but it was mostly business."

"Did you ever meet the defendant Abigail Lester?"

"Yes. On several occasions."

"Where did you meet her?"

"At Mr. Bannister's condo."

"Did you form any impressions of their relationship?"

"They were lovers."

"What made you think that?"

"Mr. Bannister told me they were."

The last two questions were objectionable, but I decided to let them go. The testimony would come in some way or other and I didn't want the jury to think I was hiding something. I'd have to take this up on cross-examination.

"Other than what Mr. Bannister told you," Swann asked, "did you have any other reason to suspect he and Abby Lester were having an affair?"

"One day I arrived at Mr. Bannister's condo, and when he invited me in, I heard the shower in his bedroom running. He told me it was Abby, and a few minutes later she came out of the bedroom. I noticed that her hair was wet."

"Were you given any explanation as to why the defendant was in the victim's shower?"

"None. And I didn't ask."

"Did you see the defendant at the victim's condo on other occasions?"

"Yes. Another time when I was at Mr. Bannister's place, the bedroom door was cracked a little and I could see in. I got a glimpse of Abby as she walked across the bedroom toward the bathroom. She was naked."

Swann walked to the witness stand and handed Tori a sheaf of papers. "Ms. Madison, have you ever seen these documents marked as State's Exhibit One?"

She took a moment to thumb through them. "I've seen them. Mr. Bannister showed them to me the day before he died. They're emails that he received from Abby."

"What was his reaction?"

"He thought she was crazy, but the last one, threatening to kill him, scared him. He'd tried to break off the affair a couple of days before and that seemed to send her over the edge."

"I have nothing further, Your Honor," Swann said.

I stood. "Ms. Madison, did you kill Nate Bannister?"

Swann was on his feet. "Objection, Your Honor."

"Overruled," the judge said. "You may answer the question, Ms. Madison."

She looked squarely at me, her face expressionless. "No, sir," she said in a quiet, unconcerned voice. She was good.

"You don't have any idea who sent those emails you identified, do you?"

"Abby's name was on them."

"Did you know that the police have determined that they didn't come from Abby's computer?"

"I heard that."

"Have you also heard that the police department's computer experts could not determine from where the emails originated?"

"Yes."

"So, wouldn't it follow that you have no idea who sent those emails?"

"I guess so."

"You could have sent them yourself, couldn't you?"

Swann was up again. "Objection, Your Honor. Argumentative. There's no evidence at all that Ms. Madison sent those emails."

"Your Honor," I said, "this witness has also testified that she has no idea if my client sent them." I knew I was beating that dead horse, but sometimes repetition will make things stick in a juror's mind.

"Overruled," said the judge. "You may answer, Ms. Madison, but then, Mr. Royal, you need to move on."

"I didn't send the emails," Tori said.

I thought I noted a glimmer of uncertainty in her voice, but I didn't think the jury would have picked up on it. That is, not until I got a quick smile from the fragrance company executive. That was a good sign. Maybe. Lawyers always play the game called "pick the foreman." The foreman is chosen by vote by the other jurors, and he or she becomes the leader. The other jurors tend to give more weight to the foreman's opinions and his view of the evidence. Or at least we lawyers thought that to be the case. Maybe we were all wet, but we played the game anyway.

When the jury is seated, we try to decide whom the others will ultimately pick as their leader. The lawyer then tries to read that person. I've probably been right in my foreman pick in less than half the cases I'd tried, and even then, it often didn't work. I would misread the foreman's reactions to the evidence, or there'd be no reaction, or any one of a myriad of other things would happen to make my mental machinations about the foreman prove completely useless.

I thought in this case that Judith Whitacre might be the forewoman, but even if not, I thought she would have significant input into the deliberations. The other jurors would respect her education and her position in her company. All in all, I thought her smiles were in my favor.

"How many times did you see Abby Lester at Mr. Bannister's condo?" I asked.

"Several times. I'm not sure of the exact number."

"Did you always see her in the evenings?"

"No. I'm pretty sure I never saw her there in the evening. It was usually in the mornings."

"Early?"

"No. Usually mid-morning."

"Including the weekends?"

"No. Only during the week. Apparently when her husband was working."

I was beginning to think Tori wasn't as smart as I had thought she might be. She was trying a little too hard to make the case that Bannister and Abby were lovers. I decided to change course. "Do you know a man named Robert Shorter?"

"No, sir."

"Never met him?"

"Not that I remember."

"Ever heard of him?"

"Not that I remember."

"If I told you that about two years ago, Robert Shorter was convicted of assaulting Mr. Bannister, would that jog your memory?"

"No, sir."

"Ms. Madison," I said, "on the day you saw the naked woman in Mr. Bannister's bedroom, did you see her later? I mean, did she ever come out of the bedroom?"

"No, sir."

"You said you only got a glimpse of the naked woman. Yet, you're sure it was Abby Lester?"

"Positive."

"You were able to make a positive identification with only a glimpse?"

"It might have been more than a glimpse."

"She was walking from your right to your left as you watched her, correct?"

"Correct."

"So you would have been looking at her left side?"

"Correct."

"Can you describe the woman you saw?"

"Well, I'm looking right at her at that table and that was the woman I saw."

"But the one in the courtroom is dressed."

"Yes. But it's the same woman."

"Are you absolutely sure? No doubt in your mind that the naked woman you saw in Mr. Bannister's bedroom is the same woman sitting at the table with me? Abby Lester."

"I'm sure, Mr. Royal. I'd met her before. I knew what she looked like. The naked woman was absolutely Abby Lester."

"Did you notice any distinguishing marks on Abby's body when you saw her?"

"What do you mean?"

"Scars, tattoos, moles, that sort of thing?"

She thought for a moment, and then shook her head. "I don't think so."

I got loud for the next question, my words dripping with anger and disbelief. "Are you telling this jury, Ms. Madison, that you did not see the long scar on Abby's left hip from the hip replacement surgery she had last year?"

Swann stood. "Objection, Your Honor. Argumentative."

"Sustained," the judge said. He was right, of course. I had anticipated the objection and the ruling.

"Ms. Madison," I said, "did you see a scar on the left hip of the woman you saw in Mr. Bannister's bedroom?"

"Now that I think about it, visualize that scene from months ago, I did notice the scar. It ran longitudinally and was probably six or eight inches long."

"Nothing further, Your Honor," I said, "but I have Ms. Madison under subpoena and may call her in my case."

"Okay," Judge Thomas said. "Ms. Madison, you are still under subpoena and will need to make yourself available to be recalled."

Swann slipped me one of those smug smiles I had become used to. He was letting me know that he'd won a big one with the issue of the scar. I sat down, and Abby leaned over and whispered in my ear. "What the hell was that all about? I haven't had a hip replacement."

"I hope you don't have a scar on your left hip either."

"I don't."

"When the jury hears that you don't have a scar, I think Tori's testimony will be worthless."

"How're we going to prove I don't have the scar?"

"You might have to show your ass to the jury."

"I'd rather get the death penalty."

"Don't worry. I'll figure it out. You can probably keep your pants on."

She nudged me in the ribs with her elbow. Hard.

CHAPTER FORTY-SIX

The judge took the mid-morning break when Tori finished her testimony. I explained to Abby that I had never heard anything about Tori seeing her naked in Bannister's condo. That had caught me completely off guard and I had to move quickly to defuse the bomb Swann had thrown into the trial. If the jury believed Tori, they would have to believe that Abby was in the condo for a tryst, and they would believe that Abby and Bannister were having an affair and that Bannister broke it off. Then the emails would start to fall into place and Abby would be painted as a scarlet woman, to use a long-outdated term. The theory that she had cracked when Bannister dumped her and killed him in a rage would become more plausible.

"Where do we go from here?" Abby asked.

"Swann thinks he scored pretty big with Tori's testimony. I think he'll call Wes Lucas next and follow the same line of questioning. If we can cast enough doubt on Tori and Lucas' veracity, the state's case falls apart."

* * *

FDLE agent Wes Lucas was called to the stand. He walked into the courtroom, nodded at Swann standing at the podium, and stepped up into the witness box. "State your name and occupation, sir," Swann said.

"Wesley Lucas. I'm an agent of the Florida Department of Law Enforcement."

"You're a sworn police officer?"

"Yes."

"Explain to the jury what your organization is all about."

"We're a statewide police agency that reports to the state cabinet. We investigate crimes that cross jurisdictions and assist when called in by local police agencies."

"As part of your official duties, did you have occasion to investigate the murder of Nate Bannister?"

"I did."

"How did that come about?"

"I was in Sarasota working on another case when the agent in charge of my office in Tampa called and asked me to meet with the Sarasota police chief on a murder that had just occurred. I went to the police department and was informed that a suspect in the case was the wife of the chief of the Longboat Key Police Department. The Sarasota chief did not think they should run the investigation because the Sarasota and Longboat Key departments often work together."

"What was the date of this meeting?"

"Monday, April 1, of this year, mid-morning. Probably around ten."

"Did you then undertake the investigation?"

"Yes, sir."

"What was the first thing you did?"

"I went to the scene of the crime. The victim's condo."

"Was the body still there?"

"No. It had already been removed to the morgue."

"Did you order a search for fingerprints?"

"No. The Sarasota detective, Harry Robson, had already done that. He went to his chief when the first run of the prints showed that Mrs. Lester had been in the condo."

"Did you determine how long Mr. Bannister had lived in that condo?"

"About two weeks."

"Did you determine that the condo had been completely painted and cleaned before Mr. Bannister moved in?"

"It had, and all the furniture was brand new."

"How many sets of fingerprints did the technicians find?"

"Ten."

"Were you able to identify all of them?"

"No, sir."

"But you identified some of them?"

"We did."

"Explain to the jury why Mrs. Lester's prints made her the focus of your investigation instead of one of the other people you identified?"

"The emails from her to the victim, particularly the one threatening to kill him. Also, we found her prints on a wine glass on a table next to the bed in the master bedroom."

"What was the significance of the wine glass on the bedside table?"

"It showed that she had been in the bedroom, and probably in the bed."

I could have objected and moved to strike that answer, but I decided to let it go. The objection would just emphasize the answer, and I thought I could undo the damage on cross-examination.

"Did you take into account the fact that the emails were not sent from the defendant's computer?"

"I didn't know that at first, but later I considered it. She could have sent them from anywhere, so it wasn't a major factor, given all the other evidence."

"Such as?"

"I talked to Victoria Madison who told me the victim said he was having an affair with Mrs. Lester. She also said she had been in the victim's condo on at least two occasions when Mrs. Lester was there; once when she heard the shower running, and Mr. Bannister told her Mrs. Lester was taking a shower, and a second time when she saw Mrs. Lester completely naked in Mr. Bannister's bedroom."

"Did Ms. Madison tell you that she'd seen a scar on Mrs. Lester's left hip?"

"Yes, sir."

The clang of the trap springing shut was sheer music. It was obvious that Swann or Tori had told Lucas about the scar during the break.

"When did she tell you about the scar?" Swann asked.

"At the same time she told me she'd seen Mrs. Lester in the victim's condo. I first interviewed her the day after I began the investigation."

"Nothing further, Your Honor," Swann said.

It was a quick and clean examination of the witness. Swann got all he needed out of Lucas and didn't push the envelope. I walked to the podium and stood looking at Lucas. He stared right back. "Agent Lucas," I finally said, "What was the name of the case you were investigating in Sarasota at the time you got the call to meet with the chief of police?"

"I don't recall. Sorry."

"Do you recall what the case was about?"

"No, sir."

"This was only a little over two months ago. You don't remember anything about it?"

"No. It wasn't anything important, and I see a lot of cases."

"But in this instance you actually called your boss in Tampa, Stan Strickland, and asked to be assigned to this case."

He sat for a moment, his face a blank. I'd caught him off guard, and he was trying to figure out how to answer the question. "Maybe," he finally said. "I know I talked to Stan that morning, and maybe I'd heard about the murder and called to let him know I was in Sarasota and would be available to get involved."

"And if Agent Strickland were to testify that you were not in Sarasota on a case? That there was no such case?"

Again, he was quiet for a moment. "You know, I might have been here on personal business. I just don't remember."

"What kind of personal business?"

"Sorry. I don't remember."

I was chipping away at him. The jury wouldn't like his fumbling such easy answers. If he would lie about something so innocuous, he'd lie about important things. "Did you think that the

Sarasota Police Department was not competent to handle a murder case?"

"I didn't think that, but if they had a conflict of interest, we'd be the ones called in."

"You didn't know about the conflict of interest until you talked to the chief and Detective Robson, did you?"

"Right."

"Then why would you have talked to your boss before you met with the chief? How would you have known about the conflict?"

"That didn't happen. I talked to my boss first."

"Are you sure?"

"Positive."

"And if Agent Strickland's phone logs and his memory contradict you, if they show that you called him before your meeting with Detective Robson, would they be wrong?"

"They would have to be wrong. How would I have known about the murder or that Mrs. Lester would be the primary suspect?"

"Good question, Agent Lucas. But you knew about the murder before the Sarasota police did, didn't you?"

"That's absurd." He was getting a bit agitated now. "How would I know such a thing?"

"Another good question. How did you know about the murder before you talked to Detective Robson?"

"I didn't."

"And, Abby Lester wasn't the prime suspect, as you put it, when you got involved in the case, was she?"

"I'd say she was."

"I think you testified that all you knew at the time you met with Detective Robson and his chief was that Abby's fingerprints had been found in the condo."

"That's correct."

"Along with prints belonging to at least ten other people."

"Right."

"Then how did that make Abby the prime suspect?"

"I guess that came about later."

"It came about when you decided to focus on Abby and no one else."

"It came about when I saw those emails."

"Agent Lucas, you first heard about the scar on Abby's left hip a few minutes ago, during the break, right?"

"No. I heard about it the day after I started the investigation."

"Did you talk to either Mr. Swann or Ms. Madison about the scar during the break this morning?"

"We talked about a number of things."

"Agent Lucas," I said, my voice rising, "if I don't get a straight answer out of you, I'm going to call Mr. Swann to the stand, put him under oath, and ask him the same question. Am I clear?"

"Objection," Swann said. "He's badgering the witness. And he can't make me testify."

"Counsel," Judge Thomas said, "approach the bench."

Swann and I and the court reporter gathered before the judge for a whispered conversation. "Mr. Swann, did you discuss the defendant's scar with Agent Lucas during the break?"

"Yes, sir."

"You may take your seat, Mr. Swann, and you may continue, Mr. Royal," the judge said.

I went back to the podium. "Agent Lucas, did you discuss my client's scar during the break?"

"Yes, sir. We did."

"I want you to take your time answering this question because you've shown a tendency to have a lousy memory and I want you to be very sure of your answer." Sometimes a little sarcasm is warranted.

"Objection," Swann said. "That wasn't a question."

"Agreed, Your Honor," I said. "I'll move on."

"Please do, Mr. Royal," the judge said.

"And this was the first time you'd heard about the scar?"

"I'm pretty sure I heard about it when I first interviewed Ms. Madison."

"Did you attempt to investigate that any further?"

"You mean the scar?"

"Yes. Did you ever tell Mr. Swann about the scar or ask him to come to me to verify whether Abby had such a scar?"

"I don't think I did."

"Why not? Would that not have been of some importance to your investigation?"

"Yes, it's important, but I had Ms. Madison's testimony that she saw the scar, and that should have been enough."

"Would it have been enough if you had found out that Abby Lester has no such scar?"

"I don't understand your question." He was playing for time, hoping to get an objection from Swann or come up with some plausible answer. He apparently wasn't going to get either one.

"Agent Lucas, if there is evidence presented in this court showing that my client does not have a scar on her left hip, or her right one for that matter, will you still stand by your answer that you first heard about the scar the day after the investigation began? Subject yourself to a charge of perjury?"

"Objection," Swann said. "Mr. Royal is badgering the witness, he's argumentative, and there's no evidence that his client doesn't have such a scar."

"I'll present the evidence at the proper time, when I put on my case, Your Honor."

"Overruled. You may answer the question, Agent Lucas."

"I think that's when I heard about the scar, but I couldn't swear to it."

"As a matter of fact, you never heard about the scar until the break we just finished."

"That may be so."

"Nothing further, Your Honor."

Swann said, "No redirect, Your Honor, and at this time the state will rest its case."

I wasn't too surprised at Swann's calling it quits. He'd done a professional job of presenting his case without trying to embellish it. I thought I'd defanged him a bit with the last two witnesses, but he'd put all the building blocks of his case into evidence, and in the absence of my being able to pick it apart or show the jury that other people had as much or more motive and opportunity to kill Bannister, he might convince the jury that Abby committed the murder. My case was about to begin, and all I had to do was plant reasonable doubt in the minds of the jurors. I didn't have to prove Abby's innocence.

"Okay," the judge said, "Do you have motions, Mr. Royal?"

"I do, Your Honor. May we approach the bench?"

He waved us up. "Judge, I only have one motion and I can be very quick with it. But I would like to ask the court's indulgence and recess until tomorrow morning. Mr. Swann has finished more quickly than I had anticipated."

"This is quite unusual, Mr. Royal."

"I know, Your Honor, but so is the entire case. I'll be ready to go first thing tomorrow."

"Okay. I'll release the jury."

"On another issue," I said, "I have Agent Lucas under subpoena and would ask the court to instruct him to be available for recall."

The judge gave the jury the usual instruction and recessed until nine o'clock on Thursday morning. On the way out of the jury box, the attractive fragrance executive shot me a quick smile.

CHAPTER FORTY-SEVEN

Once the jury was out of the courtroom, I made a perfunctory motion for a directed verdict of acquittal, which is granted only when the judge thinks there is not enough evidence put on by the state to give the case to the jury. It is a finding as a matter of law that there is not enough evidence to proceed. Swann had put on a pretty good case, hitting all the bases he needed to hit. I'd suckered him on the scar issue, but at this point, it was still a question of fact for the jury. I didn't expect to win the motion, and the judge ruled against me without even giving Swann a chance to argue.

I drove the few blocks downtown to meet with Bob Crites and review once again the contracts and other documents that Bob had found in Bannister's safe deposit box. This was one of those exercises that the trial lawyer knows is probably a waste of time. I most likely wouldn't need the documents at all, but in case I did, I wanted to be ready. We were spread out in Bob's conference room, and when we finished with the documents, he left me to prepare for Thursday.

I had a lot of work to do, other than the documents. I had already been over everything, all the depositions, and the evidence that had been admitted so far in the trial. I went over them again, I worked on the questions I would present to the witnesses, making sure I didn't leave anything out, and being careful not to make the biggest mistake the trial lawyer can make, asking a question to which he doesn't know the answer. The trial lawyer's fear of getting caught on something he had not anticipated, or had not prepared for, was nagging at me. I went over everything I could think of one more time. I expected a lot of fireworks from Swann over the next two days, and those days would be the most crucial since Abby had been charged.

When I was as prepared as I was going to get, Bob and I walked the couple of blocks to the Two Senoritas Mexican restaurant. I'd missed lunch and my growling stomach would welcome a couple of big burritos. They probably wouldn't do much for the acid that was rumbling around in my gut, but a cold beer or two might cool it off.

* * *

The sun was sinking into the Gulf as I drove onto the key. I decided one more beer wouldn't hurt me. I called J.D. "You in bed?"

"It's not even eight o'clock."

"Want to meet for a quick one at the Haye Loft?"

"Now?"

"I just crossed the New Pass Bridge."

"I'll meet you there. I've got a surprise for you."

"What?"

"It's a surprise. I'll see you in a few minutes."

"Meet me in the parking lot. I need a hug."

She laughed. "You're on, sweetie."

The last light of the day was moving over the island as I parked under the trees behind the building that housed the Euphemia Haye restaurant on the first floor and the Haye Loft bar on the second. The trees that arched over the shell parking lot blocked most of the waning light. As I parked, another car pulled into the lot and parked facing the road. I locked the Explorer and waited by the car for J.D. to arrive.

"Mr. Royal, a minute please." It was a man's voice coming from a shadow cast by one of the trees that bordered the street. I couldn't see him. He must have been in the car that arrived right after I did.

"Yes?" I asked.

"We need to talk."

"Okay."

"Over here."

"Show yourself."

"I don't think so."

"Then we have nothing to talk about," I said.

"I've got a nine millimeter pistol trained on you, and I'm a good shot. If you don't get your ass over here, I'll prove it. And you'll be dead."

"That'll cut our conversation pretty short, don't you think?"

I just needed a little time. J.D. was on her way, and she was always armed. I reached into my pocket and used the speed-dial setting to call her. The man was too far away to hear her answer.

I heard the muffled voice of J.D. coming from my pocket. "I'm on my way."

"So," I said loud enough for J.D. to hear through the phone, "you've got a nine mil and you're a good shot. I'm standing here in the parking lot like a staked goat. You're hiding under a tree. Why don't we just try to talk this out?"

"I need some information from you, Mr. Royal, but if you don't cooperate, your being dead will be good enough, I guess."

"Are you working for Mark Erickson?"

The man was silent for a moment and then laughed. "You're pretty good. A lot better than I expected from a beach bum."

I was facing Gulf Bay Drive, the side street on which the parking lot was located. I saw J.D.'s Camry turn off Gulf of Mexico Drive onto Gulf Bay. She slowed almost to a stop and then continued down the road. Maybe she was going to park farther down and sneak back. She'd better hurry or this jerk was going to take his shot.

"I have my moments," I said.

"Well, those moments are over," he said. And then, he screamed in pain.

"Come on over here, podna. Let's see who this pissant is."

"Jock?"

"Surprise."

The screams had turned into low moans. I walked toward the shadows and found Jock Algren, my lifelong best friend, standing over a large man. The tableau reminded me of those pictures you see of Teddy Roosevelt standing over the big game he'd just shot, usually with his booted foot on the carcass. The man on the ground was no carcass. He was moaning and writhing, holding his right arm, which was twisted unnaturally at the elbow, a bone poking out of his lower arm.

J.D. came running up, a pistol in her hand. "Looks like I'm not needed." She hugged me. "You okay?"

"Yes. Nice surprise. Just when I needed him."

"Who is this guy?" Jock asked.

"I don't know."

"Who is this Mark Erickson you mentioned on the phone?" Jock asked.

"A name that turned up in an investigation of the trial I'm involved in. Never met him."

"This isn't Erickson," J.D. said. "Erickson is black."

"Who are you?" I asked the man on the ground.

"Fuck you," he mumbled through clenched teeth.

Jock kicked him on his broken elbow. The man screamed. "My friend asked you a question," Jock said.

"I need a doctor."

"Tell us who sent you and what the hell this is all about," I said, "and we'll get you to a hospital."

"I ain't got anything to say."

Jock kicked his elbow again. The man screamed, and Jock squatted down and put his face close to the injured man's ear. He sad, "You need to understand something, my friend. You're going to tell me what I need to know sooner or later. I can keep kicking your elbow, or break something else, or put one of your eyes out, maybe cut your dick off, but you're going to tell me what I need to know. You think you're tough? You've never seen tough. Until now."

"Who are you?"

"Doesn't matter. Tell me what I want to know, and we'll get you to a hospital."

The guy evidently believed Jock. He started talking at about the same time I heard a siren. Within moments, a Longboat Key Police cruiser turned onto Gulf Bay Drive and pulled into the parking lot, his blue lights flashing. J.D. went to meet the officer. They chatted for a moment and both walked back toward us.

"Hey, Matt," the cop said. It was Sergeant Doug Coffman, an old friend. "J.D. filled me in. Somebody called 911 and said they'd heard screaming coming from the parking lot."

"The guy on the ground threatened to shoot me," I said. "He ended up with a broken arm, a busted elbow, and a shoulder that looks as if it's out of joint."

Doug chuckled. "J.D. tells me our buddy Jock has shown up on the island. Things always get interesting when he's here."

"He took the shooter out. Can you give me a couple more minutes with him?"

"J.D.'s in charge. Whatever she says."

"Doug, can you get an ambulance over here?" J.D. asked. "Get him a ride to the hospital and put him under guard?"

"No problem."

"Let's keep this one quiet, Doug," J.D. said. "Nothing that the press can pick up, a blackout on information going out of the hospital. At least for the next couple of days. I'll do the paperwork in the morning."

Jock walked over. "Hey, Doug." They shook hands.

"Good to see you, Jock. Glad you were here to pull Matt's butt out of the fire."

I walked back and spent the next few minutes with the man on the ground. He had become very docile and helpful. I don't think he wanted to spend any more time with Jock.

* * *

The three of us were sitting in my living room. We hadn't felt like going to the Haye Loft after the events in the parking lot. We had all calmed down, the adrenaline shock wearing off. Jock was the calmest of the three of us. He hadn't even broken a sweat putting the jerk in the parking lot out of commission. I couldn't help but chuckle at his comments to the guy he'd put down so easily.

"You've never seen tough until now?" I said. "Who do you think you are? Arnold Schwarzenegger?"

Jock grinned. "All the bad guys watch those action movies. They like that kind of stuff. Makes them think I'm badder than they are."

Jock Algren was the toughest man I'd ever met. He and I had grown up together in a small town in Central Florida, two boys from difficult homes who clung together trying to survive the perversity of teen angst and the dysfunctional families who raised us in poverty. We'd stayed close as our careers took us in different directions, Jock into government service and I into the law. Jock was a regular visitor to our key and he'd made a lot of friends on the island.

Jock had gone straight from college into the U.S. government's most secretive intelligence agency. He was a spy and a sometime assassin. He did things for the good of our country that often disgusted him, but he was good at what he did, and he understood that in our world there was a need for men like him to protect us all. So he did his duty, and when it was done for a while, he'd come to my cottage on Longboat Key and reset his life. He'd let the horror of what he'd seen and done ooze out of his system, knowing that he was among the people who loved him the most, J.D. and me. We were his family and the key was his place of refuge, a place to recharge and gather the strength to go back to the dark world where he plied his trade.

"How did you end up here?" I asked. "I didn't know you were coming."

"I didn't, either. I got a call this morning from a local cop who had been in touch with a man who needed to be escorted from Houston to Sarasota. He needed to get here quick and in total secrecy. I agreed to help. Can't very well turn down the local law."

If I were in a cartoon, a light bulb would have appeared above my head. "Favereaux?"

"Yep."

"And the cop didn't happen to be a little cutie from Longboat Key?" I asked.

"Watch your mouth," J.D. said. "Favereaux called me this morning and told me that he had followed his wife's murder case in the papers and knew I'd hit a dead end. I told him I knew she was his daughter and explained to him the DNA hits we'd gotten on Linda and Connie.

"He told me he was holed up near Houston. He's been hiding out because he thinks somebody in Homeland Security has been feeding information to the South Florida drug cartels, and he's afraid they're looking for him. He's been following Abby's trial, and he says he knows what actually happened, and he can't watch an innocent woman get railroaded. He wanted to testify, so he took a chance and called me. He said he'd come to Sarasota, but he was concerned about his safety. He thinks he knows who the rogue agent is at Homeland, and the rogue's high enough in the food chain that he would have access to all Favereaux's aliases. He could also have a watch placed on airlines, so that if Favereaux used his own name or any of the aliases, he'd place himself in great danger. The rogue would be instantly notified and alert the druggies. So, I called Jock. He worked a little magic, and here he is."

"Where's Favereaux?" I asked.

J.D. grinned. "My condo."

"How did you do it, Jock?" I asked.

"I called Favereaux at the number he'd given J.D. and told him I could get him to Sarasota. I told him my name and asked if he knew Dave Kendall, my boss. He did. I suggested he call Dave. He did and called me back. Dave sent an agency jet for us. Favereaux met me at Hobby airport, and here we are."

"Do you think he'll stick around?" I asked. "He won't just up and leave?"

"I don't think so," said Jock. "It's taken him all this time to figure out that there's a rogue in his agency. He wants to find him and take him out, but he wants to clear up things for Abby first. He'll be here."

"The rogue will disappear as soon as Favereaux shows up to testify," I said.

"My boss is working on that," said Jock. "He knows the Homeland Security director and they're having dinner this evening in Washington. Favereaux gave him the name of the man he suspects is the rogue. Homeland will lock him down, and the first move he makes when he finds out that Favereaux is testifying, they'll have him."

"I need to talk to Favereaux," I said.

"Let's go to my place," J.D. said.

CHAPTER FORTY-EIGHT

Thursday morning, the fourth day of the trial, and it was my turn at bat. This would be the day that would make or break my case, determine the fate of Abby Lester, and perhaps that of her husband and J.D. If Abby were convicted, Bill Lester's career as a cop would be finished, and depending on how he reacted to me as the one who lost the case, J.D.'s career might go down with Bill's.

Jock, J.D., and I had spent a couple of hours the evening before with James Favereaux and then talked late into the night, trying to sort out what we'd learned from Kent Walker, the man who had threatened to shoot me in the Haye Loft parking lot, and figure out how it might play into what we already knew and how I might use it in the trial.

Walker had told me he worked for Mark Erickson, the University of South Florida professor. Walker's duties had nothing to do with the university. He was employed by a charitable organization called Unlimited Futures, founded by the Ericksons. J.D. Googled it. The charity's stated purpose was to assist poor children in Sarasota County with private school and college tuition and to support other charitable organizations that assisted poor children in nearby counties.

"Did your boss think I was standing in the way of children going to college?" I'd asked Walker as he lay on the parking lot.

"Guess again," Walker had said.

He'd assured me he wasn't sent to kill me. His job was to bring me to his boss, and then, if necessary, kidnap J.D. and use her as leverage against me. They wanted me to throw the trial. Apparently, my cross-examination of Tori had rattled Erickson.

He was afraid that I was moving toward exposing his operation in which Tori played a major role. He thought I knew more than I probably did.

It was becoming obvious that Erickson was involved somehow in drug operations. He was connected to the Favereauxes and Bannister. Erickson had been with Bannister when Bannister tried to borrow money from Jon Boscia, and Bannister had transferred all his stock in BLP, Inc. to Erickson in return for ten million dollars and the promise of fifteen million more. The money from Erickson had gone into BLP, Inc., which Erickson now controlled, so the net effect was that Erickson had lent himself the money and he now owned the real estate on which the project was to be built. It was a nice slight of hand and a good way to launder drug profits. There was still the question of where Erickson would have gotten the ten million. Had to be drugs.

J.D. went to a website where she could access tax return summaries of not-for-profit corporations. Unlimited Futures showed a very high percentage of its proceeds going to administrative expenses and another large part being contributed to other charities. She could find no information on the other charities.

"My guess is that most of that money is going back into dealers' pockets," J.D. said, "but it seems like a pretty basic scheme. You don't have to look too deep to find that the money trail peters out."

"But who's going to be looking?" I asked. "You have a distinguished professor and his wife running a charity to help kids, and the administrative expenses are high but not completely unreasonable. The charities that Unlimited Futures sends money to haven't filed returns, but maybe they're so small, they don't have to file. If the charity's income is less than twenty-five thousand dollars per year, it isn't required to file a return."

J.D. took another look at the information on the computer screen. "There are a lot of charities supported by Unlimited Futures, but every one of the contributions to those entities was just under the twenty-five thousand mark."

"There you go," I said. "Unless somebody was really looking for it, Erickson would just continue to slip in under the radar."

"I'll bet you anything Unlimited Futures takes in a lot more money than it reports," J.D. said.

J.D. had made sure that Walker was completely isolated so that Erickson would not know what happened to him. She put out a press release saying that the Longboat police had found a body on the key, that of a man who had died of a heart attack. The story included an artist's sketch of Walker, but there was no identification on the body, so the police were asking the public to call if they thought they knew the victim. It wasn't perfect, but we hoped the ruse would hold for a day or two. The story ran in the Thursday morning edition of the *Sarasota Herald-Tribune*, so that by the time the trial resumed, chances were good that Erickson would think his man had not made contact with me before he died.

* * *

The show was about to begin. The jury was in the box, and it was time for me to give the opening statement I'd deferred until the state had finished its case. I planned to keep it short. I didn't want to give away any of the surprises I had in store for the day.

I wanted to hit Swann cold with the facts as they came from the witness stand. He'd have no time to prepare, to figure out how to dilute the impact of the testimony. That is, unless he knew a lot of what I'd discovered, unless he was better prepared than I thought, unless he had some surprises for me, unless he was a better lawyer than I believed him to be, unless he had not underestimated me and my case, as he seemed to have done. That little devil on my shoulder, the bane of every trial lawyer, was whispering baleful predictions of doom, and warning me of my inadequacies.

I stood before the jury, not close, no hand on the rail like they always do on TV. I didn't want to invade their personal space and make them uncomfortable. I wanted their attention. I needed to grab it and hold onto it for the few minutes I would need to make my statement. I knew the importance of not promising them evidence I could not produce. I had neither podium nor notes, and I did not smile or chuckle or try to pander to them in any way.

"May it please the court," I said with a nod to the bench. "Ladies and gentlemen of the jury, you have heard Mr. Swann's case and now it's time for me to present the defense's evidence, the evidence I believe will prove that Abby Lester did not kill Nate Bannister. Mr. Swann has done a masterful job of presenting every shred of evidence he has, and he will argue that those facts are all you need to convict.

"Perhaps he would be correct if there was no other evidence. Unfortunately for the prosecution, there's a lot more evidence, and I will present it to you over the next day or two. You will begin to see that Mr. Swann's case is very weak to start with, and it falls completely apart when you hear the testimony that will come to you today and tomorrow.

"My job is not to prove the innocence of Abby Lester, although I think you will have no doubt of her innocence. The burden of proof is on the state to prove beyond a reasonable doubt that Abby killed Mr. Bannister. The prosecution's evidence has been designed to point in only one direction, that Abby was the killer, that there is no one else who had motive, opportunity, and the means to kill Mr. Bannister. But Mr. Swann's evidence isn't all the evidence.

"By the end of tomorrow, you will have seen that there are a number of people who had better reason to kill Mr. Bannister than any Mr. Swann has attributed to Abby. You will also hear the evidence that Abby didn't even know the victim and that she certainly did not have an affair with him.

"I'm not suggesting to you that Mr. Swann has deliberately attempted to convict an innocent woman. I am suggesting that the evidence will show that the state may not have done as good a job as it should have in following up on evidence that was available to them. You—"

"Objection, Your Honor." Swann was back on his feet. I'd thought that last statement might raise his blood pressure a bit. After all, I was suggesting that he was incompetent. I expected the objection, and I was pretty sure it was not one the judge would sustain. I was walking a fine line between arguing the case and explaining to the jury what evidence I would present, but I hadn't stepped over it. Well, not more than a little bit. I also knew that the objection would focus the jury on the very point I was making.

"Grounds, Mr. Swann?" Judge Thomas asked.

"He's arguing. This isn't closing."

"I'll let him finish. I grant you that he's walking close to the line, but he hasn't stepped over it. Yet. Overruled."

"Thank you, Your Honor," I said. I turned back to the jury. A faint smile crossed the face of Judith Whitacre, the fragrance company executive. "As I was saying," I continued, "I am suggesting to you that the evidence you will see, the rest of the evidence, will be that Abby Lester has been the victim of an elaborate frame-up. You will hear from some of the players in this drama, people whom Mr. Swann chose not to call as witnesses. You will hear the reason Abby is being framed is to hide the identity of the real murderer, and you will hear of other people who had reason to kill Mr. Bannister. Abby Lester played no part in any of this, except that she was an unwitting victim herself.

"The United States Constitution says that Abby Lester cannot be compelled to testify in this trial. She cannot be subjected to cross-examination if she does not testify. But Abby will testify. She will open herself to cross-examination by Mr. Swann. She will tell you the truth. You will see the real person, this high school history teacher married to a career police officer, and you will be able to distinguish between the real Abby Lester and the calculating, sex-crazed monster that Mr. Swann has tried to make her out to be. Thank you." I took my seat and smiled at Swann.

"Call your first witness, Mr. Royal," the judge said.

"The defense calls Dr. William Sawyer," I said.

The first witness of the day was on the stand. I was standing at the podium at the far end of the jury box from the witness, the jurors between us. This arrangement required the witness to look at me and speak loud enough for me to hear and thus loud enough that the jury didn't miss anything he said while answering my questions. I wanted the jurors to get a direct, head-on look at my witnesses. "State your name, please."

"William Sawyer," the witness said.

"What is your occupation, sir?"

"I'm director of the DNA lab for Biogenesis Laboratories in Tampa."

I took him through his educational background, including his Ph.D degree, his knowledge of his field, and the years he'd worked in it. I wanted to demonstrate his expertise to the jury and the judge. When I finished, Judge Thomas accepted Sawyer as an expert in his field, thus qualifying him to give opinion testimony relating to his work.

"Have you had occasion to review DNA samples provided to you for purposes of this case?"

"I have."

"Who provided you those samples?"

"Dr. Bert Hawkins, the chief medical examiner of this circuit."

"Describe the samples for me."

"One was a blood sample, a vial of blood, obtained from a murder victim, Nate Bannister. The other was part of a bed sheet found on the bed in Mr. Bannister's bedroom."

"What was the purpose of sending you the blood sample?"

"I was not told that at the time. That's not unusual. I really don't need that information."

"Did you run the sample?"

"Yes, sir."

"Did you provide a report to Dr. Hawkins?"

"I did."

I handed the witness a copy of the report with his signature at the bottom. "Is this a copy of the report you sent Dr. Hawkins?"

"Yes, sir."

"You also received a bed sheet from which you were asked to extract DNA material."

"I did."

I handed him another report, and he verified that it was the report from the bed sheet.

"Were you able to identify DNA from that bed sheet?"

"Partially. There was DNA from two different people. One of them was Nate Bannister. The other was unknown. We could find no match in any of the databases."

"Did you also receive another blood sample from Dr. Hawkins taken from another homicide victim a few days later?"

"I did."

"What was the victim's name?"

"Linda Favereaux."

"And did you provide Dr. Hawkins with a report on this sample?"

"Objection," Swann said, rising to his feet. "Relevance."

"I'll tie it up with the next witness, Your Honor," I said.

"Overruled," the judge said. "You may answer the question, Dr. Sawyer."

"I sent the report to Dr. Hawkins," Sawyer said.

"Thank you, Dr. Sawyer. I have nothing further." I returned to my seat.

"You may inquire, Mr. Swann," the judge said.

Swann stood. "No questions, Your Honor."

"Call your next witness, Mr. Royal," the judge said.

"We'll call Detective J.D. Duncan," I said.

J.D. walked into the courtroom wearing a dark suit, white blouse, and navy-blue pumps. She looked very professional. She took the witness stand and was sworn by the deputy clerk.

"State your name, please," I said.

"Jennifer Diane Duncan."

"Your occupation?"

"I'm a Longboat Key police detective."

"And how long have you been so employed?"

"Almost two years."

"And before that?"

"I was a police officer and detective on the Miami-Dade County Police Department."

"What was your job there?"

"For most of the time, I was a homicide detective. By the time I left there to come to Longboat Key I was the assistant homicide commander."

"How many murders have you investigated in your career?"

"At least two hundred."

"So, it'd be fair to say that you know your way around a murder case."

"I think so."

"Objection," said Swann, rising from his seat. "Is Mr. Royal trying to qualify this witness as an expert?"

"I'm not, Your Honor. I've called Detective Duncan as a fact witness."

"How can her testimony be relevant to this case?" Swann asked. "It did not occur in her jurisdiction, and to my knowledge, Detective Duncan played no part in the investigation of Mr. Bannister's murder."

"Mr. Royal?" the judge asked.

"Your Honor, if I may have a little leeway here, I think the court will see that Detective Duncan's testimony will have a lot of bearing on this case."

"Okay," Judge Thomas said, "but I expect you to tie this up quickly."

"Yes, sir," I said, and turned back to the witness stand. "Detective Duncan, I want to get some personal stuff out of the way before we proceed. You and I know each other, correct?" I had to bring our relationship out in the open because Swann certainly would. I didn't want the jury to think we were hiding anything. J.D. and I had talked about how to present this.

"Yes. We're in a relationship."

I thought that would suffice. Everybody on the panel would know what she meant, and if Swann tried to make too big of a deal out of it, the jury wouldn't like it. I glanced at the jury box. They were all stone faced, except for Judith Whitacre. She looked straight at me and smiled quickly, as if saying, "good for you."

"Would the fact of that relationship in any way color your testimony in this case?"

"No."

"When did you first become aware that Nate Bannister had been killed?"

"On the morning of April 1 of this year."

"And how were you notified?"

"Detective Harry Robson of the Sarasota Police Department called me."

"What was the gist of that call?"

"Detective Robson told me that Mr. Bannister's body had been found in his condo in Sarasota and asked me to notify Mrs. Bannister, who lives on Longboat, of his death."

"Did you do so?"

"I went to her house, but she wasn't home. I returned to the station and mentioned the request to Chief Lester, and he told me he would take care of the notification."

"Were you investigating another case on the morning of April 1?"

"Yes."

"Tell us about that."

"A woman named Linda Favereaux had been murdered in her home on Longboat Key earlier that morning. I was just starting my investigation."

"Was there a connection between the deaths of Mrs. Favereaux and Mr. Bannister?"

"None that was apparent."

Swann stood. "Your Honor, this has gone far enough."

Judge Thomas interrupted him. "Do you have an objection, Mr. Swann? If so, state your grounds without any commentary."

"Relevance."

The judge frowned. "Ladies and gentlemen of the jury," he said, "on occasion the lawyers and I have to discuss legal matters that are outside your responsibility for determining the facts of this case. This is one of those times, and I will have to excuse you for a few minutes. I appreciate your patience. Deputy, please escort the jury to the jury room."

When the jury was gone, the judge said, "Where are you going with this, Mr. Royal?"

"Your Honor, I will tie this up with a few more questions. I think we'll see that the two cases are connected."

"Mr. Swann?" the judge asked.

"I can't see how the Favereaux case is possibly connected to this case. I think Mr. Royal is just trying to throw mud on the wall and see if anything sticks."

"Your Honor," I said, "just a few more questions and this will all fall into place."

"Okay, Mr. Royal, but let's get to the point. Objection overruled. Deputy, bring in the jury."

When the jury was seated, I said, "Detective Duncan, did you identify Mrs. Favereaux at the scene of the crime?"

"Yes, her maid identified her and one of our officers knew her."

"But you ordered a DNA analysis. Why did you do that if you had positively identified the victim?"

"The medical examiner routinely runs fingerprints of murder victims. It's part of a backup system that ensures we have made a proper identification. When Dr. Hawkins' office ran Mrs. Favereaux's prints, they came back as those of a woman named Darlene Pelletier who had been arrested in New Orleans twenty years ago on a minor shoplifting charge. That, of course, meant that either the fingerprints were somehow wrong, or Linda Favereaux was not the person she seemed to be."

"So you ordered the DNA analysis?"

"Yes. I went to New Orleans to follow up on Darlene Pelletier. It was important to my investigation to find out who my victim really was. It might lead to the killer."

"Why the DNA?"

"I came across a woman in New Orleans named Connie Pelletier, whom I thought may have been related to the woman we knew as Linda Favereaux. The day after I talked to Connie Pelletier, she was murdered. I asked Dr. Hawkins to run a DNA analysis on Mrs. Favereaux so that we could compare it with that of Connie Pelletier."

"Was there a connection between the two women?"

"Yes. Connie was Linda's mother."

"Did anyone accompany you to New Orleans?" This was a question that I didn't want to ask. I doubted that Swann would have known anything about J.D.'s trip to New Orleans, but any competent lawyer would ask if anybody had gone with her. My name would come out, and it would look as if we were hiding something. Which we would have been doing.

J.D. smiled. "Yes. You went with me."

"Did I take part in the investigation?"

"You were there, but you weren't part of the investigation."

"Did I have anything to do with your asking for the DNA samples?"

"No. At that time there was no reason to think there was any connection between the Bannister and Favereaux cases. If I thought there had been, you would not have been with me."

"Thank you, Detective. I have no further questions."

Swann stood, his face a mask of derision. "Let me see if I've got this straight, Ms. Duncan."

"That's Detective Duncan, Mr. Swann," J.D. said, interrupting. "I worked hard for that title. Please do me the courtesy of using it."

I chuckled to myself. That's my girl, I thought. Swann had better be careful or she'd chew him up and spit him out.

"Okay, Detective Duncan," Swann said, putting an emphasis on the title. "Let me get this straight. Mr. Royal, the defense lawyer, is your boyfriend?"

"I guess you could call him that."

"Well, what would you call him?"

"I've never thought much about that."

"Lover, paramour, sweetheart? Any of those?"

J.D. smiled. "All of those, and so much more."

I debated with myself about trying to stop this line of questioning, but one glance at the jury told me that they didn't like this kind of intrusion into a witness's private life. I decided to see how far Swann would take it.

"Are you sleeping with Mr. Royal?" Swann asked.

That did it. What a creep. I was on my feet. "Objection, Your Honor. I will stipulate that Detective Duncan and I are two single, consenting adults who are in love with each other and in a relationship. I think any further questions along this line would only serve to titillate Mr. Swann's prurient interest." That brought a few smiles from the jurors. They hadn't liked this line of questioning.

Swann was livid. "Your Honor, I don't have any prurient interests. I'm just trying to show the jury that Detective Duncan is biased." Again, he emphasized the title. Not a good move. He seemed to be mocking J.D.'s position. I saw Judith Whitacre wince slightly. If she didn't like Swann's approach to J.D., the other members of the jury wouldn't either.

"Proceed, Mr. Swann," the judge said, "but we'll have no more questions about the relationship between Mr. Royal and Detective Duncan. It's a fact in this case, and if you can show that it impacted Detective Duncan's investigation or her testimony, so be it. But you will not ask any more questions about the nature of the relationship. I think it has been adequately explained."

Swann let out a long breath of exasperation. "Detective Duncan, what is your interest in this case?" Again, the emphasis on the word "Detective."

"None."

"Then why are you here testifying?"

"I'm here in response to a subpoena to answer all questions put to me, including any that you may have."

"And you want this jury to believe that your answers are not colored by your relationship with Mr. Royal?"

"Mr. Swann, I've been a law enforcement officer for more than fifteen years—"

Swann interrupted. "Just answer the question."

"I'm trying to do that."

"I think it calls for a yes or no answer, Detective."

I stood. "Objection, Your Honor. The witness has a right to explain her answer."

"Sustained," the judge said. "Let her answer, Mr. Swann."

J.D. said, "As I was saying, I've been a law enforcement officer for more than fifteen years, and I take my job very seriously. I would never lie or shade the truth or testify to anything that wasn't absolutely the truth. I value my reputation too much to do that."

"What if your testimony would hurt Mr. Royal on his case?"

"Then I would try not to testify, but if I were required to do so, I would tell the truth and know that Mr. Royal would support me in that because he is a man of absolute integrity."

My girl was hitting them out of the park.

"Move to strike that last part of the answer concerning her opinion of Mr. Royal's integrity," Swann said.

I stood. "He asked the question, Your Honor."

"That he did. Overruled."

"Nothing further," said Swann.

"No further questions," I said. "May the witness be excused?"

"You're excused, Detective Duncan."

"Your Honor," Swann said, "may we be we heard outside the presence of the jury?"

When the jury had left the courtroom, Swann said, "Your Honor, I move to strike Detective Duncan's entire testimony. It is irrelevant and has no probative value to this case."

"To the contrary, Your Honor," I said. "My next witness will bring this all together."

The judge leaned back in his big executive chair, hands folded beneath his chin, and seemed to ponder his answer. Then, "I'm going to deny the motion without prejudice. Mr. Swann, if Mr. Royal doesn't bring this to a head with his next witness, I'll grant your motion to strike the detective's testimony. Mr. Royal, you keep promising to tie all this together. This is your last chance. Am I clear?"

"Yes, Your Honor."

"Bring the jury back," the judge said.

I had been surprised that Swann hadn't asked J.D. any questions that would have ferreted out my reasons for putting her on the stand to begin with. Now I understood. By not asking the questions, Swann was setting up the motion to strike her testimony. A good ploy. Swann did have his moments, but I was confident that my next witness would bring it all together and begin to demolish the state's case.

CHAPTER FORTY-NINE

I called Dr. Bert Hawkins. "Hello again, Dr. Hawkins," I said.

He smiled. "Always good to see you, Mr. Royal."

"Did you send a blood sample from Nate Bannister to the Biogenesis Lab in Tampa for a DNA analysis?"

"I did."

"May I ask why you sent it to Biogenesis instead of the Florida Department of Law Enforcement crime lab?"

"The FDLE lab is always backed up. It might have taken months to get the results, and I wanted them as soon as possible."

"Did you send Biogenesis any other samples from this case?"

"Yes. The police wanted an analysis of DNA found on the sheets in the master bedroom of Mr. Bannister's condo. There were semen and vaginal fluids on the sheets, and FDLE Agent Lucas wanted to determine who had recently had sex in that bed."

"Were you able to do that?" I asked.

"The semen belonged to Mr. Bannister. We could find no match in any of the DNA databases for the woman who left the vaginal fluid."

"Did you do a postmortem on another homicide victim on the same day you performed the one on Mr. Bannister?"

"Yes. On Linda Favereaux, who was killed on Longboat Key the same night that Mr. Bannister was killed in Sarasota. Actually, to be precise, Mr. Bannister was killed late in the evening of March thirty-first, and Mrs. Favereaux in the early morning hours of April first."

"Did you ask for a DNA analysis on Mrs. Favereaux?"

"Not at first."

"Why not?"

"We knew who she was, so at first I thought the DNA wouldn't be needed for identification. There was no other reason to run the tests. In Mr. Bannister's case, we were trying to determine who had had sex in the bed. However, when I ran Mrs. Favereaux's fingerprints, they came back as belonging to a woman named Darlene Pelletier."

"Your Honor," Swann said, getting to his feet. "Mrs. Favereaux, whoever she was, is not relevant to this case."

"She is, Your Honor," I said, "and the next few questions will show that."

"Overruled. Move on," Judge Thomas said.

"When did you ask for the DNA analysis?"

"A few days after I did the autopsy on Mrs. Favereaux, I got a call from Detective J.D. Duncan of the Longboat Key Police Department. She asked that I run the DNA. We always keep blood samples taken from the bodies of murder victims, so it wasn't a problem."

"Do you know why Detective Duncan asked for the DNA analysis?"

"No, and I didn't ask. I assumed it had to do with identifying Mrs. Favereaux since the fingerprints proved that she was not the person we thought she was."

"And you sent that to Biogenesis."

"Yes."

I handed the witness the Biogenesis DNA reports on the blood sample taken from Linda Favereaux and from the bed sheets found in Bannister's condo. "What are those, Doctor?" I asked.

He identified them.

"What significance are those reports?"

Hawkins studied them for a moment and then looked straight at the jury. "They are identical."

"Are you suggesting that the female DNA sample taken from the bed in Mr. Bannister's condo is that of Linda Favereaux?"

"Without a doubt."

"And that means?"

"It means that Mr. Bannister and Mrs. Favereaux had sex in that bed within a few hours of their deaths."

CHAPTER FIFTY

Swann rose and walked to the center of the podium. If smoke could actually come out of an angry man's ears, Swann would have looked like a chimney. He was demonstrably livid. Hawkins had just destroyed one of the prosecution's key pieces of evidence. Swann's theory was that there was an unknown woman's DNA along with Bannister's DNA on Bannister's sheets. That meant Bannister and the unknown woman had had sex not long before his murder. Since Abby Lester's fingerprints were found in Bannister's condo, specifically on a wine glass on a bedside table in Bannister's bedroom, and since there was evidence that she and Bannister were having an affair, and that Bannister was ending the relationship, Abby, the spurned woman, would have motive to murder Bannister.

I had stirred that pot back in April when I had argued against Abby being required to provide a DNA sample. Judge Thomas had ruled that there was not enough evidence of her guilt to require her to do so. Our refusal to allow Abby's DNA to be tested was a big red herring that I'd dangled before Swann, and he'd gobbled it up like a ravenous cat. I knew the answer to the question of whom the female DNA on the sheets belonged to. And I knew it wasn't Abby.

"Dr. Hawkins," Swann began, his voice low and tight, holding back the anger, "why is this the first time I've heard about Mrs. Favereaux's DNA being linked to this case?"

"I don't have any idea, Mr. Swann."

"You never told me about this, did you?"

"No, but then you never asked."

"How am I supposed to ask you about something that I knew nothing about?"

Swann was losing his temper. He was making a mighty effort to hold it in, but the anger kept slipping through. The last question was stupid and objectionable, but I held my seat. Swann was hanging himself, and I saw no reason to slow the process.

Hawkins rose to the occasion. He sat quietly for a couple of moments, eying Swann, a quizzical look on his face. "I take it that's a rhetorical question, Mr. Swann."

"Answer the question, please." Swann's voice was tight, his anger barely restrained.

"I have no idea why you didn't know enough about your case to ask the appropriate questions, Mr. Swann."

Swann stood silent for a moment, obviously trying to get past the anger. "Okay, Dr. Hawkins. Are you telling this jury, under oath, that the victim in this case, Mr. Nate Bannister, had sex with this woman Linda Favereaux just before he died?"

"I'm telling the jury that the DNA samples found on the bed sheet on the bed in Mr. Bannister's bedroom contained semen and vaginal secretions, the kind of fluid that would only be secreted during sexual intercourse, and that the semen belonged to Mr. Bannister and the vaginal secretions belonged to Mrs. Favereaux."

"So you can't say whether or not they had sex."

"Let me put it this way, Counselor. I can say with reasonable certainty that Mr. Bannister had sex in that bed and that Mrs. Favereaux had sex in that bed. I can't say they had sex with each other, but since there was nobody else's DNA found on the bed, a reasonable hypothesis would be that they had sex with each other. I wasn't there, so I can't swear that they actually did have sex. With each other, that is."

"No more questions." Swann stomped off to counsel table.

* * *

Judge Thomas called the morning break. I went to one of the attorney conference rooms that opened off the corridor outside the courtroom. Gus Grantham had brought Robert Shorter to the courthouse from his aunt's house in Nokomis, just south of Sarasota. I only had one purpose in calling him. I thought the best he could do was muddy up the waters a bit, but that is all part of the strategy. I had some strong evidence coming in later, but if for some reason that didn't go as I expected, muddy might have to do. One always has to have a plan B and maybe even a plan C. I didn't have a plan C and my plan B was at best weak.

I used most of the fifteen-minute break talking to Shorter about what I was going to ask him, and how I expected Swann to counter. I cautioned him to restrain his anger. "You make an ass out of yourself on the stand, and this judge will put you in jail. He doesn't put up with any kind of crap. Are we clear?"

Shorter grinned. "You're not going to beat me up again, are you?"

I laughed. "Not unless you take a swing at me."

Shorter smiled. "Not today, but I owe you one."

"We're good," I said. "See you in court."

"I don't like the sound of that," Shorter said as I left the room.

As soon as the court reconvened, I called Shorter to the stand. Swann objected. "This name's not on the witness list," he said.

"I'm calling the witness for purposes of impeachment, Your Honor," I said.

"Of what?" the judge asked.

"Some of Ms. Madison's testimony."

"Overruled. You may proceed, Mr. Royal."

Witness lists are required to be filed some weeks before a trial so that the party on the other side has a chance to talk to or depose the person on the list. However, if a witness is called in to rebut something the other party's witness said or to impeach that witness, the witness called for that purpose does not have to be on the list. Impeachment is a lawyerly term that means destruction of the other side's witness, showing that the witness being impeached lied. I was pretty sure Swann would object on the same grounds whenever I called one of the people I had left off the witness list. The jury wouldn't like that.

I had decided that Swann was so used to trying cases before pliable judges that he didn't always do his homework or think through the consequences of his actions. As far as I could tell, he had never tried a case outside his home circuit. Because of his seniority in the state attorney's office, Swann could pretty much pick the cases he wanted to handle. This gave him a great deal of leeway as to which judges he appeared before. He could pick the ones who were beholden to his boss or who were known as hanging judges, the ones who weren't all that smart and did not want to rock the proverbial boat, or who were wary of the voters and would bend toward the prosecution, no matter how weak the case. Those judges would always exercise the broad discretion the law gave them to rule in favor of Swann.

Judge Wayne Lee Thomas was definitely not one of those judges. He'd spent many years as a trial lawyer before he heeded the entreaties of his colleagues and, as they say, ascended to the bench. He was not a career judge. If for some reason he left the bench tomorrow, he would be flooded with offers from important firms across the state, dangling compensation packages that would dwarf his judicial salary.

His judicial philosophy was simple. Follow the law in a way that ensures justice is done. In the pursuit of that sometimes elusive concept, he held the lawyers who appeared before him to a high standard. He expected them to be knowledgeable of the law and the facts and to be prepared to try their case with as little drama as possible. He was unfailingly courteous, but he did not entertain nonsense from the combatants and he could be stern in suppressing it.

Swann had not factored a strong judge into his trial equation, probably because he'd never experienced one. He was before one now, and he was being knocked off stride. I was making points that I would not have made had I been faced with a better lawyer. Nevertheless, I knew better than to let my guard down.

Swann had tried a lot of cases, and I knew he could be dangerous. I also knew he wasn't the most ethical lawyer in the state, and he wouldn't be above an underhanded tactic or two.

Shorter took the stand and was sworn by the clerk. "State your name," I said.

"Robert Shorter."

"Do you know a woman named Victoria, or Tori, Madison?"

"Yes, sir."

"Tell the jury how you know her, please."

"I went to see Mr. Bannister a few days before his death. We met at his condo downtown and Ms. Madison was there."

"What was the purpose of the meeting?"

"I offered my services to him as a consultant between him and my condo association in some negotiations about shoddy work when he built our place."

"Was anyone else at the meeting?"

"No one other than Bannister and the woman. He introduced her to me as Tori, and she gave me her business card. It identified her as Victoria Madison."

"Did anyone tell you why she was at the meeting?"

"Only that the card said she was the vice president of Bannister's company. She was all for the deal I proposed. Bannister said he had to think about it, but Tori was adamant in wanting to agree to it right then."

"Did you have any other dealings with Ms. Madison after that meeting?"

"Yes. A couple of days later, on a Friday, she called me to set up a meeting with Mr. Bannister for that Sunday evening at his condo."

"That was the evening he was killed, right?"

"Yes."

"Did you go to the meeting?"

"No. Something came up. I called Tori on Sunday and told her I wouldn't be able to make the meeting."

"What was her response?"

"She was mad as hell. Said it was very important that we meet on Sunday evening. She threatened to kill the deal if I didn't show up."

"Did you ever talk to Tori Madison or Mr. Bannister again?"

"No. When I heard that Bannister was dead, I called Ms. Madison several times, but she never returned my calls."

"Did you leave a message when you called?"

"Every time."

"Did you leave your name?"

"Every time."

"Did you know Mr. Bannister before you met him that day with Ms. Madison?"

"Yes."

"Tell me the circumstances of that meeting."

"Bannister built the condo complex I live in. It was shoddy work all the way through. I confronted him about it a couple of years ago. I wanted my money back. He told me to go to hell and I punched him. I was charged with assault and battery and spent thirty days in jail."

"Did you kill him?"

"No, sir."

"Where were you on the night he was killed?"

"I was in a meeting with about thirty people. It lasted four hours, from eight o'clock until midnight."

"Did Agent Wes Lucas of the FDLE or any other police officer or agent of the state attorney's office ever contact you about Mr. Bannister's murder?"

"No."

"Nothing further, Your Honor."

Swann rose and stood for a moment at counsel table, looking at his notes. Then, "Mr. Shorter, is it your contention that Ms. Madison should know you?"

"I guess."

"And if she says she didn't know you, would you think she was lying?"

That was an objectionable question. But I wanted to see how far Swann would take this. I had come to the conclusion after meeting with Shorter on several occasions, that he wasn't as dumb as he had initially seemed. He wore stupidity like body armor against rationality's intrusions on his angry little world. I stayed in my seat.

"Maybe she forgot," Shorter said, "or maybe she's lying to cover something up."

"What do you think she'd be covering up?"

"Maybe her part in the murder of Mr. Bannister."

"Objection, Your Honor," Swann said loudly, his own anger beginning to surface again. "Move to strike the answer."

I kept my seat. "Mr. Royal?" the judge asked.

I stood. "Mr. Swann asked the question. The fact that he didn't like the response is not grounds for striking the answer."

"Overruled," the judge said.

Swann said, "But you agree that Ms. Madison might have forgotten who you were?"

"I can neither agree nor disagree, Mr. Swann. I have no idea what Ms. Madison remembers or forgets, but it's only been a couple of months and under the circumstances I doubt she's forgotten my name."

"But you don't know."

"No. I don't know."

Swann sat down. The last question was one that would have merited a first-year law student a professorial chewing out in a trial practice course. Swann had been so focused on the issue of whether Tori should have recognized Shorter's name that he missed, or didn't understand, the import of his testimony that Tori wanted him at the condo at about the time that Bannister was killed.

"I have no redirect, Your Honor," I said. "May the witness be excused?"

Swann nodded and Judge Thomas excused Shorter. I'd made sure that he would be spending the next couple of days out of the range of a subpoena server. I didn't want Swann to figure out Shorter's importance in my narrative and call him back during rebuttal, that part of the case where the prosecution could call witnesses to refute the testimony of my witnesses. I didn't trust Shorter to maintain his cool. He'd been on his best behavior today, but I had no idea of what might light off the fireworks.

We had time for one more witness before lunch. I didn't want to have the lunch break come in the middle of my next witness, and I knew the judge was a stickler for letting the juries go to lunch on time. I called Bill Lester.

Swann objected on the basis that Bill's name wasn't on the witness list. I pointed out that Bill's name was on Swann's witness list. The judge overruled the objection.

"State your name, please," I said.

"William R. Lester."

"Occupation?"

"I'm the chief of police on Longboat Key."

"Are you related to the defendant, Chief?"

"She's my wife."

"Did you, at my suggestion, take some photographs of your wife last night?"

"I did."

"Do you have those photos with you?"

"I do."

"Would you explain to the jury what the pictures show?"

"They are pictures of both my wife's hips."

"Do they show a longitudinal scar six to eight inches long on either hip?'

"No, sir."

"Does Abby have such a scar?"

"No."

"Did she ever have one there?"

"Certainly not in the fifteen years we've been married."

I handed him two eight-by-ten color photographs. Each one showed Abby. In one she was facing to her right so that her left side was toward the camera. In the other, she was facing left, and her right side was toward the camera. In each picture, Abby was wearing a long t-shirt that fell almost to her knees. She had pulled one side of the shirt up almost to her waist. She was wearing a string bikini bottom under the shirt, so that nothing was visible that wouldn't have been seen on a public beach. I handed Swann a copy of the pictures and offered another copy of each into evidence. Swann had no objection.

"I have no further questions," I said.

The judge called the noon recess. As was customary, everyone stood as the jury left the courtroom. When they were gone, the judge said, "I'd like to see Counsel in chambers before you go to lunch." We had an hour and a half to meet with the judge, eat lunch, and get back to the courtroom.

Swann sat quietly at his table, looking, I thought, a bit like a whipped puppy, although that may have been my imagination working overtime. A major part of his case had just fallen apart, and he was at least a good enough lawyer to understand that. Tori Madison's testimony would be useless, but more than that, the jury would start to suspect Swann of putting on perjured testimony. I didn't think Swann had done that. I thought he'd just assumed that he would take the beach bum lawyer apart, probably with the help of the judge, and therefore hadn't done his homework. I almost felt sorry for him, but I was going to spend the afternoon dumping such a load of misery on him that he might never get out from under it.

As I passed the prosecutor's table on the way to the judge's chambers, the young woman who was the other lawyer on Swann's team caught my eye and winked at me. She seemed to be enjoying the spectacle of her boss' fall from the pedestal he'd erected for himself.

Swann, Judge Thomas, and I were the only people in chambers. "Gentlemen," the judge said, "this morning during the recess, I took a phone call that has thrown a big wrench into the workings of this court. I want to discuss it with you both off the record, and at least for the time being, I want your promise that none of what I'm about to tell you will go out of this room. Will you promise me that?"

Swann and I nodded and the judge continued. "The governor wants me to remove myself from this case. Today."

"Sir," I said. "You can't do that without declaring a mistrial."

"I'm aware of that, Mr. Royal. I'm also aware of the fact that the governor does not have the power to require me to recuse myself. He can't even suspend me, unless I'm charged with a felony."

"There you go," I said. "But why in the world would the governor get himself involved in this case, much less ask you to remove yourself? Did he call you himself?"

"No. His chief of staff, Fulton Hancock, called. He said he was conveying the message from the governor."

"What did you tell him?" I asked.

"I told him to go piss up a rope."

I laughed. "I'm not surprised."

"There may be more crap coming down," the judge said. "Hancock said he could have me charged with a felony by the end of the day."

I was shocked. I'd never heard of this kind of pressure being put on a judge. I didn't have a high opinion of our governor, but I thought he was too smart to be involved in something as shady as trying to intimidate a judge. "What felony?" I asked.

"Something they make up, I guess. All they need is a corrupt state attorney somewhere in Florida, and they can have a felony charge. It doesn't have to stick or even be believable, but I'll be gone with a stroke of the governor's pen."

"So what are you going to do?" I asked.

"I'm going to finish trying this case and then I'm going to figure out how to fry the governor."

"He may not be involved," I said.

"I've thought of that. But I want to see how far up it goes."

"The chief of staff's position doesn't leave anybody above him but the governor."

"I know. Do either of you have any thoughts on this?"

"Hang tough," I said.

Swann spoke up for the first time since we'd walked into chambers. "It occurs to me, Your Honor, that you may think I am in some way involved in this. I assure you I am not."

"Mr. Swann, if I thought you were involved, you'd be sitting in a jail cell."

A brief smile crossed Swann's face. "I appreciate your confidence, Your Honor."

CHAPTER FIFTY-ONE

It had always been my practice to steer clear of my clients during lunch breaks. I needed the time to think, to plot the rest of the day away from the legitimate questions that clients always wanted answered. The fact that Bill and Abby were friends didn't change my habit. I'd explained this to them before the trial started, and they said they understood. I hoped they did.

On this day, I was meeting with Jock and taking J.D. with me. The night before, I had asked Jock to dig up some bank records on Wes Lucas and Mark Erickson, records that my investigator Gus Grantham wasn't able to find. Gus said the bank's security was so tight that he had no chance of breaking through. For Jock's agency, bank security was child's play.

We met in a restaurant two miles from the courthouse, far enough away that we didn't have to worry about running into any of my jurors. Jock pulled a handful of documents from a slender briefcase and handed me two small bundles of clipped-together pages. "These are the bank accounts of both Erickson and Lucas. I think you'll find them interesting. But, I've got something you're going to find even more exciting."

"What?"

"I think Favereaux is lying to us."

"Uh, oh. Why?"

"I spent some time with him this morning. There's something off about him. I can't quite put my finger on it, but I've developed a pretty good bullshit meter over the years, and it's tipping into the red with this guy. I think he's more interested in finding out who killed his daughter than he is in helping Abby. He seems to think you're the key to finding the murderer."

"I have no idea who killed Linda," I said.

"I think he knows who shot her. What he wants to find out is who ordered her killed."

"What gives you that idea?" J.D. asked.

"I asked Dave Kendall, my boss, to call the director of Homeland Security and find out if he had any information about a mole in his organization that would make it dangerous for Favereaux to come out of hiding. After he checked into it, the Homeland director called Dave back and told him that he didn't think Favereaux was in any danger, but they were looking into the possibility that there was somebody in his organization feeding the bad guys information on agents. The director's people think the cartels have figured out that Favereaux and Linda are undercover agents from one or another of the federal agencies and that there is a price on Jim Favereaux's head. The director is not happy that Favereaux went off the grid, and they want him in custody. Homeland Security's custody."

"This whole thing is odd," I said. "Who's playing who here?"

"I don't know what game any of them are playing," Jock said, "but I decided to look a little more deeply into Mr. Favereaux. These are his bank records."

I thumbed through them quickly. "Bahamian and Cayman banks?" I asked.

"Look at the numbers, podna," Jock said. "They're kind of staggering."

The accounts had grown into almost a hundred million dollars. The cash had been coming into the accounts for years, a steady run of large deposits and withdrawals from the Cayman bank and deposits into the Bahamian bank. "This is a lot of money," I said.

"No kidding," Jock said. "It looks like some money laundering going on."

"So, Favereaux's dirty," J.D. said.

"Looks that way," Jock said.

"I'll be damned," I said. "Did you leave him at J.D.'s?"

"No. I was afraid he'd figure out that I was on to him. Logan came and got him. They're at his condo doing whatever two old men do when they have nothing to do. They're probably watching TV. "

"I'm going to need him to testify," I said.

"What about the money in those bank accounts?" J.D. asked.

"That shouldn't come up," I said. "I'm sure Swann doesn't know anything about it. I'll have to keep Favereaux from testifying to anything that might be untrue, but I think there's enough important testimony there without crossing any lines."

"I hope you're right," she said.

"Jock, call Logan and tell him to bring Favereaux downtown and drop him at the courthouse. I don't think I'll need him this afternoon, but I don't want him to slip away. I never know what's going to happen to the schedule I've outlined, so if for some reason we finish early with Lucas, I'll need another witness."

"I'll take care of it."

"Jock," I said, "I've got one more little chore for you. There's a guy named Fulton Hancock who is the governor's chief of staff. He was a state senator from Tampa for a number of years, but got to the point where he couldn't run again because of term limits. When his time in the senate was up, he took the job with the governor. He's one of the most powerful people in Tallahassee." I told him about the judge's phone call. "I'd like to know what's going on, and whether Hancock is doing this on his own or if somebody else, maybe the governor himself, is involved. I'm thinking the money trail is probably the answer. If there is a money trail."

"There's always a money trail," Jock said. "I'll get the agency geeks on it. I'll have something for you tonight."

I looked at my watch. "Time to get back to the courthouse."

* * *

We were back in the courtroom, ready to proceed. The jury would be brought in as soon as the judge was on the bench. At precisely one-thirty, the judge's assistant entered the courtroom and informed us that the judge had been inadvertently detained. He could be another thirty minutes and asked us to be ready to start at two.

I sat with J.D. on a bench in the corridor just outside the door to the judge's chambers. I had told her at lunch about the judge's contact with the governor's chief of staff, and had cautioned her that she had to keep it to herself. In my years of practice, I'd never seen an effort by anyone in the executive branch to intimidate a judge. Maybe it happened on occasion, and maybe it worked sometimes, but it would be disastrous for a judge to be seen caving to that kind of pressure. The Judicial Qualifications Commission, which was an arm of the Florida Supreme Court, would remove him from the bench and the Florida Bar would most likely disbar him. He would never sit again as a judge and would probably never practice law. The penalties for that kind of judicial malfeasance are onerous, and the Supreme Court is merciless in imposing them.

We'd been sitting there for about twenty minutes when the door to the judge's chambers opened and Harry Robson walked out. "What brings you here?" I asked.

"Sorry, Matt," he said, "can't talk about it."

"I don't suppose this has anything to do with the governor's chief of staff," I said.

Harry looked surprise. "It might."

"The judge filled Swann and me in this morning."

"Then you probably know everything I know."

"What's your part in this?" I asked.

"I don't know, yet. The judge is pissed and wants to make sure that something gets done about this without interrupting your trial. My chief, the sheriff, and our state attorney are still in there."

"What's the issue?" I asked.

"Judge Thomas is convinced that a crime occurred when the chief of staff called him, but the question is whether the crime occurred here or in Tallahassee. The judge thinks either county would have jurisdiction, but he doesn't know whom he can trust in Tallahassee. He's known Jack Dobbyn for years and apparently thinks he's the best state attorney in Florida. Jack told him he could trust the rest of us."

The door to chambers opened again and a man I didn't know walked out, nodded at Harry, and went toward the elevator. "Who was that?" I asked.

"Jack Connor. He's a reporter for the *Tampa Bay Times*. I guess he and Thomas go way back, and the judge wanted a public record of this. Connor agreed to hold the story until your trial is over."

"This isn't going to help the governor's reelection chances," J.D. said. "A ton of trouble from the governor's office is going to fall on the judge as soon as this hits the papers."

"Thomas isn't worried about that," Robson said. "He's got a big pair on him. Doesn't have any fear of the consequences. He's not a guy I'd want to screw with."

"I agree," I said.

"J.D.," Harry said, "we have some work to do. You got a minute to talk?"

"What's up?" I asked.

J.D. smiled. "Police business. Can't talk about it." They disappeared into one of the witness rooms, and I perused my notes. After a few minutes, I knocked on the witness room door, stuck my head in and asked J.D. if I could talk to her for a minute. She came into the corridor.

"Call Robin Hartill," I said. "Tell her you're the most anonymous source she's ever had or ever will have and tell her she has to sit on the story until the trial is over. Tell her everything I've told you and tell her she should get down here no later than three o'clock to see Wes Lucas on the stand. Let her know there'll be more revelations as soon as the trial is over. And tell her she owes me. Big time."

"What's your plan?"

"We should finish the trial by tomorrow afternoon. The *Tampa Bay Times* is going to break the story, maybe on Sunday to get the most impact, but maybe as soon as the trial is over. Robin can break the story in the online version of the *Observer* before anybody else has it. She's been the most objective reporter on Abby's story. She deserves to be out front on this one."

"Didn't you tell the judge you'd keep this confidential?"

"Yes, but he's the one who called in the press."

The door to the judge's chambers opened and the Sarasota police chief, the Sarasota County sheriff, and the state attorney walked out. J.D. went back to the witness room, and Jack Dobbyn stopped to say hello. "I understand you're in the loop on this mess with the governor's office."

"I am."

"Matt, I've got a feeling that there's a lot more to this trial than the guilt or innocence of Abby Lester."

"There is, Jack. A lot of stuff is going to start rolling out this afternoon. You might want to have one of your people sit in."

"Bad?"

"It's real bad. A lot worse than I would have thought. It involves the feds and, obviously, Tallahassee."

"Can you link it all up?"

"I think so. I'm going to start this afternoon."

"I think I'll stick around myself. It'll get me out of the office for a change."

The court deputy stuck his head out of the courtroom and told us that the judge was ready to reconvene.

CHAPTER FIFTY-TWO

The jury was brought back in and the judge apologized to them for the delay, telling them that sometimes court business that he had to attend to intervened. He knew they'd been stuck in the jury room while they waited and assured them that he would take the afternoon recess as planned.

It was a little after two o'clock. The judge would take the fifteen-minute recess at about three. I was trying to time my witnesses so that I could end the day with a blockbuster. I didn't want to let the day wind up as I was finishing my direct examination of Agent Wes Lucas. That would give Swann the evening to prepare his cross-examination. I needed enough time to examine Lucas and have room left on the clock so that Swann would have to cross-examine before the evening break.

Every trial acquires its own rhythm as the first days wear on, so that soon enough all the actors are in tune. But the lawyers always engage in a balancing act based on informed guesses as they try to line up the witnesses to fit the time frames set by the pace of the trial. It's all part of the strategy, and it's often concocted on the run. Sometimes a witness takes longer than expected, the recesses last more than the allotted time, or the judge has to tend to some sort of emergency matter not connected to the trial.

The goal of the lawyer is to call his witnesses in an order that makes some sort of chronological sense, but also in a way that a witness's testimony will have the most impact on the jury. That's why I wanted Lucas to end the day on the witness stand. I thought I would be able to do a lot of damage to him, and I thought most of the evidence I would evince would be a surprise to Swann. I didn't want him to have time in the evening to go over the testimony with Lucas, and be fresh to start the next morning. Surprise is a powerful weapon in a trial. And so is timing.

I planned to call Lucas as an adverse witness, which meant that I could ask leading questions, something I normally couldn't do with a witness I put on the stand. Since he was the lead investigator and therefore an integral part of the prosecution's team, I didn't think there would be a problem with the judge giving me that leeway.

I needed to kill some time. If I could get a couple of short witnesses on the stand in the next thirty minutes or so, it would take the clock to near a quarter of three. At that point, I'd tell the judge that my next witness would take the rest of the day and this might be a good time for the afternoon break. If the judge would call the fifteen-minute recess, I could start my destruction of Lucas at three. By the time I finished, Swann completed his cross, and I did my rebuttal, if any, it would be time to quit for the day. The jury would leave the courtroom with the image of Lucas' earlier testimony lying in virtual tatters on the floor of the pit. They'd have the whole evening to think about it and cogitate on the weakness of the state's case. And on the next morning, I'd slap them in the face with the evidence pointing to the real killer.

"Call your next witness, Mr. Royal," the judge said.

"The defense calls Mr. Dan Kennedy," I said.

A distinguished looking man walked into the courtroom. He took the stand and was sworn by the deputy clerk.

"State your name, please," I said.

"Dan Kennedy."

"Objection," said Swann, right on cue. "Mr. Kennedy isn't on the witness list."

"I'm calling Mr. Kennedy for purposes of impeaching Mr. Swann's witness, Victoria Madison."

"Overruled," the judge said.

"Your occupation?" I asked the witness.

"I'm the principal of Sarasota High School."

"Was Mrs. Abby Lester employed by you?"

"She was a teacher in my school for many years, and hopefully will be back soon."

"In what capacity was she employed?"

"She taught history."

"Do you, as principal of Sarasota High School, keep attendance records of your teachers?"

"They're kept under my supervision."

"Have you reviewed the attendance records concerning Abby Lester at my request for the months of February and March of this year?"

"Yes, sir."

"Was there any time during those two months that Mrs. Lester was absent from school?"

"She was not."

"Not even for a short period of time during the mornings?" I asked.

"No. Abby had classes from eight o'clock in the morning right straight through until lunch at half past noon. If she had missed even one of those classes, I would have been notified and there would have been a record of it."

"I have nothing further, Your Honor."

Swann had no questions, which was a smart move. He wouldn't be able to get anywhere with the principal, and Swann probably understood that Kennedy's testimony was just another nail in Tori Madison's coffin. She was already dead as a result of the hip scar debacle. But she had also testified that she'd seen Abby at Bannister's condo on several occasions in the middle of the morning, but never on the weekend or in the evening. I'd hammer these points during my closing argument. Abby had been in school. She couldn't have been at Bannister's condo at the times Tori said she was.

I glanced at the gallery as I made my way to my seat. J.D. was there, sitting beside Sarasota detective Harry Robson. A joint task force, I thought. If I did my job right, the two of them would be making arrests before we left the courtroom for the day.

CHAPTER FIFTY-THREE

When Kennedy left the stand, Judge Thomas told me to call my next witness. It was a quarter to three and I told the judge my next witness would take up the rest of the day. I asked if he might want to take the afternoon recess now rather than break up the testimony. He agreed and the jury went out.

Swann came over to my table. "Who are you calling next?" he asked.

"Your buddy Lucas."

"He's not my buddy. He's the lead detective on this case."

"Okay."

"I don't see how you're going to take up two hours with him. He's already testified once."

"Yes, but there's a lot he knows that he hasn't told us. I plan to peel him apart, layer by layer, right down to his lying core. When I'm finished, the jury is going to laugh both you and him out of the courtroom."

"Bullshit," Swann said, and walked away.

I knew, of course, that Swann would tell Lucas what I'd said. I didn't think it would concern Lucas a great deal, but it might just make him a little wary, more determined to keep hidden the information I wanted to pull out of him. That kind of defensiveness would become evident to the jury, and the longer it went on, the more likely Lucas was to make a mistake and let the jury and me inside his snake-filled head. As I said, a trial is, in part, a head game.

* * *

Agent Wesley Lucas took the stand, smiled at the jury, smiled at the judge, smiled at Swann, and completely ignored me. I think he was trying to hurt my feelings. The judge reminded him that he was still under oath. Lucas nodded and smiled some more.

"Good afternoon, Agent Lucas," I said.

He looked at the jury, smiled some more, and said, "Good afternoon, Counselor."

"How long have you been in the drug business, Agent Lucas?"

"Do you mean how long have I been apprehending drug dealers?"

"No, Agent Lucas. I mean how long have you been the button man for Mark Erickson?"

"Objection." Swann was on his feet. "Mr. Royal is trying to impugn the integrity of a decorated police officer."

"I certainly am, Your Honor," I said, "and I didn't hear any grounds for the objection, so I can't adequately respond to it."

"Your grounds, Mr. Swann?" the judge asked.

Swann was stumped. "Improper impeachment," he said, finally, a completely useless objection.

"Overruled."

That question shocked Lucas. I saw it in his eyes, a tightening around the corners. A slight flush crept up his neck. For a split second, I saw it in his face, the killer wanting to take me out. The whole thing didn't take a second. If I hadn't been looking for it, I would have missed it. I wondered if any of the jurors had picked up on it. Lucas was good. He was a man in control of his emotions and his expressions. He favored me with a quick smile. "I don't know what you're talking about."

"A button man," I said, "is a hired gun, a man who kills for money. A man like you. Or your buddy, Kent Walker."

A stunned look momentarily clouded Lucas' face. He was surprised by my use of Walker's name. He thought Walker was an unknown heart attack victim on Longboat Key. He had to be wondering what I knew about Walker, but he was quick, and the stunned expression was fleeting. "I know what a button man is, Counselor, and I don't know anybody named Kent Walker."

"What about Mark Erickson? Do you deny knowing him, too?"

"Absolutely."

"Who is Stan Strickland?"

"He's the agent in charge of the Tampa office of the Florida Department of Law Enforcement. He's my boss."

"If there was testimony in this court that you met Kent Walker a couple of years ago while you were investigating a drug operation in Sarasota County, would you still deny knowing him?"

Lucas sat quietly, his face still as a statue. I could imagine the wheels turning in his brain. His boss at FDLE wouldn't know about Walker, because Lucas had never turned in any reports on that case. Walker couldn't have said anything because he was supposedly dead of a heart attack on Longboat Key. But even though he, Lucas, would have probably seen the sketch of Walker in the paper that morning, he would be aware that there was at least a remote chance that Walker had talked to somebody before he died.

Lucas made his decision. "I would deny it," he said, finally.

"And you don't know a drug dealer named Mark Erickson?"

"Never heard of him."

"Objection, Your Honor," Swann said. "Counsel is on a fishing expedition."

"To the contrary, Your Honor. I'll prove that Agent Lucas is not being truthful with us on each one of these issues."

"Overruled. Proceed, Mr. Royal."

"Why were you in Sarasota on April first of this year, the morning you were called in to investigate the murder of Nate Bannister?"

"I don't remember what I was working on. That was several months ago."

"You weren't actually here on a case, were you?"

"My recollection is that I was here on a case."

"You testified yesterday that you might have been here on personal business. Are you changing you testimony now?"

"No. What I meant was that my best recollection is that I was here on a case, but I might be mistaken. I might have been here on personal business."

"But you don't have any recollection of what that personal business might have been."

"That's correct."

"When you testified yesterday, you were pretty adamant that your boss, Stan Strickland, called you about this case. Have you reconsidered that testimony?"

"No, sir."

"So as you sit here today, under oath, your testimony is that you didn't call your boss and ask him to assign you to the Bannister case?"

"Yes. I'm sure that Agent Strickland called me."

"Let me show you some documents." I walked to Swann's table and dropped a copy and went on to the witness stand and laid a copy in front of Lucas.

"Where did you get these?" Lucas asked, his temper rising.

Swann was on his feet, objecting. "I haven't seen these documents, Your Honor, and they're not on the exhibit list."

"Impeachment," I said.

I hadn't gone through the normal process of getting the records. That would have involved subpoenas and notice to Swann of what I was after. Jock worked his magic and retrieved the records with little effort and, of course, no subpoena. If the judge asked about how I got them, I would plead the work-product privilege, which probably wouldn't go very far with this judge, but I was hoping Swann wouldn't take time to think through the question of where the records came from. Maybe every one would assume they came from the agent in charge of the Tampa office of FDLE.

After I had telegraphed my approach regarding the records when I cross-examined Lucas the day before, I would have thought he might have been a little less confident when I broached the subject again. I was pretty sure that he and Swann had discussed this and came to the conclusion that since I had not subpoenaed the records, which would have required notice to Swann, that I had been bluffing when I asked Lucas about what the phone records would show.

"Approach the bench," the judge said. When Swann and I got there, the judge said, "What are these, Mr. Royal?"

"Telephone records from the phone company that provides service for state agencies," I said, "including the records of all calls between Agents Lucas and Strickland on the morning of April first of this year."

"Your objection, Mr. Swann?"

"They're not on the list. I've never seen these before."

"Mr. Royal," the judge said, "are you using these for impeachment purposes?"

"Yes, sir."

"Your objection is overruled, Mr. Swann."

"But, Your Honor," Swann began.

"Sit down, Mr. Swann." The judge's voice was icy. Swann got the hint and went back to his seat. I went back to the witness stand and handed Lucas the documents.

"Repeat your question, Mr. Royal," the judge said, "and you may answer, Agent Lucas."

"Do you recognize these documents?"

Lucas had calmed himself. He looked at the documents. "They appear to be the record of phone calls."

"Do you see any phone numbers that you recognize on the records?"

"Yes. These appear to be my cell phone records."

"Do you see where you made a call at eight-fifteen the morning of April first?"

"Yes."

"To whom was that call made?"

"My boss, Agent Strickland."

"To his cell phone?"

"Yes, sir."

"Was that call the only one you made to your boss that morning?"

Lucas looked closely at the document. "It would appear so."

"Look at the second page of the documents and tell me what that is, please."

"That would appear to be the record of Agent Strickland's cell phone."

"Do you see the incoming call from your phone?"

"Yes."

"Same time as your record shows you made the call?"

"Yes."

"Are there any other calls between your cell and Agent Strickland's on the morning of April first?"

"No."

"Look at page three, please, and tell me what that is."

"That would appear to be a record of calls from and to the FDLE office in Tampa."

"Do you see any incoming calls from your cell phone on the morning of April first?"

"No, sir."

"Do you see any calls from the agency office to your cell phone on that morning?"

"No, sir."

"Are you aware that Detective Harry Robson of the Sarasota Police Department testified here that he arrived at the scene of the crime at eight-twenty that morning?"

"Yes."

"Do you remember that you testified here in this courtroom that you were first called by Agent Strickland at about ten in the morning of April first?"

"Yes."

"Then how do you reconcile that testimony with the phone records that clearly show the only call between you and Agent

Strickland on that morning was the one made at eight-fifteen by you to Agent Strickland?"

"I don't remember what that call was about, but he called me again at ten o'clock about this case."

"And on what phone would you have received the call?"

"Probably my other cell phone. I carry two, the one supplied by the office and my own personal phone."

"Did you own any other phones that day, April first?"

"No."

"Do you still have that personal phone?"

"No. I lost it a couple of months ago."

"How long did you own it?"

"Two or three years."

"Was that the only phone you had possession of on April first, other than the one issued by FDLE?"

"Yes."

"You're sure you didn't have another phone that day, perhaps one you borrowed, or one of those prepaid phones they call burners?"

"We're not allowed to carry burners, and I've never borrowed a phone from anybody in my life."

"Do you remember the number on that phone? The one you lost?"

"I'm sorry, but I don't."

"Would the number have been 813-555-3833?"

That caused a reaction, but again it was slight. I'd rattled him, but he was still stoic, his expressions subtle. "Yes, I think so."

I handed him another document. "Can you identify this document?"

He looked at it. "The phone records for my private cell."

"Do you see a call on there for the morning of April first, either an incoming to you from Agent Strickland or the FDLE office in Tampa?"

"No."

"And do you see any calls from you to either of those numbers on the morning of April first?"

"No."

"So, would it be fair to say that you did not get an assignment from Agent Strickland at mid-morning on April first?"

"I don't remember."

"Then would it be correct to say that you called Agent Strickland at eight-fifteen on April first, some five minutes before Detective Robson even got to the scene of the murder?"

"I don't remember."

When the witness starts to fall back on a lack of memory, the lawyer is winning. Juries don't like that kind of answer, particularly when the lawyer has just proved with irrefutable evidence, the written documents, that what the witness had so confidently testified to couldn't possibly be true.

Time to switch gears. "Had you ever been in Mr. Bannister's condo prior to the first time you went there as part of your investigation?"

"No, sir."

"Had you ever met Abby Lanton before you arrived here?"

"No."

"Do you know who Linda Favereaux is?"

"Only what I've heard. She was a woman who was murdered on Longboat Key at about the same time that Mr. Bannister was killed."

"Did you know that Mrs. Favereaux and Mr. Bannister had sex just before Bannister was killed?"

"No."

"Did you ever meet Mrs. Favercaux?"

"No."

"Had you ever heard of her prior to your involvement in this case?"

"No."

"Would you be surprised if I told you she was an undercover agent of the Department of Homeland Security, and was investigating Mr. Bannister for his part in local drug dealing?"

"I don't know how I'd be surprised if I'd never heard of her."

"As a matter of fact, Agent Lucas, you saw Linda Favereaux at Mr. Bannister's condo on the night he died, didn't you?"

A shadow crossed Lucas' face, a momentary breach in the cool exterior he'd maintained since I'd first met him. It was a look of fear, not unlike that of a small animal cornered by the big predator. Lucas was glimpsing his own doom. He didn't know what I could prove, but he knew I was closing in on him. He was rattled, and I expected him to deny that he'd been in Bannister's condo on the night of the murder. But he surprised me. He dropped the bomb, the one that would repudiate every thing he'd testified to, every shred of evidence he'd given in this case. He said, "I will invoke my rights under the Fifth Amendment to the United States Constitution and refuse to answer that question, Counselor."

There was dead silence in the courtroom. I stood at the podium, stunned by this turn of events. It was one of those things that often happen in trials; the unexpected turn that throws the lawyer's plans into turmoil.

I looked up at the judge, who seemed to be moving in slow motion as he leaned toward the witness stand. The rustle of shuffling papers at the prosecutor's table broke the silence, a juror coughed, a chair squeaked. The judge said, "Agent Lucas, are you seeking the protection of the Fifth Amendment to the United States Constitution against giving testimony that might incriminate you?"

"Yes, Your Honor."

"Okay," the judge said, "I'll instruct the jury." He told the jury that every witness had the right under the United States Constitution not to incriminate himself and that he could not be compelled to testify if the testimony tended to do so. The jury was not to read anything into the witness's assertion of his constitutional rights.

Good luck on that one, I thought. The second that Lucas invoked his right, every man and woman on that jury knew he was guilty of something, if not murder, and anything he'd testified to was immediately rejected.

"Agent Lucas," I said, "did you kill Nate Bannister?"

"I'll take the Fifth," he said.

"Did you manufacture the emails that were purportedly sent by Abby Lester to Mr. Bannister?"

"No."

"Do you know who did?"

He sat for a moment, mulling over the question. "I'm going to have to take the Fifth on that one, too."

"Did you kill Linda Favereaux?"

"I'll take the Fifth."

Lucas had made the calculation that by taking the Fifth he would perhaps appear guilty to this jury, but since he didn't know what evidence there was that would prove him a murderer, he would be protecting himself. The very fact that I was asking such questions would lead him to believe that there was some evidence of his guilt, but he had no way of knowing how strong that evidence was. He was probably assuming that he would be charged, but if the evidence against him could be picked apart by a smart lawyer, he could at least plea bargain to something that wouldn't include a life sentence in prison. By invoking the Fifth, he was not testifying to something that could be used against him in his own trial. The jury in that trial would never know that he'd hidden behind the Constitution in this trial.

I looked at my watch. Four o'clock. Lucas had disrupted my plan with his unexpected invocation of the Fifth Amendment. Under the circumstances, I didn't think Swann would cross-examine Lucas. I had one more major witness to call, and I'd be done. I thought I had time before the evening recess.

"Under the circumstances, Your Honor," I said, "I have no further questions."

Swann looked a little dazed as he slowly rose from his chair. He had just seen his case implode. Every lawyer who has tried enough cases has had that terrible moment when he realizes that his carefully constructed case has taken a fatal turn and he has lost the jury. It usually happens when an important witness you had counted on, or sometimes your own client, dissolves on the stand, his testimony falling apart under cross-examination that shows him to be a liar. It had happened to me once, and I knew the feeling, a combination of despair and cold anger directed at the witness stand and the person who had so completely destroyed his own case by lying under oath. I almost felt sorry for Swann.

"I have nothing," Swann said.

"May we approach the bench, Your Honor?" I asked.

He motioned us forward. "What's up, Mr. Royal?"

"Your Honor, there are two detectives in the courtroom who would like to arrest Agent Lucas. I would suggest that it might be appropriate to send the jury out so that the arrest can be accomplished outside their presence."

The judge nodded and told the jury that we would take a short recess and he would bring them right back in so that we could finish the day on time. The jury went out, and Detective Harry Robson came forward and arrested Lucas. Harry read him the Miranda rights regarding his right to remain silent and to have an attorney. Lucas nodded, his face a picture of infinite sadness. I was looking at a man whose life was over. Whatever crimes he'd committed, whatever base impulses had driven him to the dark side of a society that can only exist because the rule of law shines a bright light into its dark corners, he was still a human being, and as loathsome as he was, I couldn't help but feel pity for him.

* * *

The jury trooped back in. "Call your next witness, Mr. Royal," the judge said.

"State your name, please."

"James Favereaux."

"Where do you reside?"

"Gulf of Mexico Drive, Longboat Key, Florida."

"Your occupation?"

"I'm employed by the United States Department of Homeland Security."

"In what capacity?"

"I'm a special agent in the investigative division of DHS."

"Do you work undercover?"

"Yes."

"How long have you been doing that kind of work?"

"About thirty years, in one federal agency or another."

"How long have you lived on Longboat Key?"

"Three years, approximately."

"What brought you to the Sarasota area?"

"I was sent here by my agency to infiltrate a large drug operation."

"Did you do that?"

"I was working on it. I thought the man running the operation on this coast was a guy named Mark Erickson. I'd been working on getting closer to him for the past year."

"What kind of work did Mr. Erickson do? Other than drugs."

"He's a professor at the University of South Florida."

"Tell me about your relationship with him?"

"It wasn't much. My wife Linda and I would take Erickson and his wife Julie to dinner occasionally, and I donated a million dollars to the university to endow a chair that the Ericksons hold jointly. They're both tenured professors in the same department at USF."

"Where did that money come from?"

"It was essentially drug money that had been forfeited to the Department of Homeland Security from other operations I'd handled over the years. It was decided at the top levels of DHS that if we gave the money to the university, it would be a good use for it and at the same time, it would put me in good with Erickson. It would also show him that I had the wherewithal to be a big money player in the drug business."

"Did you have another agent working with you?"

"Yes. My daughter."

"Was that Linda Favereaux?"

"Yes."

"You just called her your wife."

"Yes. That was part of a subterfuge that we used as we worked undercover drug operations."

"She was posing as your wife?"

"Yes."

"Why?"

"Years ago, I had to pull her out of a bad situation. At the time I was an undercover agent for the Defense Intelligence Agency. My daughter was an adult by then, but needed my protection from some very bad people, some of whom suspected she was my daughter. It seemed prudent to give her a different identification and then make it appear that I'd married her, so that no one would connect her to the young woman who was my daughter."

"And you've worked together ever since?"

"Yes."

"Was she also an agent of the Department of Homeland Security?"

"Yes. A fully trained agent."

"Was Linda making any progress on the investigation?"

"Yes. She had made contact with the local money man, the guy who was responsible for laundering the funds brought in by the drug cartel. He wasn't the top guy, but she was working up the chain of command. She had found out who the money man reported to and she had begun to accumulate the evidence that would convict them both."

"Were you close to having them indicted?"

"No. We were working our way up. We wanted to find the top people, the ones who ran the whole operation."

"I take it this was a long-term investigation."

"Yes. It could take years."

"Who was the money man?"

"Nate Bannister."

Swann was on his feet, objecting loudly. "Mr. Royal is trying to besmirch the reputation of a dead man."

"Overruled."

"Did you get far enough in your investigation to determine who Bannister reported to?"

"Yes. Mark Erickson."

"The University of South Florida professor?"

"Yes. The information Linda got from Bannister confirmed that Erickson was the man who ran the operation on this coast."

"Until that time, had you been able to confirm your suspicions that Erickson was the kingpin?"

"No."

"Tell me about what was going on with Bannister."

"We'd picked up rumors among the lower level drug folks that Bannister was the money launderer. He was quite the lady's man, and Linda made arrangements for the bartender at the Ritz Carlton to introduce them. Over a couple of months they became friendly, and Bannister invited her to his condo for drinks the evening she died. She felt she was making progress. She had talked around the issue of putting some money into the drug operation. She had led him to believe that she was the disgruntled wife of a rich man who'd made his money in some shady deals. She thought if she could put some money into a drug deal, she could make a lot of money for herself and leave her husband."

"Tell me about the early morning hours of April first of this year. Did you see Linda?"

"Yes. She got home late from Bannister's. She was very upset. She told me that she'd been to Bannister's home for a drink. They had a couple of glasses of wine, and Bannister attempted to seduce her. She put him off, but he became insistent. He'd apparently had a lot to drink before Linda arrived. He was a bit loose-tongued and was beginning to open up to her about his operation. Trying to convince her that he was a big-time guy who could make her rich.

"She finally acquiesced and had sex with him. She didn't want to interrupt the flow of information he was giving her. It was the first time he'd opened up so completely about his part in the drug business and his relationship with Erickson. She wanted him to continue."

He stopped, choking back emotion. I gave him a minute to compose himself.

"Did that bother you, Mr. Favereaux? Your daughter and colleague having sex with Mr. Bannister?"

"No. She had affairs from time to time, and it wasn't the first time she'd had sex with a suspect we were working on some undercover operation. I wasn't bothered by it."

"Did anything else happen that evening, Mr. Favereaux?"

"Yes. After they had sex, Bannister went into the living room to get some more wine. Linda was in the bathroom getting dressed when she heard a gunshot. She rushed into the living room and saw Bannister on the floor with a gunshot to the head. A man was standing over the body. Linda slammed the bedroom door shut and locked it. Mr. Bannister's condo unit was adjacent to the emergency stairwell and he had installed a door from his master bathroom directly into the stairwell. I think it was his escape hatch. Linda left that way."

"Did she get a good look at the killer?"

"Yes."

"Did she recognize him?"

"Yes. She'd met him once when she was with Bannister."

"What was his name?"

"Wes. At least that was the way he'd been introduced to her by Bannister. She never heard a last name."

"Did the name mean anything to you?"

"Not at that time."

"Did Linda tell you what Bannister had to say that evening about his involvement in the drug business and with Mark Erickson?"

"Not a lot. She was going to fill me in and we'd file a full report with my boss in Washington. But before I could do that, I had to meet Mark Erickson in Bradenton."

"What was that all about?"

"Erickson had called me a few minutes before Linda got home that night. He said he needed to meet with me on an urgent matter. He asked me to meet him at a McDonald's on Cortez

Road at midnight. I told him that was an odd hour and place for a meeting, but he assured me that the McDonald's and the midnight hour would provide the anonymity that was crucial."

"Wasn't that a bit odd? Kind of cloak and daggerish?"

"Sure. But I'm in the cloak-and-dagger business. I've met a lot of strange people in a lot of strange places during my career, so I wasn't particularly surprised. He did tell me that he lived north of there on the Manatee River and he thought the McDonald's would be convenient for both of us. He also thought we'd be inconspicuous that late in the evening."

"Did he tell you anything about why he needed to meet with you?"

"Only that a mutual friend, Nate Bannister, had suggested the meeting."

"Didn't that seem a little strange to you since you had never met Bannister?"

"Yes, but then I figured if Bannister had anything to do with it, Erickson wanted to talk about a drug deal. I'd dropped some hints to Erickson, but he'd never followed up. I figured that Linda had told Bannister enough about her husband—me—that he thought I might be interested in putting some money into a drug operation. He talked to Erickson, and now Erickson wanted to meet with me."

"You've testified that you knew Erickson."

"Yes, like I said, we were social acquaintances, and I'd endowed a chair for him at USF. But we'd never talked about drugs, and Erickson had never even touched on the subject. At least not until he brought Bannister's name into the conversation on the night Linda died."

"So, even though Linda had just missed being murdered, you thought you needed to make that meeting?"

"Yes. Even more so after Linda came home and told me that Bannister was dead. Erickson was the only lead we had into the drug cartel. I thought the cartel must have found some reason to kill Bannister, and I was hoping that Erickson could tell me something about why he was killed. I thought I could better protect Linda, and at the same time make progress in moving up the chain of command in the drug cartel."

"So you went to the meeting?"

"Yes. He told me that he needed ten million dollars to finalize the deal he and Bannister had been working on. Something about a condo project over near Lakeland. I told him I would have to meet with him and Bannister to flesh out the details. Erickson told me that Bannister was no longer part of the deal and he was now the sole owner of the project. At first, he was anxious to get the money immediately, but then agreed to meet later in the week to talk in detail about the project and my part in it."

"Did he ever bring up drugs?"

"No, but I was pretty sure that was where we were going since Bannister was part of it. Of course, Erickson had no way of knowing that I knew Bannister was dead or that he was probably laundering money for the drug dealers. At least I don't think he knew. I didn't think he knew that Linda was a witness to the murder."

"How long did the meeting last?"

"Twenty minutes or so."

"Did you leave then?"

"Yes. I got a burger to go and drove back to Longboat."

"What did you find when you got home?"

"I walked into the living room and saw Linda on the floor. A man was standing over her with what appeared to be a tire iron."

"Did you recognize the man?"

"No. I'd never seen him before."

"What did you do?"

"I went after him. He turned and ran out the door toward the beach. I thought I heard Linda moan, so I stopped the chase and went back to her. She was lying facedown, and I turned her over. It was clear to me that she was dead. I left immediately and drove to the Tampa Airport."

"Why did you do that?"

"I was pretty sure we'd been compromised; that the cartel

knew we were federal agents. I couldn't do anything for Linda but I could get away and sort things out. My agency had a protocol for just such an event. I had a fake driver's license that I kept in my wallet, and that would get me on a flight out of Tampa. I called the duty officer in Washington and was told to meet another agent in Atlanta and he would take me to a safe house. That's what I did."

"Why have you come forward now?"

"I saw a picture of Florida Department of Law Enforcement Agent Wesley Lucas in the online version of the *Sarasota Herald-Tribune,* in a story about this trial, and I realized immediately who he was."

"And?"

"He was the man standing over Linda's body, holding a bloody tire iron."

It was almost five o'clock. Time to wrap up the day. My timing hadn't worked as I'd planned, but the last thing the jury would hear before they went home was the testimony that Wes Lucas, not Abby Lester, was the murderer. They would have all night to think about that. Swann would have time to prepare his cross-examination, but I was pretty sure he wouldn't be able to put a dent in Favereaux's story.

"I have nothing further, Your Honor," I said.

"We'll be in recess until nine in the morning," the judge announced. We stood and watched the jury file out. They would have a lot to sleep on that night.

CHAPTER FIFTY-FOUR

J.D. and Detective Harry Robson were in an interview room in the Sarasota police station, sitting across the table from Wes Lucas. It was almost six in the evening. After his arrest in the courtroom, a uniformed patrolman had brought Lucas to the station. The detectives had stayed for the conclusion of the day's testimony, and then arrived at police headquarters to begin the final act of the tragedy that was Wes Lucas.

"Wes," Robson said, "we've known each other for a long time. I wouldn't say we've been friends, but I'd like to think there was a bit of mutual respect between us. You were a good cop. What happened?"

Lucas was wan, his demeanor that of a defeated man. He sighed and smiled ruefully. "Fulton Hancock happened."

"The governor's chief of staff?"

"Yes. He was a state senator back then, and his son, Fulton Hancock, Jr., was my best friend. We'd grown up together, played high school football together, gone off to college at Florida State together. When we graduated, we both came back to Tampa. I hired on with the sheriff's department and Fulton Junior got a real estate license and went to work for one of the established brokerages in Tampa. He made a lot of money and was spending it on cars and women. He had a beautiful condo in one of the high-rises overlooking the bay. I didn't see much of him for about five years.

"I had just made detective when I got a call to a murder scene at a grubby little house over near Plant City. It was apparent that it was some sort of a drug deal gone bad. The place was full of drugs and cash, over a hundred thousand dollars. Three bodies were in the house, all shot through the head. One of them was Fulton Hancock, Jr."

"Was he in the drug business?" J.D. asked.

"In a big way, as it turned out."

"What did you do when you realized that your friend was among the dead?" Harry asked.

"I knew the deputy who was the first on the scene. A neighbor had heard gunshots and called 911. I had just finished a witness interview on another case and was close to the scene of the murder when I heard it on the radio. I told the dispatcher I would respond. I was at the scene within five minutes of the first deputy's arrival.

"As soon as I realized that one of the bodies was Fulton Junior, I called in and told the dispatcher not to send anymore deputies because I didn't want the scene compromised. The crime scene techs were on their way, but I figured I had about a thirty-minute window if I needed to do something to protect the Hancocks. I called Fulton Senior and told him what I'd found. He told me he didn't want to have Fulton Junior's name dragged through the mud and asked if I could get the body out of there before the rest of the investigating team arrived."

"What about the other deputy?" J.D. asked.

"That was a big question mark. I told the senator that it was doable, but it would cost some money. He gave me the go-ahead, and I approached the deputy, explained the situation, and offered him ten thousand dollars. He took the deal."

"What did you do with the body?" Harry asked. "You didn't have much time before the forensics people got there."

Lucas laughed. "That was the slickest part of the whole thing. We just put old Junior in the trunk of my department car. Even if the deputy and I had missed any evidence that there had been another victim, who's going to look for a body in the trunk of the investigating detective's car?"

"What did you do with the body?" J.D. asked.

"After we wrapped up things at the scene, I drove it to the senator's house. He got a doctor friend of his to certify the death was from natural causes and had Junior cremated that evening. Had a big memorial service two days later, and the senator was inundated with sympathy calls from the high and mighty."

"What about the deputy?" J.D. asked. "How did they keep him quiet?"

"The deputy was killed in his home that same night by an intruder who ransacked the place and stole everything not nailed down. It was chalked up to a random robbery."

"But it wasn't," Harry said.

"No, it wasn't. The senator and I had a heart to heart over the coincidence that the deputy was murdered on the same day that he found the bodies. Fulton told me that Junior had been working for him, that they were involved in the drug business in a big way and that my future would be either very bright or there'd be no future at all. He needed a man inside law enforcement, and I would fit right in. I didn't see that I had much choice, so I agreed to work with the Hancock group. Within a couple of days, I was offered the job with the Florida Department of Law Enforcement, and here I am."

"Did you kill Bannister?" Harry asked.

Lucas sat quietly for a moment or two, staring into the distance. J.D. could almost hear the wheels turning in his brain. A single tear slid out of his right eye. He swiped at it with the heel of his hand. "I'm not going to get out of this, am I, Harry?"

"Afraid not. But a confession will take the death penalty off the table."

"Yes. I killed him." Lucas had made his decision.

"Why?"

"I don't know. I was just told to do it."

"Told by whom?"

"Mark Erickson."

"The professor."

"Yes."

"You didn't ask for a reason?"

"No. This wasn't the first time I'd taken somebody out. All of the others were low-level drug dealers. Bannister was pretty high up in the organization, so it was a little different."

"How so?"

"I don't know. I was told to use a particular gun that was provided to me. I was supposed to drop it into the bay from the Ringling Bridge as soon as I'd used it. I was to wear gloves and make sure not to leave any evidence that I'd been in Bannister's condo. It sounded as if the people in the Hancock group were trying to hide their involvement in the killing. Not so much from the law, I mean, but from somebody else. Maybe other members of the group. I never found out, but it did seem like they were being more careful than usual. I'm just guessing now. Maybe I'm wrong."

"Did you follow instructions?"

"I did exactly as I was told. But there was a hitch."

"Linda Favereaux," J.D. said.

"Yes. I thought Bannister was alone, but about the time I popped him, Linda came out of the bedroom."

"You knew her?" J.D. asked.

"I'd met her once, so I knew who she was. Bannister had told me she might be the key to getting some more money into whatever he was working on with Hancock. I knew where she lived and that her husband was an older guy with lots of money."

"Why didn't you kill Linda at Bannister's place?"

"I was following very explicit orders about the hit on Bannister. They didn't include going after a witness. I got out of the place and called Erickson. He told me to go to her home and take care of her, but be sure not to use the gun. He said he'd get Linda's husband out of the house. They knew each other and were already working on a money deal. So, that's what I did."

"How did you kill her?" J.D. asked.

"With a tire iron from the trunk of my car. I went into the house by the front door and saw her in an area next to the hot tub on the patio. She was naked and had her back to me. I hid behind a drape beside the sliding glass doors that opened to the patio. She walked into the room, and I hit her on the back of her head with the tire iron. She never saw it coming. I was bending over to check for a pulse when the front door opened and a man walked in. I ran out the patio door and up the beach."

"Why run?" asked J.D. "Why not kill the witness?"

"As I said, it was a tight plan. Nobody said anything about killing the husband, and I assumed that's who he was. And if he and Erickson were working on some kind of deal, I didn't want to be the one to screw it up by killing the man."

"You were having a bad night," J.D. said. "Two murders, and both of them witnessed."

"Yeah, but I wasn't too worried about the one at the house. The husband had no idea who I was, and I didn't see any way for him to connect the two deaths. On the other hand, Linda knew who I was. She had to go."

"Do you have any other questions, J.D.?" Harry asked.

"Just one. Did you try to kill Robert Shorter, Agent Lucas?"

"Yes. I didn't do a very good job of it, I'm afraid."

"Why kill Shorter?"

"I don't know, Detective. Tori Madison called and told me Erickson wanted it done."

"Why didn't you try the kill again?"

"Shorter disappeared. I couldn't find him."

"I'm out of questions," J.D. said.

"Okay, Wes," Harry said. "Sit tight. I might have some more questions after we talk to Erickson. I'll have some dinner brought in for you. We shouldn't be too long."

"You've got Erickson?" Lucas asked.

"Yeah. He was arrested right after the court recessed for the day."

"Be careful, Harry," Lucas said. "That's one cold son of a bitch. I don't think he has a soul."

"Everybody has a weak spot, Wes. All I have to do is find his."

"I think it's his wife," Lucas said. "I'm pretty sure she doesn't know anything about his drug business and he's very protective of her."

"What's that all about?" J.D. asked as she and Harry walked to another interview room. "Why is Lucas suddenly so helpful?"

"Remorse?" Harry said. "A hope that we might give him something in return for his help? Who knows?"

"He's been in the system long enough to know that we can't do much to help him. I think Jack Dobbyn will forget the death penalty in return for a confession, but Lucas is looking at life without parole."

"Yeah. What do you think?"

"I think," J.D. said, "that Lucas sounds like a dead man singing at his own funeral."

CHAPTER FIFTY-FIVE

I was tired, the fatigue consuming my body, straining my every movement, bringing a sluggishness to my overworked brain, reminding me of why I had happily given up the life of a trial lawyer. It isn't the physical effort that the lawyer puts into a trial that drains him. It's the mental strain, the necessity of listening intently to every word said during the proceedings, the constant battle of wits with opposing counsel, and the whispers of the little bastard sitting on his shoulder telling him he's not doing enough, not prepared enough, not good enough to keep from losing an innocent client to prison, that sucks every last joule of energy from his system and leaves him feeling like a limp rag.

After court adjourned, I spoke for a minute with J.D. and Harry Robson. They were going to the Sarasota police station to interview Lucas and Erickson. "I may need to put Erickson on the stand tomorrow," I said.

"Don't you think you've got enough to prove that Abby didn't kill Bannister?" asked J.D. "What else can you need after the testimony you got from Lucas and Favereaux?"

"Nothing, probably, but I want to keep my options open in case Swann comes up with something unexpected."

J.D. smiled. "You've got this one in the bag. Take the night off and relax. I'll come by when we're finished. If Erickson has anything to say that'll help your case, I'll let you know." She kissed me on the cheek and left with Harry Robson.

I spent some time in a witness room with Abby and Bill Lester. They were both excited about the turn the case had taken, convinced that the jury would return a verdict of acquittal. I cautioned them not to get their hopes too high, that Abby would take the stand first thing the next morning, and we had to contend with Swann's cross-examination of her. Once we rested our case, Swann could put on a case in rebuttal. We wouldn't know what he might have as evidence until we saw it.

I had left Jim Favereaux sitting on a bench in the hallway. I was going to drive him to Logan Hamilton's condo where he would spend the night. We left the courthouse together and were driving north on Longboat Key when my phone rang. Jock. "Are you on your way back to the island?"

"I just crossed the New Pass Bridge."

"Is Favereaux with you?"

"Yes."

"Bring him to your house."

"Okay." I knew not to question Jock. He never did anything without a reason. "Be there in a few minutes." I hung up.

"What's up?" Favereaux asked.

"Jock wants us to come to my house."

"I thought you were going to drop me off at Logan's."

"I'll take you back later. I think Jock wants us to enjoy one of his big steaks." I was lying, making it up as I went along. "He's got a special seasoning, some sort of old family recipe, that turns really good meat into the best I've ever tasted."

Favereaux seemed to relax a little. "Sounds good," he said. "I'm hungry."

I was thinking that Jock must have come up with something in his research that concerned Favereaux. I couldn't think of any other reason for him to want Favereaux at my house, other than to keep him in sight, not give him a chance to run.

"Matt," Favereaux said, "you need to change your combination lock code."

"What?"

"That little touch pad on your Explorer's front door. The number keys that spell out 'M-A-T-T' is a little obvious, don't you think?"

I laughed. "How did you know that?"

"I used it this afternoon to put this under your front seat after Logan dropped me off at the courthouse. I couldn't very well carry it through security, could I?"

I glanced over at Favereaux. He was holding a small semi-automatic pistol, pointed at me.

"I guess we're not going to my house," I said. "What's up, Jim?"

"Sorry, Matt. I think it's time for me to disappear."

"Is this about the Cayman bank accounts?"

He seemed surprised. "You've been busy."

"Jock has. Is there more?"

"Probably. Jock's a pretty resourceful fellow. Call him and tell him you've got to go back to the courthouse. You'll be home in an hour or so."

I called using my hands-free system. Favereaux would be able to hear both ends of the conversation. "Jock," I said when he answered, "I just got a quirky call from Judge Thomas. He wants me back in the courthouse right now. I'm just about to the south fire station. I'll turn around and go back. I'll see you in an hour or so."

"Okay, podna. See you when you get here." He broke the connection.

"What's going on, Jim?" I asked.

"We're going to Vandenberg airport. You know it?"

"On Highway 301, east of Tampa."

"That's it. I'll have a plane waiting for me, heading for parts unknown. Well, unknown to anybody but me."

"Jim, you'll have every agency in the government looking for you. What do you think your chances are?"

"Pretty good. I've been working on this escape hatch for a long time. It's foolproof."

"You won't make it."

"Matt, you're a good guy. I don't want to cause you any harm, but you need to understand my position. Here are the ways the odds stack up. There are three things that can happen, three options. One, I could give you this gun and let you take me in; two, you could run off the highway or a bridge with the hope of stopping me; or three, you can take me to the airport. If I give up, you know what the agency will do with me. I'll be dead and you'll be alive. If you run off a bridge, chances are good we'll both be dead. If I survive, Homeland will kill me. You take me to the airport and both of us get out of this alive. You see the odds? I've got only one chance of survival and you have two. So let's do the intelligent thing and drive me to the airport without any dramatics."

"Jim, I don't understand any of this. If you're so concerned about your situation, why did you come out of hiding to help Abby?"

"I didn't. Abby was the beneficiary, I guess, but the real reason I wanted to testify was to nail Lucas and Erickson. It was time for me to implement my plan to disappear, and when I figured out that Lucas was the murderer, I knew I didn't have time to get him myself. I also didn't have a clue as to whom he reported, who was the boss who ordered the murder. As they say, half a loaf is better than none, and if Lucas was the only one I could get to, he would have to do. The only way I could get to him was the trial. It worked out when I got here that you had figured out that Lucas' boss was Erickson. It was just good karma, I guess. Nail Lucas and we'd nail his boss, Erickson."

"Why didn't you just use your new identity to get here? Why the big deal about an escort?"

"I couldn't use that identity. I didn't want it compromised. I'd built that for years, and I needed it for my getaway plan. I couldn't take the chance of somebody figuring it out. And I was truthful about a mole of some sort at Homeland Security. They know all my aliases."

"How do you know that?"

"When I got to the safe house in the Georgia Mountains, three bad guys showed up. I got the drop on them, killed two and wounded one, and got the hell out of there. Somebody knew where I was, somebody other than my agency colleagues. I used another one of the agency aliases to fly from Tampa to Houston, and used a credit card with that alias to check into a hotel. Another bad guy showed up that night. I saw him in the lobby when I left the restaurant after dinner. I recognized him. He was part of a ring I'd busted several years before. He'd been sent to prison. I guess he got out on parole. I went straight out the front door, grabbed a cab, and disappeared. Moved some cash around from the Caymans, lived off the cash, and never left a digital footprint anywhere."

We were traveling north on Gulf of Mexico Drive, approaching the Longboat Pass Bridge, when we came to a line of stopped cars. "Bridge must be up," I said. We stopped and sat for a couple of minutes. A Longboat police cruiser passed us in the southbound lanes, traveling at about thirty miles per hour, never slowing, the officer paying no attention to us. Another five minutes passed. "Must be a bridge malfunction," I said. "That seems to happen a lot."

The passenger door's window blew inward, spewing fragments of glass into the front seats. A hand holding a nine-millimeter Glock pistol came through the opening, the muzzle pressing against the right side of Favereaux's neck. "Drop the gun, podna," Jock said. "I don't want your blood messing up my buddy's car."

Favereaux laid the gun in his lap and raised his hands, a look of resignation on his face. "Hello, Jock," he said. "Good play."

I took the pistol from Favereaux's lap. "There's always a fourth option, Jim."

CHAPTER FIFTY-SIX

"I want a lawyer," Mark Erickson said. "Now."

J.D., Harry Robson, and Homeland Security Agent Devlin Michel were sitting at a table in an interview room at the Sarasota County jail, across from a handcuffed and very irritated Erickson.

"We've got a good case against you, Professor Erickson," J.D. said. "Wes Lucas has told us that you ordered him to kill Bannister and Linda Favereaux and that you're the guy who controls the drug operations along this coast. He also told us you report to the governor's chief of staff, Fulton Hancock. How long do you think it'll take for Hancock to drop the hammer on you?"

"I want a lawyer," Erickson said.

"You can probably make a better deal right now," J.D. said. "A lawyer will complicate things beyond belief, but in the end, you're going down for the murders of Nate Bannister and Linda Favereaux and a lot of drug charges."

"Four little words, Detective. I – want – a – lawyer."

J.D. looked at Michel and shrugged. He smiled. "It doesn't work that way, Mr. Erickson. You don't get a lawyer."

"Bullshit. I know my rights."

"Those rights have gone out the window. You're being charged as a terrorist."

"Bullshit."

"I'm an agent of Homeland Security," Michel said, shoving his credentials case across the table. "Now you're a smart man. Got a PhD. and a tenured professorship and all that stuff. Surely you know that if you don't cooperate, your next stop is Cuba."

"Bullshit. The courts have put a stop to that."

"The courts don't always know what we're doing. We're a security agency, after all."

"Then send me to Cuba. I'm not saying a word."

"Is that what you want me to tell your wife, Julie?"

"Leave her alone. She's not part of this."

"We'll find out about that very shortly," Michel said.

"Where is she? Have you arrested her?"

"She's at a private terminal at Sarasota-Bradenton Airport, waiting for one of our planes. She'll be at Guantánamo Bay in time for breakfast."

"You can't do this."

"It's done, Dr. Erickson," Michel said. "The plane has to come down from D.C., so it'll be a while before Julie leaves. You can stop that by telling us what we need to know. But you don't have a whole lot of time."

They had him. Erickson was the image of defeat. It was like the air had all gone out of him, leaving only a deflated remnant of the man he'd been moments earlier. "Okay," he said, "if I tell you everything I know, what happens?"

Michel looked at Robson. "Can you get Dobbyn in here?"

Harry made a call and a couple of minutes later, the state attorney walked into the room. "I'm John Dobbyn," he said. "People call me Jack. I'm the state attorney for this circuit. As such, it's my prerogative to bring charges for criminal offenses as I see fit. In other words, I have complete discretion to decide what charges my office should bring."

"I want to know what happens if I tell you everything I know," Erickson said.

"If you tell us the absolute truth," Dobbyn said, "leaving nothing out, and agree to testify against everybody in your network, including the top people, the federal government will drop the terrorism charges and turn you over to the state. We'll prosecute you for a number of drug offenses and murder. If you'll cop to the charges and confess, you'll be sentenced to life in prison without possibility of parole, but we'll take the death penalty off the table."

"What about my wife?" Erickson asked.

"You will not be compelled to testify against her, and if we don't find any evidence of her involvement in your crimes, she won't be charged."

"That's it? You'll just let her go?" Erickson asked.

"That's it," Dobbyn said, "but understand, if you don't cooperate completely, if you ever lie, or refuse to tell us truthfully anything we want to know, the deal is off. Your confession will stand, but the death penalty goes back on the table, and your wife will be subject to an investigation by Homeland Security."

Erickson sat quietly, turning it over in his mind. His life had changed irrevocably in a matter of minutes. "I understand. I'll take the deal."

CHAPTER FIFTY-SEVEN

"Detective Brad Corbin is in custody in New Orleans," Jock said. "Homeland Security picked him up this afternoon."

It was almost nine o'clock in the evening. J.D., Jock, Agent Devlin Michel, and I were sitting in my living room eating pizza we'd ordered from Oma's in Bradenton Beach, the little town just over the bridge on Anna Maria Island. I had given my statement to Longboat Key Deputy Chief Martin Sharkey, describing what had happened in my car on the way home from the courthouse. Favereaux was sitting in a holding cell at the Longboat Key police station, waiting for Michel to take him into custody. J.D. and Michel had finished up with Erickson and left Harry Robson to deal with the paperwork. They stopped by the Longboat police station and spent an hour talking with Favereaux. Jock and I hadn't discussed the events of the day before everybody arrived at my front door. It was a complex web, and we decided that it would be best to tell the whole story one time and let everybody add what they knew.

"Before we get into Corbin," J.D. said, "I want to know what happened with Matt and Favereaux."

I told her.

"How did Jock know you were in trouble?" she asked.

Jock laughed. "Secret word," he said.

"I don't get it," J.D. said.

"A long time ago," I said, "back in junior high, we decided we needed a secret word to let each other know if the other was in trouble. I think we'd just seen a spy movie where the protagonist had a 'safe' word that he could use if he needed his buddies to get him out of a sticky situation. It was a kid's game that we gave up within a couple of months. I think that was about the time we discovered girls. We never used the word again, other than in conversation, I guess. I wondered if Jock would remember it. He did."

"What was the word?" J.D. asked.

"Quirky," Jock said. "Matt told me he'd gotten a quirky call from the judge about coming back to the courthouse. I knew he was in trouble. He also told me exactly where he was, the south firehouse. I called Sharkey and he got the bridges up on both ends of the island, and we had patrol cars drive along the stopped cars. When one of the patrols recognized Matt's car in line at the Longboat Pass Bridge, I happened to be the closest one to him. I'd been hiding out at the curve there, back in the bushes. I thought there was a good chance they would continue north. If they'd turned around and gone south, one of the cops would have gotten them at that end of the key."

"You guys are full of surprises," J.D. said. "Tell us about Corbin in New Orleans."

"Jock made the connection," Michel said. "After they found the Cayman bank accounts that Favereaux set up, they found a regular monthly deposit made to another Cayman account. There were fairly large sums of money that had been going into that account for fifteen years. Turns out the account holder was Brad Corbin, and the only deposits into that account were those from Favereaux."

"Can you make that stick?" I asked.

"Well," Michel said, "there's more. Our people searched Corbin's house and found a pistol. The ballistics shows that it's the same pistol that killed Connie Pelletier and the record room cop, Tatum. That seemed to have broken the dam. Corbin is talking non-stop."

"I'll be damned," I said. "He had me completely fooled. What was that all about?"

"It seems that when Favereaux was in New Orleans years ago,

he was paying off a pretty highly placed detective. That detective was Corbin's mentor, and when the detective retired, he passed the deal onto Corbin."

"I don't understand why Favereaux needed a New Orleans cop," I said. "He'd moved out of that city years ago."

"There were a lot of loose ends there," Michel said. "Actually, J.D. got us interested earlier this week when she ran some more DNA tests and figured out that Favereaux and Linda were not related by blood. She was not his daughter. When J.D. first told me about that, I sent it up the chain, but the consensus was that Jim had made a mistake and he truly thought Linda was his daughter. Since we couldn't find Jim, and Linda was dead, it didn't make much difference to us at the time. When he popped back up earlier this week, and Jock called me about his agency's finding the bank account Favereaux had set up in the Caymans, everything started to fall into place."

"How did Favereaux manage to amass a fortune?" I asked. "I thought you guys had a tight rein on the money he made from drug deals."

Michel looked a little embarrassed. "We thought so, too. It seems that he was investing agency money and giving it back, plus the profits to the agency he was working for. What we didn't know was that he was investing other money he made from side deals with the gunrunners, drug dealers, or whoever else he was dealing with and keeping those profits and the principal. It was so simple, nobody in the agencies thought to check on it. Maybe there was no way to figure it out. The bad guys he dealt with weren't keeping books of account; or at least none that we found. Sometimes simple is best."

"Tell me about the loose ends in New Orleans," I said.

"The first problem was Linda," J.D. said. "Favereaux told us he never had an affair with Connie, but he was obsessed with Linda. He knew she wasn't his daughter. He started having sex with her when she was fifteen and had come to live with Connie and Bobby Pelletier. Connie knew about their affair and also knew about Favereaux's side deals with the drug people. As long as Linda was involved, Connie would keep quiet, but when Linda died, Favereaux was afraid that Connie would talk. When he heard that Matt and I had visited her, he decided he had to take action to silence her. Permanently."

"So, Linda and Jim were sleeping together," I said.

"Michel shrugged. "Regularly since Linda was fifteen."

"I'll be damned," I said.

"Was there really a mole in your organization, Devlin?" J.D. asked.

"Mole may be too strong a word," Michel said. "We had a low-level guy working for a contractor we'd hired to work on our computers. He came across some files on Favereaux and sold the information to somebody he knew in the drug business. He was told to keep an eye on Favereaux's activities, and when Jim went to the safe house in Georgia, the contractor passed it on to some bad guys and they tried to take Jim out."

"You found the guy?"

"The D.C. police found his body in Rock Creek Park. They think it was just a random killing."

"Was it?" I asked.

"Who knows," Michel said, with a leer.

"What was Tatum's part in all this?" I asked.

"Tatum's job was to protect several files that Favereaux didn't want to end up in the hands of other agencies," Michel said. "They were files that Favereaux was afraid might implicate him in the crimes of others if somebody dug too deeply. The man who preceded Tatum on Corbin's, or Favereaux's, payroll had destroyed the files years ago. Tatum was the trip wire. If somebody came looking for one of the files, he'd let Corbin know. It was a way to let Favereaux know that somebody might be on his trail. When I called about the file on Linda, or Darlene Pelletier, as she was known, Corbin got spooked and let Favereaux know about it. Favereaux ordered Corbin to kill Tatum. When Corbin told Favereaux that you and J.D. had been to see Connie, he sent Corbin to take care of her."

"Did Connie know enough about Favereaux's operation to cause him trouble?" I asked.

"Who knows?" said Michel. "But the fact is that Favereaux thought she did, and that was enough to get her killed. She and her husband, Bobby, had tried to squeeze Favereaux about ten years ago, and he killed Bobby. Connie got the message, but with Linda gone, Favereaux was afraid that Connie might go to the authorities."

"Was Linda aware of the dirty side of Jim Favereaux?" I asked.

"She was," said Michel. "In fact she was part of it. She also had a Cayman account. It was in the name of Darlene Pelletier."

"What did you get from Lucas?" I asked.

"He's dirtier than we thought," J.D. said. She told us at length what Lucas had admitted to concerning the murders and his other dealing with the Hancock group.

"What about Erickson?" I asked.

"He gave us enough to hang Fulton Hancock. FDLE arrested him about an hour ago at his home in Tampa. I don't think either one of them, Erickson or Hancock, will ever see the outside of a prison again."

"Did Erickson tell you why he put the hit out on Bannister?" I asked.

"Yes," J.D. said. "It seems that Bannister was trying to renege on the deal he'd made about the property in Lakeland, the one that is written up in the documents Bob Crites showed you. He threatened to go to the police unless some accommodation was made. He was afraid he was going to be cut completely out of the deal."

"Then why try to frame Abby?" I asked.

J.D. shook her head. "Erickson didn't know why. Tori Madison was in charge of that. Erickson didn't want it to look like a hit. He was afraid there would be too many questions if a prominent man like Bannister was found shot to death without any apparent reason. He thought it was all set up until Lucas called him after he'd killed Bannister. Nobody expected Linda to be in the condo. They were kind of making it up as they went from that point. It was important to get Lucas assigned to the case, but he screwed up by jumping the gun and asking his boss for the assignment before law enforcement even knew Bannister was dead."

"Where's Tori now?" I asked.

"Harry Robson was going to pick her up at her house in Sarasota as soon as he finished with the paperwork on Lucas and Erickson," J.D. said. "She's probably in custody by now."

CHAPTER FIFTY-EIGHT

I was standing under a hot shower, letting the warmth work through the kinks I'd developed in my shoulders during four days in the courtroom. It was almost six-thirty on Friday morning, the day that should be the last day of trial. Abby's fate would be decided before dinner. I would put Abby, my last witness, on the stand and then rest my case. I wondered what Swann had to put on in rebuttal, but I wasn't too worried about it. He'd made the decision not to cross-examine either Lucas or Favereaux, so he couldn't bring them back to use in rebuttal. I couldn't imagine who else he could put on the stand. He would probably cross-examine Abby, but given the testimony from Lucas and Favereaux, I thought he might rest his case right after I rested mine. If that happened, we would go on to closing arguments.

I heard the insistent sound of a cell phone ringing. I could see J.D. through the steam and the condensation on shower door. She was standing at the sink brushing out her hair. I wasn't sure how much good that would do given the humidity level of the room. She walked into the bedroom, and I heard her answer the phone. She was back in a few minutes, just as I turned the shower off.

"Matt," she said, "That was Harry Robson. Wes Lucas is dead."

"What?" I was shocked.

"He was found in his cell early this morning. He hanged himself with a bed sheet."

"Crap. Didn't they have some kind of watch on him?"

"Apparently not. Harry said they had no reason to think he was suicidal."

"I'm sorry he's dead. He was a real bad guy, but still, dead is forever. Maybe there was some little part of him, some spark of goodness, that we'll never see. Oh well, no big loss. I might have been able to call him back to the witness stand to admit that he killed Bannister, but I would have had a fight on my hands from Swann, and Lucas could have taken the Fifth again, regardless of what he told you and Harry. It wouldn't have been worth taking a chance."

"Why not just put Harry Robson or me on the stand to testify to what he told us?"

"That would be hearsay. The judge wouldn't let it in. Why do you think Lucas killed himself?"

"He was a very bad guy," J.D. said, "and his trial would have been a three-ring circus. He probably took the easy way out. Saved everybody a lot of trouble. But I couldn't help feeling sorry for him. It was like he had been forced into that life, and in the end wished he'd stayed an honest cop."

"We all have choices to make, and those choices always have consequences. He made a fatal choice when he picked up the phone and called Senator Hancock to tell him about his dead son. It was all downhill from there."

"There's more," J.D. said.

"What?"

"When Harry went to pick up Tori Madison last night, she'd flown the coop."

"Gone?"

"Yes. She'd packed up and left the apartment she rented near downtown. Her car was gone, too."

"Are they looking for her?"

"Yes, but so far, no luck."

* * *

Thirty minutes later, we were having breakfast at the Longbeach Café. Jock had come home from an early morning jog, and declined our invitation to eat with us. He was meeting Logan at the

Longboat Key Club for a round of golf. I didn't think that would be too pleasant. The heat was already settling over the island, and neither one of them was worth a hoot as a golfer. It was going to be a scorcher of a day, more like August than June. "I sure wish I could spend the day on *Recess*," I said.

"Maybe tomorrow," J.D. said. "I'm off, unless something comes up. We could run down to Venice for lunch."

"If the jury returns a verdict today. If not, the judge might let them deliberate through the weekend. I'd actually prefer that to a two-day break. But we only go if we win. Jock likes the food at Crow's Nest and maybe Logan and Marie will join us."

"Are you going to win today?"

"I think so, even without the benefit of Lucas' confession being admitted into evidence. Lucas didn't confess to killing Bannister in court, but he did the next best thing by taking the Fifth. I thought Favereaux pretty much nailed Swann's coffin shut with his testimony."

"Why do you suppose Tori tried to frame Abby?"

"I'd like to know the answer to that one," I said. "I think she set out to frame Robert Shorter. That would have been a pretty good plan. There was a history between Shorter and Bannister, and Shorter was known to have a hair-trigger temper. But when Shorter couldn't come to the meeting on Sunday evening, Tori had to set something else up on short notice. But why Abby? That has never made any sense. And I would have thought Tori would have had better control over the scene, that she would not have let Linda be there at the time Lucas was supposed to kill Bannister. And then, we have the question of why Tori was part of the plot to kill her boss."

"You didn't have Shorter testify about his being shot?"

"No. I couldn't show that it was connected to our case, and without that, Swann could have kept it out based on irrelevancy."

"Wouldn't Tori have had as good a case that Shorter committed the murder even if he didn't show up? His fingerprints were there. That placed him on the premises."

"Maybe the plan was to have the cops show up while Shorter was at Bannister's. Catch him red-handed, as it were. Tori could have done that with an anonymous 911 call. Lucas shoots Bannister, leaves the scene, a few minutes later Shorter shows up and finds Bannister dead, and the police arrive before Shorter can leave."

"What about the gun used in the murder?" J.D. asked.

"All kinds of possibilities. Maybe Lucas planned to wipe the revolver clean of fingerprints and leave it someplace where Shorter wouldn't see it, but the police would find it when they searched the place. Maybe they planned to kill Shorter and make it appear that it was a murder-suicide."

"But Lucas told Harry Robson and me that he was to drop the murder weapon into the bay."

"True. That may have been part of plan B, the framing of Abby," I said. "Who knows what the plan was. Unless we find Tori, we'll probably never know."

"You're ahead on points. Why not forget about putting Abby on the stand? Isn't there the possibility that Swann will make some points on cross-examination?"

"That's a chance I'll have to take. I told the jury that Abby would testify. They're expecting it. They've been watching her at counsel table all week. They'll want to hear what she has to say. And if I don't put her on, they'll wonder why. After all, I promised she would testify and they won't look kindly on me for not following through."

The café's owner, Colleen Collandra, came over with the morning's *Sarasota Herald-Tribune*. "Did you see this, Matt?"

The headline was large: CHIEF'S WIFE DIDN'T KILL BUILDER. The subheadline read: SECRET AGENT TESTIFIES THAT FDLE AGENT WAS MURDERER. The story detailed the testimony of Favereaux and Lucas and Lucas' decision to take the Fifth. I was pretty sure that each of the jurors would have read the story, even though Judge Thomas had told them at the close of each day's testimony that they were not to read anything about the trial or watch anything about it on TV. It had been my experience that the natural curiosity of the American juror overcame the judge's admonitions every time.

"What do you think, Colleen?"

"I think you're going to win, Matt."

"We'll see. I've got to get downtown. J.D. will take care of the check."

"You're a vile person, Royal," J.D. said. "Call me when you take a break. Good luck."

CHAPTER FIFTY-NINE

Nine o'clock on a Friday morning. The lawyers were settled in the courtroom, and Bill Lester sat in the gallery with few blank-faced strangers mixed in among the journalists. It was sometimes hard to tell them apart, the reporters here to record history and the watchers, those men and women who roamed the courthouse looking for a trial in progress, trying to escape a life that held little in the way of stimulus. Some of them were genuinely interested, having read about the trial in the newspapers, and some of them were street people looking for an air-conditioned place to escape the heat for a few hours. Others were just bored citizens looking for an interesting way to spend part of the day, one of an endless string of lonely days that stretched all the way to their graves. These are the widows and widowers who came to Florida with their husbands or wives, looking for a paradise in which to spend their golden years. They lose the spouse to the death that stalks us all, and find that their children, still in the northern states, are preoccupied with their own children, and have no time for an aging parent living far away. They find a trial in which they have no interest, a respite from the doldrums of life lived among strangers in a strange land, and they sit for a bit, and then move on to the next courtroom.

The court deputy entered the courtroom and announced that the judge wanted the lawyers in chambers. When Swann, his entourage, the court reporter, and I were seated and pleasantries had been exchanged, the judge said, "I want to let you know that Agent Lucas committed suicide in the jail last night. That news hasn't been released yet, so I don't think the jury will have heard about it. I'll question them on the issue if you like. I could frame the question very vaguely along the line of whether they'd heard about anything unusual happening in the jail overnight. We can put our heads together and come up with something, but we might just be putting questions in their minds as to why we're even broaching such a subject. What do you think?"

I sat quietly, watching Swann. I knew he would be trying to come up with something he could use to try to rescue his case. He said, "I move for a mistrial, Your Honor."

"Motion denied." The judge didn't even think about that one. Or maybe he'd anticipated it and already ruled it out.

"I was planning to use him in my rebuttal case," Swann said.

"I wouldn't have allowed it," Judge Thomas said. "You had your chance on cross-examination and you waived it. Anything new you could have gotten out of Lucas should have been introduced when you had him on the stand during your case. Mr. Royal?"

"I can't see any reason to even question the jury, Your Honor," I said. "Mr. Lucas' death has no bearing on the issues in this case. He's testified, been subject to cross-examination, and jailed. His death, while tragic, is irrelevant to this case."

"Mr. Swann?" the judge asked.

"In light of your ruling on my motion for a mistrial, I have to agree."

"Okay," Judge Thomas said, "that's what we'll do. How many more witnesses do you have, Mr. Royal?"

"Only one, Your Honor. My client."

"Rebuttal, Mr. Swann?"

"It depends on what Mrs. Lester's testimony is, Your Honor, but otherwise, I don't have any plans for a rebuttal."

"Okay, gentlemen. Let's finish the testimony and let the jury go while we handle the charge conference."

The charge conference is a time for the lawyers to argue which instructions of law the judge will give to the jury at the end of the case. The Florida Supreme Court has promulgated standard instructions for use in criminal cases of different types, but if the lawyers so choose they can submit additional instructions that they think might better fit their case.

"I've looked at your instructions and they all seem to be the standards. Are we going to have any objections?"

Both Swann and I answered in the negative.

"Then it'll be a short conference. We'll just make sure we're in agreement on the order in which I give the instructions. We'll start closings at one o'clock. How long are you going to need?"

"I'll need at least an hour," Swann said.

"Fifteen minutes, probably." I said. "Maybe less. Brevity is a virtue. I hope."

CHAPTER SIXTY

"State your name, please," I said.

"Abigail Lester."

"How old are you, Abby?"

"Forty."

"Your occupation?"

"I'm a history teacher at Sarasota High School."

"You're the defendant in this case?"

"Yes."

"Did you kill Nate Bannister?"

"No, sir."

"Did you know Nate Bannister?"

"I did not know him. Never met him, as far as I know."

"How do you explain a wine glass with your fingerprints being found in Mr. Bannister's bedroom after he was killed?"

"I can't explain it."

"Were you ever in his bedroom?"

"No."

"Were you ever in his condo?"

"No."

"Do you know Tori Madison?"

"I met her once."

"Where did you meet her?"

"In a restaurant in downtown Sarasota."

"When?"

"On Saturday, the day before Mr. Bannister was killed."

"How did that meeting come about?"

"Ms. Madison called me at the school on Friday. She told me

she was in charge of construction of a condo complex in Lake-land. She wanted to use an Old Florida motif on the inside of the buildings and she'd heard that I taught Florida history. She wanted to discuss hiring me as a consultant on the project. She asked me to meet her for a drink the next afternoon, and I agreed."

"What happened at the meeting?"

"Nothing of consequence. We talked about some ideas and agreed that I would put together a concept and we'd meet again in a week or so."

"Did you have anything to drink?"

"Each of us had a glass of wine."

"Do you remember what kind of wine you had?"

"The same thing I always drink. A Zinfandel."

"That's a red wine, correct?"

"Correct."

"Do you remember anything about the glass the wine was served in?"

"No. It was a wine glass, but I didn't pay any attention to it."

"Was that the only time you ever met Ms. Madison?"

"Yes."

"Can you think of any reason she would have to do you harm?"

"None."

"Where were you on the night of March thirty-first of this year? The night that Mr. Bannister was killed."

"I was home, alone."

"Where was your husband, Chief Lester?"

"He was visiting his mother."

"Is that a regular thing?"

"Yes. She's in a nursing home in Bradenton. He and I go to visit every Wednesday evening and then he goes back alone on Sundays. It gives them a little time by themselves. He never misses those visits."

"Did you ever have any email correspondence with Mr. Bannister?"

"No."

"Did you ever have any email correspondence with Ms. Madison?"

"No."

I stood for a minute, looking at Abby and watching the jury out of my peripheral vision. Abby appeared calm and relaxed, and the jurors had been attentive to her and her testimony. I thought we'd brought it off. I'd tailored my questions so that Swann wouldn't have much to cross-examine on. He could go back into the areas he'd covered in his case, but I thought, despite all his inadequacies, he was a better lawyer than that. Abby would refute each piece of the evidence against her, and it would just emphasize her testimony in my direct. There was nothing for Swann to gain by taking her on. I looked up at the bench. "I have no further questions, Your Honor."

Swann stood at counsel table, looked at the jury, and said, "I have no questions, Your Honor."

"Mr. Royal?"

"The defense rests, Your Honor."

"Rebuttal, Mr. Swann?"

"Yes, sir. One witness."

I was surprised. I ran through a mental list of all the people who might have some knowledge of this case, some evidence to present. I couldn't come up with anybody. Then it hit me. A jailhouse snitch. If someone who had been in jail with Abby came forward and testified that Abby had admitted to the murder, it would be troublesome, but not devastating, to my case. She'd only spent one night in jail, the night she'd been arrested, and that was in isolation. Still, I couldn't prove that Abby had not been in a cell for at least a few minutes with whomever the witness would be.

I looked behind me. The reporter, Robin Hartill, was sitting in the gallery, notebook in hand. Several chairs were lined up inside the rail that separated the gallery from the area where the trial participants sat. These were for members of the bar who had no part in the case being tried, but could come inside the rail and sit. I motioned Robin up to the rail and asked her to come inside and take one of the chairs right behind me. I leaned over and whispered. "Hide your notebook, and when I lean back to talk to you, pretend we're in conversation."

"What's up?"

"No time to explain. Just follow my lead."

She shrugged. "Okay."

I turned to Abby. "I want you to leave the courtroom right now. Just go outside and wait in the hall. I'll let you know when it's time to come back in."

"What's going on?"

"Trust me. Go. Don't talk to anybody."

Abby got up and left. Swann called his next witness. The court deputy stuck his head into the hall and summoned a woman who was probably in her early twenties. She was dressed in a conservative business suit, white blouse, and high-heel pumps. She took the stand and was sworn.

"State your name, please," Swann said

"Stephanie Bramlett."

"Do you know Abigail Lester?"

"I met her."

"Where did you meet her?

"In the Sarasota County jail."

"Why were you at the jail?"

"I was serving a six-month sentence."

"What were you arrested for?"

"Prostitution."

"Have I or anyone else offered you a reduced sentence on that conviction in return for your testimony today?"

"No, sir."

Swann was being very careful in how he phrased his questions. Too careful, I thought. He had specifically asked her about a reduction of the sentence on that conviction, the one she was serving time for on the night Abby was jailed. Was there another conviction? Maybe a more recent one that would merit a little help from the state in reducing the sentence?

I knew that prostitutes were arrested regularly. They would rotate through the system, paying a fine, doing a little community service, and in the rare case, a few days or weeks in the county jail. But, on occasion, they were looking at hard time. That was usually when they were arrested for prostitution but had drugs in their possession, or were selling drugs to their johns, their customers.

I leaned over the back of my chair and said, "Robin, nod your head and talk back to me for a minute. Then write something on a piece of paper and pass it up to me." She nodded and made mouth movements like we were talking. I turned back to the front.

"How did you meet Mrs. Lester?" Swann asked.

"We briefly shared a cell on the night she was arrested."

"Did you have any conversations with her?"

"Yes, sir."

"Tell me about that."

"I asked her what she had been arrested for. She told me murder. I asked her if she had done it."

Robin passed me a note that had a smiley face on it. I looked at it, and turned to her and nodded.

"What did she say?" Swann continued.

"She told me that she'd killed the dirty bastard because he was dumping her. She said he had it coming, but that her husband was a cop, and no one could ever pin the murder on her. She said she would be able to cover it up and blame somebody else."

"Did you have any other conversation with her?"

"No, sir. She made bail very quick, and was out of there."

"I have nothing further, Your Honor."

I stood and looked at the piece of paper Robin had handed me. Then I leaned down and pretended to speak to her again. She nodded, and I turned back to the witness stand. "Where do you live, Ms. Bramlett?" I asked.

"Downtown Sarasota."

"In the Sarasota County jail?"

She swallowed hard, hesitated for a moment, and said, "Yes."

"You mentioned that you were in the jail on a prostitution charge when you met my client, Abby Lester."

"Yes."

"That was not the same charge that you're presently in jail for, is it?"

"No, sir."

"So, you finished the sentence you were in jail for at the time you supposedly met Abby Lester."

She swallowed again. It was like a tell, a reaction to a question that she found threatening. "Yes. I finished that sentence."

"So, tell the jury why you're in jail now?"

"I was arrested for prostitution."

I took a blind swing, asking a question I didn't know the answer to, but a question that only had two possible answers. One would help and the other wouldn't hurt. "And you've also been charged with possession of drugs with intent to sell, haven't you?"

She swallowed again. "Yes."

"You testified that Mr. Swann had not offered you any deals on the charge for which you were in jail on the night that Abby was arrested. What about on this charge, the drug charge? Have you been offered anything in return for your testimony here today?"

Again, the swallow.

"Tell us what you've been offered."

"Mr. Swann told me that he would get the drug charges dropped if I testified."

"You were arrested here in Sarasota County?"

"Yes, sir."

"And you're being prosecuted by the state attorney's office here in Sarasota County?"

"Yes, sir."

"Do you know whether Mr. Swann is a prosecutor in this county?"

"I guess so."

"Did he tell you that he's a prosecutor in Jacksonville and he's here trying this case because the Sarasota state attorney felt that he had a conflict and his office could not prosecute?"

"No."

"Are you aware that Mr. Swann has no jurisdiction here and that he had no power to offer you a deal?"

"Oh, my God."

"You didn't know?"

"No. Does that mean that the drug charges aren't going to be dropped?"

I didn't answer her question. I glanced quickly at Swann. He sat stone-faced, not moving a muscle, still as a statue. I thought he must have glimpsed his future and found it dismal. He'd taken a chance, a stupid chance that risked his career, and he'd lost. He had bet his future against one more win and now he'd face the consequences.

I turned back to the witness. "Do you know how Mr. Swann came up with you as a witness?"

"No, sir. He came to my cell last night and offered me the deal."

"Did he bring you the clothes you're wearing today?"

"Yes, sir."

"Do you know what perjury is?"

"Lying under oath."

"Right. Do you know the sentence for that?"

"Not exactly."

"You never met Abby Lester, did you?"

"Yes, sir. I did." She was going to ride it out, hoping that I was lying to her and that Swann would fix things.

"And she never told you the tale you testified to today, did she?"

She swallowed. "Yes, she did."

"And you remember her exact words?"

"I do."

"You've got an exceptional memory, I guess. It's been two and a half months since that night at the Sarasota County jail."

"Objection." Swann was on his feet. "That's not a question."

That's what we in the profession call a dumb-ass objection. "I'll rephrase, Your Honor."

"Proceed," Judge Thomas said.

"Do you have a phenomenal memory, Ms. Bramlett?"

"I do. I remember her exact words."

"Okay. Can you point out the woman in this courtroom who admitted to you that she killed Mr. Bannister?"

The witness pointed to Robin Hartill and said, "The woman with you. The one sitting right behind you at counsel table."

I smiled at her, taking a second to enjoy the sound of the trap springing closed on her neck. "Your Honor, for the record, would the court take judicial notice that the lady behind me is not my client, that she is a newspaper reporter named Robin Hartill, that Abby Lester has blond hair and is forty years old and that Robin has dark hair and is obviously in her twenties?"

"Objection, Mr. Swann?" the judge asked.

Swann shook his head.

"Anything else in rebuttal?"

"No, Your Honor. The state rests."

Robin left her seat and went to the door of the courtroom, and in a moment Abby came back to the counsel table. "What was that all about?"

"Just a little sleight of hand. I'll tell you about it when we break, but you don't have to worry about that last witness."

I could tell by Swann's hangdog look that he was totally defeated. He'd tried a hail-Mary pass with this witness, and it had been batted down. The witness had been completely discredited, but so had Swann. It was not lost on the jury that he had gotten a witness to lie under oath, suborned perjury, which is a criminal offense. There would be consequences for him, probably a criminal charge and disbarment, his license to practice law revoked by the Florida Supreme Court. His career was over, and I thought the legal profession would be better off as a result.

"Okay then," Judge Thomas said and turned to the jury. He

explained to the jury that they could discount Ms. Bramlett's identification of the witness. He told them that this concluded the evidentiary portion of the trial, and that he and the lawyers had some matters to confer upon. He told them the court would be in recess until one o'clock at which time the lawyers would give their closing arguments.

We stood as the jury filed out of the courtroom. The lawyers and the court reporter gathered in the judge's chambers for the charge conference. Ten minutes later I was walking into one of the small conference rooms to meet Abby and Bill Lester. Abby hugged me, and to my surprise, so did Bill.

"What can I say, Matt?" Abby asked. "You were magnificent."

"Let's hope the jury thinks so," I said. "We're not home free, yet."

"Matt," Bill said, "Win, lose, or draw, we'll be forever grateful to you. There's not a lawyer in the state who's competent to carry your briefcase."

I was a little embarrassed by such an accolade, but my ego seemed fine with it. Beach bums don't often get compliments on their abilities to do much of anything. I was probably glowing a bit as I tried to bring my client and her husband down from their highs. The jury hadn't spoken yet, and until they did, Abby was still at risk of spending the rest of her life in prison, or worse.

"Thanks, guys. I appreciate your thoughts, but let's wait for the verdict before we celebrate. Y'all go on to lunch. I'll grab a sandwich and work on my closing argument."

CHAPTER SIXTY-ONE

Swann's closing argument was disjointed and devoid of passion. He hit the high points of his case, but never mentioned the lows. He ignored the testimony brought forth in my case, never mentioning the testimony of Lucas and Favereaux. He droned on, almost in a monotone, for the better part of an hour. I thought he'd lost heart, that he had resigned himself to the probability that his record of wins was about to be compromised. I wasn't so sure. There's an old saw that says it's not over until the fat lady sings. In this case, the jury was the fat lady and her repertoire contained only two songs; "guilty" and "not guilty."

I had tried too many cases to try to outguess the jury. It's a losing battle. You do your best and hope for a win. More often than not, I'd won, but I'd also lost cases that I thought I should have won. And sometimes, I won cases I thought I should have lost. The trial lawyer's thoughts often drift to his relief valve, the notion that there's always an appellate court. In the end, the mental machinations mostly result only in ulcers for the lawyer.

When Swann finished, I rose and walked empty handed to the center of the courtroom. I stood there for a moment, looking at each of the jurors individually, my eyes moving from one to the other, sometimes making contact. Judith Whitacre looked straight at me. No smile, no facial expression. Had I lost her? No telling. Maybe I never had her.

"Ladies and gentlemen of the jury. Abby Lester is not guilty of this terrible crime. Simple as that. She didn't kill Nate Banister.

"Let's look at the evidence. The only witness who really tied Abby to Nate Bannister was Tori Madison. She lied. You remember her. The one who saw the scar on Abby's hip. The scar that wasn't there. Did Ms. Madison see some other woman that night in Mr. Bannister's bedroom? Possibly, but she testified that she was certain it was Abby.

"Ms. Madison also testified that she'd met Abby on several occasions, but Abby said they'd only met once. Okay, I can't prove to you that Ms. Madison was lying about that, or that Abby was telling the truth, but when you look at the totality of the evidence you can see that the truth most likely lies with Abby Lester. Not Tori Madison.

"We know who killed Nate Bannister. Agent Wes Lucas of the FDLE was a rogue agent. He killed Mr. Bannister. Linda Favereaux saw him standing over the corpse holding a revolver. Lucas killed her later that night. Now, I grant you that we don't have direct testimony about the murder of Mr. Bannister, but we can put it together. Jim Favereaux saw the man who killed Linda, the woman he identified as his daughter, and testified here that the murderer was Wes Lucas. Linda told Jim Favereaux that a man named Wes had killed Mr. Bannister.

"Why did Lucas ask his boss to assign him to this case before, I repeat, before Mr. Bannister's body was found? There's only one explanation. Lucas knew about the murder. How did he know about it if he hadn't been part of it? And why did he insist that he head up the investigation if he wasn't trying to cover something up? How better to disrupt a murder investigation than to have the murderer in charge of investigating it?

"Let's look at the evidence that points to Abby Lester as the killer. First, the emails. They're obviously fraudulent. They didn't come from her computer. The only thing that ties them to Abby is the typed name on the bottom of the emails. Anybody could have typed those words, but it would take a person who is highly skilled in Internet technology to be able to post them through foreign servers, as was the case here. Abby didn't do that.

"We have to ask ourselves why she would have, even if she had the skills to do so. And if Abby and Mr. Bannister were having an affair, why would she have to sign the emails? It doesn't stack up. I think we can strike that bit of evidence off the board.

"Mr. Swann's theory was that Abby and Mr. Bannister were having an affair and she was angered by the fact that he wanted to break it off. On the other hand, Mr. Swann would have you believe that Abby had sex with Mr. Bannister the night he was killed. Abby was painted as a black widow of sorts; have sex and then kill your partner. That theory exploded when the DNA from the sheets told us that shortly before he was killed, Mr. Bannister had sex with Linda Favereaux, not Abby Lester.

"The wine glass in the bedroom. Now that presents a dilemma. How did it get there? Abby says she was never in that condo. The only person who placed her there was Tori Madison. The glass of wine with Abby's fingerprints would buttress the claim that she was in the bedroom, drinking wine, and presumably having sex. But it turns out that the wine glass was not from Mr. Bannister's set. His glasses were monogrammed. And if Mr. Bannister was drinking wine that night, and he surely was because the autopsy showed the remains in his stomach, what happened to his glass?

"There were two of his monogramed glasses found in the dishwasher, washed clean of fingerprints. Were those the glasses used by Linda Favereaux and Mr. Bannister? If so, who put them in the dishwasher? Does it make sense that if Mr. Bannister was going for more wine, as was testified to in this courtroom, that he would put his glass, and not Abby's, in the dishwasher? Where did the other extra monogrammed glass in the dishwasher come from? Who used it?

"The glass in the bedroom was plain, like the ones used in most restaurants and bars, like the one that Abby probably drank out of on the day of Mr. Bannister's murder, when she met Tori Madison for a drink in downtown Sarasota. How easy would it have been for Tori to slip that glass into her purse and then place it on Mr. Bannister's bedside table? And there was a smudged fingerprint on the stem of the glass. One that was not clear enough to be identified. One that may have belonged to someone other than Abby Lester, someone who placed the glass on the bedside table.

"I submit to you that the killer put the two glasses in the dishwasher, the ones used by Mr. Bannister and Linda Favereaux, and placed the glass with Abby's fingerprints on the bedside table. Was this the same glass that Abby had drunk from at the restaurant where she met Tori Madison the day before the murder? How did that glass get on that bedside table?

"Let's talk about Robert Shorter for a minute. You remember he was the man who assaulted Mr. Bannister a couple of years ago and actually served jail time for doing so. His fingerprints were in Mr. Bannister's condo. Why didn't the investigators follow up and at least talk to Mr. Shorter? He would have been the logical suspect, certainly a better choice than Abby Lester.

"Mr. Shorter was lured to the Bannister condo by Tori Madison, and an appointment was made for him to return on Sunday evening at, as it turns out, the same time that Mr. Bannister was killed. Mr. Shorter called Ms. Madison on Sunday and canceled because he had another meeting he had to attend, a meeting with thirty or so alibi witnesses. But the FDLE wouldn't have known about the alibi because its agents never interviewed Mr. Shorter.

"Who would be a better patsy for murder than Mr. Shorter? Was that the plan all along and when it fell through, somebody, perhaps Tori Madison, went to plan B? The framing of Abby Lester? It is clear that Abby has been framed. I don't have a plausible reason as to why, but somebody, most probably Tori Madison, tried to make it look like Abby killed Mr. Bannister. The evidence is strong, even overwhelming, that Agent Wesley Lucas murdered Nate Bannister. And there is no credible evidence that Abby Lester had anything to do with it.

"That last witness? Ms. Bramlett? She's a liar. She lied on the witness stand to get a reduction in her sentence for dealing in drugs; a deal that only the state attorney for this judicial circuit could make; not a deal that a prosecutor from another circuit has the authority to make. And Jack Dobbyn, the state attorney for this circuit, did not grant Ms. Bramlett any kind of immunity. I submit that the last witness was an act of desperation by a desperate man.

"Ladies and gentlemen, you do not have to find that Abby is innocent of this crime, although I think you will. It is not my burden to prove her innocence. It is Mr. Swann's burden to prove beyond a reasonable doubt that Abby Lester committed this crime, that she did, in fact, kill Nate Bannister, and that she did so with malice aforethought; that she had thought about the murder, planned it, went to his condo, shared a bottle of wine with him, had sex with him, and then shot him dead with a gun that has disappeared. The state attorney wants to send Abby to the death chamber, to execute her, to use drugs to suck the life out of a high school history teacher on evidence so flimsy that it ought to embarrass the prosecutor to bring it into a court of law.

"If you find that you have a reasonable doubt as to Abby's guilt, it is your duty to acquit. You don't have to believe in her innocence, only in the fact that the state did not prove her guilt beyond a reasonable doubt.

"Our society, our system of justice, puts a heavy burden on juries. Most of us will never have to weigh the life of a fellow citizen, to decide whether that citizen goes from this courtroom to death row or walks out into the sunshine a free person. It is a heavy burden, one that you did not seek, but one that you have accepted. I know you will do your duty as you see it, and I implore you to find Abby Lester not guilty. Thank you."

Swann waived rebuttal. Judge Thomas charged the jury with the law that they should apply to this case and sent them out to deliberate. It has been said that courts treat jurors like kindergartners when they dribble out only the evidence the judges think they should hear, and then charge them with legal principles that would boggle the minds of third-year law students. But the juries, day in and day out, in courtrooms all across the country, get it right. That fact alone boggles the minds of most trial lawyers.

We stood as the jury exited the courtroom. This is the time when opposing counsel usually shake hands and congratulate each other on having tried a good case. Not this time. Swann abruptly left the courtroom, leaving his entourage to pack up his documents and other detritus left at the end of a trial. I wasn't surprised.

I was packing up my brief case when the young woman lawyer and the intern from Stetson Law School came to my table. We shook hands. The lawyer said, "Mr. Royal, I think you just ruined old George's perfect record."

I smiled. "I hope so. He could still walk away with this one."

"I doubt it," she said. "Maybe a loss will take some of the arrogance out of him."

"He might be harder to work for," I said.

"This is my last case," she said. "My last day working for the state attorney. I start at a private firm in Jacksonville on Monday. I'll probably face George in court someday. I'm looking forward to it. And I'm not sure he has a career after that stunt he pulled with the last witness. I'd be surprised if he doesn't get disbarred. I hope you don't think I had anything to do with that."

I smiled. "That never crossed my mind. What makes him tick?" I asked.

"I'm not sure. He's a much better lawyer than you saw in this case, but he always takes the easy way out. I think his main problem is that he's lazy and narcissistic. It's too bad. He could have been a really good lawyer."

I turned to the intern. "What about you? Where do you go from here?"

"Back to Jacksonville. I'll finish the summer internship and then back to Stetson for my last year of law school. I'll see what turns up then. It was a pleasure watching you work. Smooth as silk."

I laughed. "That's the beach-bum effect."

CHAPTER SIXTY-TWO

The longest hours of a trial lawyer's life are those spent waiting out the jury. He spends it in a conference room locked up with his clients, unless they're back in a cell somewhere. It's a time when he relives every minute of the trial, trying to decipher the jurors' reaction to each bit of evidence, to consider the mistakes he made, because there are always mistakes, and wonder if one of them might have ruined the chance for an acquittal. He rummages around in his mind as the gastric juices rumble in his gut, producing yet another ulcer.

Abby and Bill sat across the table from me, saying nothing. I think they somehow knew that I needed some time to sort out the ups and downs of the past week. I was forcing myself to think pleasant thoughts that would push my fears about the trial into the back of my mind. I was enjoying an image of J.D., and my boat *Recess,* and a flat green sea as we cruised toward Egmont Key, when there was a knock on the door. The court deputy stuck his head in and said, "We've got a verdict."

If I had been attached to a sphygmomanometer, one of those contraptions they use to check your blood pressure, it would have blown a gasket. The game's over. The jury has decided. The fat lady is about to sing. Everything you've done in the past two and a half months to save your client either worked or it didn't. It all boils down to one word, or hopefully two, on a jury form. "Guilty" or "Not Guilty." In a matter of minutes, we'll know whether Abby is going to walk out of the courtroom with Bill and me, and drive to the key and find a cool bar in which to imbibe a few drinks of relief and congratulation, or leave shackled to a deputy and start the process of taking up residence at a state prison.

I looked at my watch. The jury had only been out for twenty minutes. Hardly time to elect a foreman or forewoman. Lawyers have debated for years whether a quick verdict or a drawn-out deliberation is best for the accused. It's a question that has never been satisfactorily answered, probably because there is no answer. Every case and every jury is different from another.

* * *

The jury filed back into the courtroom. Judith Whitacre was holding the verdict form. She was the forewoman. She looked at Swann, caught his eye, and smiled. Oh crap. What the hell happened? I thought surely she was one juror I could count on.

The jurors took their seats and the rest of us sat. The judge asked if they'd reached a verdict. Judith Whitacre stood and answered. "We have, Your Honor."

"Please hand the verdict form to the deputy, Madam Forewoman."

The deputy took the form and handed it to Judge Thomas. He looked at it and handed it down to the court clerk. "Please publish the verdict, Madam Clerk."

The clerk stood and read the form. "In the Circuit Court of the Twelfth Judicial Circuit of Florida, in and for Sarasota County, case number 4856, State of Florida versus Abigail Lester. We the jury find the defendant Abigail Lester..." The clerk paused. Dramatic effect? Probably not. It was only a split second, probably not even noticed by most of the people in the courtroom. It seemed like hours to me.

I was holding my breath, my heart racing. I'd had the same reaction to every verdict I'd ever heard. Abby had grabbed my hand and was squeezing hard, a look on her face that I can only describe as one of hope and resignation. The next second would decide her fate and the course of her life from this point forward.

The clerk seemed to catch her breath, inhale and said, "Not guilty."

Abby sagged against my shoulder. I looked at the jury. Judith Whitacre was grinning at me. She nodded, and I nodded back. The smile with which she had favored Swann when she walked in with the verdict in her hand had been one of derision, not congratulations.

Judge Thomas dismissed the jury with his thanks and they filed out of the courtroom. Swann and his crew left suddenly without saying anything to anybody. I was tempted to go after him, to rub in his loss and mention that never again would he be able to brag about a spotless record of triumphs. But I reminded myself that I was a better person than that. Or at least, I liked to think so.

Abby hugged me and sobbed. All the tension and fears that had permeated her senses since she had first been arrested were washing out of her system. She held me tight, wouldn't let go. I hugged back. Bill Lester came through the rail and wrapped his arms around both of us. Tears were slipping down his cheeks. "Let's go get a drink," he said. And that's what we did.

* * *

At three o'clock in the afternoon, we were at Tiny's. I'd called J.D. as soon as I walked out of the courthouse. She answered, "Well?"

"Not guilty."

"That's my man. I'm so proud of you, Matt. And happy for Abby and Bill."

"Thanks, sweetie. We're on our way to Tiny's to celebrate."

"I'll see you there."

By the time we arrived, a crowd was gathering. Word travels fast on a small island. I'd called Robin Hartill at the newspaper as soon as I hung up from talking to J.D. She put the story, including the attempted intimidation of Judge Thomas, on the Internet edition of the paper and joined us at Tiny's. Logan and Jock dragged in from the golf course. J.D. had called Gus Grantham and he was on his way. Off-duty Longboat cops were filing in to congratulate Bill and Abby. It was a gathering of the islanders, a collective sigh of the relief that one of them would not be going to prison. I got a lot of hugs and handshakes and jokes about the devout beach bum losing his status and being dragged back into the real world, all of which I denied.

The party went on into the evening. I could feel the tension leaving my body, the beach bum replacing the lawyer. Jock and Logan declined to go to lunch with us the next day and suggested that J.D. and I spend the day alone on the beach at Egmont Key. That sounded better and better. It would be a day to reclaim my rightful place among the indolent. I was looking forward to it.

CHAPTER SIXTY-THREE

Somehow, August slipped up on me. The weeks since the trial had been an easy time of good fishing and good friends. J.D. and I settled back into our routines, jogging the beach at dawn, stopping in the key's bars and restaurants for a drink with friends in the evenings. We spent a lot of time on *Recess* on J.D.'s days off, sometimes doing nothing but floating around, unanchored and unconcerned about the world. Bill and Abby Lester had gone to the mountains of North Carolina for a well-deserved rest. They came back refreshed and happy to see their lives return to normal.

The key was mostly empty, probably no more than a couple of thousand year-rounders enjoying the quiet of the summer. Word from the broader world occasionally seeped onto the key, interrupting our isolation and bringing news of the fate of the characters who had so consumed my waking moments and haunted my dreams during the months leading up to Abby's trial. Mark Erickson had pleaded guilty to a number of drug charges and murder. He would spend the rest of his life in prison. There was no evidence that his wife Julie had been involved in the drug business or that she even had any knowledge of her husband's activities. She would retain her professorship at USF. On the day of her husband's sentencing, Julie filed for divorce.

Jim Favereaux had disappeared. Homeland Security Agent Devlin Michel assured J.D. that he was in the custody of the appropriate federal authorities and would be dealt with accordingly. Jock explained to us that there were secret courts that dealt with rogue agents. A public trial would give away too many secrets. When the agents were sworn in, they signed documents giving up certain rights, including the right to a public trial if charged with a crime growing out of their activities as federal agents. If the agent was sentenced to prison, it was to a Supermax, the highest-security prison in the system. He was given a new name and a cover story that turned him into a common criminal with an extensive history of violence. I was pretty sure that was Jim Favereaux's fate.

Kent Walker, the man who accosted me in the Euphemia Haye parking lot, was in jail awaiting trial on assault charges. His use of a gun and the fact that he was trying to intimidate a lawyer in the middle of a capital murder trial, caused the committing judge to set a high bond. Walker wouldn't be going anywhere except state prison.

The governor's chief of staff, Fulton Hancock, had been arrested in Tallahassee in the early hours of the morning after Erickson's confession. Hancock was free on a large bond. He'd resigned his position with the governor, but the flurry of news reports on Hancock's transgressions had tarred the governor, despite his vociferous denial of any knowledge of his aide's criminal activities.

Detective Brad Corbin was in the Orleans Parish jail awaiting transport to a state prison. He'd spilled his guts when confronted by Homeland Security agents. It seems that there had been talk of a trip to Guantánamo, domestic terrorism, death penalties and other such nonsense. Corbin caved and confessed, and he would spend the rest of his life as a guest of the Louisiana prison system.

Judge Wayne Lee Thomas filed a grievance against George Swann accusing him of suborning perjury and making a deal with an accused Stephanie Bramlett, which he had no authority to make. The case was pending before a Florida Bar Grievance Committee in Sarasota, and things did not look good for Swann. I had not been called to testify before the committee, but I would do so if asked.

I spent a couple of weeks after the trial trying to decide whether I should approach Bill Lester about his affair with Maggie Bannister. It was really none of my business, and now that I knew who had murdered Nate Bannister, and Abby had been acquitted, the only reason I could see for my pursuing the issue was my curiosity. In mid-July, the island gossip network lit up with the word that Trip Grower, a Longboat Key police captain, and Maggie Bannister were engaged and would be tying the knot in the fall.

J.D. was as surprised as everyone else on the island, but it sent her into a frenzy of investigatory zeal. She knew that the chief and Grower had been friends since their days in the police academy, and she couldn't imagine that Bill Lester would cheat on his wife and his best friend at the same time. She'd never accepted that Lester would have had an affair in the first place.

J.D. had to be careful as she looked into the case. She couldn't compromise Cracker Dix, who had told us about the affair in the first place, nor could she smear Bill Lester by innuendo. After a week of digging, she came up with the answer. As one of the ranking officers in the department, Captain Grower was subject to call at any time, day or night, and was therefore entitled to the use of an unmarked cruiser twenty-four hours a day. Grower's car had reached the end of its service life in February and his new car was late arriving. Since Bill Lester lived on the key, and he was deskbound most of the day, he could do without his department car for a couple of weeks. He'd lent it to Grower until the new car was delivered. It was during that period of time that Cracker thought he'd seen the chief arrive at Maggie's house. Given that Grower and the chief were about the same size, it would have been an easy mistake for Cracker to make. The man he thought was the chief was actually Trip Grower.

We never did figure out why Maggie Bannister had lied about her presence in her husband's condo in the weeks before his death. Her fingerprints were found in various places around the living room, but she had denied being there. J.D. suggested that it was probably an innocent visit, but that for some reason she didn't want anyone to know about it. She might have been concerned that her boyfriend Trip would have access to the information, and would be upset to know that she had visited her almost ex-husband. Maybe Maggie thought her best defense was a denial. In the grand scheme of things, it wasn't important, so neither J.D. nor I ever mentioned the discrepancy to anyone. That old adage about letting sleeping dogs lie was often good advice.

Then, one day when I wasn't expecting it, the dog days of August fell on us like a hot blanket. The sun was intense and the days were cooled only by our afternoon thunderstorms that brought even more humidity to smother the island. It was a time to spend indoors or in a swimming pool or the Gulf waters.

It was on such a day that J.D. called me. I had been to lunch with Logan at Mar Vista, sitting at the air-conditioned bar and munching on a fish sandwich. A few hardy souls took their meals at the tables under the trees adjacent to the bay. I'd walked the two blocks home and was washing the sweat off under a cold shower when the phone rang.

"Big news," said J.D. "I'm on my way downtown to help Harry Robson interrogate Tori Madison."

"They got her?"

"Yes. She was arrested in Orlando last night. The Sarasota County sheriff sent somebody to pick her up. She should be at the jail in about ten minutes."

"How did they find her?"

"Stupid luck. She was working in a topless bar and got into a cat fight with one of the other dancers."

"She wasn't bartending?"

"Nope. Dancing. I guess she didn't have much money in her getaway stash. The story the Orlando police got from the manager of the bar was that she applied for a job as bartender, but local law required that she had to be fingerprinted and run though the local police. Not surprisingly, she refused to do that, so they offered her a job as a dancer."

"So, what happened?"

"Apparently, the fight was loud and rough. An off-duty police officer who was working security at the club tried to break it up and got punched in the mouth for his trouble. He pulled out a

Taser and quieted the girls down. When they stopped twitching, he arrested them. When they printed our buddy Tori, up popped the murder warrant from Sarasota County."

"Will she talk?"

"I don't know. Maybe we can cut a deal. Lesser charge in return for less time in prison."

"There's nothing she can add to the Bannister case. Abby was acquitted, and we know from Lucas' confession that he was the murderer. But I would sure like to know why she went after Abby."

"Me too. I'll call you when we finish."

CHAPTER SIXTY-FOUR

Tori Madison was shackled by one arm to a U-bolt in the concrete floor of the interrogation room in the Sarasota County jail. A small table separated her from Harry Robson and J.D. Duncan. Tori had dyed her hair dark brown and wore it short. Her face was as still as a mask of stone. Only her eyes were animated, darting about like a cornered animal seeking escape. "I want a lawyer," she said.

"There are a number of ways this can go, Tori," J.D. said. "One, we charge you with first-degree murder. Two, we turn you over the Homeland Security, and they arrange for a little Caribbean vacation for you at a delightful place called Guantánamo Bay, Cuba. Three, you talk to us, and we'll get you a better deal than a ride on the needle up at the death chamber."

"I didn't kill anybody," Tori said.

"It doesn't matter," J.D. said. "In the eyes of the law, you're guilty. You conspired to have Nate Bannister killed, and that makes you just as guilty as Wes Lucas. It's first-degree murder, Tori, premeditated murder. The fact that you tried to pin it on somebody else is just going to make the jury angry. Anger turns ordinary juries into hanging juries. You want to take a chance on that?"

"What kind of deal?"

Harry spoke up. "We'll take the first-degree murder charge off the table. We'll charge you with conspiracy. You confess to your part in the scheme and plead guilty to conspiracy. No lawyers. The deal is only good right now. Take it or leave it."

"I want to think about it."

"You've got ten minutes," Harry said. "We'll leave you to it." He and J.D. got up to leave the room.

"Wait," Tori said. "How much time will I have to do?"

"That'll be up to the prosecutor and the judge," Harry said. "But the death penalty won't be a factor if you plead."

"Let me think about it."

The detectives watched Tori through a one-way mirror. She didn't move during the ten minutes, and when J.D. and Harry returned to the room, she nodded. "Tell me the deal."

"We'll drop all murder charges," Harry said. "You'll give us a complete statement and agree to plead guilty to a lesser charge. You'll leave the length of the prison sentence in the hands of the judge, no deal on that, but the death sentence will be off the table. If you lie to us, the deal is off and all your statements can be used in your trial for the murder of Nate Bannister and Linda Favereaux."

"Okay," Tori said, "what do you want to know?"

"What made you decide to participate in the murder of Nate Bannister?" Harry asked.

"Mark Erickson ordered me to. He said Nate was trying to back out of an agreement that meant a lot of money to him. He agreed to give me a piece of his deal if I'd help him get rid of Nate."

"What was your job?"

"I was supposed to frame somebody for the murder. Mark didn't want it to look like a hit. He didn't think anybody thought Nate was involved in the drug business, and it was to Mark's advantage that it stayed that way. He wanted the murder to appear to be a lover's quarrel or revenge or something like that."

"So, you picked Robert Shorter as the patsy," J.D. said.

"Sure. He and Nate had a history. Shorter was a perfect scapegoat. He was going to meet Nate and me at Nate's condo on Sunday evening. A shooter would come in and kill Nate and when Shorter got there, the shooter would kill him and make it look like suicide."

"Lucas was the shooter?" J.D. asked.

"No. Erickson had somebody from Miami lined up for that job. He was trying to keep it separate from our people in this area."

"Then how did Lucas get involved in shooting Bannister?"

"The guy from Miami got held up in some way. He couldn't get here on Sunday, so Erickson called Lucas in to do the job."

"Why did you decide against the murder-suicide plan?" J.D. asked.

"It was a good plan, but Shorter called me on Sunday and refused to come to the condo that night. Erickson had a deadline he had to meet, so we had to do Nate that night. That's when Erickson called Lucas in and we went to our backup plan."

"How did Abby Lester get involved?" J.D. asked.

"She was my backup plan. After I met with Shorter, I was afraid he would back out or just not show up. He was flaky as hell, and I didn't think I could trust him."

"How did you get the glass with Abby's fingerprints?" J.D. asked.

"I called her and set up a meeting on Saturday before the murder. We had a glass of wine and talked about her helping me with a historical motif for the buildings in Lakeland. When we finished, I slipped her wine glass into my purse and took it with me.

"After Shorter backed out on us, I put plan B into operation. I couldn't take the chance that Nate would find the wine glass, so I waited in the car until Lucas killed him and came out of the building. I went right up and put the wine glasses from the bedroom in the dishwasher and turned it on. I put the glass from the restaurant on the bedside table and left."

"You didn't know about Linda Favereaux being in the condo?" J.D. asked.

"No. She must have slipped out between the time Lucas left and the time I got there. It couldn't have been more than a few minutes."

"How did you manage the emails that supposedly came from Abby Lester?" J.D. asked.

"My techie friend set those up."

"Give me the name of your friend," J.D. said.

"He wasn't involved in this. He thought it was all a prank I was pulling on a friend. An April Fools' joke."

"Give me his name," J.D. said.

"Okay. Frank Pilsheimer, but he was only helping me because I was screwing him. I think I was the little nerd's first. He never knew what hit him."

Harry Robson thought for a moment. "I don't think I have anything else, Tori, but as part of this deal, you'll have to answer any other questions I have, up until and after you're sentenced. Am I clear?"

"Yes."

"J.D.? Anything else?"

"Tori, did you order Wes Lucas to kill Shorter?"

"I passed on the order."

"From whom?

"Mark Erickson."

"Did he tell you why he wanted Shorter killed?"

"He said it was a loose end that needed to be tied off. He sure was pissed when Lucas blew it."

"Why didn't you try again?"

"Shorter disappeared. We couldn't find him."

"One more question, Tori," J.D. said. "Why did you pick Abby Lester as your scapegoat? How was she even on your radar?"

"Do you know who my father was?" Tori asked.

"I just know he was a big-time drug dealer who got busted and sent to prison years ago."

"His name was Howard McCann. When he went to prison, my life changed completely. I was ten years old when I was jerked out of private school and put in a lousy public school that was run more like a reform school than a place of learning. My mom and I had lived with my dad in a large house on the Gulf in Clearwater Beach. The feds confiscated the house, and Mom and I ended up in a dismal trailer park in Tampa. My mom had to hook to feed us, for God's sake. Sell her body to any shithead with enough cash to get her back to our trailer. She got AIDS and died because we couldn't afford health care.

"My dad died in prison, murdered during his first month there.

Do you know who killed him? No. Because nobody knows. The state didn't even try to find out who murdered him. It was probably a hit, set up by the guys he worked with before he was busted. The last time I saw him, he was in handcuffs being dragged out of our house on the beach. They wouldn't even let me hug him good-bye."

Tears were streaming down her cheeks, her voice breaking as she tried to control her emotions. She sobbed, caught herself, and said, "I've missed him every day of my life since then. And knowing that I'll never see him again, is almost more than I can bear. I targeted Abby Lester because I wanted her husband to experience the same pain I've lived with for thirteen years. I wanted him to know his wife would never be back in their cute little house on Longboat Key, to know that sooner or later, the day would come when she would be taken to the death chamber and executed. That is, unless I could figure out how to put a hit on her in prison. Like they did to my dad."

"I don't understand," J.D. said. "What did your pain have to do with either Bill or Abby Lester?"

"You don't know, Detective? You haven't been told or figured it out?"

"No, Tori. I'm sorry you've had such a miserable life, but I don't know why you would take it out on the Lesters."

"The undercover cop working with the Pinellas Sheriff's department? The one who weaseled his way into my dad's life, whom my dad trusted completely, who had dinner at our house two or three times a week, and who busted my dad? You don't know?"

"No," J.D. said.

"He was a Longboat Key cop named Bill Lester."

CHAPTER SIXTY-FIVE

Just like that, it was over. The conundrum had been solved. We had the answers, and like many solutions found in the sometimes addled brains of criminals, they made an odd kind of sense. But there are always disconnects in those confused minds, missing pieces of the puzzle that trouble the sane person who has to unravel the disparate threads of illogical thought. I always wonder what fuels the criminal mind. Perhaps it was some childhood trauma, such as the psychological devastation experienced by Tori Madison, or physical abuse suffered by some of the young people who grow into monsters, or just plain old greed as evidenced by Mark Erickson. In the end, the reasons don't matter. It's the fallout from the choices made by the crazies that hurt so many innocents.

* * *

The day dawned hot and bright and still, a typical August day in the subtropics. J.D. had taken two days off and we ran *Recess* two hours south to Cayo Costa Island, a state park just south of Boca Grande Pass. We had flat seas on the way down, a pleasant run in the sunshine, the salt air flooding our senses and bringing a feeling of relief that the whole ordeal had finally come to a conclusion. We anchored just offshore in waist-deep water and were standing near the stern of the boat, enjoying the relative coolness brought by the onshore Gulf breeze.

"Matt," J.D. said, "this all started because Bill Lester was an undercover cop working a drug ring. How did he end up working with Hillsborough County? I thought he'd spent his entire career with the Longboat Key police."

"I think the problem was that Hillsborough needed someone

who had no ties to the community to go undercover. An out-of-towner would have less chance of being compromised. Sometimes, when the potential bust is a big one, one agency will borrow a cop from another. You must have seen this in your career."

"Nope. Miami-Dade didn't borrow or lend. I guess we were big enough that we didn't have to do that. You haven't talked much about the trial, and it's been over for more than a month. Do you want to talk about it?"

"There's not much to say. I think justice prevailed, and a lawyer can ask for no better result than that."

"But how do you feel about the trial itself? Did you find that you miss the courtroom?"

I laughed. "I found the exact opposite. I used to love the battles, the mental gymnastics, the intellectual give and take, the drama of it all. But, time moves on. I've thought for a long time that I was happily finished with that part of my life. It was interesting and productive, but being a beach bum is so much better. No, I don't miss the courtroom. It's not a place for me anymore."

"So, I don't have to worry about you going back into the practice of law?"

"And take time away from being your boy toy? Not in this century, lady."

"Good. I like having you available on a regular basis."

I'd made reservations at South Seas Island Resort for the night. We'd take the boat into the marina, check into the lodge, have a fine meal in one of the restaurants, walk the beach, or not, sleep late in the morning, and then take our time meandering up the Intracoastal Waterway to Longboat Key. The life of a beach bum, or a boat bum, or a happy man looking into the future and seeing a long road of indolence and peace and happiness, is a pretty good life. The memory of the courtroom with all its stress was fading, but my resolve to never again enter the pit grew stronger every day.

I hugged my girl and thought I was the luckiest man on earth. As I felt her arms tighten around my neck, I knew I would be happy as long as she kept hugging me back.